QUANTUM SHADOWS

TOR BOOKS BY L. E. MODESITT, JR.

THE SAGA OF RECLUCE

The Magic of Recluce
The Towers of the Sunset
The Magic Engineer
The Order War
The Death of Chaos
Fall of Angels
The Chaos Balance
The White Order
Colors of Chaos
Magi'i of Cyador
Scion of Cyador
Wellspring of Chaos
Ordermaster
Natural Ordermage
Mage-Guard of Hamor
Arms-Commander
Cyador's Heirs
Heritage of Cyador
Recluce Tales
The Mongrel Mage
Outcasts of Order
The Mage-Fire War
Fairhaven Rising (forthcoming)

THE COREAN CHRONICLES

Legacies
Darknesses
Scepters
Alector's Choice
Cadmian's Choice
Soarer's Choice
The Lord-Protector's Daughter
Lady-Protector

THE IMAGER PORTFOLIO

Imager
Imager's Challenge
Imager's Intrigue
Scholar
Princeps
Imager's Battalion
Antiagon Fire
Rex Regis
Madness in Solidar
Treachery's Tools
Assassin's Price
Endgames

THE SPELLSONG CYCLE

The Soprano Sorceress
The Spellsong War
Darksong Rising
The Shadow Sorceress
Shadowsinger

THE ECOLITAN MATTER

Empire & Ecolitan (comprising *The Ecolitan Operation* and *The Ecologic Secession*)
Ecolitan Prime (comprising *The Ecologic Envoy* and *The Ecolitan Enigma*)

THE GHOST BOOKS

Of Tangible Ghosts
The Ghost of the Revelator
Ghost of the White Nights
Ghost of Columbia (comprising *Of Tangible Ghosts* and *The Ghost of the Revelator*)

OTHER NOVELS

The Forever Hero (comprising *Dawn for a Distant Earth, The Silent Warrior,* and *In Endless Twilight*)
Timegods' World (comprising *Timediver's Dawn* and *The Timegod*)
The Hammer of Darkness
The Green Progression
The Parafaith War
Adiamante
Gravity Dreams
The Octagonal Raven
Archform: Beauty
The Ethos Effect
Flash
The Eternity Artifact
The Elysium Commission
Viewpoints Critical
Haze
Empress of Eternity
The One-Eyed Man
Solar Express
Quantum Shadows

QUANTUM SHADOWS

L. E. MODESITT, JR.

A TOM DOHERTY ASSOCIATES BOOK

NEW YORK

This is a work of fiction. All of the characters, organizations, and events portrayed in this novel are either products of the author's imagination or are used fictitiously.

QUANTUM SHADOWS

Copyright © 2020 by Modesitt Family Revocable Living Trust

All rights reserved.

A Tor Book
Published by Tom Doherty Associates
120 Broadway
New York, NY 10271

www.tor-forge.com

Tor® is a registered trademark of Macmillan Publishing Group, LLC.

The Library of Congress Cataloging-in-Publication
Data is available upon request.

ISBN 978-1-250-22920-5 (hardcover)
ISBN 978-1-250-22921-2 (ebook)

Our books may be purchased in bulk for promotional, educational, or business use. Please contact your local bookseller or the Macmillan Corporate and Premium Sales Department at 1-800-221-7945, extension 5442, or by email at MacmillanSpecialMarkets@macmillan.com.

First Edition: 2020

Printed in Canada

10 9 8 7 6 5 4 3 2 1

For David, who never got to see this;
and for Jeff Garrison and Father Bob,
exceptional men of the cloth

With courage built upon desire,
The raven's simple as a fire.

QUANTUM SHADOWS

Great revelation is almost nigh.
You must wait for the raven to fly.

1

The three-forked and ornate trident stands etched in luminous black in the polished raven-gray-black stone of the wall, visible even in the darkness, as if a bolt of lightning had flared through the lightless shadows cloaking the study, not penetrating that darkness, except the man at the desk knows that the trident appeared seemingly from nowhere, and that a single long hiss filled the study as the trident made its presence known.

He studies the trident once more. To place such a trident without rendering collateral damage to the study and anyone within required far more power than that available to a mere principality, especially given the less-than-modest shadowshields that cloak his eyrie. But then, quantum transport has always required massive amounts of power.

He stands and moves toward the wall. He stops a meter away, feeling the latent heat as he studies the image, blacker than black, imbued with a light that is not light. He can also sense a residual energy, a faint aura, one unfamiliar to him, which is as one might expect of a great power invading his domain, and the quantum shadows that shield it.

A near-universal symbol, and, not unexpectedly, one with varying degrees of meaning, most of them less than auspicious. Yet an obvious one, and, because of that obviousness, one that easily could have come from at least a third of the Houses of the Decalivre, and therefore, one likely to cause quiet consternation, if not worse.

Much worse.

Raven watches from his shaded hall
still seeking foreshadows of the Fall.

2

In the lightless study, the individual who called himself Corvyn sat behind a plain black table desk. His eyes went to the trident black-etched upon the gray stones of the wall.

Under certain conditions, as he well knew, the so-called color charges represented by quantum chromodynamics, and manifested in the arrival and appearance of the trident's image, not only could vary in space and time, but could inhibit or undermine the properties of otherwise strong quantum interactions, even structured matter. That should not have been surprising to most people, but most human beings still perceived matter as solid, rather than as what it was—various levels of infinitesimal waveform energy amid vast empty space. And, given certain abilities, those possessed by powers, principalities, hegemons, and a few others, that vast empty space could be treated as and handled like shadows.

All the hegemons of the Decalivre had at least some ability with the shadows, as did others who were not hegemons, of which he was one. Also, with such powers, some hegemons believed they were gods, or some form of deity, while other hegemons, with similar powers, only believed that they were prophets or speakers for a god, while at least one House of the Decalivre had neither a prophet nor a deity. Yet all hegemons were powers with whom Corvyn had dealt and with whom he would have to deal in order to preclude another Fall. And that did not include those with lesser abilities, among them minor powers; greater powers, some of which were called angels; and principalities.

But which of the hegemons might have made such an overt and potentially threatening gesture as planting a trident in stone? Especially in another power's domain?

His eyes again went to the black impression in the stone as he pondered whether he should do what he planned. Had others sensed what had occurred? From where on the vast and high plateau of Heaven might it have come? Could he relate that trident to what he had already begun to sense? And what of the other powers?

"Cogito ergo quaero," he murmured as he gathered the aether into a flat oblong suspended between the desk and the wall, framing what might be called either inquiry or summons, but was neither.

The slight shimmer of the aether remained blank.

He concentrated again, this time, framing the search in terms of the newest loci of power.

Immediately two images formed in the oblong of aether above the desk. In one a dark-haired man stood in the shadows, looking out at those who awaited his performance, an antique instrument that might have been either lutar or lutelin held in his left hand . . .

In the other, the fair-haired figure seated at a shimmering white desk studied the boldly inked words on the parchment before her . . .

Are they the ones who will sing or pen the words that will shape the course of the next great turn, rouse the violent spirits of the age to come from amid the Houses of the Decalivre? Can either burst through the somnolence of satiety, the prurience of prosperity leavened by the stolid corruption of societal solipsism?

Or will they fail as have so many before them? And if they succeed will it usher in a revival . . . or a Fall?

Neither image bore any direct link to the trident etched into the wall. That did not mean that there was no such link. Yet they had appeared immediately after the trident. That meant he needed to watch them.

Will they reveal where other threads of power may lead?

Also important was that neither was in Helios or nearby. That, Corvyn could sense.

Corvyn held the images in the aether a moment longer before letting them dissolve into a shower of sparkling dust motes that vanished as soon as he cleared his thoughts. In turn, the aether vanished as well, since it had only been held there by his force of will, a will conflicted by other images of other times.

So many times since the Fall. The last Fall.

In time, the conflict within him still unresolved, he rose from the chair behind the desk, not bothering to open the window hangings blocking the light, and walked to the study door, opening it and stepping from the darkened study out into the airy corridor flanking the formal dining room. He paused and glanced at the full-length mirror on the wall opposite the now-closed study door. The reflected image was accurate enough—two arms, two legs, one head, short and straight black hair, gray eyes, brown-tinged skin not quite honey-colored, thin lips, and raiment of dark gray, set off by dull-polished black boots and matching belt.

He concentrated slightly, and the image faded into a shadow, then returned as he nodded. With that, he turned right and made his way to the entry hall, his boots barely whispering on the smooth gray stone tiles of the corridor, the entry hall, and, once through the silver-bronze doors and outside, the pillared atrium set between the formal gardens. Beyond the atrium the stone tiles formed a walk to the black ironwork gate that opened inward at Corvyn's touch.

He stepped out of the shade that cloaked his villa, a shade some called "shadows," rendering it somehow less than discrete while not denying the solidity of its existence. Pausing momentarily on the wide sidewalk on the west side of the Avenue Pierrot, its smooth white paving stones polished by the noonday light, he noted the reflected light graying the black tunics and trousers of the Skeptics and the unrepentant, while softening the white garments of the few White Faithful who either felt they were doing penance or were trying to convert the unrepentant, if not both, by their presence. Corvyn did not see anyone from Aethena wearing the light green of the Maid, but that was anything but surprising in Helios. Officially this was Ciudad Helios, and sometimes, more colloquially, it was called simply Hel, at least by those in Ciudad Los Santos. Not that there had ever been many of the ancient sainted who had come to Helios since its founding after the forced landing of the *Rapture* and the days of the almost forgotten First and the scattered survivors of the previous Fall. But then, that was another story, and one that he was disinclined to reflect upon, unless he felt more charitable toward the white sheep and their shepherd than he usually did. As for the other seven Houses of the Decalivre . . . only a few of their inhabitants ever graced the paved streets of Helios. That was not true of the Saints of Nauvoo, although that village of belief was more the size of one of the smaller cities of the Decalivre.

Then, too, the numbers of followers of each House varied over the years, as beliefs shifted, or were shifted by the acts and machinations of the various hegemons.

He glanced up the avenue toward the north end of the city, graced by the black stone villa of Lucian DeNoir, outlined in white light against the pale pink sky of midday, then turned south, heading toward the river. The less he was perceived to have anything do with DeNoir, the better, although it was said DeNoir was every bit as equitable as, and far more flexible than, the White One of Los Santos, whose name was best left unuttered, since names drew notice, if mentioned enough, even of other deities and sometimes of powers and principalities. As for the Maid of Aethena . . . a faint smile crossed Corvyn's lips before he shook his head.

An omnivan glided by him, the murmurs of conversation covering the faint hum of the motors powered by the solar sheets that shaded the dozen or so passengers seated on the six short-backed benches. Most of them were unrepentants. One, most surprisingly, wore the saffron of a pilgrim from Varanasi, and two were of Jaweau's faithful.

Here to confirm the existence of the Dark One, no doubt.

Corvyn concentrated, forming aether into the image of a raven, just in front of the eyes of the white-clothed faithful, holding it there until the man stiffened, then letting the raven disintegrate into briefly shining dark particles.

He heard a few of the words. "A raven . . . and it was gone . . . shadow of the Dark One."

Corvyn smiled briefly. The present incarnation of Lucian had never used darkness, and yet so many, so very many of those living in the cities governed by the Ten and their Houses, still believed that canard, when Lucian's full name meant just about the opposite. Still, Corvyn wasn't above exploiting that misbelief. He never had been.

He continued to walk down the Avenue Pierrot, although he could have tapped into the aether and flown, but other lesser powers in Helios might have noticed . . . and taken advantage of knowing his location. Possibly Jaweau and the Maid might have sensed it as well, though neither would have cared, so long as he was not in their cities. But it would have told them, and others, that he had left the eyrie, and Corvyn preferred to be noticed as little as possible. When he was little noticed, he could see and discern more. Also, the hegemons tended to pay less attention to him, which made his long-assigned duties far less difficult.

Besides, walking gave him a better feel for the mood of whatever quarter of the city he was traveling, as well as reinforced his powers in a way that did not bring comparison to those wielded by the Ten. The Skeptics Quarter, which began just south of the eyrie, always felt filled with disbelief, while the Unrepentants Quarter usually held an aura of defiant wistfulness. The location of the eyrie, at the edge of each quarter, always felt right for Corvyn, or at least as right as was possible in Helios, just as Helios was the best of the cities of the Decalivre for Corvyn himself, and for a few others every year, as it had grown, slowly and hopefully, while the populations of some Houses had declined, although not the believers of the White One, or, Corvyn had gathered, those of the Vedic faiths.

As Corvyn approached the next corner, where the Via Excellentia intersected the Avenue Pierrot, he smiled wryly as another omnivan passed, this one solely containing young men and women wearing black trousers and long-sleeved white shirts. His vague amusement faded as he sensed darkness of a different sort. Instead of continuing south, he turned right onto the sunlit via, his eyes and senses alert, scanning the shopfronts that displayed wares behind transparent impermite. A tall woman with flame-red hair eased to one side without seeming to do so as she passed Corvyn, her eyes avoiding his, despite his pleasant smile.

A little more than ten meters ahead of Corvyn, a sun-white-haired child walked down the sidewalk of the side street, small fingers grasping his mother's hand as she paused to gaze into a window displaying an array of shimmering silk scarves, the kind that captured and held light well into the evening . . . or in a darkened room.

Two shops beyond the windowfront was an unnamed alleyway, and from there issued the darkness Corvyn sensed. He lengthened his stride and moved closer to the woman and the child, who was barely more than a toddler, so that he was only a few meters behind them as they passed the alleyway. As Corvyn had suspected, behind a wavering shadowshield stood two figures, a scrawny youth in faded gray trousers and shirt, wearing a gray hood, and an older man, gnarled in spirit and frame, also in gray. Behind them within the shadowshield, and in fact generating the shield, was a twin electrobike with a cargo carrier.

Before the two could move, Corvyn stepped inside the shadowshield, his eyes on the youth. "You really don't want to be sent to Lethe . . . or to Limbo, do you?"

The youth blanched at not only the words, but at seeing Corvyn, and likely at the hint of shadow that outlined him, even at noontime. The gnarled man withdrew, backing away down the sunlit alley, as if he feared not being able to see Corvyn.

"Go." The single word was enough, and the youth turned and hurried away, not quite at a run.

Corvyn reached out and drew the remaining energy from the electrobike, leaving it stark, visible, and unpowered, leaning up against the stone wall.

A white-and-tortoise cat sitting in a tiny patch of shade on a first-story windowsill across the alley looked steadily at Corvyn, then blinked her golden eyes twice, before gracefully lifting a paw and licking it, as if to begin her toilette.

Corvyn smiled for a moment, then stepped out of the alley and looked eastward. Mother and child had paused at yet another window. He looked over his shoulder back down the alley. Neither youth nor gnarled man was anywhere in sight.

He had not quite returned to the Avenue Pierrot when a patroller turned the corner, stopped, and offered a slight bow. "Greetings, Maitre Corvyn."

"The same to you. There is an unattended electrobike in the next alley. It's unpowered, but appears to have been intended for certain mischief. I suspect those who had certain uses in mind might be returning shortly."

"At times, maitre, you do make our duties less taxing."

"Only my civic duty." Corvyn inclined his head and then proceeded. He was not about to allude to the other times. He did wonder where the ragged pair had obtained the technology, not to mention how they afforded the storage cells to power even a small shadowshield.

When he reached the Boulevard Incertezza, after waiting for a break in the line of electrobikes and omnivans, he crossed the avenue and continued westward along the boulevard for five long blocks—for all the blocks in Helios were regular, and long—until he was well within the Merchant Quarter, that section of Helios where anything could be bought and sold, so long as the transaction was freely made and so long as direct harm from any transaction was limited to the transacting parties.

In the middle of the sixth block stood a massive warehouse with heavy timbered doors, seemingly without locks, although those doors, Corvyn well knew, could not be forced by any powers less than those wielded by the Ten, and a very few others, of which he was one. He stepped toward the doors, whose crossbeams were twice the width of the thighs of a sacred Shinto combatant, moving past the heavy timber gates and down the side of the structure. He walked along the two-meter-wide space between the massive warehouse and another building with no windows on the two lower levels and but a single door facing the boulevard. He found the hidden door he had noted but never used, and manipulating a small amount of aether, opened it. After stepping inside, he sealed the door in a fashion that would not reveal how he entered.

Immediately inside was the outer ring of the garden, marked by a waist-high wall of blue and gold tiles, beyond which rose the lemon and orange trees, not to mention the perennially flowering lilacs. As with the interior of many structures within Helios, as well as other locales on the great plateau of Heaven, the garden was far more expansive than the exterior seemed able to contain. Sunlight poured through open skylights illuminating all parts of the garden, if at different lengths of time for different areas.

Corvyn took no more than two steps toward the blue-and-gold-tiled archway that suggested an entrance before Ishtaraath appeared, as if from nowhere, although Corvyn had already turned before he could have been seen by most.

"You could have at least pounded on the doors," she suggested, her voice warm, but neither husky nor sultry, not that she was incapable of uttering words in ways that would drive most men, or if she desired, most women, toward thoughts of the immediate and intensely carnal.

"Is Tammuz around?"

"He's rejuvenating himself on the Sands of Time, recalling his distant past as shepherd. He feels better doing that every so often." Ishtaraath gave the smallest of headshakes. "It's still masochistic."

"Some find it necessary," replied Corvyn mildly.

"The Sands are expansive enough to accommodate such necessity and the bodies of those who fail."

"The Dunes offer a certain form of immortality, or at least longevity."

"I tend to prefer greater certainty." Ishtaraath turned toward the archway. "You might as well come into the garden, Corvyn."

"Since it's an invitation . . ." He smiled and followed her.

The two seated themselves at a table in an alcove surrounded by Damascus roses and clustered bellflowers, a rather odd combination to Corvyn, but the blue of the bellflower suited Ishtaraath, since it matched the color of her eyes, and the shade of the fabric of her jacket and trousers. Despite the white sunlight streaming through the skylights, the garden was cool, and the fragrant air gave the impression of being blue, the blue of long-lost Earth-Eden.

Ishtaraath tapped her long fingernails on the gold impermite of the table. "You would not have come here, on foot, no less, aerial spirit, unless you had a matter of import to discuss."

Corvyn nodded. "An interesting thing happened last night . . ." He went on to describe the trident and the power behind it, then watched for her reaction, but saw only the slightest of frowns.

"Have you any idea who dispatched it?" she asked. "The trident's not a formal symbol from any of the Decalivre Houses. Even Shiva doesn't use it symbolically."

Corvyn did not mention that symbols didn't have to be mentioned symbolically to be representative . . . or effective. The trident also represented three points, so to speak, and that trinity did exist elsewhere among the Houses of the Decalivre, in more than a few Houses. "Any of the Ten have the power to do that. Even a few heads of the larger villages of belief might have been able to. I can't see any reason for any of them to do it, though. Whoever did was powerful enough to remove any aura. I have my doubts that it was DeNoir, though." He was not about to explain that his doubts were a certainty.

"But it did penetrate your considerable defenses, it appears," she added.

Corvyn waited, then said, "This morning, when I sought future pivots, the aether showed me two images, a dark-haired singer and an older fair-haired poetess. The singer was male."

"Both wordsmiths, but opposites of a sort. Designed to appeal to you." She paused. "You know, you've recited a few lines of verse, but never shown me any in written form."

He smiled and recited:

"At the sight of Ishtaraath in green light
The words of the poets take flight."

"Flattery, yet."

"But based on what I've seen."

"Most men would say, 'based on truth.'"

"I'm not most men, as you know, and the word 'truth' has moralistic overtones that I dislike."

"You've mentioned that occasionally."

"More than I should have." After the briefest of pauses, he went on. "Neither has any link to the trident, either. Not that I could detect."

"That is disturbing. Do you know in which House the two reside?"

"There was no indication of that."

"What *did* the aether tell you?"

"They're about the same. The aether never equates powers." Corvyn smiled. "You know about them already, don't you? What about the mirror?"

"You're rather difficult to deceive."

"Difficult, but not impossible, as you well know. The mirror?"

Ishtaraath frowned. "Their light balances are identical."

"You told me that wasn't possible. There's always a difference in illumination between individuals, even identical twins."

"Don't be dense, Corvyn."

"You think Jaweau? Their illuminations overlit?"

"That's more likely, although Zijuan might do something like that to keep the other hegemons off-balance. DeNoir couldn't care less, and that would be counter to everything the Maid stands for. They won't be in Los Santos, whether or not Jaweau is behind either of them. Whoever it is will let them test their mettle away from him."

"Him?" Corvyn raised his eyebrows.

"Do you really think the Maid would stoop to something like this? With a trident, especially?"

"Why would any of the Ten want change?"

"Why indeed?"

Corvyn could have used the irony in her voice as a concealment, so heavy was it that it could have curdled light. "I see."

"I believe you do."

"Will you inform Lucian?"

"No. I'll leave that to you, if indeed you prefer to."

Corvyn laughed, a sound more like the soft croak of the raven he sometimes was.

"I thought not. What will you do in the meantime?"

"I haven't visited the Houses of the other nine recently. And I might visit a village or two." *Far better to run to than from.* He glanced at the nearest Damascus rose, before his eyes shifted to the blue of the bellflowers.

"You find the garden intriguing, and you shouldn't," declared Ishtaraath.

"Why not?"

"I'd think you'd be more attracted to shiny and bright things, things that would glitter in the shadows of your eyrie. Or is your eyrie that dim once within the shadows?"

"Words also glitter, and not always in the best of ways. That might be one reason why, although I am attracted to brightness, glitter lost its enticement long ago." He stood, as there was little more to be said, and

Ishtaraath had long since lost any interest in wordplay for the sake of wordplay. *We tend to refine ourselves to our essences, for better or worse.*

And that was a tendency against which he had struggled for far too many years. "Until I return."

She nodded. "Until you return."

Living life, be not so proud,
the raven's flight is not loud.

3

The following morning found Corvyn at the rear of his eyrie, completing a last check of the items in the two cases laid out on the bench in his spotless workroom. Each container was no thicker than a spread handspan. One contained what garments he would need and a spare pair of boots. The other contained items that he hoped he would not need, but could prove useful if he did. Then he looked up at the slender dark man who stood by the door.

"I will be gone for some time. You and Muninn know what to do."

"Yes, sir."

Corvyn lifted the cases and took them from the workroom to the adjoining bay, where he slipped them into the concealed spaces in the fenders of the rear wheel of the electrobike, then sealed them in place. Finally, he adjusted his black hat, an uncommon but not unheard-of stedora, and sealed his riding jacket. Then he mounted the electrobike and eased it out of the bay it shared with the seldom-used electrovan, glancing back to make certain the doors slid together to reveal nothing but blank gray stone before turning onto the alleyway heading south.

The two sweepermen at the end of the block did not even look up as he glided past. Two blocks later, he turned the electrobike west on the Via Excellentia, after first checking to make certain the dubious individuals he had encountered the previous day had not returned. There were no other darknesses lurking in the early-morning light of the alley on the far side of the via. Early as it was, he expected few other vehicles or electrobikes, and he saw but a handful, and only a few sweepers on the walks and streets attending to their chores. The sullen windowfronts awaited the opening of the lightpipes, when the shops would be ready to beguile shoppers.

The Via Excellentia stretched westward before him, seemingly for milles and milles, narrowing to a white line merging with the endless shops, none of them more than three levels, establishments renowned enough that purchasers had been known to come from far Varanasi or even from the distant headwaters of the River of the Unknown. Some items in his tool case had been purchased in certain of those shops, though not by Corvyn himself.

Although he traveled at a slightly more than moderate speed, almost an hour elapsed before the last of the shops was behind him, and he passed the twin gray pillars marking the western boundary of the city of Helios proper. The gray stone pavement here turned to white, although the lands of the Skeptics stretched all the way south to the waters of Lake Lethe, and hundreds of milles to the northwest, bordered on the west by the River of the Sun and on the east by the Ragged Mountains, and farther south by the River Acheron. While it would have been far faster to simply follow the other white stone-paved road south along the river part of the way to Los Santos, and then go back upstream along the River Sanctus to Marcion, that route would not suit his purposes. Nor would it allow him to discover how much of a threat the power behind the tridents posed. Was that power merely attempting to enshrine a new faith? Or was it attempting to conquer all other faiths . . . which the long history of humanity indicated would inevitably result in terror, chaos, and catastrophe?

Corvyn had a vague sense of foreboding, but just feeling that offered neither insights . . . nor proof. Only by visiting the cities of the Decalivre could he obtain either. He took a deep breath and tried to concentrate on the road before him.

Ahead, still milles away, stretching even farther into the distance, were low hills, most of which were devoted to vineyards. Between Helios and the hills were tilled fields, pastures, and orchards, with dwellings and other utilitarian structures set alongside lanes, far more randomly than was the case around Los Santos, or in those cities of the Decalivre situated to the north or northeast of Helios, with, of course, the exception of Aethena.

He rode past almond orchards, orange and lemon orchards, fields with crops in various stages of growth—seasons on Heaven were largely in name because the temperature and precipitation seldom varied that much over the year in any given locale. In Limbo, below the Edge of Heaven, and in the high reaches of the Celestial Mountains to the north, the same definitely could not be said. But in terms of mildness of climate the vast plateau of Heaven was relatively blessed. *If a thoroughly boring climate can be considered a blessing,* reflected Corvyn, even as he recognized that such boredom differed in each of the lands controlled by the different hegemons or the chiefs of towns or villages of belief.

By midmorning he reached the base of the hills, occasionally passing lorries and omnibuses. He saw only a handful of electrobikes, most heading in toward Helios, and exactly one pedal-pushed bike.

By midafternoon, he was definitely tired of the almost predictable repetition of climbing past lovely, east-facing vineyards to reach a low rise, then descending past woodlots and west-facing terraced fields into fertile bottomland, over a bridge, past more crop-filled bottomland, and then once more climbing past vineyards to another rise, slightly higher than the previous one. This ascent and descent pattern continued until, late in the afternoon, when the sun hung just above the hills generally behind Corvyn, he came to a flattened and paved area on the north side of the road. A waist-high gray stone wall surrounded the pavement, and beyond the wall for a good mille, there were only meadows, because the ridgetop where he paused was the highest point on the road between Helios and Marcion, and the pavement dated back almost to immediately after the Fall.

Corvyn nodded as he guided his bike off the road and onto the paved area, stopping just short of the wall, and stepping off the bike. He set the bike on its stand and stepped toward the wall. Then he looked back in the direction of Helios, not that he saw anything but the hills. The air was still a trace warmer than he would have liked, with a dusty smell. As he turned to look westward, toward the soon-to-set sun, two women appeared near the north end of the pavement and walked toward him.

They were anything but simple hikers or followers of the Maid. That,

Corvyn could sense, despite their walking sticks and light khaki hiking clothes. He waited until they stopped several meters away.

The tall blond woman surveyed the electrobike, then Corvyn. "You trust yourself to that? One such as you?"

Corvyn took her words as those of courtesy, not of knowledge. "It's not a matter of trust," he replied equitably. The Lances of Heaven would have turned upon him if he carried the cargo held in the hidden spaces of the electrobike into the skies, just as they had swept the skies of all mechanical fliers or even biotech creations much larger than a human being, unfailingly and invariably, over the eons since the Pearls of Heaven were first strung. "Have you come all the way from the Celestial Mountains? Or elsewhere?"

The blond woman only smiled.

"Where is Asgard these days?" Not that he was unaware that currently there were two villages of belief that claimed that name.

"Where we come from matters little," responded the second woman.

"Still seeking Valhalla?" he asked with gentle irony. "Or merely valiant warriors disenchanted with their villages of belief or those desperate to leave Limbo?"

The blond woman studied Corvyn, and her fingers tightened around the walking staff that was far more than most eyes could see. But she did not speak.

His eyes turned to her companion. "And you, Kara?"

Both looked back at him, their deep blue eyes as hard and cold as sparkling lapis.

"That time is past," he lied, knowing that such time had never fully passed and that it never would . . . even after another Fall. "Along with rings of fire . . . and bronze armor." Except that their sun-bronzed skin had been enhanced so that it functioned like armor for the two warrior maids who still clung to an almost vanished faith.

"You think so?"

"I hope so, Brynhyld."

Abruptly, she nodded to her companion, and the two stepped back, then continued walking southward, eventually toward the Edge of Heaven, he supposed, and the descent into Limbo. They would easily reach the trees to the south of the road before the white sun set.

Corvyn took his time surveying the vistas in all directions before getting back on the electrobike and continuing westward and downhill into the vale immediately below the viewing area, where he stopped at the Ridgetop Inn. He had lost count of the changes in name and décor that the inn had endured, but the present incarnation—that of a mountain villa—was pleasant enough and far more to his liking than had been the chalet-filled small village that preceded it.

A stocky man, with short blond curly hair and a swarthy complexion, walked out from the receiving chamber to meet Corvyn. "Haven't seen a bike like that before. Not one built that sturdy. Must draw a lot of power."

"Not so much as you'd think. It's ancient, but it does what's necessary. That's true of a lot that's ancient."

"You here for the night?"

"Assuming you have room."

"Plenty right now."

Corvyn withdrew the Helios card from his inner jacket pocket and extended it. The name on the card was C. O. Poe—one of several names and cards, all legitimate, insofar as all could draw on Corvyn's considerable credit balance, and all of which were linked to his biometrics, as were all cards in Heaven, although theoretically and in practice, in most cases, no individual possessed more than one card or one identity. He carried only the one, of course, because scanners would have detected the presence of a second, and that would have caused definite complications.

The innkeeper glanced at it, then at Corvyn. "Maitre Poe. Looks like you all right. Biometrics match, too. For the night will be twenty. My name's Jared. Jared Hansen. Use my name on the inn-net if you need anything."

"Thank you."

After a moment, during which he passed a scanner over the card, the innkeeper asked, "Where are you headed?"

"Where the road takes me. Marcion for a beginning. Have you heard any news from there?"

"Nothing that's not netwide."

"I saw a pair of Valkyries walking the ridgetop toward Limbo. That's a long trek."

"If they're Valkyries, they've got time."

"You see many?"

"Every so often some traveler sees some. I can't say I have."

Most likely because you don't look. "How long have you had the place here?" Corvyn knew it had been less than ten years, because that was the last time he had stopped at the inn, and old Samaha had been running it. While Corvyn hadn't cared for the chalet style, he had liked Samaha.

"A little over eight years. Samaha was my uncle. No one else in the family wanted the place. They all liked home."

"Where is home?" If he had to wager on it, Corvyn would have bet it wasn't Helios. Samaha had never said where he'd come from, and Corvyn had never felt the need to ask.

"Nauvoo."

That did surprise Corvyn, given that the inhabitants of the overlarge village of belief that claimed that name and had sought to be a full House of the Decalivre—and failed—seldom ventured beyond their lands, not since the time of the pogrom of the missionaries, when all the cities of the Decalivre—and the Lances of Heaven—had forcefully reinforced the point that beliefs were restricted to their lands. Not only that, but innkeeper Hansen didn't have the always-cheerful smile that so many Saints had, even if he did have the blond hair. But then, neither had Samaha. "Why did you want the place, then?"

That question brought a rueful smile. "Let's say that Nauvoo didn't have the same attraction for me and my partner. He and I felt a change was for the best."

"But Helios was a bit too different?"

"You might say that. Ridgetop suits us fine. Your room is sixteen. Bottom level on the far end."

"Is the café still open?"

"Open now, until midnight. Open at dawn."

Corvyn nodded.

He rode the bike the hundred meters or so to just before the door to his room, then stopped and got off, looking up into the deep rose sky of early twilight. He could just make out the five visible Pearls of Heaven evenly spaced out across the sky, each a silvered pink, just half of the ten circling the world beyond the shields. They'd shine a brighter silver once true night fell.

Since no one had attempted to link Corvyn, there was no need to check for messages, not that there had ever been that many, not in recent decades, in any case. He wheeled the bike into the room, where there was a stand for it, as well as a charger that the bike didn't need, given its energy-absorbent surface.

After taking care of a few matters and washing up, Corvyn made his way from his room to the café, leaving the stedora on the narrow dresser. He wondered what sort of fare Jared and his partner presented, hoping more imaginative cooking than he recalled from his previous visits to Nauvoo and other Saint offshoot villages. A single electrobike—the lightweight and slender kind mostly used for local travel—was linked to a charging rail outside the café.

When Corvyn entered the café, the piped light, simple blond-wood chairs, and plain impermite tables gave him the impression of having been specifically chosen to create a feeling best described as cheerfully nondescript and clean.

"Any unoccupied table that suits you," offered the man carrying a tray with two platters on it. "I'll be with you in a moment."

Corvyn glanced around. He was almost the only one in the café besides a young man sitting alone in one corner and a dark-haired pair of men wearing the loose-fitting tunics and trousers and sandals that suggested they were likely Tianese, or possibly from Keifeng. After looking over the tables and counting them—eleven—Corvyn smiled. Some superstitions persisted, as if any of the Ten would have cared about whether a café had exactly ten tables. He walked to a circular table roughly equidistant from the other patrons and seated himself. The menu appeared, displayed by the table.

After scanning the items, he was pleasantly surprised—three kinds of pasta entrees, beef, veal, bison, trout, and fowl, with a variety of vegetables and greens. Although the "meat" would be entirely replicated from protein bases, the vegetables, fruits, and greenery would be local, or regional. So the quality depended on what was available locally and the skill of the cook.

Not that it's ever otherwise.

Corvyn looked up as the trim figure who had delivered the platters returned, carrying the empty tray.

"Good evening, sir. I'm Jason, chef, server, and anything else that needs to be done. Might I answer any questions?"

"Which one would you eat tonight?"

"I had the veal in the port reduction with mushrooms, with the egg noodles. I'd still have it again. The fowl and rice with lemongrass is a bit lighter."

"I'll try the veal, with the mixed greens and your dressing. Whatever light red wine you'd recommend."

"I'd go with the Vulcar."

Corvyn nodded.

After Jason left the table, Corvyn tried to pick up the conversation of the two men across the café, but could hear nothing, although their lips were moving.

Screened. That was more than interesting, given that no one sat close enough to overhear, suggesting that the pair had something to hide . . . or came from a background where *everyone* had something to hide, which suggested they were more likely from Tian than from Keifeng, although the Taoists could certainly be indirect. Rather than use the shadows, he sharpened his eyes and focused on the man who half faced him, trying to read his lips. Even so, he only picked up phrases.

". . . three societal nodes are unstable . . . animists don't count . . . barbarians of the north . . . Valkyries . . . Saints . . . the moment it appeared they might rise again . . ."

After a time, precisely when Jared returned with the salad and a goblet of a dark red wine, Corvyn suspected that the older man was Tianese and possibly a wandering Confucian scholar and the younger man his disciple rather than his paramour. *Or . . . that could be a cover.*

The man sitting alone left the café while Corvyn ate the greens, which served their purpose, neither too substantial nor so delicate as to be fragile. Corvyn sensed the power shift as the departing diner unlinked his electrobike, suggesting to him that the link mechanism could have used cleaning.

The veal was tender, the mushrooms a touch too earthy, and the port reduction quite good. Not outstanding, but far better than he had expected.

The scholar was still pontificating to his disciple when Corvyn left the café wondering why the older man bothered with screening. Only those with certain capabilities would even notice. *Unless the screening is to draw attention to him and away from others . . . or to draw attention that will soon be dismissed.*

Both could be true, or yet a third possibility that Corvyn had not considered. Even the Ten missed some possibilities.

In the eyes of the raven
all are unfaulted, uncraven.

4

For various reasons, Corvyn found that he was not ready to leave Ridgetop until the pure white sun was up enough to color the sky the full pink of day and the Pearls of Heaven had faded to near invisibility. His late awakening did not disturb him unduly, for Marcion, the Cite Christos, lay less than a full day away even along the highway of the hills, and he had no desire to enter the domain of the Paulists any sooner than necessary nor to remain within it any longer than required to discover what he must and depart. While it was likely that the so-far-unknown power had embedded the flaming trident emblem elsewhere, given the powers of each House of the Decalivre, he would need to visit each to determine whether to act or not. On the one hand, his failure to act might lead to another Fall. On the other and more disturbingly, acting might precipitate such a Fall as well.

But Corvyn had always preferred sins of commission over sins of omission. So he departed Ridgetop on the ancient electrobike, heading northwest on the white stone highway that had never aged and never would, descending and then ascending, before descending again, each descent greater than the succeeding ascent, reversing the pattern that had taken him to Ridgetop.

While the terrain was similar, the crops were not, since those in the Cite Christos had long since forsaken the fermented fruits of the land, as declared by the prophet of the Paulists, and the only vineyards were for grapes to be eaten or turned into raisins. There were, on the other hand, groves of olives, oranges, and lemons, and fields of other crops . . . and long patches of trees, including the massive cedars. The spacing of dwellings along the highway of the hills was not quite random, but certainly not so ordered as was the case in the lands surrounding other cities of the Decalivre. The one possible exception was the lands of the Skeptics, given the far lighter hand of rule by Lucian DeNoir, a style of rule quietly mocked by some, particularly the White One of Los Santos and the Disciple of the Twin Masters of Tian, as allowing chaos and disruption to flourish and to encourage the evils of disbelief.

Just after midday, Corvyn neared Komnenos, a town whose name had lost its antecedents even though they postdated those of Marcion, but remained a comfortable place to stop. At least it had been in the past. Chestnut trees grew everywhere, along with beech and hornbeam, and more than a few oaks, but most important and famed were the sweet chestnut trees. These were made possible by Lake Sinop and the long ridge to the north of the lake, which trapped the moisture from the River Sanctus and the evaporation from the lake. Otherwise the fertile lands surrounding the town would be far, far drier and hotter, more like Marcion.

On the outskirts of Komnenos, he passed the tannery, known for the leather produced with the tannins from the local chestnuts, and an adjoining building which housed a natural shoemaking enterprise for those who eschewed replicated footwear—and who were able and willing to pay the supradeital price. Corvyn had a pair of boots made from that leather, and while comfortable, they were not one of the two pair he had brought with him. Beyond the tannery began the stolid stone houses, all of ashlar masonry, if in occasionally differing rectangular patterns of the various kinds of local stone.

Near the center of Komnenos was a square, around which stood a number of two-story structures, some offering forms of cuisine, others featuring other commodities suitable to Paulists. Corvyn dismounted from the electrobike in front of the same establishment where he had eaten on a previous visit. Although the Bridge styled itself a bistro, so far as Corvyn could determine, it was a café that had long since forgotten that it once had pretensions, with dark tables so polished by time and olive oil that the chestnut wood now resembled dark impermite. Black cords tied back the red-and-white checkered curtains, and that, in a fashion, Corvyn found fitting, the black restricting the less restrained primitive that followed early sophistication in the years after the days of the First on Heaven.

Although most of the tables were taken, for it was midday, a dark-haired, black-eyed, and honey-skinned woman greeted Corvyn. Her pale blue chiton over a darker blue sadin was cinched with a wide belt of the same darker blue. Even the leather of her soft boots matched the belt. She motioned him to a corner table for two and pointed to the menu, chalked on a slate board, with the fish and vegetarian dishes written in pale green and the few meat dishes in red. There were no beverages listed, but Corvyn knew what was available besides the grape juice and nonfermented apple cider permitted to the Paulists of Marcion.

He removed the black stedora and set it on the other chair before seating himself and briefly studying the bill of fare. "I'll have the lamb and lentils, with the beer."

"Thank you." She nodded and slipped away, returning shortly with a tall mug, setting it on the table, and departing without another word.

Corvyn sipped, ignoring the covert glances he sensed. The saffron-bittered honey beer, clearly provided for non-Paulists, fell somewhat on the sweet side, but was acceptable for a change, although in continuing draughts it would have been far too cloying.

He listened intently. Most of the conversations were hushed and private, but his eyes and ears told him that both men and women were eating there, in roughly equal numbers, one of the better aspects of the Marcionic influence on Paul's generally misogynistic approach to faith. On the other hand, he suspected that both men and women were grateful that Marcion's views on sensuality had not taken hold, or would have been grateful had they even known those views.

Before long, the woman who had greeted him and provided the beer returned with a large bowl set on a larger platter. Beside the bowl on the platter was the customary flatbread, topped with sprigs of rosemary. She also set a carafe of olive oil on the table in front of him. Before she withdrew, her eyes lingered on him for just a moment.

The lamb, with lentils and yogurt, was tender, and it was lamb, and not mutton. The mixed tastes, with a hint of lemon as well, called up a memory of another meal, and another time, almost as far back, or ahead, as the days of the twisted cross, when the Pearls of Heaven had just been strung, and he had dined in the twilight with the woman who had yet to become Ishtaraath, and her laughter had been more intoxicating than the red wine of Champagne-Nouveau. He also recalled the words he did not speak, not then, words cribbed from farther in the past:

The old becomes the new, if as in rhyme,
cause leading to cause, each in its time . . .

He did not finish that thought, for he preferred to leave the last words unthought . . . for the present.

When he finished, he set aside his utensils, and took a last swallow from the mug. The beer was better with the lamb than either juice or wine would have been. Seeing his server, he gestured, and when she stopped at the table he said, "The lamb was very good." He offered his card.

The woman looked at the card, and the name, and frowned, if momentarily, then shook her head, if barely, as she scanned it. "We all have our secrets and reasons. Yours are more . . . shadowed, honored one."

In turn, Corvyn smiled, recognizing the woman who had been a girl on his previous visit. He did not protest the appellation, undeserved as it may have been, because the protest would have demeaned her courtesy. "Tell me what might be new of Brother Paul, Miriam."

"What is there to tell? He does not change. Few of power do, and few of them travel. You do not travel much, unless there is a reason. I'd rather not ask such a reason." She returned his card.

Corvyn smiled, this time at her words. "I've heard murmurings of a new trinity of power. I thought I might seek it out." And that was true, because the trident represented a trinity of sorts.

"The old trinity is all that Brother Paul will accept."

Corvyn laughed softly. "That has not changed."

"Have you, honored one?"

"More than you would believe, and less than I should have, I fear."

"Then I will mourn for the old ways, and pray for you."

"Pray for my success, if you would."

"That, also."

"And keep the money. It's real." He smiled again as he stood. "Thank you. It is a joy to see you." All those words he meant, and not just in the moment, for words that were honest only in the instant were little better than lies . . . and often worse. He lifted the black hat from the other chair as he left the table.

When he was back on the electrobike and riding westward out of Komnenos, Corvyn considered the meal at the Bridge with an expression half thoughtful, half regretful. Miriam seemed not unhappy or displeased with her circumstances, and there were so many who were neither happy nor pleased, even in Heaven . . . as well as those powers and principalities, or those even greater, who would have exploited those who felt they had been deprived.

Has it ever been otherwise?

His eyes focused on the road ahead.

The words of gospels set in oak
turn to ashes at Raven's croak.

5

As he entered the city proper of Marcion, where the highway of the hills became the Avenue of the Light and the Way, and the white stone turned a very light gray, Corvyn's eyes discerned absolutely no change in the dwellings and structures he observed within the city proper, although there had been minor changes beyond. Nor had there been any new dwellings or other structures, suggesting that Miriam was correct, that nothing had changed, and that Brother Paul's view of faith had neither increased nor decreased the number of his followers significantly—although Corvyn would have wagered on a slight decrease, if one not large enough to be easily noticed.

In Komnenos, the houses were built of stone because the chestnut trees were too valuable for timber. In Marcion, located on the eastern side of the River Sanctus, the houses were of brick and stone because trees were rare in any close proximity to the city. The prevailing winds, almost invariably blowing from the south, were bone-dry after traversing the Sands of Time that began—or ended, depending on one's perspective—less than three days' travel from the southern bank of the River Jordan, its closest proximity to Marcion being another three days' travel south of the River Sanctus.

Rooftops glistened with solar sheets and films, as did all rooftops on Heaven, and the air was warmer than it might otherwise have been from the heat discharged by all but the very meanest of dwellings. In the distance, at the far end of the avenue stood the Basilica Vera, as it had since before the establishment of the Hegemony of the Decalivre. The basilica overlooked the river from its low hill above the river, circled by the Damascus Road. Its dome shimmered in the early midafternoon, reflecting light almost bright enough to be a second sun, albeit one of golden radiance restricted to the environs of Marcion, rather than the pure white light of the primary radiance that bathed all Heaven, an oddity of sorts, given the pink sky.

Marcion was far smaller than Ciudad Helios, possibly, Corvyn suspected, because Hel was the sole city for Skeptics, while the other nine hegemonic cities each catered to and were supported by those inclined, at least generally, to the beliefs theoretically embodied in each hegemon. Then, he reminded himself, that might just be his rationalization, something he attempted to guard against. Such a use of logic tended to become easier with age, and he had fought that battle for longer than he wished to recall. Even so, Marcion was not small, and it took him almost another hour on the avenue to reach the basilica.

Once close, Corvyn guided the electrobike to the row of stands in the parking area to the south of the Great Square of the Faithful. He found a vacant stand, locked the bike in place, added a few additional protections, and then walked toward the basilica. He did not, however, head to the main steps. Instead he walked along the side of the building, occasionally melding with the shadows as he made his way to a small locked door on the north side of the building, a door actually under the side of the north staircase. He unlocked the door with the experience of age and certain other abilities and stepped inside, leaving it locked behind him. Lightpipes illuminated the corridor at a comfortable level, diffuse enough to keep normal shadows from forming. After several meters, the corridor made a right-angle turn toward the center of the basilica, ending in a small anteroom.

Seated there at a table desk, a functionary in a tannish-brown robe looked up in surprise, if not shock. “How did you get here? This is—”

“For the truly faithful, no doubt.”

“Dark gray raiment. You are either an outcast or a citizen of Hel—”

“Perhaps both, perhaps neither,” interrupted Corvyn cheerfully, once again. “I could also be a Taoist priest on a pilgrimage, or an undecided Wiccan in exile. That is not material. I'm here to see Brother Paul."

"The unrepentant, or those who are not believers, must first request an audience with Father Meander or Father Simon." The functionary's voice was politely firm.

"Is either of them free?" asked Corvyn, already knowing the answer, given that the full name of Father Simon was Simon Magus.

"Alas, not for some time."

"There wouldn't be a Father Tertullian, would there?" Corvyn let himself appear open, almost naïve.

"Not that I've heard," replied the functionary in light brown, frowning.

"That's probably for the best. Where would one find the best fare in the Cite?"

For a long moment, the man, for all functionaries of Brother Paul were men and always had been, said nothing before finally replying, "For a believer or an unbeliever?"

"Excellent should be excellent to any palate, I would think," replied Corvyn.

"I don't believe I can help you. In any case, you need to leave." The man stood, as if to escort Corvyn back the way he had come.

"I will depart in my own fashion." Corvyn shrouded himself in unseen shadows, vanishing from the sight of the functionary in light brown. Then he waited to see what the man would do.

Predictably, the functionary looked around the antechamber. Less predictably, he opened a narrow drawer from which he took an energy scanner and played it across the space. When it failed to register anything, since the energy waves simply bent around Corvyn, he took a deep breath, and gestured.

"Yes?" answered a voice without an image.

"A man in dark gray appeared and asked for you. When I suggested that he should first see others and that neither Brother Simon nor Brother Meander was immediately available, he asked for where one might find the best fare in the city. I attempted to escort him out. He vanished."

While the man spoke, Corvyn discovered what he needed to know.

The unseen voice replied, "He has either discovered what he needs to know or has not and withdrawn. In either case, there is nothing else you can do. Resume your vigil."

"Yes, Brother Paul." With a barely audible sigh, the functionary seated himself.

Corvyn continued onward to where the internal communications led him, that is, to a study behind the transept and apse within the Basilica Vera—both much larger than would have been the case in a traditional basilica, but far simpler than in a cathedral. The neither cramped nor commodious stone-walled chamber contained a desk and a comfortable chair, a closet for vestments, and a small altar on which rested a single leather-bound volume within a gold outer case, recently altered, or defaced, depending on one's perspective. The closed volume rested on a stand beneath the simple cross.

Corvyn smiled as he sensed the volume. Then he moved to a position just inside the door and studied the Apostle, a man of slightly more than middling height, with a strong but not aquiline nose, short but straight legs, and a full head of hair and a neatly trimmed beard, both sprinkled with some gray, clearly an affectation, since graying had long since been unnecessary in the realms of Heaven, where death rarely came from physical aging.

After a moment, he emerged from his shadows. "Greetings, Brother Paul."

"From which dark depths have you emerged, creature of shadows? Or are you Stolas from the depths?"

"That's a bit illogical, Brother Paul. Without the light there are no shadows. I'm no more a creature of darkness than you are."

"For as others have transformed Satan himself into an angel of light, so would you claim the same of yourself?"

Corvyn shook his head, smiling as he did. "I'm neither of Satan, nor of the darkness, although I've certainly been known to use it, as have you, you must admit, if you be true to yourself."

"I have had no fellowship with the unfruitful works of darkness, but rather have reproved them."

"That you have, and that is how you have used the darkness to spread the words of the One True Gospel." *That is, the one you believe to be true.*

"All words have but one truth, and that truth is the true Christos."

"There is truth as perceived, and fact as it is. So often they are not the same, and you, of all apostles, should know that."

"*You* would judge me, shadowed one?"

"Spare me the words about when judging another, one condemns himself. I've long since understood and accepted that."

"You would still place yourself above the Lord."

"I presume you don't mean the Jaweau of Los Santos." Knowing this already, Corvyn offered the statement for where it would lead.

"Though there be those who are called gods, whether in Heaven or elsewhere, every soul is subject unto the higher powers, and there is no higher power than the Lord, and even you in your shadows cannot escape his powers."

"I agree that we're all subject to higher powers, Brother Paul. I've never questioned that. I do question what and who the highest power might be . . . and for that matter what higher power has burned a trident into the impenetrable cover of the One True Gospel. The one you call the original, I mean." Corvyn's words were merely to call attention to the trident burned in luminescent black into the gold outer cover of the volume bound in leather on the small altar, or the One True Gospel, which should really have been known as the Book of Marcion.

"What? That minor miracle of a Fallen technology?"

"If it has penetrated your aetherial shields, Paul, it is not minor, nor is your black-flamed trident the only one embossed throughout Heaven. You might wish to talk to Jaweau. Or are you considering that the trident upon your gospel is unique and signifies that the time has come for the Fisher of Men to come once more and unite Heaven under one true faith?" Corvyn smiled. "I rather prefer to think of it in the context of Thomas, the doubter. Or perhaps, as you have said, even here in Heaven, we see through a glass, darkly, and there are shadows, even in full sun."

Brother Paul's eyes blazed, and small lightnings issued from his fingertips. "Begone, dark one!"

Corvyn considered remaining, but that would have been merely further baiting Brother Paul, and to no purpose. Besides, bearing those forces would be painful. Even before the lightnings more than brushed his gathering shadows, he withdrew and departed in his own way, leaving the Apostle alone in his stone study.

The bombs will fall, the bullets fly.
The raven watches, standing by.

6

Men in black uniforms, trimmed in silver, the only insignia on their tailored jackets a double jagged lightning bolt, marched rhythmically. The synchronized steps of thousands of boots shook the smooth paving stones designed to last a thousand years. Behind them the twisted cross of silver and black led black metal monsters. Yet the cadence of the marchers and the deafening and continuing cheers of the spectators who lined the great boulevard, and those who watched from the heights of more distant buildings, drowned out the impact of the monsters' oiled metal treads on the stone.

Graceful metal birds of prey, also emblazoned with the twisted silver cross, swooped down, racing along the line of march, before angling into the brilliant blue sky . . .

The sky split . . . and separated raggedly . . . each torn blue half sliding out of sight down into the distant horizon, revealing only an unending sky, blood red, where the birds of prey each found themselves the target of endless legions of smaller, uglier, stronger flying metal reptiles that spit forth glowing metal pellets that seared, crippled, and killed. Metal pellets that, when missing their aim, cascaded down upon the once-jubilant spectators, torching some, rending others, and leaving others so terrified that their hearts stopped instantly. Still others fled, that flight prolonging their lives only a few additional moments.

Even when the first graceful birds of prey had been shredded from the sky, the metal reptiles continued to spit forth their glowing metal missives of death and destruction. Long after the buildings flanking the great boulevard, as far as the eye could see, were shapeless rubble, death missiles pounded rubble into dust. Trails of thin black smoke rose into the blood-red sky, long after the last spectator had expired . . . except Corvyn.

Corvyn wove every shadow he had ever known, dancing, evading, twisting, to escape the dance of devastation he had attempted to forestall in so many ways. Dashing, dancing, appearing, vanishing, he evaded devastation missile after devastation missile, trying to reach the sole white structure in the star-distant time so far beyond . . .

Corvyn woke, sweat-covered, burning, yet shivering.

Always a variation on the same theme . . . for how many eons?

He rose. He knew he would not sleep longer.

In his mind, the rain came down in sheets from the dark clouds overhead, and then poured in cataracts off the partial and ruined roofs of the houses lining both the narrow lanes and angled streets off the broad boulevard leading to the twin stadiums that once held over a hundred thousand spectators.

How long will the past be prologue? Or was it ever?

He no longer knew . . . if he ever had.

Although you wake at break of day,
the ravens have yet to fly away.

7

Once he had settled down and washed up, knowing that he would not sleep further, Corvyn dressed and then sat on the single chair in his rented room and concentrated, gathering the aether into the customary, for him, flat rectangle suspended before him, framing his search for the newer loci of power—first, the poetess. For a time, the faint sheen of the aether remained blank; then an image appeared.

Corvyn immediately saw that either what he beheld in the first aetherial vision had changed . . . or he was mistaken, for the poetess—if she was indeed that—was not so fair as he had thought, but possessed a complexion more like the color of amber honey, and her hair was silver-white, while her face was without lines. The irises of her eyes were deep gray, and her expression somehow tired-looking. She was not writing or thinking words or entering them into some repository to hold them for later presentation. She just stood, looking into a distance that the aether could not convey, a single sheet of paper in her left hand. She stiffened slightly, and Corvyn wondered if she sensed his observation.

He concentrated on the sheet she held, and the image changed to reveal the words, written in a tongue he had not expected, but poetic in any language.

The threefold, eternal dream, conscious stream
Winds, falls, through all time, a deceiving seam . . .

Belief in posing honor, lying pride,
and humble faith, deities undeified . . .

While he smiled at the words and their accurate, if poetic, depiction of the state of Heaven as it was and had been for some considerable time, he pondered how such abstruse verse could pose a threat to the Hegemony and to Heaven itself. Still, it was interesting that the poetess had tapped into power. That could prove even more intriguing if she intended to take up a particular perversion of an ancient myth that contained a tiny enough sliver of truth to persuade people, men especially. Men could so often be turned to the evil they would prefer, by the comfort of logic and cold rationality that lacked the truth of honest emotion.

He let that image fade and called up the other.

The tall, dark-haired man with the slightly squared chin stood in front of a hall that might have held two hundred people. He sang as he played a comparatively new version of an antique instrument, likely constructed to complement his voice. Corvyn had not seen or heard a lutelin in more years than he wished to count. Every person in the hall sang with the dark-haired man, word for word, creating another kind of power. Corvyn concentrated, moving the image to take in the audience. They were participants as well, yet the intensely vacant expression on each face told Corvyn that none of those passionately singing the words offered by the singer understood what those words signified . . . or cared. They only wished to be one with the singer, seeking a kind of near-mindless rapture.

Corvyn had no doubts that the singer knew exactly what he was doing, for all that tapping the power of music was one of the most ancient of powers, often squandered on meaningless causes, less often marshaled in the quest for dominance, but usually evil when so employed, and seldom appreciated or employed in its highest form, although too many purveyors of blind faith had insisted that such was the highest function of music.

After releasing the aether, he sat there in the darkness before dawn for a time, contemplating the trident and the two individuals he had viewed. Together they were also three, and that troubled him not a little.

As before, his investigations revealed that neither was that close geographically to him, and thus not within the sphere of belief of Marcion.

Some time later, Corvyn left the room in the structure that was neither inn, caravansary, pension, hotel, motel, nor boardinghouse, but which partook in part of each, in that it catered to travelers and their mode of transport, and that what it provided was serviceable, but not luxurious. He walked along one side of the courtyard, which contained no camels at present, and entered the café, although Marcion in his day might have called it a taverna.

He was among the few there, unsurprisingly, since the sun had yet to rise, but an older woman in a darkish brown chiton and underdress immediately appeared. He could tell she was older, because her features lacked the softness and roundness of youth, having become sharper, some would say more refined, with age, since radically visible aging was rare anywhere on the plateau of Heaven. In the lower and hotter depths of Limbo, that was not always the case, and certainly not in the even hotter and lower depths beyond Limbo, nor would it have been so in the bitter cold of the Celestial Mountains, had anyone been permitted there . . . or able to survive there.

She smiled politely. "Sir, would you care for juice or tea?"

"Tea, please."

"Strong, sweet, or both?"

"Strong, not sweet, thank you." Bitter as what he had dreamed and seen had been, the cloying sweetness of Paulist tea was the last thing he wished.

The platters the server set before him contained fresh figs, slices of melon, eggs scrambled with mushrooms, potato cakes, and flatbread with honey.

"Are you doing penance?" she asked, taking in his dark gray garments.

"Not in the sense of the faith," he replied, carefully not implying any particular belief, "and not any more so than on any other day. Do you see many penitents or pilgrims here?"

"A few. Most prefer the hostels closer to the square. We get more merchants. Most are coming from or going to Yerusalem."

"How many still use camels?"

"Very few anymore. They say most of the camels are used by those who travel the road to paradise and also trade with the small villages scattered throughout the Sands of Time." At the mention of the Sands of Time, she paused, then added, "I'll be back to see if you want more tea."

Corvyn ate slowly. The melon was good, the figs better. The potato cakes were too heavy, and he only had two bites, but the eggs were light enough that he finished them, along with a bite of the flatbread with just a smear of honey. Then he sipped the tea . . . slowly, enjoying the strong but not bitter taste that only came from the terraced plantations south of Keifeng.

When the server returned and refilled his mug, he asked, "Are there Saint converts heading up the river these days?"

"There are always a few. Mostly young men. The only true saint is Brother Paul, but they don't understand that. Some never do."

"He can be most impressive."

"Have you heard him preach?"

"No. I met him briefly. You might say we've established that we don't agree on certain matters."

For a moment, the server seemed to freeze. "He doesn't meet many outlanders."

"I've heard that. I was fortunate to talk with him even briefly. He is a powerful speaker with firm convictions."

After the slightest hesitation, she replied, "That's a great honor, you know, especially for an outlander."

"It is indeed. I certainly won't forget it." Corvyn doubted Brother Paul would either.

The server smiled, and Corvyn handed her his card. She studied it for a moment. "Poe . . . I've never seen that name before."

That was not surprising, seeing as C. O. Poe only existed as one of Corvyn's sub-identities, although sub-identities were officially prohibited in Heaven.

She scanned the card and extended it in return. "You have a good day."

"I hope to." *Or at least a productive one.* He accepted the card, then stood, and slipped from the taverna.

Once the basilica opened to the public, Corvyn joined the thirty or so who waited to behold its inner splendors. He was just another stranger who had come to Marcion to marvel at the Holy Temple to the Unseen Trinity that ruled Heaven and the universe beyond, for was that not what the One True Gospel preached? Inside the outer doors, but outside the gate, he, along with the others, donned the woolen foot covers over his boots—dirt, sand, and other grime must not mar the mosaic floors—then followed everyone else, led by a deacon.

He ignored their guide easily enough, and instead surveyed the interior of the basilica, to refresh his recollections. The floor plan was simple—an atrium at one end, and a transept with a large apse behind it at the other. The atrium lay beyond the comparatively narrow narthex; then the long nave, flanked by aisles on each side, extended to the transept. The nave contained twenty-four marble columns, twelve on each side, each representing an apostle. On the upper level, above the columns on each side of the nave, stained clerestory windows depicted various scenes from the life of the true Christos—except for the last window on each side. Each showed a man standing on a road, transfixed by a beam of light, his companions wincing and turning away, but the renderings of the two differed slightly, and that had always puzzled Corvyn, given the usual fixity of true believers, whatever their faith.

Corvyn's eyes moved from the northern window of Paul on the Damascus Road to take in the carved capitals of the columns, ornamented by acanthus leaves, twisted as if being whipped by the winds of a storm. Then he studied the mosaics on the walls at the outer side of the aisles, again all scenes from the ancient Acts of the Apostles, reminding Corvyn, not for the first time, that Brother Paul had perhaps strayed the least from the antecedents he claimed, especially compared to the other nine hegemons.

As the group moved forward toward the transept, Corvyn looked at the curved wall of the apse and nodded. There, above and behind the shimmering silver altar, a large mosaic portrayed the Christos, his arms extended as if to his worshippers, within an oval of gold braid and olive leaves. On each side were clouds, and within each cloud was an archangel, the one on the right with a flaming sword, the one on the left with a golden trumpet.

Those images, Corvyn knew, were not theological inventions or religio-mythic fictions, nor was Brother Paul as simple as he seemed.

The tour of those areas open to visitors took slightly more than an hour, and Corvyn learned little more of what he sought. Just before the tour ended, he stepped into the shadows cast by one of the marble columns and departed in his own fashion, eventually finding his way to Brother Paul's private refuge on the northwest side of the basilica. The walled garden was far larger than Paul's study behind the apse, and certainly more pleasant, with the fountain in the center and the olive trees spaced around the stone walls. Within the scope of the olive trees, the garden was divided into sections, one of flowers, dominated by anemones and lilies; one of spices, including black mustard, lemongrass, and coriander; and one containing several fruit trees, most prominently several pomegranate trees, but also a fig tree and a trellised grapevine.

Rather than attempting to maintain the shadows that concealed him, Corvyn manifested himself as a slightly overlarge raven, largely concealed in the most ancient of the pomegranate trees that shaded the table and chairs in the open space not all that far from the fountain. While he waited, he spent the time considering the various possibilities. Although he doubted that Brother Paul had any connection to the appearance of the tridents, he preferred to learn more so as not to be required to return to Marcion, for while the city was pleasant enough in climate and appearance, it had always been far less to his liking than many other cities of the Decalivre.

Well over an hour had passed before three men walked into the garden from the tunnel leading from the basilica and seated themselves around the table.

Paul looked to Michael.

"We're shielded. The entire garden."

"What have you discovered?"

"One of the visitors vanished this morning," offered Michael, who bore a remarkable facial resemblance to the archangel with the sword. "He looked like the intruder you encountered yesterday afternoon."

"Who is he?" asked Paul.

"He spent the night at the Road's End. The account that paid for his room and his breakfast is listed to a C. O. Poe, out of Ciudad Helios. The funds and the identity are verifiable, but there is no address."

"Then Poe is just a sub-identity," replied Paul.

"More than likely," agreed Michael.

"Those are forbidden by the Decalivre," pointed out Gabriel. "That means he's an agent of DeNoir."

Michael shook his head. "DeNoir doesn't have any agents. He never has. He doesn't enforce the ban on sub-identity."

"It's too bad that's not something subject to the Lances of Heaven," said Gabriel.

Michael offered a condescendingly superior expression to Paul, as if to suggest that the other angel should have known better.

"Then this Poe is either a rogue or a power in his own right," Gabriel said, unabashed.

"There's another thing," said Paul. "He didn't *know* that there was a Satan's pitchfork flamed into the gold, but he wanted to see if one had been. That doesn't sound like DeNoir is the power behind the pitchfork."

"Unless he's attempting to cloud the waters," rejoined Michael. "The Dark One is anything but straightforward."

"That can't be discounted," mused Paul, "but the appearance of the shadowed one is too obvious for DeNoir . . . unless he had nothing to do with the appearance of the pitchfork and is trying to discover who is behind it."

"He's traveling by electrobike. If whoever sent him received a pitchfork at the same time," declared Michael, "this Poe had to have come from Los Santos, Helios, Nauvoo, or Yerusalem. There aren't any cities or villages of power close enough for him to have gotten here from farther away."

"Unless he's an aetherial and picked up the electrobike near here," replied Michael, "and is trying to hide the extent of his powers."

"That might be. It's old," added Gabriel.

From his perch in the pomegranate, Corvyn would have smiled, but a raven's beak wasn't suited to smiles.

"You're forgetting one thing," said Paul. "To travel the aether, or the shadows, for any great distance takes endurance and power, even for those who hold the powers of their Books. Such lengthy travel also risks triggering the Lances of Heaven."

That last sentence was not true, although what preceded it was, and Corvyn wondered if Paul believed what he said, or wished the two angels not to know that the Lances could not penetrate full shadows.

"I can have the doves follow him, if you wish," offered Gabriel.

"Let me think about that for a moment."

"Why would an aetherial do anything that might benefit DeNoir?" asked Michael.

"Why does an aetherial do anything?" replied Paul dryly.

"There's a raven up there!" exclaimed Gabriel, abruptly staring at Corvyn, almost as if he had noticed the corvid earlier and waited to draw attention to it.

Michael was on his feet, seemingly far taller and more imposing than he had been instants before, with a long sword of fire in his hand.

"Don't damage the pomegranate," ordered Paul.

Corvyn dived at the archangel, veering past his face before angling around the fig tree and past a lemon tree toward the wall. He had just cleared and dropped below the wall when the flame and power of the sword swept above him, its edge clipping him and nearly throwing him to the ground. He landed heavily, resuming his normal form, concealed by shadows. Only the fact that the smaller manifested size of the raven gave him greater protection allowed him to survive the power of the archangel's blade without injuries he would rather not endure.

Hugging the various walls, he slowly and laboriously made his way from the grounds of the basilica. Despite the fact that the sword had only struck Corvyn's protections, Corvyn's upper back and right shoulder tingled with an uncomfortable burning. He also knew he would have bruises before long, and that it would be several days before the pain and tingling totally subsided.

He had learned what he came to find out, as well as a bit more, without crippling injuries, if barely.

Michael's sword was also a reminder that each of the hegemons controlled powers that could prove devastating, and so did some of their retainers. *Something you have a tendency to forget over time.*

The truth may seem, but cannot be,
nor will doves learn what ravens see.

8

Although Corvyn could detect no sign of either Michael or Gabriel, or any of their minions, tracking him once he left the environs of the Basilica Vera, he saw no point in remaining in Marcion any longer than necessary. Since Paul might well change his mind, a confrontation would only reveal too much to too many of the powers and principalities of Heaven, with the always possible, if unlikely, risk that Corvyn might not survive . . . or survive so badly injured as to be unable to discover what he must or to be unable to act to prevent another Fall.

Ignoring the pain and the tingling still burning across the back of his shoulder, he returned to the Road's End, gathered his limited belongings, and loaded them into the electrobike. Less than an hour after his hurried departure from Paul's garden, he sat, somewhat uncomfortably, on the electrobike, heading northwest on the Boulevard of the Transformation. More than fifty meters to his left was the River Sanctus, some ten meters lower than the boulevard. Two terraces filled the distance between the roadway and the river. The lowest and widest terrace stood only a few meters above the normal water level, the second and narrower one was but a meter below the stone pavement of the road. Dryland gardens filled the lower terrace with winding paths that meandered through the bushes and scattered wildflowers. A well-trimmed false-olive hedge dominated the upper terrace, where Corvyn saw several robins picking at the small and bitter fruit.

The neat stone dwellings on the right side of the boulevard remained modest for the first mille or so from the end of the basilica grounds, then increased in size as dwellings for traders—who appreciated the river view and could pay for it—replaced the houses of the most faithful. But then, almost everyone in Marcion was faithful to some degree, as was true in every city, town, and village of belief—except for the lands of Helios. Paul, especially, would not have had it any other way, nor would the other hegemons. Among other things, that was why there were parish churches located in every neighborhood of the city.

Corvyn continued on the boulevard for slightly over an hour before the more closely spaced houses and structures of the city gave way to olive and lemon orchards and dryland pastures and fields. The boulevard became the river road to Nauvoo, once more pure white eternal stone, but still paralleling the watercourse. On the hills to his right sparse pastures alternated with woodlands that featured junipers and scrub pines. Beyond the river to the west, the great cedar forests filled much of the land between the River Sanctus and the River Jordan, and some stretched to the Celestial Mountains far, far to the north.

Two hours later, Corvyn pulled off the road at one of the frequent turnouts overlooking the river. He moved the electrobike close to the waist-high stone wall and looked down at the river nearly twenty meters below. The afternoon sunlight glinted on the gray-blue water. He stretched, gingerly and carefully, grateful that the burning and tingling were not so intense as they had been. They should fade over the next day—provided he didn't create more difficulties for himself.

A flicker of something like a shadow intruded upon his greater senses, and he turned slowly, then smiled wryly as he beheld two white doves that had just alighted upon the far end of the semicircular stone wall. The doves belonged to Gabriel, and they would follow him until the archangel recalled them or until something ill befell them.

For the moment, there was little point in having the doves meet with an accident. They might prove useful in certain circumstances. He returned his attention to the river. A powered launch made its way upstream, carrying youthful-looking Saints, young men and women both wearing dark trousers and white shirts. They were most likely returning from their educational tours of either Los Santos or Marcion, the only sort of outreach attempted by the Prophet, Seer, and Revelator or, more accurately, by the minions who had controlled his image ever since the pogrom of the missionaries.

The doves remained perched on the end of the wall when he remounted the electrobike, but when he returned to the road, they took flight.

Another two hours brought him to the outskirts of Corinne, a town built on several hills, the upper slopes of which offered a view overlooking the river to the west. To the east stretched the level plain that had likely been a lake in some far distant past, and beyond that the beginning of the Ochre Mountains, which were as hills compared to the Celestial Mountains demarcating the northern border of the great plateau of Heaven.

Unlike the city of Nauvoo itself, or Brigham, some fifteen milles farther along the road toward Nauvoo, or for that matter any other of the towns or villages in the Saint territory around Nauvoo, the restaurants in Corinne offered wines, beers, and assortments of teas and coffees. Corvyn thought about where he should eat, but he really could not resist the lure of the only establishment he had ever frequented in Corinne—La Caille. So that would be where he dined—after a stop at the inn where he could change into attire more suitable for La Caille.

The Gentile Inn was two blocks or so to the east off the river road, which did not become Main Street or Center Street, as it did in Nauvoo and in all other towns or villages in the Saints' domain, according to the dictate of an ancient prophet, but remained River Road. The inn was a handsome two-story building of red brick with limestone quoins, window frames, and lower sills, and a dark split slate roof. An actual garage offered locked stalls for electrobikes, but Corvyn drove up to the main entry and eased the bike into one of the stalls under the shelter of the roof that extended across the entry. Then he walked inside to the counter in the antique-style entry foyer.

"I'd like a room for the night." Corvyn smiled and extended a card.

The blond-haired and dark-honey-skinned young man standing behind the counter took it and scanned it, then looked at the display before him, clearly surprised. "It's been a long time since you were here last, distinguished sir. Before my time. I never would have guessed it. I'm Adam, if you need anything."

"It has been a while," replied Corvyn, understanding from Jared's words that the inn's system identified him as a possible power or principality. "There are times to travel and times not to, and times when one has no choice." He smiled politely.

"Just the one night, sir?"

"Yes. Unless something unexpected happens."

"Yes, sir. Would you prefer a suite on the upper or lower level?"

"Upper, if you have one."

"The Apple Suite is available. At the far end. The door is coded to your card."

"Thank you. I'll be leaving my electrobike in front for just a little before I go out for dinner."

"Yes, sir."

Corvyn retrieved his two cases from the bike and then returned to the inn, where he climbed the wide steps to the upper level. The rooms were distinguished by numbers on the doors; however, at the far end were two doors without numbers. One had a fruited apple tree upon it, the other a lemon tree. At the other end of the long hallway, as he recalled, the two suites had doors with an olive tree and a pomegranate.

Once inside the modest suite—sitting room, bedchamber, and bath chamber—he removed his riding jacket and outer garments, washed up, changed into another set of grays, with a more formal gray shirt, and then added a darker gray dinner coat. After sealing and concealing the cases, he left the suite.

When he stepped out into the covered entry to the inn, Corvyn noted, unsurprised, the two white doves perched on the brick wall connecting the outer pillars supporting the entryway roof. He did not acknowledge their presence in any way, but merely eased the bike from its supports, mounted it, and then drove away from the inn, following his memories as they guided him to the wide avenue that curved up a gentle slope. Halfway up, on the right, he reached a large area sculpted out of the hillside. Two black stone pillars with white capitals framed the beginning of the entry drive, paved in a fashion that Corvyn had never seen anywhere else in Heaven. Jet-black but nonreflective stone paved the right side, while white stone surfaced the left side. In contrast, the curb stone and walk on the white side were black, while the curb and the walk on the black side were white.

Some fifty meters past the gardens he came to the oval swan ponds, each perfectly circular and a good hundred meters across. In keeping with the color scheme, the pond on the right was ringed by black stone, with a black stone fountain in the shape of a swan set in the center, while the pond on the left was similarly arranged, except in white. A pair of swans swam gracefully in each pond, white swans in white, black swans in black.

La Caille was built of pure gray stone in the style of an ancient château. Whether architects based it on an actual château on long-lost Earth, Corvyn could not have said, not after all the eons. He passed several private vehicles parked on one side of the drive and then dismounted outside the entrance, where he turned the electrobike over to a young man wearing formal uniform, a white tunic over black trousers, then walked through the heavy oak double doors that were swung back.

The man waiting at the archway beyond the entry foyer frowned as Corvyn approached. "Monsieur, we have—" He broke off his words as Corvyn looked at him. "This way, monsieur."

"Thank you," replied Corvyn pleasantly.

Corvyn found himself at a small table for two, discreetly separated from others, as with all the tables in La Caille. He recalled that the servers were both men and women, attired in black trousers and vests with white shirts, their complexions ranging from light-honey to rich brown, a range common in most Saint communities.

The server who waited upon him was male, neither young nor old, and he offered an ornately printed menu and wine list. "There are no special entrees this evening, monsieur."

"Is there anything that you would especially recommend?"

"The Veau du Diable is quite good, as is the chateaubriand."

"I'll have the veal, then." Corvyn had had the chateaubriand more than a few times—many more. He just hoped that the diable reduction did not rely excessively or exclusively on the cayenne pepper. Raw heat and power left a great deal to be desired, whether in cuisine or in other aspects of life. "With the portobello mushrooms and the truffled red potatoes.

Mixed greens to begin with, just a touch of the house balsamic. Would you suggest a Lambrusco or a Gamay with the veal?"

"The Gamay Meridional might be better."

"I'll try that, then."

"Very good, monsieur." The server glided away.

Corvyn studied those at the few tables he could see. All were attired far more elegantly than was usual in either Marcion or Nauvoo, although there were doubtless a handful of other establishments that catered to elegance in those cities.

A goblet of red wine appeared, so deftly presented that most would not have noticed it. Corvyn lifted the goblet, enjoying the restrained aroma, and took a sip. The vintage was among the better he had tasted, but then, that was one of the reasons why he chose La Caille.

The mixed greens that appeared next included thin slices of a powerful sweet basil, offset by a tangy arugula and small crumbles of goat cheese. The veal was perhaps not quite so good as the Gamay Meridional, but intriguing, with just the proper balance between the sweetness of the apple glaze and the bite of the cayenne pepper.

As he finished the last of the veal and portobello mushroom, a woman slipped into the empty chair opposite him. She was small, slender, and almost wiry, and clad in a high-necked, floor-length gown of shimmering, copper-brown silk that flowed with every movement. The sleeves extended to her wrists, wrists at the end of arms that were just a trace too long for her frame. Her skin was more the color of dark amber than honey.

Corvyn smiled, but waited for the other to speak.

"You can call me Sunya, Corvyn."

Despite the feminine huskiness of the voice, the essence across the table from him confirmed the identity of the power that, contrary to myth and legend, could be either male or female, or even something not quite human, not that being human had any great cachet in terms of virtue, or lack thereof. Corvyn knew that all too well.

"You're rather far afield . . . Sunya."

"So are you, dark one."

"Not nearly so far as you. Might I ask what brings you here? Perhaps your health?"

"What else? The Auspicious One is less than pleased with my latest jest. The blue-faced one would like nothing better than my immediate and very humiliating comeuppance, and has voiced such thoughts to Kartikeya. Even Garuda believes the jest was excessive. I think you, of all powers, would understand."

"It sounds as though the Auspicious One might be slightly on edge, not that he would wish it known, despite legends of his once being a doormat, so to speak."

"Have you ever told him that?"

"Would you?" replied Corvyn.

Sunya grinned, but shook her head. "You've always been skeptical. How have you survived so long?"

"I always have reason for skeptical thoughts of the hegemons, if for differing reasons involving each."

"Is there a one who isn't skeptical of you?"

"I wouldn't be who I am if at least some of them aren't skeptical. You might be welcome in Keifeng or Tian, I'd think."

"Neither the Jade Emperor nor the First Disciple is looking favorably on me at the moment. Don't ask. Just be aware of that. I'd rather roam until things settle down with the Auspicious One and his eldest son."

"Is Kartikeya . . . ? I thought the problems were with Ganesha."

"The god of battles has been traveling. It is rumored that he is trying to convert some of the villages of belief to his standard."

"What else might be new?" Corvyn laughed softly.

"This is different." Sunya's voice lowered and darkened.

"How might that be?"

"Just different. Worse, I fear, than with Kali."

"Dealing with multiple manifestations of power again?"

Sunya shrugged. "That's nothing new. No . . . there's something else. With Shiva. I can't say what." She shook her head.

Corvyn debated pressing her, but decided she had said all she would say. "So what mischief are you here to cause?"

"That's your skeptical nature speaking again, dark one."

"You aren't thinking of stealing the golden plates again, are you? It didn't change anything the last time. He just claimed that he returned them as requested."

"I try not to repeat myself. That gets boring."

"Then I won't inquire further."

"That's kind of you. I don't believe I asked you what you might be doing here."

"Let us say that I'm conducting a survey of sorts."

"You're not known for relying on quantifications of opinions. Have you changed?"

"No more than you."

"You do have evil thoughts, you know."

"Speaking of that, if you see a pair of white doves, I'd appreciate it if you'd let them be." Corvyn doubted Sunya would even have considered doing anything to the doves.

"Have you upset Gabriel again?"

"Most likely, but you'd have to ask him."

"I just might . . . after I'm finished here." Sunya smiled, then rose. "It's nice to see you do leave the shadows occasionally, Corvyn."

"And that you enter them," he replied, watching as she turned and walked through one of the archways leading into another dining area. He couldn't help visualizing a tail or a differing physique and wondered what might be powerful enough to encourage such a power to leave Varanasi, even temporarily. Although he suspected that Shiva was anything but pleased with the appearance of a trident that was not a manifestation of the true trishula, Corvyn wondered if it had that much bearing on the appearance of the power calling itself Sunya . . . or why Kartikeya tried to rally others to his standard.

Then again, Shiva might have sent Sunya to see if the trident might have come from the only city of Heaven that was not part of the Decalivre as a declaration of power, something Corvyn doubted, or, conversely, to see if the Prophet had received one even though Nauvoo was not a city of the Decalivre.

Sunya as an agent of Shiva was highly unlikely, but with the Auspicious One anything was possible. And Corvyn could not rule out the possible, no matter how unlikely, given the very unlikelihood of Heaven itself, or the fact that something as powerful as the entity behind the trident might well wish the destruction of Heaven and another Fall.

When he paid his server, he left an obscenely large gratuity, another form of disruption, but one that would be useful in that it would provide a distraction of sorts.

Once outside, in the warm but not unpleasant air of early evening, when the Pearls of Heaven began to glow faintly pink in the night sky, Corvyn covertly observed that two white doves perched on two of the gargoyles beneath the roof. He did not look back at them once he mounted the electrobike and rode not quite sedately back down the black-and-white drive.

When he arrived back at the Gentile Inn, he wheeled the bike into the stand inside the garage across from the main building. There, he inspected it closely, finding the tracer under the rear fender. He nodded and left it in place, then locked the bike into the stand, as well as adding his own precautions. As he straightened and moved away, he sensed a tall figure in the darkness outside the garage.

Once he stepped out into the pale light of early night, only that of the stars, abetted by the glow from the Pearls of Heaven, he addressed the one who clearly waited for him. “Greetings.”

Even in the dim light, Corvyn could make out the big-headed, red-haired, and red-faced giant who strode toward him, a lancia in one hand and a straight-sword in the other. While he had never encountered the other in person, he had called up that image in the aether, one of the avatars of the deity known as Ares, although if not any time remotely recently. “I wouldn’t expect to see you here, Rudianos.”

“Prepare to meet your doom, winged nemesis!”

“What exactly have I done to merit that?” asked Corvyn, shadow-slipping away from the thrust of the spear-like lancia, similar to, but distinct from, the bronze spear favored by the deity when he appeared in his true form.

The blade of the straight-sword glowed with black fire, outlined in the ash red of coals.

Corvyn withdrew slightly, evading the sword.

“You are merely a shadow, not the true Dark One. You are not fit for the challenge.”

“However we come to be, we’re all created in the same image,” replied Corvyn dryly. “Just with slightly varying capabilities.”

Rudianos did not reply with words, but with the blurring speed of the blade. The power of the black-fired blade was not as great as that of Michael's great flaming sword, Corvyn could tell, but getting struck with it would be exceeding painful, if not worse, and Rudianos did not appear rusty with age, for all of his lengthy history. "Don't you think you should leave that to the one who dispatched you, old man?" Corvyn barely escaped being bisected, and then spitted, then danced aside even more quickly as sword and lancia blurred and bore in on him.

Reluctantly, he sought the shadows and eased back, concealed and silent, as Rudianos swung his weapons through the spaces where Corvyn had recently been.

"The shadows will not save you, dark one. This time, perhaps, but not the next." Abruptly, the red giant was gone.

Corvyn frowned. Had Rudianos even been there? Certainly, the power of the weapon had been, but to move an entity through spacetime took massive amounts of energy, enough that whoever or whatever was behind Rudianos's appearance had to be either a hegemon or one with equivalent power. And given that Rudianos was an avatar of Ares, ruler of Ilium, a city of belief, and not a House of the Decalivre, the fact of his presence and attack was definitely worrisome.

Remaining within his shadows, Corvyn made his way to his temporary chamber, where he scanned for forces and intruders. Finding none, he emerged from his wreath of protection, and, eschewing all illumination, sat down in the barely comfortable and slightly overstuffed armchair to think, to rest from the exertions required to utilize the shadows . . . and to prepare for the day to come.

The raven's wings expose the light
of false belief, the Fall of night.

9

The images switched seamlessly from input node to input node, moving from the view dispatched by the Napali scanner, then the one from Haleakala, and then the orbital view from the Pacific geocentric station . . . scanner after scanner. The controller just monitored them, analyzing the components and comparing them to projected patterns.

Suddenly, the command data traffic flowing through the network accelerated, even as the outsystem datalinks vanished.

Outsystem comm links inoperative this time. Declaring RepCon Three.

The controller adjusted the security settings and relayed the orders to the local defense nodes and to its overseer.

Corvyn took over for the monitoring system.

Ten standard minutes later came the next comn.

WestCom Prime neutralized this time.

Neutralized? From the datastreams Corvyn controlled, it appeared that the military orbit control station, as well as all the major comm nodes, had been totally obliterated, most likely from a horde of sharp stones with no energy or electronic signatures.

RepCon One! Repeat. RepCon status is one!

Corvyn knew what that meant. The war had already begun. The war that would bring on the second Fall.

All units. RepCon One! RepCon One!

If Corvyn could have winced, he would have. Megatons of nuclear weapons were airborne, all headed for the Middle East and toward various points on the moon.

Then the western sky turned brilliant white, so white that Corvyn would have been blinded, had he been on the ancient lava peak where the scanner that relayed the image was situated . . . in the nanosecond before it was incinerated by the energy wave front that followed the searing incandescence.

"Lucifer has fallen!" Those words flashed through the comm system long before the speakers in the command center announced them in words slow by comparison to the direct links that Corvyn monitored.

Even in the depths of the control room, Corvyn could feel the heat welling up around him.

Sweat poured from his forehead before redness flared around him and he struggled for breath . . .

Abruptly, he found himself struggling awake trying to sit up in the wide bed of the now too-warm room in the Gentile Inn.

Where did that come from? Even as he thought the question, he knew the answer. Rudianos had triggered visions of the one Fall he had not witnessed, the one Fall of which he had no memories, although he certainly knew the details that had led to rendering more than ninety-five percent of Earth-Eden uninhabitable for almost an eon . . . before the rebuilding that had led to, of course, the third Fall . . .

Corvyn used the edge of the sheet to blot his forehead, thinking of how history had not merely rhymed, as one ancient writer had put it, but also repeated itself. Each Fall had been greater than the last, beginning with the first mythical Fall from grace, followed by the second Fall, the one that had "merely" rendered ninety-five percent of Earth-Eden uninhabitable for tens of centuries, to the third Fall, the one that had destroyed Earth-Eden and Mars, to all the others, each one leaving a lifeless husk of a world, if that, all the way to the Cluster War that had made a half score of habitable worlds uninhabitable . . . with only one massive ship surviving—the not quite mythical *Rapture*.

You don't know that whoever planted the trident will take things that far.

Except . . .

The ancient Newton's first law also applied to leaders who put faith ahead of everything else.

Corvyn decided he wouldn't sleep longer . . . or not well.

I knew a raven in my youth,
So let them have their truth.

10

Much, much later Corvyn breakfasted at the Gentile Inn, choosing the eggs Bernadine to complement the apple pancakes and crisp bacon, while savoring the fullness of the bergamot tea before he once again set forth, after first removing the tracer from the electrobike, heading northwest on the white-paved road that hugged the eastern bank of the River Sanctus.

In less than an hour, he saw ahead another white-paved road, narrower than the river road, branching off to the right. The signpost, the first he had seen since leaving Marcion, showed an arrow and a name—FAR WEST. The name still amused Corvyn, since Nauvoo was located closer to the Great Western Canyon than any other large concentration of population in Heaven, and Far West was the easternmost Saint town in the area holding a predominance of those believers.

An hour later, more or less, he saw a large town ahead, spreading to the east of the road and the river, and shortly thereafter, the electrobike carried him past a statue of a bearded man standing beside an ancient handcart. There were two white doves perched on the handles of the handcart, and the plaque on the gray stone pedestal below bore one word—BRIGHAM. The town, named after the second of the ancient Saint Prophets and the greatest of the ancient Saint Revelators, greatest in the misty memories of the saints, at least, and also as referenced in their Doctrine and Covenants, could have been a pleasant enough place to look upon, especially if passing through, reflected Corvyn.

Living there, on the other hand . . . even ravens would have blanched, not just at the arbitrary dietary covenants, some not even in keeping with Saint history, since in the time before the Fall, the true ancients had once endorsed sacramental wine, and even possessed a church vineyard, but the name Tocquerville had never appeared anywhere in the lands of Heaven.

But then, arbitrariness was the hallmark of all belief. That, Corvyn knew all too well, and was the reason why he had attempted to believe in no fixed doctrine except that of not believing in anything that was not verifiable, as least so far as he was able to do so.

Soon, he passed the neat houses and other buildings of Brigham, and its wide and tree-shaded streets, as well as scores of the smiling Saints, still disproportionately blue-eyed, if generally far darker in skin color than their ancient predecessors. He continued on the white river road until, even from ten milles away, he could make out the Temple at Nauvoo, standing upon a perfectly symmetrical hill at the far end of the long mall connecting it to the white stone missionary building on the east bank of the River Sanctus. Not that the Saints dared to call the structure that. Officially, it was the Educational Travel Center, and it dispatched hundreds of students on their educational "tours" every year, some of whom did not return.

The Temple itself was of perfect white alabaster, the stone enhanced to a smooth hardness that might well outlast Heaven itself, with three tall arched doors at the top of white alabaster steps that climbed the incline from the white stone walkways of the mall to the wider steps of the Temple itself. From the front of the Temple rose a hexagonal tower, the bottom section of which was one-third the height of the main part of the Temple. The next section of the tower, roughly the same length as the base, was also hexagonal and gave way to a low dome, from the center of which rose the shimmering golden image of the Angel Moroni, facing east, trumpet to his lips.

Corvyn did not bother with the Temple. His primary interest was not in structures, but in visiting the First Counselor to the current Prophet, Seer, and Revelator, and that was why he took the side road well short of the mall and headed east.

The hill on which the Temple stood was actually a long flat ridge with a square holding walkways and gardens directly east of the Temple. East of the square was a massive oblong tabernacle in which the Prophet appeared to periodically address the most blessed of the faithful Saints. A smaller gray stone building, nondescript, sat on the north side of the Temple Square. That was where Corvyn guided the electrobike, shading himself and the bike as he neared and then entered the underground parking, easing past the sensors that should have detected him. He parked the bike in one of the spaces reserved for messengers, since he was a messenger of sorts, carefully placed the black stedora in the top of the left cargo case, then made his way to one of the ancient lifts.

With certain manipulations, he bypassed the equally antique quantum security system and rode the lift to the fourth level, the highest level permitted by the Prophet, since the highest level could not exceed the second level of the Temple. He stepped out and found himself face-to-face with an Avenging Angel, from whose energy projection coruscated low-intensity stunner bolts that, after the first jolt, Corvyn bent around him as he made his way to the study of the First Counselor. First Counselor Joseph Smith Cannon would be there. He usually was, because Saints were the most well-organized and regimented belief in Heaven, even though Nauvoo was not recognized as a House of the Decalivre. The faith was also noted for a financial acuity that would have been termed greed had it been exhibited by any individual.

A young man wearing an incredibly antiquated, but clearly often-worn, black jacket and trousers, with an equally black cravat, and a brilliant white collared shirt sat at a table desk in the anteroom outside the study. Corvyn was about to appear from his shadows when the First Counselor opened the study door and said, "You can shed the shadows, Corvyn."

Corvyn did, nodding to the startled functionary at the desk.

The counselor stepped back into the study, leaving the door open.

Corvyn followed him, closing the door behind himself and noting that another man rose from a chair at a small circular conference table.

"I don't believe you've met Tanner Oaks. He's the most recent Apostle."

Most recent, Corvyn knew, was relative for Saints. The darker-skinned Oaks had been one of the Twelve for over a decade. Corvyn inclined his head politely. “It’s good to put a face to a name. In person, that is.”

Oaks inclined his head in return, as little as possible.

“I might have known you were the one who triggered the angel,” said the First Counselor. “Couldn’t you have just avoided it?”

“I was preoccupied, Joe.”

“You haven’t been in Nauvoo in years.”

Decades. “It’s been a while.”

“I’m curious,” said Oaks, his voice not quite pleasantly flat, and just short of grating. “Were you ever one-eyed?”

“Any man is one-eyed who sees only what he wishes,” replied Corvyn, giving a truthful answer to a different question and knowing that the inquiry came from the Asgard of Oaks’s ancestors before they capitulated to the golden tablets and manna of Moroni.

“Are thought and memory your ravens?”

“Thought and memory come in all colors, from the gray sorrow of regret to the still-burnished crimson of past desire.” *As did once the raven . . .*

“You won’t get any more answers than those on questions like that,” observed Cannon. “Why are you here, Corvyn? You never travel for leisure or pleasure.”

“You might say that I’m pursuing a flaming trident that leaves its imprint in stone . . . or perhaps into the cover of the oldest Book of Mormon.” As he spoke his senses studied both men. There was enough reaction that he said, “So it’s also imprinted on a stone wall in the study of the Prophet.”

Oaks didn’t bother to conceal his surprise.

Cannon offered the same friendly and warm smile that he would have used in dispatching a Danite or blessing a baby. “You said also. Where else?”

“Burned into the impenetrable cover of the One True Gospel, the one Brother Paul calls the original.”

“The heretical Book of Marcion, you mean?” commented Oaks sardonically.

“This particular trident seems to force itself on either books or stone.”

“What is your interest in the trident?” asked Cannon.

"Mere curiosity." Corvyn smiled. "It's more interesting than shiny things."

"You'll pardon me if I express a certain skepticism," replied Oaks. "Even if I'm not from Helios."

"The trident is a most interesting symbol. It's three-pronged, and three has several meanings of import to Saints, the three kingdoms—"

"You're stretching, shadowed one." Oaks's voice was tart.

"I don't think so. Three and the trident have meanings to quite a few Houses of the Decalivre. Each bears upon their particular truth, not always easily." Corvyn considered mentioning that an agent of the Auspicious One might also be seeking what Corvyn was, then decided against it. Cannon, like most Saints, gave lip service to virtues discarded all too often for expediency or gain, and, besides, Sunya was far less duplicitous.

"There is only one truth," said Oaks firmly and quietly.

"Yes, you have your truth. So does each House of the Decalivre."

"You're thinking that whoever placed these images was attempting to assert a theological primacy?" asked Cannon.

"That . . . or possibly to cause a conflict over primacy . . . or even to raise questions over the basis of faith."

"The basis of faith is faith," replied Oaks.

"Exactly," said Corvyn, standing. "Thank you both."

He withdrew into the shadows, but did not tarry, knowing that the First Counselor could detect his presence, linked as he was to some of the most sophisticated technology in Heaven. Besides, Corvyn would learn nothing from remaining, and Apostle Oaks had begun to wear on him. Then, the more recent Apostles usually did.

Just because Cannon would expect it, if nothing more, Corvyn made his way to the study of the Prophet, Seer, and Revelator.

The study was small, simple, and plain, with just a wide table desk of the whitest marble, a single spotless white leather armchair behind it, and three books on stands on the desk, each open to a particular passage and facing the armchair—the Book of Mormon, the Pearl of Great Price, and Doctrine and Covenants. The desk faced a wide window without blinds or shades that overlooked Temple Square.

As Corvyn had suspected, the trident was etched in luminous black on the white stone of the wall behind the desk. The First Counselor had already taken the precaution of covering it with a thin veneer of white stone, indicating his reluctance to remove it immediately, and also, most likely, his understanding that the power required to do so could not be concealed. Even so, Corvyn could sense the residual power behind that new stone veneer, most necessary because, for the Saint faithful, the Prophet was always there, in his study, and a black trident would have been most inconsistent with the visions of the Prophet. But then, inconsistency had never bothered a faith that began among the blond and blue-eyed and steadily absorbed those with more melanin in their skin, and those whose spacefaring created the same effect.

Corvyn smiled and once more withdrew.

Throw your words against the wind, into light.
Neither man nor god knows the raven's flight.

11

Having no desire to spend the night in the lands of the Saints, still referred to by some as Deseret, and by others as Kolob, Corvyn reclaimed his electrobike, donned the black stedora, and proceeded another several milles north on the river road, past the seemingly endless wide streets of Nauvoo, until he reached Lee's Ferry, located in the far northwest part of Nauvoo. Just before he reached the inclined gray-paved road leading down to the ferry slip, he passed a small brownish stone dwelling situated on a squat point overlooking the river. Although the structure bore no appellation, Corvyn knew its name—Lonely Dell—and that of the scapegoat who inhabited the original house of that name before the Fall.

As he rode down to the slip, he saw that the top level of the waiting ferry shimmered like black glass under the white light and pink skies of Heaven. That blackness soaked in all the photons possible in order to power the ferry across the river and not to be carried downstream by the considerable current, a task that faced all ferries, since the Lances of Heaven enforced the prohibition on bridges, or for that matter, cables or other connections, crossing the ten major rivers of Heaven, the waters of which all eventually flowed into Lake Lethe.

Once at the slip, Corvyn slowed the bike to a stop and handed his card to the ferryman standing by the gate.

In return, the ferryman scanned it without really looking at it or Corvyn, returned the card, and said, "Stowage for electrobikes is forward on either side of the drop ramp."

"Thank you."

Corvyn eased the bike across the ramp and onto the gray metal of the deck, then forward to the front end of the vehicle deck, where he locked the bike in place, then walked back to the steps leading to the passenger deck and took them up one level. Perhaps a score of passengers stood on the open deck surrounding the windowed passenger cabin, seldom used except for the few times that it rained, usually, but not always, at night.

While there were several groups of passengers, including two parties of men in white thobes, clearly Poetics, and most likely merchant traders, Corvyn next turned his attention to those in pairs, beginning with the two women in the green trousers and tunic-like blouses of the Maid, both black-haired, olive-skinned, and of indeterminate age. The Poetics avoided glancing at the pair in a fashion that was more studied than an inspection could have been.

At that, Corvyn allowed himself a brief smile of amusement, continuing his quiet scrutiny of the others, passing over the two Judaics in black, and the two less-than-comfortable young Saints in their white shirts, black trousers, and cravats. His eyes finally turned to a man with a slightly weathered face the color of dark honey with black hair and well-trimmed beard. The man's white thobe had a forest-green lining, suggesting certain possibilities to Corvyn. He held no aura of energy, or other indication of power or principality, which suited Corvyn quite nicely.

As Corvyn approached, the man looked up and offered an amused smile. "The black hat doesn't change anything, you know, veiled one?"

Corvyn smiled in return, if slightly surprised that the man could sense auras or at least shadows that were not seen by most. "If I were Al-Muqanna, or Borkai, if you prefer, honored alim, I would most likely be in white, not gray, and riding not an electrobike, but a gray camel—not the one that stopped Abu Jahl."

"Your refutation is a proof of sorts."

"It likely proves that I know a small bit of history about the Poetics," replied Corvyn. "Just enough to cause confusion and trouble."

"Has that not always been the profession of the gray man? There are unseen shadows around you, and those are of the veiled prophet."

"There are shadows, and there are shadows."

"Shadows under the light of the Pearls of Heaven are not so dark as those you cast."

"You're speaking metaphorically, I trust," replied Corvyn with a gentle laugh.

"If I were speaking metaphorically, I might claim to be Abu Sufyan. I'm not. Jemal Quarysh, at your service."

"Perhaps Imam Alim Jemal Quarysh?"

"A wise man never claims titles."

"You can call me Corvyn. It's what I usually answer to, and it's also my name."

"One of them, anyway," returned Quarysh.

"The green of your thobe lining might suggest an interest in or an affinity with nature."

"It could suggest that. Or not."

"Just as gray can suggest shadows, or not."

Quarysh inclined his head, politely, but asked, "Why are you on the road to Yerusalem? I presume that is your immediate destination."

"I'm undertaking a survey." Since his words embodied both the literal and metaphoric truth, concealing as much as enlightening, Corvyn was happy to utter them.

"What sort of survey?"

"A cultural survey, one dealing with the manifestations of the triad in belief."

"The Triangle of Manifestation has long since been disproven."

"Only in the sense that space is an affect of energy, but in pragmatic terms space, time, and energy still form a triad that we see and experience even in these enlightened times."

"Those who have lived in most times, even before and after the Fall, believed that they were enlightened. This has not changed even under the Pearls of Heaven. I suspect you know this all too well." Quarysh paused as the ferry's whistle announced its departure, a departure so smooth that it was almost imperceptible, then continued conversationally, "The waters of the River Sanctus are a deeper blue than I'd thought. They say that each of the rivers of Heaven is a slightly different color."

"I'd never thought about that," replied Corvyn, a statement truthful only in its words. "What color would you say the River Jordan might be?"

"It's more greenish, as I recall. I've never really looked at it the few times I've passed through Yerusalem. What about the River of the Sun at Helios?"

"Bluer than the Sanctus, as I recall."

"Have you ever seen the citadel of the Dark One?"

"DeNoir? Anyone in Helios can see his villa. It's certainly not a citadel."

"You have not been inside it? With the shadows that surround you, I find that hard to believe."

"I'm not who you think." With those words, Corvyn avoided an outright lie.

"Perhaps not who, but most likely what," replied Quarysh. "Why are you undertaking this . . . survey?"

"Oh, it's a very real survey. The purpose is almost exactly as I stated. What do you think about the forms of the triad in belief, in your particular faith?"

"I cannot say that anything dealing with three has nearly the significance to those of the words of the Prophet and of Allah as it does to the Paulists or the followers of Jahweh. I would not wish to speculate on the views of those who follow the White One of Los Santos, since he is, shall we say, more focused on faith than upon the basis of that faith."

Corvyn would not have put it that way, but also would not have argued against the observation. "Your words are interesting," he mused. "A great deal of Poetic art is based on geometry, and the triangle is an integral part of that art, both in mosaics and other forms."

"You mentioned belief, not architecture or art."

"Can you separate what is built and displayed by those of faith from the faith? What is built can give lie to words merely spoken."

Quarysh stiffened.

Corvyn smiled pleasantly. "I won't trouble you further, Imam Quarysh. I've enjoyed our brief conversation." He nodded politely, turned, and walked to the forward railing, where he stood and looked toward the approaching shore, still a good third of a mille away.

No one approached him for the remainder of the crossing, and shortly before the ferry entered the slip on the west side of the river, Corvyn descended to the vehicle deck, which also held five camels, and unlocked his electrobike, noting that no one had triggered the protections.

He was the first to ride off the ferry and into the town of Rockwell, well suited as a complement to Lee's Ferry. The causeway from the ferry led right into Center Street, which at some point near the middle of town intersected Main Street. As in so many Saint communities, nondescript grays, whites, and browns dominated the buildings and houses, each set discretely apart from every other structure, as if the very buildings required personal space.

Although it was barely past midafternoon, Corvyn knew he would need to find lodging for the night, unless he wanted to spend it in a caravansary with less than optimal amenities, something he would have to do in any case on the following nights as he made his way to and through the land of milk and honey—and to Yerusalem.

Rockwell was laid out in the same fashion as every other Saint town, although the land on which it stood did not technically belong to the Prophet, Seer, and Revelator, a distinction that allowed certain liberties to the inhabitants of the town. The wide tree-lined streets boasted sidewalks that seldom held many people, and more than a few electrovans filled with families of four, as in Nauvoo and every other Saint town, a compromise required by all Houses of the Decalivre in the aftermath of the pogrom of the missionaries, a massacre not just of missionaries, but one necessitated by Saint intransigence and carried out by the Lances of Heaven.

Corvyn did not stay on Center Street long, but turned right on the first street that headed north paralleling the river, since the better neighborhoods were usually upstream rather than downstream. Although, given Saint neatness, that was likely to be less certain in Rockwell. After three long blocks—all the long blocks were long in Saint lands, as a result of eons of tradition dating back to Earth-Eden before it was destroyed—he could see that the size of the dwellings increased slightly, and before long he found himself nearing the Palmyra Inn, a structure graced by a round stone portico in the middle from which two wings of a single level extended.

He left the electrobike in front, albeit with certain precautions, and made his way inside, where a tall woman with mahogany hair smiled brightly as she rose from behind a table desk. "Welcome to the Palmyra Inn."

"I'd like a room for the night, if one is available." Corvyn extended his card.

"We have several," replied the clerk, accepting the card and scanning it. "Just one night, Mister . . . Poe, is it?"

Corvyn had almost forgotten that the Saints tended to use "mister" as a form of address, and he paused momentarily before replying, "Poe, that's correct, and just the one night."

"Would you like a suite? Or a grand suite?"

"A small suite would be fine."

"Your suite is on the north end overlooking the river, number three." She returned the card, along with another. "There are bike lockers by the north door. You can access them with the room card. Can I help you with anything else?"

"The name of a good place to eat." Corvyn could have accessed the net to determine proximity, but not anything relating to opinion, a limiting parameter of which he approved and with which he had long since been all too familiar.

"Near here, there's the Beehive and Sundance. They're both good."

Corvyn smiled. "Which serves the widest range of beverages?"

"Both serve hot beverages. The Sundance also offers most spirits."

"Thank you." Corvyn inclined his head, then left the entry.

He quickly secured the bike and carried his cases into the small suite, which did in fact offer an excellent view of the River Sanctus—before he closed the shades and darkened the sitting room. After seating himself on the not-quite-uncomfortable chair turned away from the table desk, he called up the aether, gathering it into a flat oval this time, suspending it before him, first seeking the poetess.

This time she sat in the shade, looking out over a balcony at a city that could be one of several, although it was certainly not Marcion or Nauvoo and highly unlikely to be Yerusalem. Her gray eyes were slitted against the white light that fell just short of her. On the table beside her were several sheets of paper, and Corvyn shifted the focus of the aether to read what he could.

Sequestered sensibilities serve ages
Of strident sycophantic sages,
Ensconced too easily in ivory cages
Their words all penned from puissant plundered pages.

Almost as if she sensed his intrusion, and perhaps she could, she reached out and turned the paper facedown on the table before he could read more.

Short as what he had read happened to be, his lips quirked in amusement, in part because he agreed with the sentiment, the meaning, and the parodying style of the words, and also because her awareness of his observation indicated that she was more than a mere passive piece in what just might be a highly convoluted but hidden struggle between those who sought power and those who sought to break it.

He returned his concentration to the aether in order to seek out the singer.

The dark-haired singer stood alone in what could only be a studio of some sort, playing the lutelin and singing. Abruptly, he stopped, frowning. He resumed singing and playing, then halted once more, clearly dissatisfied.

Corvyn observed for a time longer, then let his control of the aether lapse, thinking. The singer had been working on perfecting either another song or a way of delivering that song, if not both, and that was scarcely unusual for a performer. Yet . . . there had been something . . .

Corvyn shook his head.

"Quaero, sed non invenio." Except he had found another thread in the current tapestry of the Norns, or of Arianrhod, or Neith, or . . . Clotho and her sisters. The names of the Fates were endless, singular and plural, but too often the tapestry of Fate produced the same result, regardless of the intentions of those who wove the fabric of belief.

Should you call up any of the Decalivre? With a wry smile, he shook his head. Then they would know for certain that times were perilous, and their desires for their beliefs to at last triumph would only increase the possibilities of another Fall. *No. Matters, as before, must be handled in the shadows.* A lesson he had learned too late and too painfully.

After considering the situation for a time, he stood and let the light flood back into the sitting room. Then he freshened up, darkened the color of his jacket, checked the location of the Sundance, and left the suite. Once outside, he walked four long blocks, past several low structures behind gray stone walls that were clearly private residences, before coming to yet another low and long structure, comprised of massive peeled logs above low walls of mortared boulders, yet with wide windows as well.

He took the polished stone walk that extended some twenty meters and entered through a honey-gold wooden door.

"Might I help you, sir?" A greeter stepped forward, a tall, lean woman with gray eyes, wearing a slate-colored jacket and trousers, complemented by a cream blouse and gray boots of the type once associated with grasslands and ranching.

"I know it's a bit early, but is dinner being served?"

"It is, in both the Smithy and the Arboretum."

"And you would suggest?"

"I wouldn't presume, sir, but you might better appreciate the Arboretum . . ."

"The Arboretum will be fine." Corvyn's smile was part appreciation and part amusement at her effort to suggest that a man of refinement and taste would prefer the more elegant and doubtless expensive restaurant. "How long has the Sundance been here?"

"Well before my time, sir. I couldn't say. You'd like a window table?"

"Yes, please."

As indicated by the name, the Arboretum consisted of a large space with tables on slightly different levels, each surrounded by living greenery of some sort. Corvyn was surprised to see that of the nearly twenty tables, almost a third were taken, despite the early hour. The greeter escorted him to a circular table with a wide window on one side and the arc of a gardenia hedge on the other, just high enough to shield him from those at other tables, or them from him.

The greeter departed, and in moments, a server appeared, an attractive brunette of approximately the same age as Corvyn appeared to be, if with a hint of hardness on an otherwise pleasant face. "Might I get you something to drink?"

"What might be the best dry white wine you have?"

"The driest white is Atacama Pinot Grigio; the best of the drier whites is the Sundance gris."

Anything with the name Atacama was likely far too dry for Corvyn. "I'll try the Sundance."

"If you touch the miniature bronze there," said the server, pointing, "that will call up the menu." With a smile, she turned and left.

Corvyn studied the piece he had thought to be a decoration—a nearly solid bronze miniature of a barred window on top of a stone wall. Definitely one of the more bizarre menu bars he'd seen over the years. He touched the metal and perused the menu, noting the menu items, and the considerable prices of each, but nodded at several. He paused to listen to two men in somber brown garb at the nearest table, one clearly older than the other and doing most of the talking, loudly enough that Corvyn didn't have to strain.

". . . beliefs are stronger than science, because they rest on what makes beings capable of thought comfortable. Actual thinking has an unsettling tendency, and being unsettled weakens the thought being expressed."

"Capable of thought? That's an interesting way of putting it."

"Perhaps I should have said theoretically capable of thought. In any event, that's why Jaweau and the old ones discourage thought. It weakens their power."

"Brother Paul isn't known . . ."

"Not here," said the older man quickly. "We're talking about other hegemons."

"What about the Hegemon of Helios? There's never much said about him."

Of course there isn't, reflected Corvyn, *for good reason.*

"Little is said, but dark shadows always have power."

"Because they conceal what men do not wish to be seen?"

"More because people believe that to be true."

Isn't that always the case? Corvyn smiled sardonically even as he wondered just what the two Paulists were doing in the vicinity of Nauvoo, but the next sentences reflected on the food, as if neither had wanted to talk about Lucian DeNoir, or shadows.

Corvyn turned his attention to the couple next-nearest him.

". . . keep track of who crosses the river . . ."

"Sundance isn't Saint . . . don't report . . ."

"Danites have their ways . . ."

Corvyn shook his head. As if the First Counselor and his aides had that much interest in who drank spirits or met with those to whom they were not married for time and eternity. The ward bishop perhaps, if he happened to be petty enough, but not the First Counselor or the Danites. Their powers were concentrated on other matters in order to deal with those high in the Decalivre. *Or you, if they but knew.*

A few moments later, the server returned, presenting a goblet and a carafe. "The Sundance gris, sir."

"Thank you. I'll have a small house salad and the cranberry orange duck with the rice occidental and green beans almandine."

"That's a good choice. The duck is always good. The owners raise them on a place farther up the river."

"Do you live on this side of the river?"

"Most of us working here do. The ferry's not cheap if you have to take it each way every day."

"Does serving spirits affect who chooses to work here?" Corvyn offered a smile with a hint of warm amusement.

"Definitely. The perquisites and gratuities are far better, and the clientele far more interesting. You're not from around here, not anywhere close."

"From where would you say I hail?"

"You're older than you look, and you've seen more." She shook her head. "I'd say, that wherever you lay your head most nights, even for years, it's not home."

"You see more than most."

"Most of us here do. Those who don't get uncomfortable after a while." She looked to the goblet. "You'll like the Sundance." With a cheerful look that wasn't quite a smile she turned.

Corvyn took a sip of the gris. It was good, not great—the taste crisp, but not too edged, and definitely not buttery, because, for him, too buttery brought up the memories of the decadence that had preceded too much destruction.

As he waited for the salad he knew would not be all that long in coming, he realized something else. The Sundance was shielded from the intrusions of almost all powers and principalities, except for those on the level of the heads of each House of the Decalivre. That partly explained the couple nearest him—and the prices.

He took another sip of the Sundance gris, enjoying it more than he thought he might.

If sleep, perchance, shall lead to dreams,
the raven drinks at Heaven's streams.

12

Two days later, the electrobike carried Corvyn through the sandy hills a good hundred milles northwest of the Sea of Galilee. While he could have covered the distances he had traveled more quickly by using the shadows, he would have been exhausted by such long shadow travel, and needed time to recuperate. Not to mention the fact that he would have been limited to what little he could carry, and he would have been unable to see the people and the lands through which he had passed. And that would have been a loss, because the people often revealed what a hegemon did not.

Much farther behind him to the northwest were low mountains, a puny extension of Celestial Mountains so much farther to the north, but on that extension now towered mighty cedars, their metaphorical roots in long-gone Lebanon. The most pious of the Judaics still trekked to the northwest periodically to obtain that prized wood, but only periodically, mindful of the fate of those first mighty cedars whose descendants had fared far better than those of the even once-mightier sequoias.

Corvyn's immediate objective was the River Jordan, where the road turned to follow the southeastern course of the river as it wound toward the Sea of Galilee and Yerusalem beyond. What he would find in Yerusalem was another question, at least beyond another possible trident, for the Judaics were fragmented in all aspects of their faith, except in the Torah and belief in a deity whose name should not be often spoken and that no individual, and perhaps no rabbi, was above another in closeness to that deity.

While traveling, he had summoned the aether, but found nothing different about the singer and the poetess, except they were still not close, nor had they moved from wherever they had been before.

Ahead, near the top of a hill, he saw a shepherd boy with a border collie, moving a flock of sheep up the slope. The young man wore a long-sleeved shirt and trousers of khaki so washed out that the color was more like tannish white, and a broad-brimmed hat of a similar shade and color. His staff was likely a stunner in order to deal with the coywolves that lurked amid the hills, but his steps were measured as he climbed the boulder-studded and mostly grassy slope.

Corvyn smiled and continued along the road.

More than two hours later, he neared the point where the hill road met the river road at the town of Aenon. While there were no springs there, the water of the Jordan was clean, as were all the waters of Heaven, but Corvyn had more interest in getting something reasonably tasty to eat for a late midday meal.

After passing several establishments that were either closed or had a feel to them that was not terribly interesting, he finally eased the electrobike to a halt in front of a building that looked like an overlarge stone cottage. A small signboard bore the name RIVER'S EDGE—a name appropriate because the cottage-like building sat only a few meters back from a stone wall that angled down to the greenish water of the river. A very restrained and barely discernible sense of power also enfolded the building and gardens that stretched northward, encompassing several other structures.

The interior space looked more like an ancient public room—except far cleaner—and was empty except for an older woman walking toward him.

"Are you open?"

"From sunup to midevening, every day. What else would I do?"

"Then you're the proprietress?"

"That's me—Siduri Brightstone, the one and only. Window table suit you?"

"If it suits you," replied Corvyn cheerfully.

With a broad smile, she gestured toward a square dark wooden table set before a window overlooking the river, then led him there. Cutlery and utensils rested on a pale blue placemat.

Corvyn took the seat that allowed him to look downstream as well as in the direction of anyone else entering the public room.

"Cautious type, aren't you?"

"Habit. It's been years. What would you suggest?"

"I do have a braised lamb shank with polenta, and a wild green salad. The greens aren't that wild, though. They come from the garden."

"The lamb sounds good." Corvyn hadn't kept up with the Judaics' calendar—there was something about some Judaics not serving lamb during Passover and others believing lamb was a special dish for Passover. He supposed it wouldn't be served if it happened to be against the faith of the proprietress. "Do you have a wine that will go well with it?"

"Lamb's always good. I have a half bottle of a Tempranillo reserve that's fairly good."

"Fairly good?"

"It's very good, but it's pricy. Fairly good for the price."

Corvyn laughed softly. "I'll try them both . . . if you keep me company while I eat. That's if no one else shows up."

"I've had better offers. Also had much worse. You'll have company, after you're served."

The name Siduri was somehow familiar, but Corvyn could not place it. Finally, he accessed the net and asked the origin of the name. When the answer came up, he smiled. Then he made another inquiry and came up with a second name, just in case.

He was still thinking in which of the many possible fashions Siduri had ended up on the edge of Judaic territory when she returned with two goblets and a half bottle, which she opened so deftly that Corvyn could not even hear the emergence of the cork. She did not pour, but said, "I'll be back in a moment."

She was indeed, carrying two platters, one small, with the greens, and one larger, with slightly raised edges and containing a single lamb shank and the polenta, both lightly covered with a sauce that offered familiar scents in an unfamiliar combination. "There you are." After setting them before him, she seated herself across from Corvyn.

He lifted the bottle to pour.

"Just a finger or so."

Corvyn obliged, then filled his goblet a little more than half full, after which he lifted it, knowing she would lift hers, which she did.

"To the fruit of the vineyard and the bounty of the land." He took a sip of the Tempranillo, enjoying the robustness that was not too much, with a certain . . . piquantness. He nodded. "Better than fairly good."

Siduri had also sipped. "A bit better."

Corvyn was not about to dispute her on that. Instead, he cut a morsel of the lamb and ate it, enjoying the restrained fusion of lemon, thyme, rosemary, and tomatoes . . . and, of course, olive oil. After several mouthfuls, he said, "I'm surprised you aren't busy all the time."

"You'll see why when you pay," she replied with a smile.

"Then you must have a stable of regulars who enjoy fine cuisine."

"Enough."

Corvyn enjoyed several more small mouthfuls before speaking again. "You have a vineyard here and others farther away?"

"I do. The Tempranillo comes from the hill vineyard."

The lamb shank was just the right size for Corvyn, or almost so. He left a bit of the lamb and quite a bit more of the polenta, finishing his dinner with the greens.

"You eat in the older style," she said. "I thought you might."

"I eat in the style suggested by the food and the provider." He lifted the half bottle and poured another finger into her goblet and refilled his, then took another modest swallow. "You enjoy it here?"

"More than I would most places."

"You've been doing this for a while, Siduri . . . possibly you knew a man named Gilgamesh?"

"I might have, a long while ago, Enlil."

Corvyn shook his head. The name was the other one about which he had inquired. "I could be, but I'm not." That was true in the strictest sense, but the distinction his statement implied was without a difference.

"You're older than you look, and more powerful."

"So are you."

Siduri shook her head. "I'm less than a principality, and that suits me these days. It's enough to deal with small difficulties, and not enough to attract larger troubles and powers."

Corvyn nodded, understanding all too well what she meant. "Do you ever have any Paulists visiting?"

"I'm sure we have, but I don't ask. Most don't mention where they come from."

"Then I will. Helios."

"I visited there once." She smiled softly. "There was a garden there, and I spent a little time with a friend. But there were far too many powers, principalities, and others who would challenge the Dark One."

Ishtaraath had never mentioned Siduri to Corvyn, but then there was much that Ishtaraath neglected to mention, and Corvyn wasn't about to mention Tammuz to Siduri, for obvious reasons.

"You know her, don't you?"

"I do. We're on friendly terms." Most of the time.

"You're even more cautious than you look. But, then you would be. Why are you here? Certainly not to see me."

"I'm here in this room because I was looking for an excellent meal, and I sensed a restrained sense of power that suggested I'd find what I was first looking for."

"Then . . . why are you headed to Yerusalem?"

"To see if a black-flamed trident has burned itself into some holy aspect of the Temple."

Siduri frowned. "The Dark One's pitchfork? Why would he do that?"

"I doubt that he did. Some power arranged for one to appear on the cover of the holy book of the Paulists, and in the stone of the study of the Saints' Prophet, Seer, and Revelator."

Siduri shivered. "I cannot say that I like that. That can only raise troubles across Heaven."

"That's obvious," agreed Corvyn. "The question is twofold. Who is behind the tridents, and what do they hope to gain from creating such unrest?"

"Poseidon is only revered in the tiniest of villages, and you wouldn't be here if the Dark One of Helios were behind the tridents. Shiva's never been one to announce his intent. He tends to wait and then overact in nasty ways."

"Your thoughts are similar to mine," said Corvyn.

"If . . . if what you say turns out to be true in the other Houses of the Decalivre, it would suggest that a power is building to declare itself the One True God of Heaven."

"That is exactly what I fear." Corvyn's words were totally without deception or evasion.

Siduri rose just before the door to the public room opened and a couple entered. "I wish you well, ancient of shadows."

"Thank you." Corvyn handed her his card.

She scanned it and then showed him the amount on the scanner, an amount equivalent to the most expensive prices of high cuisine in Helios or anywhere else in Heaven. Corvyn added a fifty percent gratuity, then approved it.

"Thank you," Siduri replied.

"It's been my pleasure." And for Corvyn, it had been indeed. He stood and inclined his head. "Do take care, Siduri. I'd like to find you here in the future."

"That is up to you, I believe." Her smile was not quite impish. "May the light not extinguish your shadow."

"Thank you." Corvyn could not resist smiling in return before he made his way out to the electrobike to continue his journey.

Always, Heaven's purest light
shadows Raven's every flight.

13

Corvyn spent that night in Galilee, little more than a fishing village, unsurprisingly, since it lay within the lands claimed by the Judaics, and not within the lands of the Paulists or the followers of Jaweau the White, or even of the Poetics. The Sea of Galilee was, as had been its namesake, a large lake, one more than three times the size of the original, some thirty milles long and twenty wide, and likely with better fishing, if fewer storms. He left early the next morning because it would take him until late afternoon to reach the outskirts of Yerusalem.

Yerusalem, like its original namesake, was not located on the River Jordan but some milles east of it, unlike the namesake, which had been to the west of the original River Jordan. But then, Heaven did not always provide the expected. One expectation—or rather the result of that expectation—Corvyn fervently did not wish to see fulfilled. That potentially disastrous expectation would be most unlikely to be fulfilled, or even supported, in Yerusalem, since it was the only House of the Decalivre that had no head, no grand rabbi, not even a successor to the legendary Maimonides. There was no overriding Sanhedrinic council, and each of the branches of Judaism had its own version of the halakha.

All this led Corvyn to wonder whether he would discover anything at all of use during his visit, and what impact, if any, the black-flaming trident had in that holy city.

By early afternoon, he neared the road to Jericho, less than ten milles from the river. The air was definitely warmer and drier than in Nauvoo, and olive groves grew seemingly on every third hill. There were also lemon trees, but those tended to be inside walled gardens close to the houses. The road to Jericho and on to Yerusalem remained one of smooth, impermeable, and almost eternal tan stone.

Corvyn turned onto it and, within a hundred meters, had to ride around a cart pulled by a donkey led by a youth in a brown thobe who did not even look up as Corvyn passed. Neither did the donkey.

After another two hours, Corvyn slowed the electrobike at the crest of a hill where he could look out over Yerusalem, then guided the electrobike to the side of the road before stopping. From there he studied the city that filled the entire valley below, in the center of which was the Temple, to be precise, the Third Temple.

The Third Temple occupied a raised square on the Temple Mount, but then, every one of the previous incarnations of the Third Temple had been on a flattened hill called a mount. The Temple itself was of white marble and shining bronze, theoretically similar in appearance to the Second Temple, but not employing gold, because that would have been heretical for reasons that had never been clear to Corvyn.

Even from the hillcrest some ten milles from the Temple and the center of Yerusalem, Corvyn could sense the interplay of currents of power, very different from Nauvoo, Los Santos, or Marcion, where all the currents centered on the head of that House, or Helios, where all currents, especially those around DeNoir's villa, were muted. But then, he knew the reasons for that. He decided to head for the quarter of the city closest to the Temple where that interplay appeared to be the greatest.

In time, he entered a yellow brick building with an air of history and the name of the King David. The concierge looked at Corvyn with initial skepticism, which vanished as he accepted Corvyn's card.

"You will be staying how long, sir?"

"Two nights." That might or might not be, but Corvyn suspected that what he needed to do in Yerusalem might be even less straightforward than it had been elsewhere.

"I can give you a suite on the sixth floor, sir. If you don't mind not having a Temple view."

"That will be acceptable."

"You're fortunate it's not Passover, Pentecost, or even Tabernacles. You know, we even get Poetics and Saints for the Feast of Tabernacles."

"Many of them?"

"Around ten thousand, sometimes more," replied the concierge. "Not all at the King David, of course."

"Of course."

"You have a vehicle?"

"Merely an electrobike for local transportation."

"Ah, yes." The concierge returned Corvyn's card with a second one. "The suite pass will open any bike locker that's not taken. Once you open that locker only your pass will unlock it." He paused. "You know, the lockers at the base of the Temple Mount are not that secure."

"That does not surprise me. Thank you."

Corvyn dealt with the bike, extracted his cases, and carried them to the lift that transported him to the sixth floor. Even before he stepped into the sitting room of the suite, he knew that someone of power awaited him, and took appropriate precautions.

The power who stood by the window was both tall and of extreme beauty, of the type once called androgynous, with golden curly hair and deep gray eyes that seemed sad. The angel wore a white shimmering thobe, but displayed no wings, although Corvyn believed the angel could have, if ever the necessity arose.

He did not recognize this particular angel, but that was scarcely surprising. While he knew the ranks of the Judaic angels and their names, there were no descriptions available, or rather, since they could take on a variety of guises, only the patterns of their powers revealed their identity. Corvyn had never needed to make himself more than casually acquainted with any, and that left him at a certain disadvantage.

"Which dark one are you?" The voice was musical, but neither particularly masculine nor feminine.

"You must know by now, if you're already here," replied Corvyn.

"Your card tracks to Helios, and the depths of your shadows rival those of the Dark Hegemon. Since Lucian DeNoir, as he prefers to be called, at least occasionally, is not known to travel widely, it would appear that you are the shadow raven, otherwise known as—"

"There's no need to go there. That was many lives ago."

The angel's laugh was like wedding bells at a wake.

"I'm merely visiting Yerusalem. What is your interest in me?"

"Neither the raven nor DeNoir *merely* exist, or *merely* visit, and nothing is the same after either passes."

Under the circumstances that might yet occur, Corvyn certainly hoped that matters would change as a result of his travels. "That remains to be seen."

"There is enough difficulty here with the present dark one."

"Samael, you mean?"

"Is there any other in Yerusalem? Until you arrived, that is."

"What do you want, then?"

"No more than I've always wanted . . . to bring all of Heaven together in harmony."

"There's more than one kind of togetherness," replied Corvyn. "Should I call you Sandalphon or Sandalphel?"

"Does it matter? I am what I am."

"Only for convenience."

"Since most would prefer Sandalphon, call me Sandalphel, if you need a name at all."

"What do you want of me?" Corvyn emphasized the last two words slightly.

"I can compel nothing. That is not my nature. I would request that you consider just how your dark chaos will affect Yerusalem and all of Heaven."

"I have already considered that. From what I've seen, my not traveling will be far worse than what my travels may bring."

"Did you believe that in the time of the golden ring? When the others of power were not enough to hold Metatron's Cube together and the Second Home was consumed in fire?"

"I did not travel far enough then. Would that I could have."

"Metatron did not record that you were absent."

And as the recording angel, Metatron would know. "Acting from within was not sufficient. It seldom is. We're too often blinded by what we wish to see, or how we wish to see it."

"For what has come of your shadows . . ."

"For what has come from what was later laid under my shadows," corrected Corvyn. "Not that my inability was not a great fault. I acknowledge that fault."

"I cannot console you for that, nor will I."

"Nor should you."

Sandalphel shimmered more brightly, then vanished amid the light, as Corvyn did amid the shadows.

Metatron, the highest of the angels of the ancient deity, had reputedly not spoken to any entity not a power since the first Fall, the one so long ago, long before the destruction of Eden Earth, the Fall obliquely mentioned by Sandalphel, yet Metatron and Sandalphel were greatly troubled by Samael? That did not bode well. Was there an unseen connection to the creator of the tridents?

For all that, Corvyn was hungry, and Heaven would not fall in the immediate future if he sought out a good meal. *Not yet, in any event.*

Rainbow of the distant past, white star,
Raven alone sees all things as they are.

14

Corvyn slept later than he had planned and woke troubled by vague dreams he could not recall, but such dreams were far better than those he could remember. Far better. In time, after he had roused himself, refreshed his person, dressed, and eaten, he called up the aether, not even to observe either the poetess or the singer, but to ascertain that they were not near Yerusalem, which they were not.

That task accomplished, he walked out onto the streets of Yerusalem and made his way, as any visitor might have done, toward the Temple Mount, not that he would be admitted to the Temple as an unbeliever, but as a visitor whose purchases would contribute to the well-being of Yerusalem, his presence near the Temple would not be unwelcome.

He knew that the trident would not have been burned into the innermost and sacred chamber designed for the Ark of the Covenant, because that chamber was the most sacred, and totally empty, reflecting the loss or destruction of the Ark millennia in the past. At the thought of a sacred and empty chamber, he smiled fleetingly, if with wry amusement.

As he neared the walls surrounding the Temple Mount, he sensed the representative emptiness of the Temple, as well as the currents of power manifested by the remaining angels of the Almighty, one in particular, whose presence did not surprise him, but whose absence would have. Cloaked in shadows, Corvyn let the currents of power guide him to where the trident had been burned into the white marble of the Temple—on the wall just inside the Temple proper.

Beneath that black-flamed image stood a group of rabbis, largely but not exclusively in white robes with white caps, all of whom were engaged in a discussion about the black-flamed trident emblazoned into the white marble above them. What surprised Corvyn was not that there had been a discussion, but that it was continuing, given how long it had been since the trident appeared.

Still cloaked in shadows, Corvyn listened.

". . . when Herod placed the Roman eagle over the gate of the Second Temple, there was a revolt . . ."

"That was a symbol of temporal authority over the supremacy of the Almighty, and all revolted for that reason, not because there was any Talmudic conflict . . . or question of faith . . ."

"In Maimonides' treatment of Attributes, he states that faith is not a mere attitude of mind, or an innate state of consciousness. Nor is it immediate comprehension of intuitive knowledge, which is but mysticism, but rather the positive intellectual certainty arrived at after a process of ratiocinative reasoning. Ratiocinative reasoning suggests that neither the Almighty nor one of his angels would place a symbol such as a trident inside the entrance to the Temple. Therefore, the placement of this symbol must be from a temporal source here in Heaven, and from one attempting to assert spiritual primacy through temporal means—"

"That is not how Maimonides applies to this abomination. That trident can only be an attribute of the person, power, or being that created it and placed it here. As an attribute, it is not only a symbol, but a part of that power which placed it here, and by following that attribute, one should be able to discover that principality or power."

"Exactly how do you propose to follow that attribute to its creator?"

"That is a matter of technology and mechanics. Isn't that your specialty?"

"If it's beyond technology, it's yours. As Maimonides said, descriptions of metaphysical phenomena are beyond human comprehension, which comprehension is limited because the majority of people can only recognize physical bodies . . ."

Corvyn eased away, doubting that he would find anything resembling such a drawn-out discussion in other venues where the trident had appeared. While the number three had certain meanings for the Judaics,

Corvyn was not aware of a particular Judaic meaning for the trident, but then he certainly had had little to do with the Judaics, except through what aspects of their faith had been incorporated into the beliefs of the Paulists and the white ones of Jaweau.

He was about to make his way from the Temple when he sensed a strengthening of a particular dark power, one of those whom he suspected might well be interested in his presence in Yerusalem. And that dark power was within the vacant Holy of Holies, which was also a mockery of sorts, even if not recognized by the Judaics.

Corvyn shrugged and made his way there through the shadows.

A figure with black-edged wings of otherwise heavenly aspect awaited him, an angel who could be none other than Samael. Corvyn had not expected otherwise in the vacant space that would never see the Ark of the Covenant for which it was designed, which, in an abstruse way, represented a testament to the triumph of faith over reality, while demonstrating its futility.

"Who sent you?" asked Corvyn, knowing the question was meaningless, but not wishing to impart any information first.

"You know that question is without meaning."

"I was being polite. Inquiries have meanings beyond the mere words, as you well know. How is Lilith these days?"

"Tempting, as you also know."

Corvyn waited.

"Your presence here, given that your usual abode lies a considerable distance from here, suggests you are pursuing something or merely stirring up trouble."

"Merely?" questioned Corvyn mildly.

The black-edged wings fluttered slightly as Samael offered an amused laugh.

"I've always wondered if you were the one who actually cast the golden apple onto the banquet table in the Halls of Olympus . . ."

"Why would I have concerned myself with that?" asked the dark angel. "I had no concern with deities who were but the personification of excessive adolescent fantasies."

"Because it led to war, and war, or the threat of war, particularly when involved with seduction and beauty, has always increased your power."

"In the past, you also received certain . . . benefits."

While that was not true, Corvyn ignored the implications and said, "You would call them that."

"And you?"

"Curses, but that was in another country, and those goddesses have long since . . . descended."

"Your language is always . . . precise. I notice that you are traveling in a most pedestrian fashion, hardly suited to an aerial spirit. One might think that you were attempting to avoid the scrutiny of the hegemons . . . except traveling in a manner unbecoming an aerial being creates a certain harmonic dissonance that, in the end, creates more notice."

Just in the end. "Only if someone happens to be looking."

"You aren't that far below notice, spirit of the raven."

"Nor are you, Samael. Was the trident I just observed sent to the Temple . . . or to you?"

"Poseidon's long gone."

"Drowned in the sea of space and the culture of information and explanation, no doubt," replied Corvyn.

"Which should have happened to you, by all rights."

"Except that the bright shiny bits of knowledge that I've found and hoarded, and then disbursed, have their use." *As do deep-rooted archetypes.* "As does the educated religious group democracy of your Judaics—"

"They're not mine."

"Then why are you here, in the Holy of Holies? Or is your presence here merely a mockery of the beliefs that sustain you? Your strength and presence are a testimony to that unacknowledged religious democracy."

"I'd prefer another word to the abomination called democracy, which always degenerates into the rule of those with the most votes, the principal question being what items are being used to purchase those votes. The chosen people at least require logic in their theology."

Corvyn kept his amusement to himself at Samael's defense of the

Judaics and pressed harder. "Except that logic applied to questionable premises results in questionable logic and unpleasant results."

"Questionable logic is always preferable to anarchy or illogic. Or to faith inherited and held on to through custom and lack of scrutiny."

Corvyn was not about to argue that point, not logically or any other way, although he had seen enough times that illogic would have been preferable to any form of logic. "You do have a way with words. But then that is the tradition from which you draw."

"I draw nothing. They draw from me."

"Why do you tolerate the trident?"

"It wasn't my doing, but it will plague those who have rejected me. It affords me a certain satisfaction, unlike you."

"I beg your pardon, font of logic and puissance," replied Corvyn sardonically, even while withdrawing more deeply into the shadows before Samael could touch him with either the power of destruction or the hand of death . . . for quite a few reasons, including the fact that, regardless of long-standing myths, Corvyn was anything but a masochist.

Both the blast of power and the chill of death found nothing.

Corvyn smiled again, because Samael would either have to remove signs of his presence in the Holy of Holies caused by the flames that did not strike Corvyn . . . or leave them, with the unpleasant implications they would create for the Judiacs . . . and Samael.

As he made his way from the Temple, still within his shadows, he was aware that yet another power followed him, if at enough of a distance that he could not determine anything more than the fact that he was being followed and by a power greater than a mere principality. He found that acceptable for the present, given how many more Houses of the Decalivre he needed to visit, especially since Samael's disavowal of the trident had the ring of truth.

Once several blocks from the Temple, still cloaked in shadows, he slipped into an alley and shed them, stepping out into the sunlight and turning his steps back toward the King David under the pink sky of Heaven, tinged in the north by wisps of clouds.

Do not carrion birds still mourn the dead,
and ravens grieve where those bright banners led?

15

From a perch on a blackened girder, twisted and half melted, protruding from hundreds of meters of snow-covered ice, the raven surveyed the panorama of whiteness that stretched in every direction. The only colors visible were those of the predominant white, tinged with the blue of ancient upraised ice, and the black and rust of scattered metal skeletons—all that remained of the city that once extended hundreds of milles north, south, and west, along the continental coastline. Besides the raven, there were no visible signs of life under the white sun that provided light, but seemingly no warmth.

Under the ice, the old coastline was still there, the raven knew, but the present coastline was more than a score of milles to the east, and also buried under ice, the result of centuries of increasing cold and snowfall and decreasing ocean levels.

Spreading his wings, the raven rose from his iron perch and climbed into the chill and bright blue sky, pristine, without even a trace of smoke, for any fire built by the scattered remnants and descendants of those who built the great cities lay more than a thousand milles to the south, beyond the reach of the ice and snow.

As high as the raven climbed, he saw nothing but ice and snow, with the exception of the tallest of steel shards men had once thought challenged the sky. Clear the air was, and bitingly bitter cold, with the ice of the present and the memories of the past . . .

A chime struck, built . . . and died away.

A far softer light surrounded Corvyn, and he sat up abruptly in the spacious bed in the King David. He shivered, despite the fact that the room was anything but chill. But he recalled the ice all too well.

Ice colder than anything in the Celestial Mountains, ice no one else remembers, or would want to.

Those memories, memories not technically his, but memories long since his, nonetheless, that seemed so recent, and yet so distant, and the dream, told him that it was time to leave Yerusalem.

The Ten must seek the defeat of error.
The raven sees the beginning of terror.

16

A day after leaving Yerusalem and crossing the Jordan on an open ferry with camels and traders, Corvyn spent a night in a less-than-distinguished caravansary. The following morning, he departed early, and, in time, a good hour after midafternoon, he came to a side road of white stone, one far narrower than the main road to Jannah that he had been traveling. There was no sign, nor had there ever been one. He stopped the electrobike and debated whether he should take the road to the place with no name, a place he had only seen through the use of aether, but one of which he had long been aware.

When will you likely be this close again? And will a day make that much difference with all you have before you? Besides, he knew the only other place to stop would be yet another caravansary, and one scarcely to his liking.

Then, as he thought it over, he saw the pair of doves that had, for some reason, been less than visible in Yerusalem. Each was perched on a boulder rising out of the soil that was mostly sand.

Thinking of Gabriel, and knowing how Brother Paul disliked those at the end of the white stone road, with a wry smile he turned the bike onto the narrow white road and proceeded.

He did not have to travel far, only slightly more than an hour, before he came over yet another rocky hill dotted with tufts of grass and scattered shrubs and saw his immediate destination. Everything in the Mazdean community was white, every single structure, and the houses and outbuildings were constructed in circles or at least in arcs, so that from the sky the town might well have resembled a multi-petaled exotic flower. Only the solar panels half concealed on the roofs were dark. Likewise, from what Corvyn could discern, the only shadows of power were those he brought. On a grassy slope on the far side of the neat but slightly sprawling town, he saw a herd of goats, accompanied by a shepherd and dog. Given the beliefs of the town, he knew full well that he would see no cats, although there would be terriers to deal with rodents.

A handful of electrovans moved through the streets, as well as an electrobike or two, but fewer than he would have seen in a town of the same size in the lands of the Saints, and far fewer children as well. He continued down the slope toward the central plaza, which was also a circle, rather than a square.

Before long, he parked the electrobike in a public stall and looked around slowly. Small shops surrounded the plaza, two cafés that Corvyn could see immediately, and several other low-domed buildings he did not recognize, although he suspected that one might be a fire temple.

A young man in white saw Corvyn and immediately turned in to a narrow alleyway, walking quickly in the other direction. A woman a few meters beyond the alleyway averted her eyes from Corvyn, and turned, taking a small child by the hand back down a side street away from the plaza.

Corvyn continued to walk toward the nearest café, where two older men sharing a table watched him approach. Then from the nearer of the domed buildings beyond the café, a slender man emerged, moving briskly across the plaza in Corvyn's direction, confirming in Corvyn's mind that the domed structure likely had some connection with faith.

Corvyn turned and waited.

The man who approached wore a pure white high-necked jacket and trousers. Even his boots were white. His only adornment was a gold medallion, that of a winged disc. He stopped a yard or so from Corvyn and inclined his head politely. "You have the aspect of a daeva and are clad in the same way." He smiled. "Few daevas would come here so obviously."

"I'm not here in service to untruth," replied Corvyn. "You might say I just stopped for a respite."

"Respite? Then this is not where you should have come. There is never a respite in the struggle to reclaim Heaven." For all his words, the athornan smiled. "My name is Alhazen, Alhazen Ibnsina."

"I wasn't aware that Heaven had fallen," replied Corvyn. "You can call me Corvyn."

"Join me for coffee, or tea, if you are so inclined, and we can discuss the matter." Alhazen gestured in the general direction of the café.

"Thank you. I'd like that, both tea and the discussion." *And possibly a meal, if the café is good.*

The athornan walked beside Corvyn, and the two proceeded to the café, where Alhazen walked to a shaded table under the awning. Corvyn took a chair that allowed him a view of both Alhazen and the square.

"The shadows behind and beyond you are deep," observed the athornan.

Since Corvyn could sense no particular power surrounding Alhazen, the man's observation was either a considered guess or the result of excellent perception. "You're more perceptive than most. On what are you basing that observation?"

"Your shadow is distinct and unblurred at the edges. Under the light of the sun, as modified by the Pearls of Heaven, the shadows of us mere mortals blur at the edges. Even the shadows of lesser powers and principalities, or lesser daevas, blur slightly."

"I wouldn't think you'd seen many of those here."

"We don't." Alhazen glanced up at the wiry and honey-skinned man who stood far closer to him than to Corvyn. "My usual." He looked to Corvyn.

"Tea. Not too sweet."

"Thank you, sir." The man retreated toward the natural shade of the interior of the café, not looking back.

"What brings you here?" asked Alhazen.

"I told you. A respite from my current pursuit."

"I'd be curious to know what a power of shadow might pursue or might even need to pursue."

"That which should not arise in Heaven. A certain shadow of the past, if you will."

"A power based in shadow pursuing a shadow of the past . . . I cannot say that I find that, in the words of those from Varanasi, auspicious."

"You've been to Varanasi?"

Alhazen shook his head. "Not for more years than I'd wish to count. In my youth, I visited every city of the Decalivre, even yours."

"Mine?"

"Where else could you come from, except Helios? Only the city named for the sun allows so many shadows."

"Rather a witty observation."

"Just an observation. All the worlds of men have been filled with two types of individuals, those who have wit and no belief, and those who hold to belief with no wit. Heaven is no different, except some of those with wit have power, and some of those with power have little or no wit." The athornan paused as the server, who also appeared to be the proprietor, returned with the coffee, milk, no sugar, Corvyn knew, and the tea, as dark as the coffee would have been without milk.

Alhazen sipped his coffee.

Corvyn sipped the tea.

"So you pursue evil?" Alhazen raised his eyebrows. "To what purpose? To vanquish it nobly and forever, as so many paladins have attempted in vain for so many eons?"

"My goals are not that absolute." Corvyn smiled sardonically. "What your ancient one understood was that to fight against evil, one perpetuates it. Evil cannot be vanquished by force of arms, because violence in service of anything merely begets more evil."

"Then why do you even pursue, if the end is vain?"

"Sometimes," rejoined Corvyn, "violence is necessary to prevent greater evil. Do you dispute that?"

"Violence ostensibly in the service of good can only forestall greater evil, but cannot vanquish evil itself."

"Then you will admit that there are times evil must be forestalled?" Corvyn took another sip of the strong but not bitter tea.

"Define evil for me," countered Alhazen.

"Any act or lack of action that results in harm to another." *That will do for a start.*

"What if any act to prevent harm to another will harm the actor or others? Or what if the other is convinced that your way of life is harmful to him and that your way of life justifies his actions as preventing harm to himself or those who believe as he does?"

"Isn't that the rationale behind the Lances of Heaven?" asked Corvyn. "To forestall mass action against others whose beliefs are different?"

"The Lances have proven to be necessary," admitted Alhazen. "They do not address the question I raised."

"If we are going to discuss the reasoning behind the Lances of Heaven and such," said Corvyn with a brief laugh, "I need to eat. Would you care to join me?"

"Of course. How often does a mere athornan have a chance to dine with a power of darkness?"

"Not a power of darkness," corrected Corvyn, "a power cloaked in shadows. There is a difference. I do not serve Ahriman or his attributes, nor, for that matter, the Dark One of Helios."

Alhazen stiffened for an instant before saying, "I did not wish to offend."

"You did not, but it is best to be clear about certain aspects." Corvyn gestured to the proprietor, who hurried to the table.

"Yes, maitres?"

Corvyn turned to Alhazen. "What would you suggest?"

"The aash, the lamb stew with the stuffed grape leaves on the side, with the Ramian Shiraz."

Corvyn nodded. He'd always been fond of good lamb. He just hoped the café would provide such. He finished his tea. "You were saying that the Lances of Heaven do not address the question, or perhaps, the intersection of belief and violence."

"They merely forestall extreme violence."

"On that, we agree. Is that so bad?"

Alhazen shrugged. "It is necessary. Would that it were not."

"But those of strong beliefs so often wish to impose those beliefs on others, in the name of one deity or power or another. Each group of believers insists that its deity is the supreme almighty. Too many of them wish to impose their beliefs on others. Every time a mighty power has attempted that, the result has been terrible . . . or worse."

"That desire, in itself," replied Alhazen, "would indicate that they do not worship the true Ahuramazda, because in the supreme being, essence and existence coincide."

"Couldn't you say that of most higher beings?" asked Corvyn.

"Not even of powers and principalities, or of the hegemons, for how often is their essence contrary to some form of existence? And if their essence denies any form of existence, then they cannot coincide with what is."

"You make a good point, not that most of the hegemons would accept it." At that moment, Corvyn stopped because the proprietor arrived with two goblets of wine and two very small bowls of aash, which appeared to be a stew-like soup. He tasted it, at first gingerly, trying to determine what it resembled, then gave up, although while he could not pick out specific herbs, he could taste the lentils and the barley noodles. The small bowl was just right. When he finished, he looked to Alhazen. "That was good."

"You'll like the lamb more, I think."

Corvyn suspected that he would, but continued the discussion. "So . . . you seem to be saying that no deity is supreme." That was not what Alhazen said, but Corvyn wanted more of a response. He lifted the goblet and inhaled the scent of the wine, which was promising, then set the goblet down.

"None of those in Heaven claiming to be such, or allowing others to claim such, are supreme."

"Then . . . perhaps there is no supreme deity . . . or that supreme deity has a myriad of attributes, reflected in the variety of the hegemons."

"The variety of the hegemons reflects only the variation in believers, and the unwillingness of the majority of them to accept what lies beyond their own wishes for a deity."

Corvyn doubted he could have phrased that concept better himself. He decided to refrain from more discussion for the moment, because the lamb stew arrived, served in a wide shallow bowl, the lamb over basamatic rice, accompanied by a small side plate with two stuffed grape leaves. The stew portion was modest, almost small. He took a small mouthful . . . and could not help smiling.

"I said you'd like it."

"I do. Very much." Corvyn took a sip of the Ramian. It, too, was excellent, flavorful and rich, yet not heavy. After several bites of the lamb, he tried a dolma, which, if anything, was better than the stew. He decided to enjoy the meal and return to the discussion once he finished eating.

In time, he looked at the empty bowl and platter, then took another small sip of the Ramian and asked, "What do you think the purpose of Heaven is . . . assuming you think it has a purpose?"

Alhazen offered a sardonic smile. "Perhaps to prove that men are incapable of understanding fully the divine. Or to limit them until they can comprehend the divine, and to show, in the meantime, as Plato once imagined, that we see only shadows of reality, yet believe that we comprehend the universe."

"But Plato was talking about men who were prisoners chained through their lack of education," Corvyn pointed out.

"Is there any difference between being prisoners through lack of education or prisoners through lack of understanding?"

"The point is taken." Corvyn laughed, softly, then asked, "How would you remove those shackles?"

"No man, no woman, no power can remove the shackles of willful ignorance. You already know that, or you would not be asking the questions that you have." After the slightest pause, Alhazen added, "Ahuramazda is beyond all beliefs."

"I think that's a good place to leave the matter," replied Corvyn, beckoning to the proprietor, then handing over his card. "Where would you recommend I spend the night here?"

"Our atashkadeh has a modest guesthouse. I'd be honored if you would accept the offer."

"I'd be pleased to accept. I've enjoyed the time."

"As have I."

Corvyn meant what he had said, more than the words would indicate, although he felt a certain sadness as he walked from the café with the athornan, for the tasks that lay ahead of him would be so unnecessary if more in Heaven thought as Alhazen did. Yet the fact that so few did also reminded him that the wisdom of the athornan's beliefs did not translate into physical, technological, or, Heaven forbid, military superiority.

The two rose and walked toward the fire temple, and then beyond to the guesthouse, a small domed structure well apart from the temple.

Alhazen stopped short of the door. "It's open for you. Good evening, Corvyn of the shadows."

"Good evening." Corvyn inclined his head, then watched as the athornan turned and walked toward the temple, still without any hint of power, not that there should have been, because that would have shown that the unnamed town was not what it was.

As Corvyn started to enter the guesthouse, he saw the two doves descending to alight on the roof. He smiled, then stepped inside the small dwelling, noting that it had no locks, only a simple door bolt. Nor could he detect any other shadows or powers.

But then . . . why would they bother?

Those in the town without a name were hardly likely to support any of those involved in the shadowy contest to place Heaven under one hegemon . . . or any single belief.

Neither will they fight, except reluctantly.

Corvyn could scarcely blame them.

Raven seeks the hostile unfamiliar space,
leaving hallowed truth behind in place.

17

Another day and a half passed before Corvyn finished making his way through the lands of the Poetics to reach the outskirts of Jannah itself, the city that many of the Poetics would have preferred to be named after their original sacred city, but that unmentioned name was too sacred to be used for a successor too far away in time and space, as was the name of the city where the Prophet was buried. Now and again Corvyn caught sight of the doves, enough to see and sense that the poor birds were looking more than a little ragged.

Since Jannah proper was only open to true believers, Corvyn took a room in the adjoining city of Ummah, where outsiders were free to come and go and conduct commerce, or almost anything else permitted elsewhere in Heaven. The exception was the availability of alcoholic beverages, but then, Corvyn was also fond of tea, especially bergamot tea. He settled into the Al-Houda, hoping the name was a favorable omen, not that he believed in omens. He decided on a meal in the hotel and then returned to his room, where he sought out the singer and poetess through the aether. After discovering that neither was near, he went to bed. Eventually, he slept, if fitfully.

Just after dawn, he woke, showered, and dressed, then headed down to have breakfast.

The lobby of the hotel was moderately full. He was among an obvious handful of individuals not in a thobe or the equivalent, and even fewer were fairer than he was, although, in Helios, his natural complexion would have been considered on the swarthy side. The hotel restaurant was as yet uncrowded, and the host seated him at a corner table. Corvyn called up a menu and made his choices by the time a server appeared.

"Peace be with you, sir."

"And with you," returned Corvyn, smiling warmly. "I'm thinking about having the chicken omelet with sheermal, figs, and tea."

"That is the meal of a man who has a long day before him."

"That is very likely," replied Corvyn. "Most days are long at present."

"Then it would be a good meal."

"Thank you. As for the tea, which would you recommend to go with the omelet, cardamom or black?"

"That's a matter of taste, sir. We have both."

"The cardamom, then."

"That's a good choice." The server smiled, an expression of approval, then turned and moved away.

Seemingly, in instants, a small tea glass, a pot of tea, and a bowl filled with small clumps of raw rock sugar appeared.

Corvyn did not attempt to drink the tea with the rock sugar in his mouth but dropped several lumps into the pot, waiting slightly before pouring the tea into the glass, then sipped the tea, which he found satisfactory.

While he waited for the remainder of his breakfast, he surveyed the restaurant, now partly filled. He could sense several glances in his direction, but none of them appeared prolonged, as if the stranger had been noticed, assessed as likely in some business or another, and relegated to the background. For the moment, that was more than acceptable to Corvyn.

His breakfast arrived. He ate all of it, then paid and left a generous gratuity, before returning to his room.

There, he considered his options for undertaking what he felt necessary, much as he knew that what he might face could be painful, if not worse, unless he was both prepared . . . and careful. Deciding that procrastination, as well he knew, only created more agony and increased the odds of failure, he set forth amid his shadows. An open approach to his immediate destination would only result in some form of confrontation before he was close enough even to sense, let alone view, what he must in the way that was necessary.

Unlike Yerusalem, the focal point of Jannah was not white and gold, but white and black, a black cubical building, the Kaaba, made of white polished alabaster, of which the upper four-fifths was covered in black silk, a practice dating back to Earth-Eden and the prophet and only true voice of Allah the Poetics recognized. The Kaaba was surrounded by a mosque of white stone, ornamented in gold. Only the angels of Allah were permitted to worship in the Kaaba, and only the most faithful of the Poetics were allowed to enter the circular court around it to pray. Since the angels were well-versed in blocking the approach of lesser powers by concealing themselves among worshippers, unless Corvyn wished to create a great deal of consternation and conflict, he would need to use other means to determine if a trident had arrived near or in the Kaaba, whether it remained in place, and how the Poetics had dealt with it.

Clad in unseen shadows, Corvyn assumed the countenance and shape of a raven, leaving only the raven form visible as he flew across Ummah and over the streets and white buildings of Jannah toward the mosque that surrounded the Kaaba. Descending toward the mosque, he located a near-empty balcony and perched on the white stone railing. The location mattered little, since the mosque was circular. He sensed that the trident had been embedded in the white alabaster shrouded by the black silk, but was now covered by a thin layer of alabaster, the only practical way of dealing with it, since the power necessary to remove it might well damage, if not destroy, the Kaaba.

Since the Poetics were similar to the Judaics in one respect—that there was no single leader of the faith—the only questions that remained were which angel would appear and in what guise to deal with the shadow interloper.

Those questions were partly resolved with a blinding glare and a wall of pure white light which encircled Corvyn. Since remaining in the form of a raven was confining, to say the least, Corvyn resumed his proper form and stood behind the white stone balcony wall, shielded from view of the worshippers in the mosque or in the courtyard below.

Within the circle of light appeared an angel, a figure imbued with overwhelming power, not to mention projecting a sense of absolute right, a figure so bright that most could not have looked directly at the angel.

"Creature of Iblis, without fear,
Why are you presently here?"

"I'm neither a creature of Iblis, nor a djinn, and I'm here to behold the Kaaba."

"Here only the faithful may pray.
Depart now, for you may not stay."

"I mean no harm to those who believe," replied Corvyn, and those words were absolutely true, not to mention accurate, for truth and accuracy were not always the same, especially in the nether regions of theology.

"Allah on high weighs those who cry lies,
Binds them to fire that never dies."

Corvyn noted that the words were more than chanted, less than sung, and melodious, nonetheless. They also revealed the angel and his purpose. "I never knew you were so poetic, Azrael."

"He knows the souls who offer false praise,
And will dispatch the fallen to the Blaze.
Those who disbelieve the Prophet's signs
Further Iblis's unholy designs."

"I don't disbelieve the signs, Azrael," returned Corvyn pleasantly. "They just don't happen to apply to me."

"Which of God's bounties will you deny?
Which of his commands will you defy?

Refuse him and face a fire of molten brass
And torments in Gehenna that will never pass.
Iblis refused the signs and gloried in the earth,
Lusting after fame, followers, and passing worth.
Although you fly, your raven wings will fail
For all you came to Heaven by starry sail."

With the last of those words, the light surrounding Azrael turned eye- and soul-searing, as well as hot enough to incinerate anything.

Corvyn had already removed himself, knowing of Azrael's lack of patience with those intemperate enough to resist his warnings and blandishments.

He waited until the containment vanished and the area returned to a reasonable approximation of normality and then reappeared, once more as a raven, wondering, with wry amusement, which of the angels would next appear.

The reverberations of a distant trumpet and another wall of light suggested the identity of the next angel, who did not speak.

Resuming his human form, Corvyn said mildly, "Welcome, Israfyl."

"*When that trumpet is blown with a mighty blast*
Shouting the end of days at last
The Terror shall come and Heaven shall be cleft
In its frailty and the faithless left
In the desolation of the Fallen past."

"You might be right about that, angel of the trumpet, but I'd rather that we not go through that again. Humanity's had enough Falls already, don't you think?"

There was a time of silence before Israfyl replied.

"*For the righteous read the book in their right hand,*
But others scorn it in their left and will forever stand
In the depths of Gehenna and the fires of hell,
Because they turned from faith and fell.
Do not obey those who cry lies.

Do not heed those who compromise.
Ignore those who claim faith is dead,
Or that science rules instead."

Corvyn nodded. "Very poetic, and I'd expect no less from the angels who serve the Almighty and protect the words of the Prophet. But what about the other people of other Books? You know, those in the other mansions of Heaven? Or those who are good without a Book. Aren't they worth a look?" Even before he sensed the sonic, the spiritual, and the pure energy about to be focused within the circle of light, Corvyn withdrew into the shadows and made his way back toward Ummah.

There was little point in tempting a third angel, for that angel would doubtless have been Mikail, or possibly even Jibreel, and he might just have arrived in full power and not been in a mood to listen, and that would have been unnecessarily painful for Corvyn, if not worse. It also would have accomplished nothing that his conversations, if they could be called such, with Azrael and Israfyl had not already achieved, or for that matter, failed to achieve.

Certainly, the amount of power focused on where Corvyn had not been was significant and had to have been noticed by some, if not all, of the other hegemons besides Jibreel, not to mention registering within the systems of the Pearls of Heaven.

In the shadows, Corvyn took the equivalent of a deep breath, then made his way across the two cities, both of which seemed somewhat larger than when he last visited, and emerged into his temporary quarters, where he made preparations to set out once again.

While it was more than clear that no one in the cities he had visited thus far had the power to embed the tridents, Corvyn had only narrowed the most likely prospects to powers in those cities of the Hegemons that he had not yet visited . . . or other places as well.

While silver birds look grave and proud,
the raven flies through time's last shroud.

18

Directly to the east of Jannah lay only the Sands of Time, the Torrent of the River Styx, the Great Cataract, and Lake Lethe. Corvyn could have retraced his way back north to the River Jordan, then followed that river road to the last town close to Lake Lethe and then crossed the hills to Los Santos. For reasons he could not have logically stated, that route did not feel right. That was why, two days out of Jannah, he rode the electrobike eastward along a way little wider than a path that might or might not have existed prior to his arrival. Each individual traversed the Dunes of Memory created by the Wind of the Past on the Sands of Time by himself, even when accompanied. At the same time, even if unaccompanied, a traveler was never long left alone, especially not with his or her thoughts. That said, it was still often better to travel alone, if one remained strong of will. If one did not, traveling the Sands of Time was almost invariably fatal.

Corvyn had not seen Gabriel's doves since slightly after he had entered the Sands of Time and feared they would not survive, but there was little he could do, for only Gabriel could recall them, and Corvyn doubted that would occur, not given the rigidity of purpose of the Paulists.

The white light that flowed from the Pearls of Heaven was pitiless in what it revealed and concealed amid the sands that constantly shifted, with or without wind.

To Corvyn's left, almost unseen, protruding from the white sands, was a robotic sampling arm, a device of metal both shining and yet pitted by time, doubtless connected to a larger device deeper beneath the sand. As Corvyn rode past, the arm stretched, impossibly beyond its physical capability, and touched Corvyn's shoulder. An electric-like jolt convulsed his arm, enough that his eyes watered momentarily.

That shock was only the beginning, he knew, but that was another reason why he needed to take the path he had chosen.

Perhaps an hour later, he saw an object that appeared at times to be an octahedron and at times a sphere, hovering over the top of a dune. As he neared the object, it began to spin, then vanished. A flash of light washed over Corvyn. For an instant, he felt as though he had been bathed in acid, if without the long-term effects.

He racked his memories for what that object might have been, then winced as he recalled the interlaced web of those octahedrons moving across a jade-green sky, turning all beneath them the gray of a long-dead world as they passed, a gray that remained for eons.

Despite the vividness of what he saw and sensed, and the sometime violence, only once in a great while did either the rough beasts or the avatars of sophisticated technology of destruction or deception escape the Sands' clutches.

His thoughts circled like metal replicas of carrion birds, devoid of blood and sinew, lacking feathers, but well-endowed with claws sharpened by time.

He looked ahead and smiled, seeing sandships scudding across the flats that were not open to him, for the flats held the memories of what might have been and never came to pass. These ships searched endlessly and vainly for forgotten canals that were never built on the Sands of Time, nor had they existed anywhere except in the histories of the might-have-beens. Yet as memories of dreams, that recollection pleased him. The dreams that never came to pass offered both hope and consolation, and far too often in the length of history, both had been rare.

He continued onward, east toward the lake that he would not reach or choose to bathe in. *For who else is left who wishes to remember?* Especially what Corvyn continued to have to recall.

With that realization, he almost slowed the electrobike, but did not, since that would merely have added to the memories likely to assault him in any event, so he continued eastward.

Somewhere ahead, he sensed a rawness. Possibly a recent violent death or a disruption that should not have existed in the Sands, and that disturbed him. Immediate and violent deaths, rare as they were in Heaven, belonged in the lands of the Decalivre and the villages of belief, not in the Sands of Time, which were meant for other deaths.

The sense of rawness, recentness, and wrongness grew as he proceeded toward it, for, being who he was, he could do nothing else, at least not while amid the Sands of Time. An hour passed, more or less, before he rode slowly between two dunes and beheld the abomination—two figures laid out in rings of fire, Brynhyld and Kara, the two Valkyries he had encountered on setting out from Helios.

Their blue eyes were open, but unseeing, and their faces were frozen in an expression of disbelief, with a preservation field around them that faded and vanished as Corvyn neared, as did the two rings of fire. The right hand of each held the sword that was the true shape of the walking sticks that they carried when they had conversed so briefly with Corvyn. Neither the swords nor their sun-bronzed skins, stronger than armor, had sufficed against the power that ripped them from the hills through which they had proudly strode. That transition had indeed been abrupt, given the freshly dismembered small leaves and pine needles strewn around them.

The immense amount of energy required for that transition, for the instant death of two Valkyries more or less invulnerable to most weapons, especially those powered by mere muscle, and for the field that had surrounded and preserved the two, suggested that no minor power or principality could have accomplished the abomination. Added to that, the field had been attuned to release itself at the arrival of any power or principality, or less possibly just to Corvyn . . .

. . . and the perpetrator has to be one of those heading a House of the Decalivre or an unknown of equal power.

The other factor that bothered Corvyn, more than a little, was the cold-blooded killing of two Valkyries who, insofar as was possible, were essentially minding their own business and had been murdered by a power to whom they posed no threat.

Or did they?

Were their deaths meant as a message to Corvyn? Yet that made no sense, because neither Brynhyld nor Kara knew anything about the tridents, and Corvyn had never offered a threat to any House or even to any but the most misguided of villages of faith.

Except to preserve Heaven from another useless Fall.

And that made the killing of Brynhyld and Kara even more despicable.

In the end, all Corvyn could do was to use his powers to create a pyre and to stand a short vigil while it turned the two warriors into ashes and smoke. While he watched, he sensed no other observers, although the Pearls of Heaven observed everything.

Then, with heavy heart and renewed worry, he once again proceeded along the narrow path, for all paths through the Sands of Time were narrow.

After some distance, sensing movement, Corvyn looked to his left, where, perhaps a third of a mille from his path, half buried in the sand stood a construct of brass and steel. The exposed section protruded some three meters out of the sand, its internal parts moving seamlessly and so quickly that they blurred. Standing beside it, her eyes fixed on a place only she could see, was the dark-haired priestess-goddess of algorithms and the mysteries of metal minds, oblivious to the flood of stereotype plates that flowed from the mechanism as they likely had, or had not, for eons.

From that construct flashed a jagged bolt of silver lightning, likely unseen by anyone or any power but Corvyn, which crossed the intervening distance and drove like unseen needles through his eyes and deep into his memories. The jolt and pain were not quite excruciating.

He shuddered, managing to remain on the electrobike as he continued eastward. Behind him the goddess remained as oblivious to his departure as she had been to his arrival.

Once more he continued under the pitiless light, until, as if rising from the black depths of the deepest ocean in all the worlds visited, a dull gray hull, whale-like but resembling equally a mechanical leviathan, burst upward through the white sands that had impossibly turned to ice splintering away in shards. From that wound in the protective ice, water sprayed upward like a geyser, throwing bodies of all sorts into the suddenly airless sky, where, one after another, they fragmented in explosive decompression, forming a gray haze that shrouded the distant red sun whose rays were undistorted by any atmosphere, only by that haze and the fast freezing spray, drops, and goblets of water.

The chill of airless space froze Corvyn solid, halted the electrobike, and vacuum wrenched breath from his very lungs as a larger black metal globe descended toward the broached leviathan and tractor beams lifted it up and away from the sundered ice and the geyser that still gushed water and shredded life. The metal globe, larger than many moons, its spawn recovered, retreated from the devastation it had created . . . and from the frozen, silent Corvyn.

In time, Corvyn recovered, and it felt as though shards of ice flaked away from him and the bike as he again resumed his progress. He would have preferred not to have revisited that particular Fall, for all its senseless ugliness.

But then, all Falls are senseless and, in the end, ugly.

When midday came, he stopped and took a long swallow from the single water bottle he carried, his eyes surveying the dunes that never looked the same, not even from moment to moment, dunes that, even when they shifted into forms that should have cast shadows, often did not, and, at other times, cast shadows that were optically impossible.

A dune to his right shimmered, shivered, and then reassembled itself into the semblance of a cliff, abruptly becoming just that, with a low mansion standing before the base of the cliff and a full lawn leading from the shaded veranda toward Corvyn. A waist-high wall surrounded the veranda. A red-haired woman stood behind the wall, her head turned from Corvyn, eyes gazing not at the ocean she could see, but into the golden-green sky.

Corvyn swallowed, and his eyes burned. After he blotted them clear, the woman and all around her had vanished, leaving only a ridge of sand.

He took another swallow from the water bottle, then sealed and stowed it, and resumed his progress.

Several milles passed before the pink sky above him turned into the deep maroon of a place he once knew too well, with multicolored stars filling the late twilight. Then, in an instant, the deep maroon split to reveal a wedge of brilliant orange, and the metallic blue wedges of lightships poured through the cleft in space. From the maroon skies on each side of the wedge, silver-gray needles raced toward the lightships, and with each needleship that struck, a greenish-yellow flash annihilated both ships. Particle beams of coruscating gold lanced out from the invaders, claiming far more of the defending needles . . . and the orange cleft widened with the oncoming hordes of lightships that hammered the needleships from the sky.

Corvyn looked away, even as the orange sky descended and enveloped him in fire, piercing him like the sting of a thousand hornets . . . before the physical pain passed.

Then . . . for a time, perhaps hours, Corvyn continued past little more than sand and more sand, under the pink sky and pitiless light of the sun and the scrutiny of the Pearls of Heaven, glad for the respite, yet knowing there were other sights to see, other Dunes of Memory.

In late afternoon, after experiencing several other occurrences of events that might or might not have happened, Corvyn sensed something ahead, and felt a growing chill.

Walls of impossible ice rose from the path before him, and waves of life-stealing chill ripped warmth from him, and a darkness of a different sort shrouded the space around him. A roughly feminine figure stood in the middle of the path as he neared, her presence forcing him to come to a complete stop, not that it was absolutely necessary, but given the impact on his perceptions, halting was more advisable.

One side of her face was blue, as was the long hair on that side, while the other side was pasty white, with straight blond hair. Both eyes were black and cold. "Have you come to grant me my due, raven of time?"

"I've always granted you your due . . . and more." *So much more, through my failures, and failed efforts.*

"You could not do otherwise, though I must point out that, of recent, you've been most stingy."

"There have been neither great battles, nor great deaths nor great heroes." *And that is as it should be.*

"For now, dark one. Only for now. One can only forestall the serpent of time for so long."

"That may be."

"That *will* be." The words seemed to fly from her and wrap themselves around Corvyn, seeming to leach every calorie of heat from his body.

"Only when I fail." *Only when I fail.*

The darkness and chill vanished as she and the walls of ice faded into the Dunes of Memory.

Gathering himself together, Corvyn again proceeded, knowing that, for all else he would encounter, and the pain that would accompany each encounter, the worst was past. Besides, all things had their price, and this part of his journey was necessary to pay part of that price . . . and for other reasons.

Above the clouds or perched on stone,
the raven remains all alone.

19

Close to midday three days and several living nightmares later, Corvyn stopped the electrobike on the top of a ridge, in the narrow gap in the low wall of what appeared to be brown quarzitic sandstone but was not, being far more durable. The wall embodied properties that restrained the Sands of Time from sweeping over the ridge and into the River Jordan valley and stretched southeast to Lake Lethe and northwest almost to Yerusalem. The narrow stone-paved road that began in the gap between the walls was dark gray and extended northeast into the valley to the River Jordan and eventually to Cammat Landing, where he planned to take the ferry across the river on his way to Ciudad Los Santos.

Corvyn did not look back as he left the Sands of Time. There was no need. Even Gabriel's doves had not been able to follow him through the Sands. While he would like to have thought they managed to return to Yerusalem, that was likely a vain hope. He had seen no sign of them in days. The doves, being naturally skittish, would have avoided whatever power killed the Valkyries, if they had even come close, but would have easily fallen prey to more subtle twists of reality. Still, he had wished the doves no harm, and that was more than he could have said about other beings.

He guided the electrobike down the long slope. Artemisia bushes grew on either side of the road, spaced irregularly, and with barren ground between them. If Corvyn cared to look closely, he knew he would also have seen scattered clusters of prickly opuntia, at least for the next few milles, before he reached the more fertile and wetter lowlands closer to the river.

After traveling close to three milles, and descending a few hundred yards, he came to the first of the olive groves lining the valley. On the next lower terrace, he passed a grower repairing a stone wall. The man stared, not quite unbelievingly, as Corvyn passed, for seldom did many leave the Sands of Time. Another mille went by before he reached Arbel.

While it was a small town, it would have an inn, if seldom used, and that was fine with Corvyn. He needed a meal, since he was far from certain when he last ate or drank.

One block off the main square, he found the Hillside Inn, an oblong building of beige sandstone, constructed so long ago that it felt as though it were an extension of rather than an addition to the ground beneath. Leaving the electrobike by the door, he stepped inside the small front room and was vaguely surprised to see a young woman wearing a khaki shirt and trousers instead of a traditional robe, with a wide brown belt and boots. She was seated at a desk, an elaborate data matrix projected into the air in front of her.

After seeing him, she blinked, and the matrix vanished. Then she stood and smiled pleasantly. "You seem surprised. Are you looking for a room?"

"I am. Also, something to eat. And yes, I was surprised."

"We're not as traditional here as people are closer to Yerusalem. That shouldn't surprise someone like you, surely."

"It wouldn't, not usually, but I spent a long three days on the Sands of Time." Corvyn smiled wryly. "At least, I think it was three days. Sometimes you can't tell."

Her thick black eyebrows rose. "You make a practice of traveling there?"

"Only when necessary."

She shook her head. "Better you than me. You mentioned food. We can do that, provided you don't mind simple fare."

"Simple fare will be just fine." Corvyn extended his card.

"You haven't seen the room or sampled the fare."

"Just take the information and enter it later."

"You're either very trusting or even more powerful than you appear."

"I could say I'm neither, some of which would be true, but the answer is that anyone handling a multilevel spatial matrix can't possibly be bothered with either incompetence or small-scale theft."

"And if they could, they won't be handling matrices long," she replied, taking the card and scanning it without even looking.

Corvyn had no doubt that she'd discover everything she could later, and that was fine with him.

"Do you want to eat first?"

"If that's easily possible."

"It is, and it's more convenient now, since I was going to fix something anyway."

"You do everything?"

"We don't get many visitors, but I agreed to keep it going for the sake of the town. Besides, it's more interesting. Your only cost for the meal is my company."

Corvyn decided against saying that he might be getting the better bargain because he could be wrong, although he sensed none of the signs of a principality or power. By itself that meant nothing, but the odds were strongly that she was neither. What else she might be was another question.

"By the way, my name is Jael. The end room is the best. It's clean. It's not locked, and there's a locker outside for the bike. You can put your things there and freshen up quickly, then join me in the dining room." She looked toward the archway on her left.

"Thank you. I'm Corvyn." He smiled again, then turned, and made his way outside, where he wheeled the bike to the last room. It was clean, spacious, spare, but well enough appointed that his stay would likely be comfortable. There was a faint scent of tarragon, doubtless from the large bush growing at the edge of the garden that adjoined the inn. He recalled another time.

When fulsome herbs grew so green and wild
In the eyes of one never a child.

Once his cases were in the room, he washed his face and hands. The shower he craved could wait. Then he returned to the front of the inn and entered the dining room.

"Seat yourself," called Jael, presumably from the kitchen.

As he sat at the table set for two, Corvyn hoped she did not arrive with a bowl of milk, although that struck him as unlikely.

She did not, instead bringing two platters of what appeared to be a chicken curry of some sort with warm flatbread and sliced fresh figs on the side, setting one platter at each place. "White wine acceptable to you?"

"So long as it's not too sweet."

"I'll be right back."

Corvyn studied the curry, which also appeared to contain raisins as well, and was served with linguine, rather than rice.

"You'd have to call it mixed cuisine," explained Jael as she returned with two wineglasses and a large carafe, from which she deftly half filled both glasses before seating herself. "Or, as Shelad calls it, 'mongrel cooking.'"

"Shelad?"

"My handyman and general assistant. He calls himself a dispossessed Poetic, dispossessed because he followed Chana here and persevered until she agreed to marry him."

"That sounds like quite a story." Corvyn lifted his glass. "With thanks to you."

"Wait until you taste it."

Corvyn sipped the wine, trying to place what it might be, similar to a clean Viognier, not a flowery one, such as Condrieu, not that many on Heaven would recall that ancient vintage. Then he took a bite of the curry and nodded. "They go together quite well. A local vintage?"

"It is, a Viognier varietal. The climate here isn't the best for Chardonnays."

Corvyn nodded, keeping his surprise—and confirmation—to himself. He took several more mouthfuls before speaking again. "The curry is excellent as well."

"I started cooking curries for Shelad and Chana, and discovered I liked the variety of what I could do. He never learned to cook, and she wasn't about to try curries. Her family is rather traditional."

"This close to the Sands of Time, that's not surprising. Traditions are also often walls. How often do you see creatures escaping the Sands of Time?"

"Very seldom. I wouldn't call it escaping. Most perish away from the Sands. You know that."

Corvyn did. He smiled. "Most . . . but not all."

"Hosea told Shelad he saw a rough beast last week."

"A rough beast?" Corvyn raised his eyebrows. "Just beyond the wall restraining the Sands?"

"No. At the edge of the groves, heading west."

"Slouching and heading toward Bethlehem, no doubt."

"He didn't mention slouching, but making its way in that direction."

"Did he say what it looked like?"

"Not in any coherent sense."

"It would have been coherent to you, had you seen it."

"Oh?" Jael offered an amused smile.

"How long have you been a guardian?" That was the only possibility Corvyn could think of for someone of her abilities to be in a small town at the edge of the Sands, that and the multilevel spatial matrix.

"Let's just say long enough to be older than I look. Are you really as old as the Pearls of Heaven?"

"No." He was far older, if memories reflected age, but there was little point in admitting it, since no one, not even a guardian, would have believed it.

"But close."

Rather than comment further on that, he asked, "What about you?"

"I'm no Yael, nor Deborah, nor Judith. I'm here to do a job, fill a function, if you will. Most of the Sands creatures can't survive elsewhere, but those that can . . ." She shook her head.

"What did you do about the rough beast?"

"Nothing. I tracked it. It decided it wasn't up to a . . . rebirth, if you will. It returned to the Sands. What about you?"

"Periodically, I find myself there. Traveling the Sands is . . . useful."

"Would you care to explain that usefulness?"

"The Sands hold more than history, more than dreams, even more than illusions and delusions. It's useful to be reminded how dangerous some of those ideals, dreams, and delusions can in fact be . . . and have been." He took another bite of the curry and then another swallow of wine. "You're aware of those dangers, I'm sure."

"More from the perspective of the beastkeeper. I'd rather not enter that cage, or arena, if you will."

Corvyn smiled ironically. "Not all of those failed or lost ideals and misguided dreams remain lost. Some periodically emerge from the Sands to infect yet another generation of misguided idealists or manipulative demagogues, some of whom may even be demigods. At those times, the cage is not terribly useful."

"You sound as though you're tracking an escapee."

"Not yet. More like trying to determine exactly what has already escaped and is manipulating who else."

"You don't believe in letting failed ideals expire once more on their own?"

"History has shown that the collateral damage can be far too high."

"And you would decide that?"

Corvyn laughed, even as he saw the hardness behind her seemingly trusting eyes. "The judgments of those who head the Ten Houses have never agreed. That is why there are ten Houses and hundreds of villages of belief. The ultimate delusion is there is a belief or a theorem that supersedes all others in excellence and suitability, and the penultimate tragedy is that millions believe it, and other millions reject it."

"Penultimate? Not ultimate?"

"The ultimate tragedy is what comes after that."

"You're rather cheerful, for all your shadows of doom, gloom, and grief." Jael lifted her glass to her lips, but barely sipped.

"We can learn to control what we feel, even if we should not control others."

"That's a rather interesting way of putting it."

"At times, often many times, there are those who control others. Whether one believes that such control is good depends on what one believes about others. If one believes most people to be sheep or wolves, one likely believes such control is necessary, either to keep the sheep from being eaten or the wolves from slaughtering them and fighting over the spoils."

"Wolves aren't like that."

Corvyn smiled again. "You're right. They're not. No animal other than humans is, and that's the problem."

"So . . ." She drew out the word. "Who are you? The name you gave does not exist anywhere. Your card offers a sub-identity. Yet sub-identities are prohibited. That places you on a level close to the heads of the Decalivre, but the nets show only that sub-identity. You carry the hints of shadows that cannot exist, but do."

"I told you. I'm Corvyn. No more and no less. I'm not a sub-identity of any House or village." Which he was not, although he used sub-identities and always had.

Jael smiled sadly and shook her head. "I'm glad I'm only a guardian."

So was Corvyn, for more than a few reasons. "Is there more wine? I'd like to hear more about Arbel."

"There is. Let me refill the carafe."

Corvyn finished the last few morsels of curry, and the next to the last slice of the figs, before Jael returned and refilled their glasses.

"I reported your arrival here."

"And?"

She offered an amused smile. "I was thanked, told to learn what I could, and to enjoy your company before you vanished or otherwise departed."

"What do you want to know?"

"Who or what you're searching for."

Corvyn smiled wryly. "If I knew that I wouldn't be searching. Some power, although it could be power, principality, or even the head of a House, is defacing the actual sanctuaries of at least some Houses of the Decalivre with an ancient symbol. That symbol is ambiguous, representing evil to some faiths and mastery of the mundane to others. I'm interested in learning who is behind this ritual defacement and what end they have in mind." That was not strictly accurate, because Corvyn had a very strong suspicion of the end, but certainly not who the perpetrator was or why the perpetrator had chosen this particular time.

"Defacing . . . how?"

"I'd prefer not to say."

"Meaning that you have no intention of saying more."

"I've told you more than I've told anyone else."

"Why me?"

"Why not? You're not in a house of belief. You're isolated, and you're a guardian."

She frowned for a moment, then slowly nodded. "You actually want me to report that. Why?"

"It's obvious, if you think about it."

After several moments, she nodded. "I think I see."

Corvyn had no doubt that she did. She had no agenda, which any head of House would have, and no head of House would know from where the information came, except that it came from the Pearls of Heaven, because that was to whom the guardians reported. Some might soon suspect, but they would not *know*, and that was enough for Corvyn's purposes.

"Did you come looking for a guardian?"

He smiled. "Not in the slightest, but I'm not loath to take advantage of an opportunity when it's offered."

"That's the only opportunity I'm offering."

"No. You're also offering intelligent conversation and information without an agenda, and I intend to take advantage of that opportunity." He took another sip of wine, then asked, "Were you from the Jordan Valley originally?"

"Not the valley, but the hill country east of Yerusalem. I grew up in Shivta."

Corvyn frowned, but was pleased. He had never heard of the town. "Tell me about Shivta."

"It's actually one of the older towns on Heaven, but there's a fault line there, and that's why the old-time elders decided to keep it small . . ."

Corvyn took another sip of the wine, better than he'd expected, and continued to listen, enjoying a conversation without an agenda.

Rivers flow from hill to lake.
Ravens slight the ferry's wake.

20

Corvyn woke late, readied himself for the day, enjoyed a leisurely breakfast with Jael, and then wheeled the electrobike out to the edge of the gray stone road that led to Cammat Landing.

Jael stood by the door of the inn, an expression of amusement on her face as he looked at her.

"Going back to your matrices? Or hunting escapees from the Sands?"

"I thought I might investigate a little history," she replied.

"Just don't believe everything you find. Even historians have agendas."

"*Even* historians?" Her tone of voice was amused. "Everyone has agendas, especially those who cloak themselves in shadows."

"I don't deny it, but make sure it's my agenda and not someone's superimposition of their belief about my agenda."

"I should know that?"

"Now that we've conversed, you might have a much better idea." He offered a last smile. "Enjoy your days, each of them by itself." Then he swung onto the electrobike. He did not look back.

As he headed down the hill, he had to admit that the brief time he spent since leaving the Sands of Time had been the most enjoyable interlude since sometime before he left Helios. Perhaps he should visit Arbel again.

He shook his head. Some things were best experienced once and remembered often, rather than the other way round.

In less than an hour, he neared the outskirts of Cammat Landing.

The fact that Cammat Landing was located on the River Jordan and not on the Sea of Galilee had always irritated Corvyn. But he'd been only one of the First on Heaven, and not one with the power of official nomenclature, so that naming authority had gone to one whose ignorance had trumped any knowledge of history on the part of his subordinates. As a result, the river town had been named Cammat Landing, and so it remained, even while Zafon was the name given to a town on the Sea of Galilee, not that anyone on present-day Heaven would have known, or particularly cared.

Like the buildings in Arbel, the buildings in Cammat Landing were largely, but not exclusively, of one story and constructed of beige sandstone. The roofs were single-slanted, rather than pitched from the center, given that snow seldom fell on the southern part of the great plateau and that the rains were usually gentle. The air was far damper, unsurprisingly, since the town occupied part of a narrow river valley surrounded by hills, and the air was fragrant with mixed scents, two of which Corvyn thought were myrtle and rockrose.

The gray stone road took him directly to the ferry slip, where he waited, almost alone for more than half an hour, before the ferry returned and he wheeled the electrobike to the front, where he again waited, if only for perhaps a quarter hour, before the whistle sounded, and the ferry departed. Although the Jordan was wider than near Yerusalem, the single ferry at Cammat Landing was far smaller, at little more than twenty meters in length, than those at Lee's Ferry or south of Yerusalem. In the late morning, Corvyn was among a handful of people on board headed for Plymouth.

Standing beside the electrobike as the ferry pulled away from the slip, he looked to his right, to the southeast and in the direction of Lake Lethe and its waters of forgetfulness some hundred or so milles away. The stretch of lakeshore between where the Jordan and the Sanctus entered Lake Lethe was called the Beach of Forgetfulness, although it almost might have been called the Sands of Death, because most who bathed in the waters of the Lake to forget their past not only forgot that, but also forgot most of those behaviors associated with survival, unless they were fortunate enough to be rescued by the Brothers and Sisters of

Mercy. But then, Corvyn well knew, anyone who wished to forget who or what they were was seeking death of another kind in any event.

His eyes turned to the handful of others standing near the front of the sun-powered ferry, taking in first the tall blond man who stood beside the only four-wheeled vehicle, a sedan with aerodynamic curves that were hardly necessary considering that the curved roads of Heaven, smooth-paved as they were, did not lend themselves to excessive speed. On the other hand, the vehicle contained considerable forms of protection hidden under those curves. The sedan's driver, for he was the only one near it, was lightly tanned and wore a white jacket, white shirt, white trousers, white shoes, and presumably white socks. His not-quite-chiseled features suggested comparative youth. His apparel suggested that he was some sort of junior functionary, either commercial or financial, but not ecclesiastical, although the strict whites indicated that those who employed him might well have some relationship with the White One. Either that, or his apparel was designed not to be offensive to anyone in the lands of the White One.

Corvyn concealed a momentary smile and walked toward the young man, who carefully avoided looking in Corvyn's direction. "Greetings."

"The same to you. You're a ways from the abode of the Dark One."

Corvyn smiled pleasantly, but not warmly. "Actually, I just came from the Sands of Time."

For a moment, the other said nothing, then finally replied, "You're fortunate to be here, one way or the other."

"Aren't we all fortunate to be here?"

"That's true enough. What took you to the Sands of Time?"

"The usual. Revisiting illusions and shattered dreams. Cataloguing and analyzing delusions before proceeding to Los Santos. What about you?"

"Business in Bethlehem, Bethsaida, and a few other places."

"Bezalel's descendants?"

The man in white shrugged. "There's always a market for good jewelry."

"And it's less expensive on this side of the river."

The other shook his head. "It's not that at all. The artistry is more unique."

Corvyn understood that. The Sands of Time were close to the south side of the river, and artistic genius, illusions, and madness have always had a special relationship. "Artistry is not always what it seems, but I wish you well."

"Artistry is what it is."

"Exactly," replied Corvyn. It was what it was, and not necessarily what people saw in it, which might have been why, often, the best artistry was unappreciated, and the most outlandish praised for its "originality." He smiled again. "I'm sure you do well in Los Santos." With that, he turned and walked back to the electrobike.

A woman in a long brown robe and matching brown shoes or perhaps ankle boots approached him.

Corvyn looked at her openly, noting her age, evident only in the fineness of her features. "Yes?"

"Are you truly a Skeptic from Helios?"

"How much of a skeptic depends on the situation, but I am from Helios."

"It's a stupid question, but I've always wondered what the appeal was of doubting everything. My son tried to explain it, but . . ." She shook her head.

"He left and went to Helios?"

"He did. He vanished. I haven't heard from him in years."

Corvyn frowned. "I'd be surprised if he's in Helios, then. The Dark One allows anyone who obeys the laws to stay, but not to become invisible."

"I heard that . . . but . . ."

"You thought people were just telling you something that might be untrue?"

She nodded.

"He's likely in a village of belief, somewhere on the fringes of the lands of Helios."

"But he doubts everything."

"There are those who believe in doubting everything." Corvyn did not point out that belief could often have little correlation with either factual accuracy or logic. "There are invisible villages."

"Why?"

The barely concealed anguish in her voice moved Corvyn enough that he said, "Sometimes, even the highest cannot answer that question, much as some of them would like to."

"Thank you, kind sir." She eased away from him.

No one else approached, and Corvyn turned his attention to the town on the north side of the river. He had no idea why those of the First named it Plymouth, except for the possibility that the name once signified both a point of departure and a point of arrival, and the Plymouth where the ferry had begun to dock was certainly both for the lands of the White One of Los Santos.

The stone quays and river walls were white, as was the ferry slip, and most of the buildings that Corvyn could see—as he knew from previous visits—were also constructed of white stone, except, of course, for the dark rooftop solar collectors. Likewise, the majority of those in the land were fair-skinned and light-complected, with an extraordinarily high percentage of blonds, although many of those were the result of genetic engineering, either in the present or by ancestors.

When the ferry came to a halt in the slip and the ramp lowered into place, the crewman gestured to Corvyn, who mounted the electrobike and rode slowly off the ferry and onto the North River Road, not that he would remain on it for long—only until he reached Appalachian Street, which turned into the Appalachian Trail Road on the north side of Plymouth.

In riding through Plymouth, Corvyn was far more watchful than in other towns, because in Plymouth, Los Santos, and other towns under the white shade, there were fewer electrobikes, and small lorries or sedans were more numerous than elsewhere in Heaven. Corvyn had never been able to determine if that preference was primarily cultural or whether it had some basis in genetics, but given that use or analysis of any genetic material of an individual for any purpose involving anything but the health of that individual was strictly forbidden and resulted in immediate banishment to Limbo, on principle alone, and one with which he agreed, he had never had any desire to investigate his suspicions.

He followed a white lorry, not that the lorries in Plymouth appeared to be any other color, for almost half a mille past various shops, eateries, and other establishments, noting as he had before that most residents preferred to eat or conduct other business inside rather than outside, even given the comparatively pleasant climate along the Jordan. All those he saw wore white garb, or garb that was white and barely tinged with the faintest shade of some color. Those who dared to wear such faint shades were often considered less reputable or more risk-seeking, if not both. With all the buildings of white stone or other materials also treated to be white, Corvyn found it difficult to easily determine whether there was any great distinction between structures and especially between houses.

He was more than happy to turn right on Appalachian Street and make his way to the northeast past the seemingly endless expanse of white, and the glare reflected off all that white. Los Santos would be worse, but he would face that when the time came. As he neared the northern edge of Plymouth, the dwellings became larger, set on larger plots, with emerald-green lawns precisely set between houses and walks and the street, and perfectly trimmed trees and gardens, except . . . all the flowers he saw were white, which always struck him as ironically accurate in terms of the faith and doctrines of the White One. For some reason, the flowers also reminded him that his was the only gray electrobike he had seen since he rode off the ferry, yet electrobikes came in all colors . . . except in the white lands.

Before long he was on the Appalachian Trail, riding up the first steep hill on a road with sweeping curves, taking in the barely visible scattered homes set within forests of beech and maple trees as well as a variety of pines, but largely white pine. All such homes were self-powered and contained, as effectively required, since the Lances of Heaven periodically destroyed unpowered structures more than a few meters square, supposedly when no one was present, although Corvyn always had some doubts. The rules were simple enough—maintain the structures and use the land wisely without degrading it. Those who lived there had come to prefer matters that way, since living on the rugged hills without shelter was less than pleasant and usually eventually fatal.

The Appalachian Hills were not especially wide near Plymouth, perhaps some sixty milles across, although a hundred and fifty milles to the northwest they extended close to two hundred milles from southwest to northeast. The distance was measured as how the raven flew, and the road covering those sixty milles in front of Corvyn was closer to a hundred and eighty milles. After four more hours of climbing rock-punctuated rugged forest land and descending into narrow valleys or vales where he might or might not see a dwelling or two, Corvyn began to wonder if he shouldn't have stopped in Plymouth and allowed an entire day to cross the hills.

That was when he saw what might have been an inn set alongside the white stone road on a rise before yet another twisting climb. Corvyn did not recall the inn, but then, it had been years since he traveled this particular road, and he had more than a few memories buried deep in his thoughts. He decided to investigate and eased the electrobike off the road and onto the drive leading to the low stone structure, which seemed almost part of a stone outcropping just below the top of the rise.

When he stopped under the roof of the pillared portico, he glanced around, then saw a small sign proclaiming the Redstone Inn. He found no sign of shadows other than his own and no indication of other powers in the vicinity of the inn itself. Beyond that . . . he had some doubts. The structures were neither new nor ancient, but appeared well-maintained. The reddish stone of the building was offset by the white trim, sashes, and doors. He placed the bike in one of two stands, opened the door, and stepped into the small foyer, which contained little besides a counter of polished pine. In the wall behind the counter was a door, which opened, presumably at the hand of the man who stepped through it and behind the counter.

The innkeeper stood well over two meters tall, with sandy-blond hair and the typical not-quite-pasty fair skin that dominated in the area, especially in the hills away from Los Santos itself. He looked at Corvyn and then through the windows flanking the door at the electrobike, not quite frowning. "That's an old bike."

"It does what I need."

"Don't see many of you folks this far south."

"That's true." Corvyn smiled. "Not many from Helios get this far. Most just take a quick look at Los Santos and leave. But then we don't see many of the White One's faithful in Helios, either."

"You'll be staying just for the night then?"

"Just for the one night." Corvyn extended his card.

"Poe . . . that's an old name," mused the innkeeper as he scanned the card and returned it. "Seems like it's familiar, but I couldn't say why."

Corvyn ignored the implication that his skin was likely several shades too dark to be local. "It is an old name. It goes back a long ways."

The innkeeper smiled professionally. "It's slow right now. Any of the five rooms are available. Take whichever you please. If you'd like supper, we serve from five to seven. Café door is on the road side at the end."

"I would, and thank you." Corvyn paused. "I take it that you have some locals who occasionally eat here as well."

"There are a few most nights, seeing as we're the only place in twenty milles. Even the best cooks need a break at times." The innkeeper paused, then added, "There's a locker for bikes outside each room. Bears, you know."

Corvyn hadn't known, he realized surprisingly, and said, "Thank you."

"We don't see them often, but if they smell food, they can make a mess. Wouldn't want to have one of them rip up your bike."

Corvyn nodded, then turned and left the foyer, feeling the innkeeper's eyes remain on him for a time. He looked briefly into each of the rooms, but they were close to identical, and, in the end, he took the one farthest from the inn foyer. After putting his things in the room and locking up the electrobike, he stood in the middle of the spare, clean, and nondescript chamber and called up the aether, searching first for the poetess.

She appeared standing behind a low stone wall, one that might be white, light gray, light pink, or even light blue, given the lighting, and looking out over what appeared to be a city. What city it might have been, Corvyn could not tell, save that it was unlikely to be Los Santos. She gestured, and the image vanished, although the oblong of the aether did not, indicating that she had both the awareness and power of at least a principality. It also indicated that she had recently been taught the ability to block aether imaging . . . or that she had known all along and had now chosen to do so.

He frowned. The first times he had called up her image, she had seemed unaware. The last time, she had turned the sheet holding verse so that he could no longer see it. This time . . .

Corvyn concentrated on the singer, and found . . . nothing.

"Interesting." In fact, it was more than interesting, since it indicated that both were more than they initially had appeared, but there was little enough that he could do about it at the moment, nor was he so inclined. Not at the moment.

Rather than worry, he decided to walk down the path that led east from the small inn for his own reasons. Those reasons included a feeling that something of interest lay along or at the end of the path. Within fifty meters, greenery surrounded him. Thick undergrowth flanked the path under the canopy of much taller trees, some of which he recognized as maples.

He walked along the well-trod path toward what felt like a shrine, although what sort he wondered. A half mille farther east the path ended in a small clearing, which was anything but natural. The north side ended at a flat stone wall carved out of a rock outcropping that rose roughly four meters, and white stone tiles formed a pentagon some ten meters on a side. In the center of the pentagon stood a four-sided white stone obelisk three meters on each side at its base that rose some thirty meters, tall enough to be impressive, but lower than the ancient white pines that ringed the clearing. From the growth of the vegetation immediately around the space and the weathering of the stones, the pentagon had been there longer than the Redstone Inn.

Corvyn looked up, noting that tree branches overarched much of the clearing, and that the pink sky was visible only for about five meters on each side of the obelisk. Corvyn felt no active energy sources, although he had the feeling that there might be stored energy somewhere nearby.

There were no markers, no explanations, but Corvyn scarcely needed one, not considering the unmarked white obelisk. The original had vanished with the destruction of Old Earth-Eden, and its meaning had been far different from what the white obelisk had long since come to mean. He shook his head, then turned and walked back toward the inn.

An hour later, he stepped inside the café, faintly surprised that three of the nine tables were already occupied. Although he had half expected to see the tall innkeeper, the server was an older woman, also fair-skinned and blond, as was everyone in the café except Corvyn.

She smiled and said, “Any table that’s empty. I’ll be with you in a minute.”

He took a table for two against the wall, seating himself where he could view most of the other patrons. A young couple, dressed in tan leather jackets and plaid shirts, sat at a corner table, while two older couples in white shared a four-top. A family of sorts, also garbed in white, gathered around the large circular table, a man, two blond women of approximately the same age, and three children, whose ages, Corvyn estimated, ran from mandated attentive silence to polite comments.

The server returned before Corvyn had a chance to begin eavesdropping and offered a professional smile. “We’ve got two choices tonight. Old-style pot roast with potatoes, carrots, and onions or fried chicken, with mashed potatoes, white gravy, and kale.”

Since Corvyn had never cared much for fried chicken, he immediately said, “The pot roast.”

“We don’t have much variety in drinks, just ale and lager, either light or dark in either.”

“Pale ale, please.”

“You’ll like it. I’ll have your food out shortly.”

“Thank you.”

She hurried out to the kitchen.

Corvyn had thought to eavesdrop, but found he didn’t have to in order to listen to the two couples at the four-top.

“. . . don’t care what you say, Matt, there’s no way you can raise artichokes here. Besides, who’d eat ’em?”

“I would, for one. I get tired of pole beans and collards and kale.”

“. . . it takes forever to cook ’em, and they don’t much taste without oversalted butter . . .”

“Still say it’d be good to have a choice . . .”

“You’ll be the one picking and cooking ’em . . .”

Corvyn turned his attention, but not his eyes, to the much lower-pitched words being exchanged at the family table.

“. . . don’t stare . . . not polite,” murmured one of the women to the youngest child.

". . . one of the dark ones?" whispered the older-looking boy.

". . . could be from Helios, Marcion, Keifeng . . . few other villages . . . now eat your dinner."

The couple in the corner ate without exchanging words.

Before that long, the server returned with a large mug of pale ale and a healthy platter of pot roast and the assorted vegetables.

Neither the pot roast nor the remaining conversations were terribly interesting, and Corvyn ate what he needed, drank all of the ale, and then retired to his rented chamber.

Were the raven's wings once white,
just before the Fall of night?

21

By midmorning, Corvyn was milles and milles northeast of the Redstone Inn, moving along a section of the road that extended the length of a narrow valley between two forested hills that were high for the plateau of Heaven, but less than foothills in comparison to the Celestial Mountains far to the north. A certain sense of gloom came from the unending greenery, as well as the lack of vibrant colors . . . or odors. While he had slept well enough, and breakfast had been better than the dinner the night before, his thoughts kept going back to the two Valkyries and the white obelisk in the forest east of the Redstone Inn.

The obelisk had been four-sided and not three-sided, and it had been set in the center of a regular pentagon, not a pentagram, although the central pentagon of a pentagram could also be regular. But the fact remained that it was a white obelisk, a symbol that had less than favorable memories and connotations for Corvyn. He couldn't help wondering whether Jaweau knew. The fact that there were no energies surrounding it suggested that those who had erected it did not want to call any more attention to it than necessary.

Still the existence of the obelisk raised questions, one of which was just how many others were scattered through the hills and dales surrounding Los Santos. If there were others, Jaweau could not be totally unaware of them, and that raised certain questions, especially about the True Faith of Los Santos. Then, there were also other questions, such as those surrounding the abilities of both the singer and the poetess, and why they had appeared at the same time as had the black tridents.

Corvyn was still half pondering those and other questions when he began to sense the gathering of power even before the whirlwind came out of the north, a funnel darker than the night sky without the Pearls of Heaven. Above that blackness was a cloud of flame, infolding itself, with an amber brightness that rivaled that of the white sun at noon. As the funnel and the cloud swept over the lower ground to the left of the road, the conifers withered under the flame and turned to blackened shards.

Yet Corvyn could see that the trees behind the cloud were untouched, even as a wave of heat cascaded over him.

Sophisticated imagery, possibly reflected and/or directed off the shields of one of the Pearls of Heaven.

Lightning flashed, thunder rumbled, and four winged figures appeared, each with the shape of an androgynous human, one with the face of a man, one with the face of a lion, one with the countenance of a bison, and one with the head of a sun eagle.

Corvyn felt no change in the electric potential around him and none of the pressure changes that should have accompanied such an impressive display. Still . . . even what he was seeing, feeling, and hearing demanded a considerable amount of power . . . more than he would have wanted to spend . . . or pay for. He brought the electrobike to a halt and waited. Trying to deal with that power and sophisticated imagery while riding would only have been more difficult . . . and less effective.

". . . you have been impudent and stiff-hearted . . . what you think to do is of the wicked, and I have laid a stumbling block before you. Any righteousness that you have done will be forgotten, and all the evils that you have done over the centuries shall be multiplied manifold in the minds of all creatures in Heaven, both now and forevermore.

"Can you not see this, raven of the night? Can you not recall when your plumage was of the rainbow? Can you not recall when the Light was yours, and you forsook it? Poor raven, see what I return to you."

With a hiss and a flash, the image of the trident appeared on the paving stone two yards in front of the electrobike—the same image that had appeared on the stone wall of his study, cut into the stone itself and black deeper than the lightless night sky that Heaven had never seen, at least not since the Pearls of Heaven were strung. Then the glowing whirlwind and the dark funnel that had somehow been amber as well black vanished.

That image and the black flamed trident cut into the stone before Corvyn chilled him, because whoever, whatever, had projected the image and marshaled the power it took to focus it on a relatively isolated and remote road seemed to think that he was the source of the trident.

Or wanted you to think that the power believes you're behind it.

But any hegemon or other power able to muster that much force should have known that the trident had never been the symbol of the raven. So why the deviousness? Why not a direct attack, rather than the charade? *Unless the being behind it cannot muster that much power at a distance . . . or isn't yet ready for such an attack.*

None of the possibilities pleased him.

He studied the black-flamed trident once more. It appeared identical to the others. That did not bother him so much as the possibility that the power behind the trident might have access to the Eyes of Heaven . . . and might well gain access to the Lances of Heaven as well.

He shivered, despite the warmth of the day.

The raven claims no city's sacred fire
but seeks the truth beyond desire.

22

By an hour past midafternoon, Corvyn had begun the descent into the southern reaches of the city proper of Los Santos, an expanse of white buildings and white streets, with the only visible darkness under the pink sky of day being rooftop solar collectors and the green of vegetation. Behind closed doors, though, there were more colors . . . and shadows, to which Jaweau, the White One, had never voiced public objection. While many of the various scattered dwellings and holdings Corvyn had passed in the Appalachian Hills displayed colors other than white, even that limited palette of colors had almost totally disappeared by the time he reached the clusters of homes on the outskirts of the city. In turn, the Appalachian Trail had become the Boulevard Sanctus, its center divided by a wide strip of perfect green grass and well-tended gardens. There might even have been flowers in those gardens in colors other than white, not that Corvyn had ever seen any in his infrequent but continuing visits.

Just as the colors were limited, so too were the fragrances, so that Los Santos seemed to have the faintest scent of electric fields and ozone, rather than odors of food, or flowers, or humanity, or even trees.

In passing, Corvyn reflected, as he had more than once over the long years, that although white light contained all colors, those who claimed the virtue of white light or whiteness seemed far too often to deny the colors embodied in the white light they exalted.

Unlike Helios, or the cities and towns he had so far visited since he departed to seek out what he could about the mysterious tridents,

Los Santos boasted a profusion of modestly high structures. None challenged the Cathedral Los Santos, which dominated the low and perfectly circular hill in the center of the city. Shimmering white walls girded the hill itself, with no breaks except for the Avenue of Redemption, which extended from the Port of Hope on the Sanctus River due south to the cathedral, a thoroughfare even more impressive than the Boulevard Sanctus on which Corvyn traveled toward the center of the city, a city that had grown significantly since he last visited.

That also raised the question of what cities or villages of belief had shrunk to support such growth in the faithful of the White One, a question of lesser import than the matter of what aspect of the White Faith had changed enough to engender such added support. *Or to what unspoken but inferred prejudices has the White One catered without seeming to?*

Corvyn knew all too well that his cynicism might have been excessive at times, but he also knew that support for faiths, of whatever type and stripe, grew only when they promised something, and in Heaven, where the vast majority of material needs were met, the most likely avenue for gaining support was promising superiority of some sort.

Not only was Los Santos a sparklingly clean city, but there was also little crime. How could there have been? Every square millimeter of the city was under surveillance every moment . . . and each of those moments was analyzed and scrutinized by the quantum intelligences in the vast chambers beneath the great white cathedral. Only that which took place in the few shadows that did exist in the city escaped such scrutiny, and only if every trace remained in the nearly nonexistent shadows.

Since Jaweau would know exactly where Corvyn stayed, and since the cost of lodging was the least of Corvyn's concerns, he directed the electrobike to the Domus Aurea, one of the premier lodgings near the cathedral, not just because of the closeness and the hotel's two excellent restaurants, but also because of the irony of that name. That irony was likely lost to anyone but Jaweau, who would not raise the issue and thus resurrect it, for all that he believed in other resurrections.

A doorman clad in a spotless white coat, trimmed with the thinnest of gold piping, waited as Corvyn guided the electrobike into the covered portico. "Welcome to the Domus Aurea, honored sir." The doorman's voice was cheerful and welcoming, without a hint of condescension as he looked toward the antique-appearing electrobike.

Corvyn removed the two cases from the rear fenders and bestowed them on the bellman, who followed him to the reception counter, constructed of gleaming, gold-threaded white marble, presided over by a blond woman in white.

She took his card, then returned it almost instantly. "You have the Helios Suite, sir. Welcome back to Los Santos. Would you like reservations at the Garden at seven? Or perhaps the Paradise?"

"The Paradise this time, I think."

"Very good. Enjoy your stay."

As he followed the white-clad bellman to the lift, Corvyn found himself both amused and slightly concerned. Clearly, Jaweau's surveillance and analysis systems had greatly improved since Corvyn's last visit.

The Helios Suite was on the ninth floor of ten, and the highest floor for guest quarters, the tenth floor being reserved for the Paradise. Behind the white door were a spacious sitting room and an adjoining bedchamber. The sitting room faced north and offered a view of the city all the way to the Sanctus River. The suites facing west and looking toward the cathedral were for the faithful or for the heads of other Houses of the Decalivre, should they ever visit, although Corvyn was not aware that any such visits had ever occurred, at least not openly.

It was not all that long before dinner, and he immediately made preparations, including a long, hot shower, which, antique as it was, he much preferred to more modern methods of personal cleanliness. Slightly before seven, wearing a shimmering gray jacket and trousers, a darker gray shirt, and a much lighter gray cravat, he presented himself to the maître d'hôtel at the Paradise, who also wore a version of the white and gold livery of the staff.

"Yes, sir. Your table is ready." After escorting Corvyn to the table, the maître d'hôtel removed a card with the emblem of a raven and departed.

Corvyn smiled at the quiet reminder that everyone knew who he was. *Jaweau can't resist such touches.*

His server appeared, a woman in the same gold-trimmed white as the rest of the hotel staff and functionaries, and handed him an actual physical menu—one single stiff white sheet edged in gold, but, thankfully, with all the items printed in black.

"The small Caesar salad and the lobster bisque, with pita bread, rather than a baguette, and a carafe of the Appalachian Viognier." Those were more than enough for Corvyn after the heavy food of the last day, although the lobster bisque would be rich and creamy.

"An excellent choice, sir." She nodded and slipped away.

Corvyn always studied any chamber in which he placed himself, and the Paradise was no exception. The tables were set far enough apart that personal eavesdropping would be difficult, but most likely everything said was recorded and analyzed with the result that little would be said that was not meant to be overheard. The walls and high ceiling were a pale blue verging on white, with darker blue trim, while the table linens were that same pale blue, and the napkins matched the darker trim. Those dining were a varied group, with perhaps half white-clad, and the remainder in various garbs in an assortment of colors. They included a man in a purple thobe, and a woman in a scarlet and gold tailored trouser suit, and a couple in formal green singlesuits, possibly from Aethena, although Corvyn had his doubts. There were also two men in high-collared shimmering silk jackets, one teal and the other maroon, likely from Tian.

The carafe of Appalachian Viognier and a wineglass appeared. Corvyn tasted and approved the wine, and the salad followed in due course. Corvyn ate the perfectly crisp romaine lettuce, with the touch of anchovies and tiny croutons, and just the right amount of dressing. When he finished, the server immediately removed the salad and, after the slight and proper delay, presented the lobster bisque.

As Corvyn looked at the bisque, he noticed that a musician had taken her place on the small slightly raised dais set to the side, and was tuning her harp. He smiled faintly, then tasted the bisque, excellent, without any hint of the bitterness that might have come from shells handled improperly, although he doubted that it could have been anything other than outstanding at the Paradise.

The first selection that the harpist played sounded as though it was a hymn performed in a style he would once have called refined classical.

The second short piece she played reminded him of something ancient, although he could not remember the composer or the title. None of the other diners, it seemed, even noticed her skill. The third selection was the melody of "Purity of Light," a hymn that Corvyn had heard a handful of times and recalled only because of its melodic banality. He was scarcely surprised at the light scattered applause around the dining room. Well-recognized banality almost always triumphed over the excellent unknown.

He studied the harpist as she played. While her features, form, and skin appeared young, their refinement and her skill, not to mention her repertoire, suggested that she was anything but in first youth.

The fourth selection was from *Fall of the Redeemers*, a long-forgotten virtual opera, and one Corvyn would have thought might not have exactly had Jaweau's approval. Then he nodded. That selection was an invitation . . . and possibly a trap.

Still . . . it might be interesting.

The harpist performed for another half hour, by which time Corvyn had finished his bisque, and most of the selections were versions of hymns, if masterfully played, by which time Corvyn had also finished the crème brûlée and was sipping his bergamot tea. When she was about to either take a break or leave, he stood and walked to meet her.

She did not look surprised at his approach, but waited, standing in a tailored cream jacket with matching trousers.

"I greatly appreciated the selection from *Fall of the Redeemers*. I haven't heard that in years." *More like decades, if not longer.*

"Thank you. If you liked that, you might drop by Lucifer's Basement later this evening."

"Can I find it?" Corvyn asked with an amused smile.

"I believe you could find anything, but it's three blocks south and one west." There was just the tiniest emphasis on the word "you."

"I just might."

"Then I might see you." Her smile was pleasant, but there was glint of humor in her eyes. "Now, if you will excuse me . . ."

"Of course." Corvyn nodded and returned to his table, where he finished the last of his tea before leaving the Paradise and returning to his room.

Once there, he spent some time perusing the area around the hotel for the shadows of power, of which there were only a few, and fleeting. None interested him. He then made several brief preparations before leaving the room and taking the lift down to the main level. From there he walked outside onto the street, turning south. With all the white buildings, and the incandescence of the cathedral, night in the center of Los Santos did not really exist but had been superseded by a glowing white twilight that apparently encouraged people to be out, because while it was not late, neither was it early, and Corvyn saw people everywhere, but generally as couples or individuals, rather than as larger groups.

He walked the three blocks and turned west. Not quite a block farther, between a bistro and a shop apparently catering to women, which was closed, he observed a staircase heading down, and over the archway at the bottom of the white stone steps were letters engraved in black, and outlined in thin red light, spelling out LUCIFER'S BASEMENT. The door set back into the archway was a lurid red. Corvyn descended. As he neared the door, it slid into a recess, and he proceeded into a dim foyer.

"Good evening, sir. Might I scan your card?" The androgynous individual who offered the question wore antique black and white formalwear and would have looked suited to fit in some virtual drama, save for the red horns protruding from the short dark black hair and the equally red tail that snaked out from beneath the black jacket.

Corvyn offered the card.

The functionary scanned it, then stiffened momentarily. "Thank you, sir."

Corvyn suppressed the smile he felt . . . and the datasurge from the greeter. "I understand there's live music here."

"In the showroom in about ten minutes. Enjoy yourself."

The door beyond the greeter, also lurid red, opened, and Corvyn stepped through it into a red-illuminated room that, except for the illumination, looked little different from all too many taverns or bars that he had entered over the years. Half the backed stools at the bar were taken, as were perhaps six of the thirteen small tables. Another horned individual stood behind the bar.

Corvyn made his way through the next doorway, where another red door opened at his approach, into what had to be the showroom. He had no more than stepped inside than another greeter of sorts appeared, also dressed in formalwear but with the head of a shepherd guard dog. "Welcome to the Music of Lucifer, most honored Raven."

"Thank you." Corvyn was only modestly surprised, even though his card was linked only to the Poe identity. "Only one head this evening?"

"We are in formal attire. Your table is the one edged in black." The dog-person gestured to the far side of the showroom, which had twenty-seven tables of different sizes and shapes, all draped in crimson linen, but many edged in diverse colors, and most of which had already been taken by the audience of perhaps seventy people. Their garb was as varied as the edging colors and table sizes, and a number wore dominoes, as if such provided much disguise. The table to which Corvyn was directed was at the side, against the wall, yet provided an unobstructed view of the low stage, currently empty.

A server, also in the formal devilish garb, but definitely female, took his order for a glass of whatever Viognier the establishment had, since Corvyn did not like to mix drinks, although it was unlikely that he would finish the wine, which arrived as the performers entered through a door at the side of the stage. Most carried instruments, all of which Corvyn recognized immediately, that were strictly acoustic. Each wore a black formfitting singlesuit, with glowing red piping down the sleeves and legs, and black boots. The woman who had played the harp at the Paradise carried a viola and bow. The other instruments were a trumpet, a clarinet, a balalaika, and what looked to be a five-string acoustic bass guitar. Given the five instruments, Corvyn was prepared to be surprised. He also wondered about the choice of the three stringed instruments—three strings, four strings, and five strings.

The quintet began with a piece Corvyn knew, "The Devil's Sonata," although it had long since fallen out of favor, possibly because it was far too short to be a sonata. What followed were a series of works, each featuring a different instrument. The one for trumpet could have been called "Lucifer's Call for Judgment Day," but Corvyn had no idea what the real title might have been because the players announced nothing. They just played. Then came a work that was similar to, but not quite the same as, "Satan's Son," that featured fingering on the viola that Corvyn would have doubted could even be played on the viola if he had not been listening and watching the musician.

The set ended with several more upbeat, almost musically mischievous pieces.

Shortly after the musicians left the low stage, the violist who had been the harpist at the Paradise reappeared and walked to Corvyn's table, where she seated herself. "You came."

"How could I not? I was slightly surprised at the name of the club. It is a club of sorts, is it not?"

"It is. I told the manager to expect you. Otherwise . . ." She laughed softly, but throatily. "Otherwise, you would have been turned away or required to use certain abilities. Either seemed . . . unnecessary."

"Why did you want me to come? Just to hear the music? By the way, you're impressive musicians. I couldn't believe what you did on that one piece. Was it a riff of sorts on 'Satan's Son'?"

She smiled. "You could call it that. Violinists who play intricate works swiftly and accurately have often been called the offspring of the devil. Most violists won't try something like that."

"You're obviously not like most violists."

"That's why we play here."

That definitely made sense to Corvyn.

"You see. I didn't even have to explain." She smiled.

Corvyn could sense a sadness of sorts beneath the smile. "You play the music for the sake of it," he went on pleasantly, "but music is often used to move people in various ways. The way you played the harp, for example, was designed to put people at ease, so much so that it took a moment for me to recognize the source of the fourth selection."

"Only one such as you would have been able to do that."

"The guitarist . . . he's good also. But that made me think. I heard about a singer who uses what I'd describe as a lutelin, or a lutar. Have you ever seen or heard of anything like that?"

She frowned, after waiting slightly too long. "I've never heard of anything like that, but I can see why a singer who wants to stand out might develop an instrument that's particularly suited for his voice."

"I just wondered."

"Even if such a singer were from Los Santos, he wouldn't stay here."

In turn, Corvyn frowned. "Even in a place like the Basement, here?"

"A singer like that usually wants more."

"That's true. Some singers live for more than the music, and that can be a problem."

"Oh?"

"Music can lift civilizations and societies, but it's also been used to destroy them, often with what the users claimed were the best intentions." What Corvyn voiced was a truism, but one particularly accurate, unlike some.

"Sometimes, they've just used music to depict the great cycle."

"The ring, if you will?"

"That's as good a term as any." Her words were pleasant, matter-of-fact.

"Music and words do move people, though," Corvyn asserted gently. "Certainly, music and words together can be most powerful, given that those caught in sensual music all neglect monuments of unaging intellect. At other times, words alone have played a part in Falls." He paused, as if considering, before he added, "Even poetry, at times, especially in the years when the stars threw down their spears." He laughed ruefully. "But I doubt we have poets . . . or poetesses . . . like that in Heaven today."

She nodded politely. "Who am I to doubt the shadows of a Skeptic?"

"Then where . . . ?"

"Jaweau might know, the Maid, more so." She smiled warmly. "I'm glad you came and enjoyed our music. I'd stay, but I need to get ready for the next set. It's a bit . . . more lurid." She stood.

So did Corvyn, knowing that he had gotten all the answers that she was willing to give, and that to press more would only endanger her and gain him little. "Thank you, again."

Once she had left the showroom, so did he, making his way back through the bar and up onto the white twilight of Los Santos.

From the violist's words and unseen but perceived feelings, she knew about the singer, but not about the poetess. It would be interesting to see what Jaweau had to say, assuming the White One did not avoid him.

He walked at a deliberate pace back to the Domus Aurea.

Tell the raven where past years are,
unlighted by the morning star.

23

Corvyn stood in a narrow alley between tall, thin houses with steeply pitched roofs. The heavy night air smelled of burning wood and other substances. The few windows overlooking the alley were dark, but thin slivers of light at the edges of one or two told him that the windows were heavily curtained for a definite purpose. The faint glow of a light on the street less than a block away barely penetrated the brownish-black darkness of the alley, and the only other light was a reddish glow barely perceptible above the dull slate roofs of the buildings to his right.

He walked toward the streetlight, knowing the library was somewhere beyond, slowing as he neared the street, not all that much wider than the alley, lined by shops on both sides closed and shuttered for the night.

"What are you doing in that alley?" The words issued from a tall man in a black uniform with a strange silver insignia on his shoulder boards and his belt buckle, words spoken precisely and harshly in an ancient tongue. Corvyn understood it and replied in the same language. "I'm trying to find my way to the library. I don't want to miss anything."

"Over there." The soldier gestured to Corvyn's right. "They've just started. You'd better hurry."

"Thank you."

Corvyn walked swiftly along the street toward a small square, in the middle of which was a fire, more like a bonfire. Close to fifty people circled it, throwing billets into the flames. As Corvyn approached the square and the crowd, he saw a slightly larger structure ahead and to his left, the only one with the doors open, from which people hurried down the wide stone steps with their arms full of books, passing them out to those around the fire—who then tossed the volumes onto the flames. Each book seemed to flare as the flames touched it.

Corvyn knew such a flare was an illusion, but still winced as he angled his way toward the library. As he reached the base of the steps, another man in a black uniform appeared. In the firelight reflected on his face, the man took on the appearance of another kind of being, except he carried no trident. "Just keep to the square. They'll bring the forbidden books." The officer's eyes narrowed, and he looked more closely at Corvyn, then gestured abruptly.

Two troopers in brown uniforms with red armbands hurried toward Corvyn, who side-kicked the officer in black, then shoved him toward the brown-clad troopers, before turning and racing toward the steps, dodging between the young people carrying the stacks of books toward the ever-growing bonfire.

He almost made it to the library door before the sky split and fire engulfed him.

Abruptly, Corvyn sat up, throwing off the damp and clinging white sheets. Sweat streamed down his face as he stood in the coolness of the luxurious bedchamber and stepped away from the capacious bed, its disarrayed white spread thrown back from Corvyn's uneasy slumber.

He blotted his forehead with the back of his forearm as he walked into the larger sitting room. Slowly Corvyn paced, considering the dream, which was and was not a dream. He had dreamed it many times, for it was one of the oldest, dating back to a time before he had become what he now was, yet that memory had become his own over the endless years.

That he had dreamt it now—that was disturbing . . . and possibly revealing.

For all the vanity of light,
bare truth prevails in Raven's night.

24

Once Corvyn woke, breakfasted, and readied himself, he set out for the cathedral in his own fashion. He emerged from the shadows at the base of the Avenue of Redemption. The long incline of the avenue traversed from the level of the rest of the city up the gentle north slope of the Mount of Faith to the Cathedral Los Santos itself. He considered whether he should walk, then shook his head and reentered the shadows, guiding himself to the anteroom to Jaweau's private sanctuary, situated behind the Altar of Light that dominated the cathedral. The wall separating the two might well have resisted the powers of an ancient space dreadnought. While Corvyn could have entered the private sanctuary directly, he opted for a mannered approach and appeared in the anteroom.

The white-clad functionary at the white table desk did not seem surprised. "He's expecting you, dark one." As he spoke, the white door irised open.

"Thank you." Corvyn stepped inside, into the momentarily blinding white light, and the door closed behind him.

The sanctuary of the White One was unlike any other in Heaven. The north half of the chamber held a simple altar with a shimmering white cross suspended in midair above it, and the south half held a white desk with chairs facing it.

As soon as Corvyn entered, he saw two, and only two, dark objects, one of which was the black trident burned into the white stone above the small altar on the north side of the room. He let his eyes fix on it, waiting to see Jaweau's reaction.

"I assume that's what you were looking for." From where he sat behind the desk amid a cloud of light, now somewhat subdued, Jaweau gestured to the dark gray chair, the only such in the spotless white sanctuary that still felt more like an office or study to Corvyn. "Do you care to tell me why?"

"Because some power burned one into my study. The more I looked at it, the more it annoyed me. So I went looking to see if I had been singled out." Corvyn seated himself.

"You obviously haven't." Jaweau gestured to the black trident, but his seemingly guileless blue eyes remained on Corvyn, his shimmering blond hair faultless.

"And you left it there?"

"For now. Until I'm ready to deal with all that lies behind it. Besides, the only ones who could discover that it's here would probably already have been visited with their own tridents. Some force greater than mere powers or principalities is behind it." He smiled at Corvyn. "You've obviously discovered something along those lines already."

Rather than answer the question, even indirectly, Corvyn said, "I'm surprised you're so accessible."

"Only to you. Only because it's far less trouble to see you immediately. If I refused to see you, you'd make your way here anyway . . . or skulk around Los Santos where your shadows would disturb people more."

The absolute truth behind Jaweau's words—not that Jaweau was seldom other than truthful, if sometimes only on a superficial and literal level—bothered Corvyn even as he replied sardonically, "Nothing to tarnish or dim the light of faith."

"I will convert even you someday, shadowed one, or at least all those in the shadow lands. As you know, I can be most patient."

Corvyn was well aware of that and nodded.

"And," continued Jaweau, "the light always prevails, because light holds the truth, and a true belief is truth. It cannot be otherwise."

"But where there is light, there are always shadows."

Jaweau seemed to ignore Corvyn's response as he said, "By the way, did you enjoy Lucifer's Basement?"

"I enjoyed the music there more than at the Paradise. I'm not terribly partial to hymns."

"So . . . what do you want?" asked Jaweau. "Or are you here on behalf of Lucian?"

"You know we don't talk. We never have."

"Then perhaps someone else should be hegemon."

"Anyone else as the head of the House would be intolerable."

"Except you."

"You should know more than anyone that I have no interest in that."

"Not now. Still . . . others might prefer someone besides Lucian." Jaweau didn't look angry, just offered a sad-eyed and superior expression. He waited for Corvyn to speak.

"You know Lucian and I don't talk. Why don't you two?" Corvyn knew the answer, but needed to ask the question to avoid revealing that he knew.

"You'd like to know, wouldn't you?"

"That's up to you." Corvyn shrugged.

"Let's just say that it's far more than a difference of opinion."

Isn't that more than enough for you? Corvyn did not voice that thought, but merely nodded in response and waited.

"Where are you headed? Across the central hills and up the lesser rivers?"

For as long as Corvyn had been acquainted with Jaweau, he had referred to the Acheron and its tributaries as the lesser rivers, even though their flows and length were greater than those of the River Sanctus. "What you do think?"

"You've obviously seen all that you care to in the Houses on the Greater River. The only real question is whether you end or begin with the Maid."

"Is that what you think in that devious mind?"

"Devious?" From amid the cloud of light, Jaweau raised a hand, and small lightnings played around his fingertips.

"I didn't say dark. I said devious."

"With your reputation, Corvyn, you call me devious?"

Corvyn laughed. "Questions instead of answers." What he did not say was:

The rhetorical rhymes of olden times
Avoid replies that only can be lies.

"The answers are always in the light, not the shadows. One only has to look. Questions lie in the darkness and shadows." After the briefest of hesitations, Jaweau added, "And occasionally . . . information."

Corvyn managed not to show any reaction to the veiled probe. "You can find information anywhere."

"Obviously, but information always reveals its source, especially in the light of truth."

Jaweau always had the skill of conveying righteousness with every word and gesture, and this moment was no different from any other time Corvyn had met with the White One. "We agree about the looking," answered Corvyn, "but it's interesting that you only mention the Maid, as if she would ever deign to become involved in something like this."

"What is 'this'? How much more do you know than you're revealing? I have a dark trident here in my sanctuary. Embedded with power and skill. You say you have one, too. From where you've been, I gather that there are other tridents. What else do you know besides the presence of the trident?"

"Not much," replied Corvyn. "What about the Maid?"

"Don't you find it interesting that you've found nothing except the tridents? Is there any other House besides hers that any know so little about?"

Corvyn frowned. "There's much known about Tian or Sunyata, but little of import."

"I could say the same about Helios."

"No, you couldn't," countered Corvyn, "not if you stand by your vaunted honesty."

"It's too bad you're not the head of the House of Skeptics."

"I prefer to remain in the shadows."

"I'm certain Lucian prefers that as well." Jaweau paused, then smiled. "In any event, you might find a trip up the Maid's river to be of interest. Think about it."

Corvyn could sense that he had learned all that Jaweau would say, so he rose from the dark gray chair that had doubtless tried to discern his thoughts and physiology—and failed.

Jaweau seemed to have come to the same conclusion, because the sanctuary filled with blinding light that concealed the departure of the White One.

Corvyn slipped into the unseen shadows in a far less ostentatious departure.

Yet he wondered, moments later, about Jaweau's departure. Had the White One even really been there in person? Yet what would he have gained by not being there? It wasn't as though Corvyn could have threatened him. And why had there been the allusion to information in the shadows unless Jaweau had discovered the signals from the control station?

After more thought, Corvyn moved through the shadows, where he observed, briefly, worshippers in the cathedral being bathed with a warm light of reassurance and certainty based on the One True Faith. *Not that all faiths aren't that one true faith to their believers.* Jaweau had simply gone to greater lengths to reinforce that certainty. At least from what Corvyn observed. *Although Brother Paul has tended to dispatch Gabriel's doves to remind straying believers.* Corvyn just wished Gabriel hadn't sent the doves after him. The birds deserved better than the Sands of Time.

From the cathedral proper, he used the shadows to pass through the chambers that held the quantum intelligences deep beneath the cathedral, chambers holding only a few organic intellects, to scrutinize the continuous collection of data and visuals. Given his observations and the myriad of technologies, some of which employed quantum shifting, it just might be possible that Jaweau had discovered a certain signal and the control station that it identified. That was not the best of omens. Yet, without investigating every last console and quantum intelligence, there was no way to tell. At the moment, without proof, he could not transgress certain ancient limits. Observations from the shadows were one thing; physical entry and systems invasion were another, as had been imprinted on his very being.

From beneath the cathedral, he returned to Jaweau's sanctuary, but the White One was definitely gone and nowhere close enough to sense.

It seemed as though Jaweau did not wish to spend more time with Corvyn, which led to a variety of suspicions, even if the White One had never liked to spend much time with Corvyn.

So Corvyn began a wider search of Los Santos, always from the shadows.

That search took the remainder of the day, and he found no trace of Jaweau in the city itself. Corvyn saw little point in taking the time necessary to cover all of the lands belonging to the House. In that amount of time he could visit other Houses, quite a few of them. And Jaweau might have used the shadows to travel beyond his own domain.

But you may have to return here.

That was also possible, and more than likely, but it was six in the afternoon and Corvyn was tired. Searching from the shadows was exhausting, and a good dinner at the Paradise followed by a good night's sleep, hopefully without nightmares, had come to sound very appealing before he resumed his search.

The glittered dross the pirates took
beguiles not the crudest rook.

25

After deciding that at the present time, and for various reasons, there was little point to remaining in Los Santos, Corvyn rose the next morning and prepared to leave the Domus Aurea. Well before eight he rode the electrobike down the Avenue of Redemption to the Port of Hope, where the River Sanctus was indeed wider than the Jordan, and where Corvyn waited almost an hour for the ferry to pull into the slip. When the ferry arrived, Corvyn smiled. It had slipped his mind that, unlike every other conveyance in Los Santos, the ferry was red and gold because the gaming salons across the river in Portroyal owned it.

Had it been late afternoon, or even late at night, the wait would have been much shorter because more ferries were available to accommodate those frequenting the variety of gambling establishments beyond Jaweau's reach. As Corvyn rode the electrobike onto the ferry, along with perhaps thirty others who had been waiting, most of them on foot, he recalled the myth that the Lances of Heaven had destroyed the angels of vengeance Jaweau had dispatched to destroy the gaming salons and their money changers. The events of the mythic story had never transpired, although the Lances of Heaven would certainly have been unleashed had Jaweau been foolish enough to send any forces.

After only a few minutes, the boarding ramp lifted, and the ferry left the slip, churning northeast across the river.

Corvyn felt both worried and glad to leave Los Santos. He had left matters unresolved, but knew that without visiting other hegemons he would not find the evidence required for him to act. He also hoped to find either the poetess or the singer, preferably both, before returning. Or at least discover enough to ascertain that neither bore directly on the matter of the tridents.

He stood beside the bike near the end of the ferry closest to Portroyal, looking out across the deep blue waters of the Sanctus. Colorful structures clustered together on the northeast side of the river above the stone river walls with low rolling hills beyond. Portroyal was more than a town but less than a city, and while geographically close to Los Santos, it was actually under the governance of Helios. It was also one of the older towns on Heaven, having sprung up soon after the establishment of Los Santos, as soon as it was clear that the lands on which it was established would be governed by the City of Skeptics—and thus could offer gaming and certain other . . . services . . . not openly permitted in Los Santos.

In less than a quarter hour, the ferry neared the black stone river walls of Portroyal and slid easily into the one open slip of the five in a row—the others being occupied by other off-duty ferries, all in gold and some other brilliant color, emerald green, magenta, fuchsia, and lazuli blue.

As the ramp extended to the dark gray stone pavement leading from the slip, Corvyn studied the buildings set higher on the gentle slope. The most prominent was the Gold Doubloon. Keeping with the ancient antecedents of Portroyal, the black-walled structure flew an enormous black flag displaying the skull and crossbones, while behind the salon a small hill designed to resemble a volcano occasionally belched steam. Corvyn decided to begin his search there, since the harpist had been familiar with the singer and since gaming establishments had always been a place of employment for entertainers for as long as there had been those who gamed.

He was among the first to leave the ferry, easing the electrobike over the ramp and along the short lane to the boulevard paralleling the Sanctus. After making three turns and close to a mille later, he guided the bike into the underground parking spaces of the Gold Doubloon, secured it in a bike locker, and made his way to the lift, which he took to the main level. He stepped out into an area that appeared to be stone-walled, but the ashlar masonry was set far too irregularly for the precision dimensions of stone blocks of Navaho sandstone, as opposed to the volcanic stone that might have been used in the original Portroyal. Nor would there have been the black-trimmed crimson hangings framing the alcoves in which stood statues of piratical figures, none of which Corvyn recognized, not that there was any reason why he should have.

He could have used the shadows, but it would have taken more time and effort than being direct. He merely approached a man dressed in inauthentic pirate garb. "I'd like some information, please. I'm looking for the entertainment director."

The young and fresh-faced functionary took in Corvyn's shimmering grays, then paused, clearly sensing that he was more than he appeared. "Ah . . ."

"I'm not looking for employment, but for information. Don't misdirect me. That wouldn't be advisable." Corvyn smiled pleasantly.

"Yes, sir. Ah . . . that would be Maynard Roberts. Take the small lift around the corner and go up one level."

"Thank you."

The small lift required a code, which Corvyn bypassed. When he emerged, the image of a pirate, if a man in a tattered thobe carrying an antique slugthrower rifle could be called a pirate, appeared and asked, "Your business, sir?"

"Entertainment, Maynard Roberts."

"The third door on the right."

The door was locked, and after sensing someone inside, Corvyn used the shadows to slip beyond the closed door.

Roberts looked up from the series of images projected before him in puzzlement for an instant before the images vanished.

"I'm investigating a matter. I was hoping you might help." Corvyn smiled warmly. "I'm trying to trace a singer. He's dark-haired and plays a rather unusual acoustical instrument, something you might call a lutelin or lutar, a cross between a guitar and a lute." Corvyn didn't want to explain that lutes and guitars were essentially variations on the same instrumental theme. So he didn't.

Roberts frowned. "What did he do?"

"He seems to be gathering those who love his music and then moving on. We're interested."

"I can't say I've run across him or even heard of someone like that."

Corvyn could sense both the honesty and the disinterest in the other's voice, but asked, "How long have you been in entertainment here?"

"A little over eleven years."

"Thank you. That's all I need to know. I appreciate your time." With that Corvyn turned and left the small office, conventionally, making his way to the lift, and from there out of the gaming salon.

From the Gold Doubloon, he proceeded to the Silver Reef, with a similar lack of results, and thence to Sinaia, the Estoril, Wolfwoods, the Casino Wiesbaden, where none of those dealing with entertainment had ever heard of such a singer.

The seventh establishment he visited was the Dragonara, where he met with the assistant to the entertainment director and asked the same questions. This time the answer was different.

"We never had anyone like that, but I think there was someone like that at Lasseters. You might ask Robyn Lezli there."

"Thank you." Corvyn nodded politely and departed, again conventionally, having no immediate need of the shadows. Equally conventionally, he and the electrobike made their way to Lasseters, where he met with the brown-eyed and red-haired Robyn Lezli and posed the same question.

"Singer with a lutar?" Lezli laughed. "That had to be Bran Denu. He played here until two years ago in the tea garden. Late-afternoon gigs. Good voice, the pleasant sort. Nothing special, but the older women liked him."

Bran? Corvyn hid the wince he felt, for, if that name had been chosen with forethought, matters were worse than he had thought, for "bran" was the word for "raven" in an ancient language, and he suspected that he knew all too well what "denu" meant. *Lure or not, you still need to find him.* "How long was he here?"

"Three, maybe four years." She shrugged. "I thought he'd stay longer. He was a good fit. Warm voice, not pushed. He liked people and seemed to enjoy what he did. He didn't seem to want to go anywhere else, and that was fine by me."

"Why did he leave, then?"

"He said he'd discovered that he wanted to use his music for a greater cause. When I asked him what that might be, he just smiled and said that if he was successful, I'd find out in time, and if he wasn't, then that was probably for the best."

"Did you think that a rather odd response?"

The redhead smiled. "Who am I to say? Most musicians, the good ones, especially singers, aren't like other people. They're all a little driven, some more than a little. Some even more than that."

"Did he mention what this greater cause might be?"

"Something about ending the unending cycle of goodness repressed."

Corvyn nodded, even though the theological implications of those specific words chilled him. "Very idealistic, it would appear."

"More like gently bombastic," suggested Lezli.

"That, too," agreed Corvyn, thinking about how "goodness" imposed by power was seldom regarded as such by those on whom it was imposed. "Do you know where he went?"

"I asked him. He just said that he was going where people would listen," replied the redhead. "That could be anywhere."

More like everywhere. "I won't take any more of your time. Thank you."

She frowned. "Somehow, you look familiar. Have you been here before?"

"I've never been in Lasseters. I was in Portroyal years ago."

"Oh . . . somehow . . . I'm sorry."

"Sometimes, people mistake me for someone else." *Usually someone else well-acquainted with the shadows.*

"That must be it. Good luck with your search."

"I hope so."

Corvyn smiled wryly as he left. It took him exactly nine inquiries to discover who the singer was—far too easy. Theoretically, with Denu's name, accessing information on him wouldn't be difficult given Heaven's requirement for single identities.

In a short time, he was on the electrobike heading toward the Shakuni, one of the two gaming houses he had not visited, the other being Hollidays, for a total of ten, exactly the same number as Houses in the Decalivre, an odd sort of symmetry. He wondered what the ownership might be. *But then, the official ownership is not likely to be always the real ownership, even in Heaven.*

Using equipment built into the electrobike, he accessed certain data sources. None of them indicated information on Bran Denu after his employment at Lasseters, though certain perturbations suggested that had not always been the case. That meant that more than a few matters were not at all as they seemed. He wondered exactly how painful finding out what they were would be.

He met with entertainment personages at both the Shakuni and Hollidays, and no one could tell him much more about Denu, except that the entertainment director at Hollidays vaguely recalled auditioning Denu and finding him totally unremarkable.

From pleasant-voiced and totally unremarkable to a singer who can move hundreds, if not thousands?

Corvyn continued to mull that over as he left Hollidays and mounted the electrobike, heading toward the River Acheron and the river port of Volos, more than two hundred milles to the east-northeast. There he hoped to catch one of the high-speed courier boats to take him to Keifeng and Yu Huang, the Jade Emperor. While Denu could also have taken a boat directly to Helios, Marcion, or Nauvoo, Corvyn had sensed no disruptions likely from his presence in any of those cities. Nor were any present in Jannah or Yerusalem. In turn, such absences confirmed that Corvyn must play out matters in other cities, towns, and Houses, for the present. He could only hope to learn enough to act before others, always for the best of motives in their own eyes, precipitated another Fall—one that might be the last.

This time is the reversal of an age
and the ancient raven becomes the sage.

26

After seven long hours on the electrobike riding up and down the fertile rolling hills that supplied much of the wine to Helios, or Hel, as it was sometimes referred to by those with highly fervent beliefs and biased adverse opinions formed without factual bases, Corvyn pulled off the gray stone road at the top of the rise overlooking the River Acheron and the river city of Volos. The port of Volos shipped many of those vintages throughout Heaven except, of course, to Nauvoo and Jannah, or at least not with the approval of the hegemons of those two lands.

Even from the top of the rise, several milles from the river, Corvyn saw that Volos had grown since he last traveled there. But then, some towns grew and others dwindled, even in Heaven, although few would have dared to voice that today might not be as perfect as yesterday or that tomorrow might be more perfect.

Depending on the faith of the believer.

Corvyn smiled sardonically and started down the gentle rise toward the center of Volos, a town close to the size of the Saint town of Corinne and considerably larger than Portroyal.

Unlike any town or city through which he had passed on this journey, the houses and other structures were all finished with stucco and colored in every shade of light pastel possible, with the doors and trim in a darker shade of the same pastel. The light-colored buildings gave off a certain glare, but the black of his stedora absorbed some of it.

Although he had stayed at the Aetalos long before, Corvyn did a quick search and decided on the Polyteleia, much closer to the courier boat piers, if he even needed a place to stay, since a courier boat could be leaving that evening.

Less than a quarter hour later, he arrived at the courier pier, where there were no boats in sight. Still, he made his way to the small office, then entered after securing the electrobike outside.

An older man looked up with a momentarily bored expression until he saw Corvyn's shimmering grays. "Honored sir, what can we do for you?"

"I'm looking for passage on a courier boat to Keifeng."

"Keifeng? The first boat for Keifeng won't be leaving here until two tomorrow afternoon. There is a salon suite free, but other than that . . . well . . ."

"The salon suite will be fine." Corvyn tendered his card.

The clerk scanned the card and barely looked at it, as if he did not wish to know anything more than necessary about Corvyn. He quickly handed it back and said, "If you would be here a half hour before departure, sir, that would be more than helpful and assure that there are no delays in departure."

"I will be, thank you." With a smile, Corvyn replaced the card, nodded politely, and departed the small office.

From there, he rode the two short blocks to the Polyteleia, a handsome three-story edifice of pale blue formulated stone blocks with dark blue trim. A portico supported by fluted columns of the same formulated stone as the hotel proper covered the entry. Rockroses, larkspurs, and violets filled the raised stone beds on each side. Corvyn smelled the roses even before he got off the electrobike and left it in the temporary care of the doorman. He smiled, because the sweetest-smelling roses were the thorniest. He then entered the Polyteleia.

"A large suite or a small one, honored sir?" asked the man who rose from behind the table desk in the spacious entry foyer.

"A small one, if it has a river view."

"Yes, sir. On the third level? How long will you be staying?"

"Just tonight and until midday tomorrow. The third level will be fine."

"Excellent, sir. Your room is the Larkspur Suite."

Again, Corvyn tendered the card.

When the manager swiped the card, a faint smile crossed his lips, suggesting that the hotel's information system had alerted him to the fact that C. O. Poe was likely at least a principality. He handed the card back. "Take any bike locker beyond the roses on either side. Touch your card to the lock plate and that locker is yours. The concierge this evening is Aspasia." He gestured toward the woman seated at a small table desk to the side. "Is there any other matter in which we might be of service?"

"What might be the best restaurant in Volos?" asked Corvyn. "In terms of the cuisine, I mean."

"The best restaurant in Volos? The Apollon," replied the manager with obvious enthusiasm.

"It's the largest good restaurant," interjected the concierge, "but the very best is the Diamond Z. It's small enough that every dish is outstanding."

"Only if you like outstanding exquisitely prepared blandness," returned the manager, turning to Corvyn. "You see how I indulge Aspasia."

"The Apollon specializes in excesses of garlic and opinion," rejoined the concierge politely. "Miltiades has to support the Apollon because his second cousin is the sous-chef. A sous-chef there is one step above the dishwasher. The chef at the Diamond Z is Zaphir Rennopoulos, and any information search will show how noted he is."

Miltiades shrugged. "He is a good chef. But the pasta at the Apollon is better."

"You'll hear better conversation at the Diamond Z," added Aspasia.

"This distinguished personage might prefer quiet to opinion."

"All good restaurants in Volos have conversations," returned the concierge. "The question is which ones are worth listening to." She looked to Corvyn. "Which would you prefer? It might be less . . . interesting if I made a reservation for you."

Corvyn laughed. "It might at that. How far is the Diamond Z?"

"Two blocks north, and two east to the river."

"A half hour from now?"

"Three-quarters," suggested Aspasia.

Corvyn nodded, not quite hiding his smile.

Aspasia's estimate was far closer to the actual time it took Corvyn to stow the bike, get to his small suite, freshen up some, and then walk to the Diamond Z. He left the stedora in his room. When he neared his destination, he studied the comparatively small building, just a single-story structure of cream-white stone with teal-colored trim and front door. The brasswork on the door shimmered without a mark or smudge.

After stepping inside, Corvyn discovered that the Diamond Z was indeed a small restaurant, with but eighteen largely filled tables if his quick tally was correct, a count which he barely finished before a trim dark-haired woman appeared.

"Seigneur Poe, I believe?"

"That's my reservation," replied Corvyn, not wishing to speak the sub-identity aloud any more than necessary, a habit of reticence most likely useless now, but one still ingrained by years of caution.

The woman, who wore a teal jacket above shimmering white trousers, gestured and led Corvyn to a table set slightly apart from the other tables. The table linens were white, but the napkin at the one set place was dark teal. She handed him a single sheet, which bore the feel, consistency, and strength of parchment, but which was not. After he seated himself, she asked, "Would you care for an aperitif?"

Before answering, he scanned the bill of fare, laid out in an ornate but readable calligraphy he recognized but did not immediately recall. "The Malbec Volos."

"Very good, seigneur."

"And if you can convey the order, the dumplings and the lamb mavrodaphne."

She smiled. "I can do that, since I'm also the one serving you."

"Thank you."

"We will ask a favor of you, though."

"Oh?"

"Zaphir would like a few moments of conversation with you later."

"I'd be delighted."

As she left the table, Corvyn noticed several covert glances in his direction, but no one seemed to want to look directly.

She returned almost immediately with the Malbec, which Corvyn sniffed, then sipped, finding it more than acceptable and hoping the rest of the meal would be as good. As he savored the wine, he surveyed the others seated around the restaurant, noting that all were well-dressed, some of the men in jackets, a few with cravats. While he used the shadows to eavesdrop, something he refrained from in Los Santos, he overheard nothing of import except a few words of curiosity about his identity.

The dumplings arrived shortly, and Corvyn took his time eating them, and found them not only flavorful, but lighter than he expected from their description—filled with a feta cheese mousse, pistachios, sun-dried tomatoes, olives, and topped with a piquant pomegranate sauce.

The lamb mavrodaphne with the spinach pastitsio was equally good, and Corvyn silently thanked Aspasia for contradicting Miltiades. In the end, he decided on the baklava, made with the purest of clover honey.

He was sipping some excellent bergamot tea when a blond older man in the whites of a chef appeared and seated himself on the far side of the table.

"Zaphir Rennopoulos, shadowed one."

"The dinner was excellent," replied Corvyn, "especially the dumplings."

"Thank you, and thank you for allowing me a few moments of conversation."

"It's my pleasure, but before we begin on that, might I ask a simple question?"

"Of course."

"Have you heard of a singer who only accompanies himself on a guitar-like instrument that might be called a lutar or a lutelin? It's not the same as a bouzouki. It doesn't have a double course of strings. He may go by the name of Bran Denu."

Rennopoulos shook his head. "I would have heard if such a singer appeared anywhere in Volos."

"I'd thought as much." *For more than a few reasons.* "Thank you. Was there a particular conversation you wished to begin?"

"There is." The chef smiled, if slightly tentatively. "I've always wondered why Helios is called the City of Skeptics, when it seems to me that I see and hear more Skepticism here in Volos."

"The simple and largely accurate answer is that it suits Lucian

DeNoir to have Helios known as such. The fact that Volos also holds Skeptics just reinforces the idea that Volos belongs to the Dark One."

"And what of you?"

"I've always been more in favor of enlightened skepticism than blind faith."

"Even in Heaven?"

"Especially in Heaven," replied Corvyn.

Rennopoulos frowned, then said, "Because you're of the shadows, the shadows of Helios, I would wager that you are a personage of intellect. Because you are a person of intellect, I would ask you to define a skeptic."

Corvyn did not reply immediately, considering how best to address the question again, since it was one he had pondered for many years. Finally, he said, "My short answer would be that a skeptic is one who believes that, while many truths have been discovered, such truths may not be the entirety of what they involve, but that it is theoretically not impossible that the whole truth might be discovered. At the same time, I am doubtful that there is any universal single truth."

"Yet here on Heaven we have the ten Houses of the Decalivre and hundreds, if not thousands, of villages of belief," declared Rennopoulos. "All profess a different view of truth, and one must admit that many of the heads of these Houses possess some intellect."

"Anyone who can speak, and some who cannot, possess intellect," said Corvyn dryly. "The question is always the amount of that intellect. Dogs have intellects of a sort, as do certain types of cats."

"Ah . . . but how do you know that?"

"I do not *know* that absolutely. I do not deal with dogs or cats as a scholar. I accept the proof of scholars, and you can assert quite rightly that is a form of belief, not proof. The question in our lives is not *that* we believe, but what we believe, from what sources come those beliefs, and why we believe what we do." *And the fact that from beliefs come the differences in faiths that lead to Falls.*

"Are not most beliefs based on the sources we find necessary to support what we wish to believe?"

Corvyn smiled. "That is what the ancients should have called the 'natural state' and did not. The true skeptic is the one who questions the very basis of his beliefs, particularly those he does not think of questioning or does not wish to question."

"Such as our senses?"

"The question is when to trust our senses and when not to. Our senses are sometimes most reliable, within their specifications and limitations, and within our design parameters, but the universe is far more diverse than the environment for which we are optimized. We can physically perceive gravity when standing or resting upon a body above a certain mass, but not in space when we are not close to any such body, or when we are orbiting that body. That we cannot perceive what we conceive of as gravity does not mean that such a curvature of space-time does not exist, only that our senses are not reliable in those circumstances. My senses, on the other hand, are sharp enough to ascertain that you are indeed physically present and resemble a living being."

"We could both be illusions, and those senses illusory."

"Any illusion that complete is, in effect, indistinguishable from reality. Given that, what we perceive is real, but how we perceive it is illusory. Thousands of years of science have shown that everything we have so far encountered in the universe is a combination of energy, usually energy structured in some fashion, and space, with far, far more space than those points of energy, yet we perceive and act as if that energy has solidified the space it binds. Our senses interpret those energy levels they can perceive as colors, and we know that different individuals can identify differing ranges of what we call colors, but we have yet to determine accurately that the way in which I perceive blue is the same as the way in which you perceive blue. Which is the true blue? Or, for that matter, the purest white?"

Rennopoulos raised his bushy eyebrows. "And your point, honored shadowed one?"

"One kind of skeptic would doubt any other true blue except the blue that he or she vouchsafes. A second would say that the true blue can never be discovered, and a third would say that the truth of blue has yet to be discovered, but might be, and in the meantime, the color perceived at four hundred and fifty-five nanometers is a workable approximation." Corvyn laughed softly. "Or, put more practically, everyone is skeptical. It's what they're skeptical of that defines them. If they're so skeptical of anything that's unfamiliar that nothing can change their minds, then they're dogmatic Skeptics, or perhaps True Believers. I suppose I'd call a true skeptic one who doubts anything that has no absolutely verifiable evidence, but who proceeds on the best available proof, changing his views as his knowledge and perception increase. Those skeptics are rare. Too many who call themselves Skeptics believe they have a duty to relieve others of the false pretense to knowledge and wisdom. No one can change another's deeply held beliefs. Only the believer can make that change, and, unhappily, most changes in beliefs occur when those in power with views no longer supported by fact die off, that is, if they're replaced by those with changed views."

"That is an academic observation, since there is seldom change in Heaven," Rennopoulos observed sardonically.

"Seldom, that's true. But not never, and great and sudden changes in any society or culture have seldom resulted in anything beneficial or any lasting good. Nor has an insistence on the acceptance of one great and fixed truth ever resulted in anything other than renewed conflict."

"Do your departure from Helios and your appearance here foreshadow such drastic change? Or conflict?"

Corvyn smiled politely. "That remains to be seen."

"Then you are indeed the Raven . . . and we may see troubled times."

"I've been called that, but be skeptical of names and what you believe of them as well."

The chef smiled. "I'd say that you belong more in Volos than Helios."

"That might be true, but I am here this evening. Because Heaven is as it is, most times I need to be in Helios." *And most likely anywhere but Volos.* "But I did enjoy the dinner . . . and the conversation."

Rennopoulos inclined his head. "I will not trouble you further, but your words were . . . enlightening . . . perhaps revealing . . . and a little disturbing." He eased out of the chair and inclined his head once more, then turned and slipped away.

Corvyn took a last sip of the bergamot tea, then nodded to his server.

She immediately moved to the table. "The dinner is our pleasure, seigneur."

"You won't allow me . . . ?"

She smiled. "Your presence will more than repay us."

Corvyn did not argue, but stood, took her hand, and briefly and lightly pressed his lips to it. "My appreciation."

Then he eased his way from the restaurant, well aware than many of the diners had remarked upon his presence. Whether that would prove beneficial or immaterial remained to be seen. *But it was an excellent dinner.*

Those souls who threaten Raven's shade
may find their holy truth unstayed.

27

Corvyn slept well, and without dreams, for which he was grateful, not that he would not have more nightmares, for such were his lot, given who and what he had been for longer than he wished to recall . . . and perhaps a good dinner and interesting conversation might have been one reason for his comparatively untroubled sleep. He breakfasted adequately at the Polyteleia and arrived at the courier boat dock almost an hour before the scheduled departure time.

The boat was a deep blue with white edge piping and roughly forty meters long with essentially no decking, hardly surprising, given the speeds at which most courier craft traveled. The name on the stem plate read *Blue Dolphin*.

Even before Corvyn got off the electrobike, a crewman in blue singlesuit appeared.

"Seigneur Poe? Might I assist with stowing your conveyance?"

"Thank you. You might, once I remove my travel cases."

In moments, the one crewman had taken the bike to one of several lockers in the rear of the superstructure and linked the lock to Corvyn while a second crew member—an older dark-haired woman—escorted him to the salon suite, a slight misnomer. The quarters consisted of a sleeping chamber barely large enough to accommodate the moderately spacious bed, a small bathroom, and a modest sitting room with a small table and two chairs set beside the window that took up most of the outboard bulkhead.

Before his escort could leave, Corvyn asked, "When will we arrive in Keifeng?"

"At nine tomorrow morning, sir."

Corvyn mentally calculated, then asked, "How many stops?"

"Three. Each an hour. The first is at Ilium, then Lothal. HoiAn is the last stop, but you're likely to still be sleeping then, unless you're a very early riser. Is there anything else you'd like to know?"

"No, thank you."

Once the attendant left, Corvyn moved the two cases to the narrow space between the inboard bulkhead and the head of the bed, then returned to the "salon," where he seated himself at the table, on the side where he could look forward. As he waited for the crew to finish departure preparations, he considered what might or might not lie before him. Shortly, the lines were cast off, and the *Dolphin* moved smoothly and almost silently away from the pier and toward the middle of the river on electric drives.

Once in deeper water, the *Dolphin* accelerated and rose smoothly onto its hydrofoils, and Corvyn turned his attention to considering possible ways to shorten his inquiries. Close to three hours later, with little real progress, he decided to find some nourishment, although he did not expect to find much variety on a vessel that carried at most thirty-nine passengers.

The restaurant was small, with just nine tables. While Corvyn doubted omens, the three threes of the arrangement bothered him nonetheless, although he knew that the restaurant couldn't have been arranged just to discomfit him. He took the sole remaining window table, facing forward and looking toward the hatchway into the compartment. After noting the limited menu displayed on the dark blue impermite surface of the table itself, he touched the two items that he wanted—bergamot tea and the lamb souvlaki wrap. He just hoped that the tzatziki was not too bitter.

Less than ten minutes later the single server brought him his order, along with a large napkin, also dark blue. "Would you like anything else, sir?"

"No, thank you."

He took a sip of the tea, not outstanding, but not terrible. The lamb souvlaki wrap was slightly better, simply because the flatbread that wrapped the lamb was fresh, the lamb warm, and the tzatziki mild. He finished eating—he could not call it dining—just as the courier boat slowed, then slowly settled off the hydrofoils and into the yellow-green river water.

Once fully in the water, the craft angled to starboard and headed for the light gray river walls of Ilium, which formed a massive stone prow separating the waters of the two rivers—the Yellow and the bluer waters of the River Acheron. Upstream on the Acheron more than two hundred milles lay Aethena, the City of the Maid. While he would likely need to go to Aethena, it made more sense to start in Keifeng and work his way back eastward, since he had strong doubts that the Maid had much to do with the tridents—especially anything involving the killing of the two Valkyries.

At the same time, the courier boat would be stopping for roughly an hour, and Corvyn decided that it wouldn't hurt for him to at least walk along the river and get a feel for Ilium, since it was unlikely he would visit the City of Ares any other time soon.

Once the courier boat docked, Corvyn waited for disembarking passengers to clear the gangway before making his way onto the pier. Everywhere that Corvyn immediately looked, he saw dull gray—from the clean lines of the stone piers to the high stone river walls and even to the buildings on the crest of the point overlooking the junction of the two rivers. The stones were all cut and fitted precisely.

With military precision.

With a wry smile, he walked toward the gray stone structure set back from the pier and raised several meters, most likely the domain of the portmaster. Even the few dockworkers that he saw—both men and women—wore gray. The omnipresent gray exuded the feel of storms, even though the pink sky was clear and the sun still well above the horizon. Ilium definitely looked and felt like the city of the war god.

Corvyn had almost reached the ramp leading up to the portmaster's building when he saw a young man, neither thin nor burly, nor tall nor short, walking toward him. The man wore a gray officers' uniform, with thin red piping on the long sleeves and the trousers. He seemed most unremarkable until he drew nearer, and Corvyn sensed the projection of fear emanating from him. That, along with the fiery red eyes, told him who he was about to meet. The uniformed young man stopped short of Corvyn, who also halted and waited to see what the other had to say.

"Are you visiting as the harbinger of war, raven god?"

"I'm no god, Phobos. Are you here at your father's bidding?"

"He would bid you welcome, especially if you're inclined to stay awhile. But he is currently occupied and sent me in his stead."

"I'm honored and appreciate the courtesy. I'm but passing through, and I thought I might take a brief walk before my boat continues on."

"Up the Acheron, perhaps?"

"No. Up the Yellow River."

"There's little in Keifeng, and less of honor."

"Oh? How would you define honor, then?"

"Honor cannot be defined. It can only be earned through triumph in battle. Any other so-called honor is empty."

And war is peace, and freedom is slavery. "You do sound like your father, Phobos. Hasn't the time for war passed?"

"The universe is based on war, honored Raven, from the very beginning—matter triumphing over antimatter, force over passivity, men wrenching iron from the ground and turning it into tools and the weapons that forged civilization and advanced it." Fires flashed from Phobos's eyes, and each word issued forth like a flaming missile.

"I can see you feel strongly about the need for war," replied Corvyn evenly.

"War alone imposes the stamp of nobility on those who have the courage to make it."

"I see. And against whom would you think to make war? And with which allies? Those in Keifeng? Or elsewhere?"

Phobos laughed, a not-quite-maniacal sound. "You cannot trick me into revealing what has not yet occurred. But there will be war. There will always be war, because men need honor, and only war can provide that honor."

"There has been no war in Heaven . . ."

"What about the pogrom of the missionaries?"

"That was the slaughter of misguided innocents and a few handfuls of even more misguided Apostles of the Saints."

Phobos laughed again. "You see, honored Raven . . . you agree with me. There is no honor in Heaven, and the only violence was that of a slaughter of those without honor."

Corvyn did not agree, but Phobos would see what he would see, like all those so wrapped in their truths that neither facts nor the feelings of others could dent that armored certainty. "You may have a long wait for the honor of war."

"I can wait until the universe is a cold cinder."

That, Corvyn could believe. "Is there anything else from your most honorable sire?"

"Nothing, except his respects, despite your differences."

"I appreciate his felicitations and bid you convey my respects to him as well."

"I will do that." With a smile simultaneously both open and sly, Phobos inclined his head, then turned and walked rapidly away, vanishing into the shadows after a score of steps.

Corvyn resumed his walk, wondering if Ares was somehow connected with the tridents, but Poseidon's symbol had been the trident and once upon a time, the two had been opponents, not allies. *But then, using an opponent's symbol would certainly confuse the matter. Except Ares is only a city god and far weaker than a hegemon.*

He kept walking for a time, but sensed no other powers or principalities. Finally, he turned and headed back toward the *Blue Dolphin,* having gained only the impression of a city governed by rules without a deeper meaning, despite all of Phobos's words about war and honor.

When Corvyn had almost reached the *Blue Dolphin,* a half-familiar figure stepped forward. An unseen red shadow suffused the personage, or rather the power.

Corvyn stopped and addressed the other. "Why are you using the avatar of Rudianos, honored God of War? Is that so you don't anger the Maid? Or is there some other reason for taking another form in your own city?"

"Neither happens to be the case. This way, I'm not required to destroy you, Raven. In fact, I'm here to offer you some friendly advice. I suggest that, even with the shadows at your beck and call, you consider not traveling farther on the water."

Because the water limits the power of that red-fired black blade of your avatar? Corvyn did not voice that thought, but nodded.

"It might be best if you left the courier boat," added Rudianos quietly.

"Why, might I ask?"

"Just friendly advice. It's up to you." With that the red-haired and broad-shouldered warrior turned and walked back along the gray stone pier without hesitation or a glance back, not that Corvyn would have expected that.

What was that all about? Frowning, Corvyn attempted to shadow-sense Rudianos/Ares, but the ancient had vanished and was now beyond his senses, suggesting that he had used the shadows to move well away from the courier boat. *And why would he suggest I leave the* Blue Dolphin*?*

Corvyn had no desire to repeat what had happened outside the Gentile Inn in Corinne, yet there had been no animosity in Rudianos's words, a fact that seemed strangely at odds with their last encounter. And why had Ares manifested himself as Rudianos while instructing Phobos to greet Corvyn and tell him that his father was occupied elsewhere? Why the words about not having to destroy Corvyn? What power would have compelled that of Ares?

You're missing something. But there were so many possible interpretations of the situation, and given what Corvyn didn't know, in the end, he decided to return to the *Blue Dolphin*.

Once aboard, he walked to the rear observation area and watched from there as the *Blue Dolphin* left the gray stone piers at Ilium and turned westward to head up the Yellow River, quickly picking up speed. He was about to return to his quarters when another blue-singlesuited crewman approached him.

"Sir, Seigneur Poe?"

"Yes?"

"Did the messenger get to you?"

"Was he a broad-shouldered redheaded man?"

"Yes, sir."

"He found me on the pier."

"Very good, sir. I just wanted to make sure. He said he had an urgent message for you. He said it was important."

"I did get his message. Thank you for checking."

"My pleasure, sir." The crewman nodded, then turned and left the observation area.

That didn't make any more sense than what Rudianos/Ares had said. Why had he tried to kill Corvyn at the previous meeting and then suggest he leave the courier boat, almost as a warning, the second time?

Still puzzling over the matter, Corvyn made his way back to his quarters, using his senses and the shadows to inspect the boat the best he could, but he sensed nothing amiss. Once in the salon, he inspected his quarters as well, most carefully, and also found nothing. After reading some of a tome of ancient poetry, or what would have been a tome had it not existed in a far more compact form, he finally readied himself for sleep, hopefully without disturbing dreams.

A raven beyond Heaven's wall, enthroned,
pinions blackened from the Fall, intoned.

28

Blinding light surrounded Corvyn. Even before he fully woke, he instinctively threw himself into the shadows, but the shadows that largely shielded him twisted as if the very fabric of space-time had been violently warped. He felt as though he flew through some of that light upside down, pinions heat-blackened, before slamming into something unyielding.

Swirling cold ripped through the shadows, and Corvyn was tossed about in waters with hot and cold currents alternately buffeting him. Somehow, he made it to the surface, trying to breathe and clear his throat.

How . . . how did you get in the river?

Then he recalled the heat and blinding light and his instinctive flight into the shadows, and he shivered, not just from the chill of the water, but from the realization of what must have happened. He trod water, trying to get his bearings, until he saw points of light gathering on the shore. He began to swim in their direction, not that he would likely make it to them, given the current, but if he could keep swimming, he would have a chance to make the shore farther downstream.

How long it took, he did not know, but his legs were numb and his arms not much better when he finally reached the lower river wall. He half climbed, half crawled out of the water, wearing little but the shorts in which he had been sleeping, when a voice called out.

"There's someone here!"

Two figures hurried toward him, and lights flashed across his figure. The two immediately ran toward him.

"Can you move? Are you hurt?" asked the man as he neared.

"I . . . don't . . . think so . . ." Corvyn managed. "Just numb in places . . ."

"Are you sure?" asked the woman.

"I'm . . . not sure of anything . . . but . . . I don't think so."

With that, the woman helped him the rest of the way out of the water.

"Were you on the boat? Or were you on another boat?" The man helped Corvyn to a sitting position on the grass bordering the stone of the river wall.

"I was on . . . the courier . . . boat . . . *Blue Dolphin* . . ."

"What caused the explosion?" asked the woman as she wrapped a thin thermal sheet around him.

"I don't know," answered Corvyn honestly. He had his suspicions, but he didn't know. *Not yet.* "I was sleeping. Then there was light, and I felt like I was being seared, and then I was in the river."

The woman played the light over his face and neck. "You're red in places, and that's after being in the water. The immersion might have mitigated the worse of the burns. We'll have to see once we get you to the clinic."

"Where am I?" asked Corvyn. "Besides on the bank of the Yellow River, that is?"

"Luoyang. Baiyin's the nearest big town. It's thirty milles upstream."

"How far from HoiAn?"

"Forty milles or so," replied the woman.

"Can you walk, if we help you?" asked the man.

"I should be able to," Corvyn replied.

The man offered a hand, and Corvyn took it, levering himself up off the grass. He felt sore in places and suspected he would feel more so by the next day. "Did you see what happened?"

"There was a brilliant light and then an explosion. It was on the river. So it had to be a boat," replied the man.

"It was a courier boat headed for Keifeng," Corvyn explained.

"Of course," said the woman. "All the *Dolphin* boats are couriers."

As he walked slowly away from the river, helped by the pair, Corvyn thought more about what happened, and the fact that it had definitely been a direct attack on him. Whoever it was knew that trying to enter the shadows was close to impossible from water. Given his disoriented sleep, just using the shadows to shield himself from either explosives or the directed energy beam, whichever had caused the high-speed hydrofoil to explode, was close to a miracle—not that Corvyn believed in the traditional definitions of miracles.

He thought about accessing the news, then shook his head. At the moment, he was not linked to Heaven's system, and it might be best if he remained off the system for some time, at least until he was in a position where he could activate another sub-identity, since "C. O. Poe" should be presumed dead, at least for quite a considerable time. The most immediate question was exactly how the hydrofoil and everyone else on board happened to be destroyed. The most obvious method would have been by the Lances of Heaven, in order to stop Corvyn before he discovered who might have gained control of the Lances, but, given the safeguards surrounding them and the Lances, that was improbable. The most likely possibility was the use of traditional explosives, suggesting that the power involved needed to destroy or delay Corvyn. *Or to discover any weakness you have.*

"There's a small community van we can use to get you to the clinic."

Corvyn could sense that the man was worried that Corvyn might be in shock. Which he was, except not physical shock, but the mental shock from the idea that anyone would use that much power and that much effort against someone as much in the background as Corvyn had always been. *And not care in the slightest about what happened to all the others on the boat.*

"Oh, I don't believe I gave you my name. I'm Wang Chao."

"And I'm Liu Min."

Corvyn thought, then said, "Stafie Corbin." The name meant "shadow crow" in a long-lost language, and it was also a sub-identity he hadn't used in generations, although any search for that name would provide confirmation that such a person existed in a small town within the considerable ambit of Helios and that Stafie Corbin was more than financially solvent.

"It's not that far to the van," said Wang Chao.

That was fine with Corvyn, whose legs felt shaky by the time the two helped him into the van, a conveyance that barely seated four but that drove itself smoothly to the Luoyang Community Clinic. A sleepy-eyed physician waited, a very young professional most likely recently certified and serving in a small community to pay off her education.

Ten minutes later, or thereabouts, Corvyn emerged from a diagnostic console and gratefully sat down opposite the physician.

After studying the diagnostics, she looked at Corvyn. "You're very fortunate, sir. You have some heat damage to your dermis and some bruising. Most likely the immediate immersion in the river mitigated some of the burns." After a slight hesitation, she asked, "Do you have any idea how the explosion occurred?"

"There was an intense flare of light. That's all I recall."

She nodded, then asked, "Did you see or hear anyone else?"

"I didn't. One moment I was sound asleep. The next there was the flash of light, and then I was in the river." All of what Corvyn said was true. He had just not told what happened between those moments.

"It's amazing that you survived . . ."

Corvyn knew that it was even more amazing than the physician realized, but merely nodded as she continued.

". . . you will likely be stiff and sore in places for the next several days . . ."

When she finished, she looked expectantly at Corvyn.

"I don't have my card or anything, just the shorts in which I was sleeping. I can connect you to my data if you have a full-access capability."

"Oh . . . that won't be necessary. The clinic is rated for emergency care."

Wang Chao nodded in turn. "You can stay with us tonight. In the morning, we can take you to the Bank of Baiyin here in Luoyang."

That was a polite way of suggesting that if Corvyn were a fugitive or giving a false name, he'd be caught immediately if his name and biometrics did not match.

"That would be much appreciated. I'll need to purchase clothes and personal items, and an electrobike to continue my journey to Keifeng." Corvyn turned back to the physician. "Thank you so much. Is there anything special that I should do?"

"Light to moderate exercise would be fine, but nothing excessively strenuous for a few days. And if anything really gives you pain, see a physician or a clinic immediately."

After nodding to the physician, Corvyn left the clinic with Wang Chao and Liu Min, sincerely hoping that events would not require anything strenuous, at least not immediately.

As the three sat in the van returning them, presumably, to the couple's quarters, Liu Min said, "You might have to hire a van to take you to Baiyin if you wish to purchase an electrobike."

"First, he needs to get some rest," replied Wang Chao. "In the morning, we'll see how he feels."

"You'll see how he feels," she said with a hint of a laugh in her voice. "I have the early shift, remember?"

"The first thing I need is some clothing," Corvyn said. "I'd rather not appear at the bank in just my sleeping shorts."

"You can borrow something of mine," replied Wang Chao, "until you can reestablish the links to your resources."

"I won't be imposing too much on you?"

"Not at all. We have a spare room with separate facilities. Liu Min's brother was staying there for a while, but he's in Tian now."

"Oh?" From what Corvyn knew there was little philosophical love lost between the Taoists and the Confucians, just as the Paulists and the White One didn't get along. That had so often been the pattern in history, that the most violent conflicts had occurred as a result of schisms in a faith, schisms that seemed insignificant to outsiders. Then again, planetary destruction had also occurred as a result of conflicts between radically different belief systems.

"He was always a Confucian at heart, not like the rest of the family," explained Liu Min. "That's why he lived with us while he finished his training."

"You must care a great deal for him."

"Someone had to." Liu Min quickly added, "Do you have any siblings?"

"Not that I know of." Corvyn injected a wryness just short of being bitter. "My . . . family is . . . rather dysfunctional . . . and scattered. That's why I live in Diakrino."

"I can't say that I've ever heard of it," said Wang Chao cheerfully.

"I'd only heard of Luoyang in passing," replied Corvyn, "until I found myself here . . . and I'm very grateful to be here, especially in one piece."

Liu looked to her partner. "You've been tracking what the other rescue units have been doing. Have they found anyone else?"

"They haven't found much besides small scraps of material, but that's not surprising from the force of the explosion."

"Does anyone have any idea what caused it?" Corvyn asked, already knowing that the practical causes had to be limited.

"Not really. The most likely explanation is that the entire stored power system blew. It happened on the River Sanctus once, Feng Wen said, but that was almost thirty years ago."

"How could that happen?" Liu Min frowned.

Wang Chao shrugged. "Anything can happen once in a while. Even on Heaven."

Even when it shouldn't. As Corvyn thought that, he found himself yawning.

"You must be exhausted," said Liu Min sympathetically.

"I don't know how you managed to swim in from close to the middle of the river," added Wang Chao.

"I swam as much as I could with the current. The river's a lot stronger than I am."

"Most people wouldn't think that way."

"It took everything I had just to get partway out of the water."

"Don't worry. We'll be home in a few more minutes, and you can get some sleep."

Sleep was something Corvyn definitely looked forward to, although he suspected that the bed would be somewhat firmer than he was used to, but he had definitely slept on much worse.

If he could sleep. He worried that one of the hegemons might have gained partial access to the Lances of Heaven, even though he knew how unlikely that was. He shuddered at what he would have to do if that turned out to be true, or if even one of them was on the verge of obtaining such access, unlikely as it might seem.

A vixen's charming and inviting eyes
ensorcell none who wear the raven's guise.

29

Corvyn woke in the small room in which he had gone to sleep. The sun was up, but from the angle of the light, it had not been up that long. The bed had definitely been firm, but that hadn't kept him from sleeping. He glanced around, but nothing appeared different—the same spare room, with the same light blond wooden table desk, chest of drawers, and chair, the adjoining bathroom, and the window shades. And the lack of wall ornamentation, which struck Corvyn as more Taoist, but that just might have been the way he perceived Taoists.

Corvyn rose slowly and gingerly, which turned out to be a good idea, because he was indeed sore in more places than he wanted to count. Because Wang Chao had laid out toiletries and a robe the night before, as well as a set of loose-fitting exercise clothes, Corvyn had no trouble in showering and dressing, except he felt guilty about using too much hot water, and cut off the shower, good as the heat felt on his sore body. Once dressed, he made his way to the kitchen.

Wang Chao immediately rose from the small table. "Tea or café?"

"Tea, please . . . black if you have it."

"That I have. Liu Min is the one who likes green tea. Do you like cream?"

"No, thank you." Corvyn eased into the straight-backed chair and, in moments, was looking at yellow wheat noodles accompanied by sliced pears, with a cup of black tea beside the platter. He took several sips of the steaming tea, then tried the noodles, which were hot and spicy, but not overpowering. His eyes didn't quite water, and he was hungry enough that he ate all the noodles, and then the slightly crunchy pears. "That was very good. Thank you. I was hungrier than I realized."

Wang Chao laughed. "You worked hard swimming last night."

"Harder than I've worked physically in a while."

"You never did say why you're going to Keifeng."

Corvyn smiled wryly. "It seemed important yesterday." *And it seems more important today.* Not that he was about to say that. "I'm actually trying to find a musician with a particular talent. No one knows much about him, except he's a fine singer and accompanies himself on an instrument that is a cross between a guitar and a lute. I've heard rumors about him, but the people don't seem to remember his name, just his musicianship. I heard he might be in Keifeng. He doesn't seem to stay anywhere long."

"I can't say I've ever heard of anyone like that. I'm more into instrumentals." After a brief pause, Wang Chao added, "As soon as I clean up the dishes, we can walk to the bank. It's only about half a mille."

"That would be fine." The sooner Corvyn left Luoyang the better. While his image or voice could not be used on any publicly accessed media without his permission, the newsies could still report that the sole survivor of the disaster refused media coverage, and that would have strongly suggested to whoever was behind the attack on the *Blue Dolphin* that Corvyn was still alive and functioning. Corvyn would prefer they be left guessing, at least for a while, and his staying with the couple would have made tracking him slightly harder.

The other question that nagged him was why Rudianos/Ares warned him not to stay on the boat, especially since Rudianos had earlier tried to kill him. *If he truly wanted to kill me, why would he warn me?*

Corvyn knew the most likely answer, and if that answer happened to be correct, then whoever was behind Rudianos was definitely connected to the tridents. Having Rudianos warn him was a masterstroke indeed, and he had no doubts that, if he had taken the warning, something possibly just as catastrophic would have occurred in Ilium. But Ares had set it up so that Corvyn's remaining in Ilium was highly unlikely. *Because he didn't want anything to point directly to him.*

For the moment, Corvyn had more immediate worries. He couldn't resume his search, or go anywhere, without clothing and funds. So he needed to activate the Corbin sub-identity and then leave Luoyang quickly. As of the night before, only the clinic and rescue squad knew that he existed in Luoyang, but before long, traces would appear. *Only the faintest of traces if you leave quickly.*

A half hour later, he and Wang Chao walked down the sidewalk beside a street narrow enough to suggest that the town, or at least its center, was much older than Corvyn had thought. *You should have known that.* Except, after all the years, the memories of the smaller towns tended to blend together. The air was also moister and cooler, unsurprisingly, since Luoyang was more than twelve hundred milles north of Los Santos, as well as almost a thousand meters higher.

An older black stone building housed the Bank of Baiyin at Luoyang, but the recently refurbished interior was bright.

Wang Chao led Corvyn to a rear office in the comparatively small structure, bowing slightly to the woman behind the polished black table desk, seemingly bare, although Corvyn could sense the systems concealed within its clean lines.

"Assistant Director Wu Mei, might I present the honorable Stafie Corbin. He is the sole survivor of the courier boat accident last night. He lost everything but his sleeping garments."

"He wishes to reestablish links to his assets?" Assistant Director Wu Mei, while not particularly large, reminded Corvyn in a vague way of another Wu, also a woman.

"I do, Assistant Director."

"Your assets are located?" Her voice was pleasant, but direct.

"The Banque Helios," replied Corvyn.

"That shouldn't be a problem, then."

If you're telling the truth was really what she meant, because all the financial institutions on Heaven were linked, albeit with elaborate security protocols.

"If you'd enter the booth, sir?" She gestured toward the shielded booth in the corner of the modestly sized space.

The shields enclosed Corvyn as he stepped into the booth, ready to employ shadow manipulation if necessary, but he sensed that the links connected smoothly, and in moments the shields around him vanished.

Wu Mei's eyebrows rose slightly as she looked at the data readout appearing within the surface of the table desk and visible only to her. "You wish the same card terminal as before?"

"If that wouldn't be a problem," Corvyn answered politely. "I do have considerable business ahead."

The assistant director manipulated certain data, then said, "If you'd place your hands on the flat screen."

Corvyn did so.

"Thank you. That will be enough. It will be just a minute or two."

Corvyn waited. In perhaps two minutes, the booth produced a card.

"Now, if you'd use the card there in the booth to link with your banque, just to make sure there's no problem."

Corvyn did that as well.

"Excellent. You should be fine, sir."

Corvyn stepped out of the booth and inclined his head to Wu Mei. "Thank you. I do appreciate your expertise and assistance."

In the next hour, Corvyn purchased an outfit consisting of a dark blue jacket and trousers, a burgundy shirt, and black boots, along with a few other items. After saying his good-bye to Wang Chao and surreptitiously transferring funds to both the rescue workers, he purchased passage on the next van headed for Baiyin.

By late midmorning, he was seated on the left side of the twenty-passenger van viewing the Yellow River intermittently as the van headed northwest on the dark gray pavement. The haze was just thick enough that the Pearls of Heaven were effectively not visible.

The van was only half full, and the other passengers included a woman and two children, both of whom were playing some sort of visio-structure game; three young men, all differently attired and carefully avoiding each other; an older man and a younger one, most likely his son; and the older woman sitting on the seat even with Corvyn on the other side of the van.

Up to this point, Corvyn had not accessed any media, and especially not anything about the destruction of the *Blue Dolphin*. Since, under the privacy rules of Heaven, neither the passenger list nor the names of any survivor could appear in any media without the consent of the individual or that individual's heir, Corvyn should have some time before the power behind the attack would be able to determine if he survived, although it was certain that the attacker would believe he survived once any report of a survivor appeared. That was one reason why he wished to make his way to a larger city as soon as practicable.

The older woman wore black trousers and a black tunic emblazoned with what appeared to be abstract designs, or stylized Taoist emblems, suggesting she was neither financially strained nor especially well off. With an amused smile, she turned to Corvyn. "You seem rather an unlikely man to be riding a van."

"My previous form of transportation suffered a breakdown in Luoyang. The breakdown also destroyed everything I wasn't wearing." Corvyn shrugged. "This seemed the only timely option."

"You're not from here."

"No. I'm from Diakrino."

"I've never heard of it. A white town?"

Corvyn shook his head. "It's barely within the lands of the Skeptics."

"A dark town, then."

"More like lightly shadowed," replied Corvyn with a humorous smile. "No matter what anyone says, there aren't dark shadows anywhere there."

"You must travel often."

"Not nearly so much as when I was younger." That was definitely accurate.

"That's true for many of us, but you don't look that old."

"Thank you," replied Corvyn, adding, after the briefest pause, "Are you from Luoyang or Baiyin?"

"Baiyin. I occasionally visit friends in Luoyang." She paused, then said, "If you're looking to purchase transportation, you might want to stop near Zhengyi Square. That's on the southeast side on the way in."

"Are you going to be on the van then?"

She nodded.

"Then I'd appreciate your pointing it out, because I haven't been here before." That was a lie, but telling the truth would have been worse, because it had been so long since he was last in Baiyin that he remembered little, and he didn't look anywhere close to that old.

"I'll let you know." She turned to look out at the meticulously terraced green hillsides that rose to the northeast away from the river road.

"Thank you. I appreciate that."

In less than a quarter hour, the van reached the outskirts of Baiyin, where most of the houses were of a dark brown stone with roofs of greenish-gray tiles. The dark stone and the omnipresent greenery imparted a more somber air to Baiyin than to any of the locales Corvyn had thus far visited. *But environments eventually take on the coloration of the beliefs they encompass.* At the same time, he knew that, sometimes, the environments changed the beliefs, usually when technology was less than impressive or did not change rapidly.

"Zhengyi Square is ahead, just after the curve."

"Thank you." Corvyn directed his voice to the van. "If you'd let me off at the square."

"As you wish, sir," the van replied.

A few minutes later, the van glided to a stop, and the side door opened.

"Be kind to them . . . if you can," said the older woman as Corvyn stepped toward the van door.

Seeing no point in protesting or explaining, Corvyn replied, "That's always a good idea, if possible." He smiled pleasantly, then stepped out of the van into air slightly cooler than he anticipated. He thought he smelled a pine-like scent, but that vanished, to be replaced by the faint odor of cooking oil.

The van pulled away, and Corvyn turned his attention to what lay before him. The yellow-green tiled roof of the building in the middle of the square curved up at the ends, as did those of all of the temples in Keifeng and the other towns and cities under the sway of the current Laozi. The fact that the shade of the tiles was not that different from the color of the waters of the Yellow River was scarcely lost on Corvyn. Formal gardens bounded by low stone walls immediately surrounded the temple.

Corvyn sensed neither powers nor principalities and made his way along the stone walk toward the commercial structures farther toward the river. Several people glanced at him briefly, decided that he was a traveler from elsewhere, and continued about their business without breaking stride.

In time, he located what he sought in a building constructed of polished black stone with a set of bronze doors. Brass letters in an antique serif type stood out tastefully against the polished black stone. They read CUSTOM TRANSPORT. Corvyn entered the large open space.

A youngish woman in shimmering dark green trousers and a high-collared matching jacket rose from behind a black table desk and walked toward him. For but an instant, a look of surprise crossed her face.

"Honored sir, how might I be of assistance?"

"I'm new to Baiyin, but I presume that your establishment can formulate custom transportation on very short notice."

"We can. The time will vary depending on the complexity of the vehicle."

"If you have a design console, I can provide the template of what I require."

"You are a designer?"

"Among other expertises . . . yes."

"This way, sir." She guided him to a small space that contained a console and a chair, and little else.

Corvyn seated himself and immediately accessed certain specifications from locations not accessible to others. The sales associate's eyes widened as she realized what he was doing, and she slipped away, returning shortly with an older woman. Neither spoke as they watched. In less than a quarter hour, Corvyn completed the template and rose from the design console. "That is what I require. You should be able to fabricate it in a day, if not sooner."

The older woman looked to the display suspended in midair over the console. "Can I access the data?"

"You can access all of it, but it's currently frozen. If you need to change anything, let me know."

The older woman nodded and settled before the console. After a few minutes, she turned to Corvyn. "We can have it ready by tomorrow morning." She projected an accounting. "As you specified, that is the cost, all items included."

Corvyn scanned the accounting, and the total, slightly more than he'd anticipated, but not by much. "Half now, half when I find it acceptable and take delivery?"

"That is standard practice."

Corvyn extended the card he recently obtained.

"For this, you'll need to use a secure access. If you'd follow me, honored sir."

Corvyn did, noting that the sales associate did not, and found himself in a small chamber shrouded in privacy shields that even he would have had difficulty getting through from outside, and certainly not quickly. He walked to the small console and waited until the older woman entered the immediate amount due. Then he inserted the card, waited until the transfer was complete, and retrieved the card. As was usual, the console did not reveal the source of the funds to those in Custom Transport.

The older woman looked at him. "All our transactions are confidential and will remain so. Especially yours."

She might as well have spoken the words "most honored unaging one," but Corvyn didn't mind being classed as an immortal, because that was less revealing than his true identity. "Thank you. I appreciate that. What time in the morning?"

"Any time after eight."

After Corvyn departed Custom Transport, his next task was to find an appropriate place to stay until his new electrobike was ready, and after that, to find a clothier who had or who could quickly fabricate some additional raiment for him.

Less than an hour later, he had a spacious room in the Inn of the River's Happiness. Once he was alone, he accessed the news, routing the request through the hotel's system, rather than directly to his subidentity account, although that resulted in additional charges from the hotel. There were several media accounts of the disaster. All of them agreed on the cause—an explosion created by a malfunction in the courier boat's power system—but no account revealed any speculation on what had caused that malfunction.

What Corvyn found interesting was the responses from the various Houses of the Decalivre to media inquiries, inquiries obviously being made because of the rarity of such an explosion in Heaven.

Brother Paul was among the first to comment, saying, "It might be possible that agents of darkness inadvertently unleashed forces that they could not control, and innocents thereby perished."

Laozi's response to the question of why it might have happened within the bounds of the lands of Tao was simple and direct. "We had nothing to do with the unfortunate explosion and are investigating the matter. Initial discoveries suggest that determining the exact chain of events will be difficult, if not impossible."

Jaweau's representative declared, "We deplore the violence and the loss of life, and will do our best to support the investigation, as well as continue to support the values of purity and light necessary to strengthen Heaven against those who threaten our hard-won comity."

The Prophet, Seer, and Revelator offered prayers for the departed and the bereaved, while the chief of the Rabbis' Council in Yerusalem declared that the destruction of the *Blue Dolphin* was most likely a terrorist act, and an illogical anachronism from the distant past, a past concealed by inappropriate Poetic pseudo-justifications, and that such aberrations needed to be immediately removed from Heaven—without saying how or just who the terrorist or terrorists might be. *But clearly hinting at the Poetics.* The Poetics replied by noting that such acts only occurred whenever logic attempted to surmount faith.

Not surprisingly, Lucian DeNoir offered no comment, but he almost always remained silent. No one from Aethena or Sunyata commented, but Corvyn wouldn't have expected that from either the Maid or the followers of Siddhartha. He was surprised that no one from Tian or Varanasi had commented.

After mulling over the implications of the responses and lack of such from the assorted hegemons, he visited two clothiers and arranged for various articles of clothing to be delivered to the inn, including a second pair of boots. He decided not to replace the stedora, at least for the present time. He also purchased grooming aids and toiletries.

Then, with nothing pressing that he could presently address, he decided to visit the temple dominating Zhengyi Square, a temple he found open to both worshippers and nonbelievers, unlike many of those in the southern reaches of the Celestial Mountains, perched on tall jagged peaks dwarfed by the northernmost peaks.

He nodded politely to the two monks at the entrance and made his way inside, where he studied the statues representing the three purities. They did not look terribly different from those he beheld before the last Fall . . . or the Fall before that. They were male, with beards and mustaches, and far heftier than anyone presently inhabiting Heaven. He wasn't quite sure what to make of the small altar to the blue-green dragon, and nodded to the one for Hebo, the god of the Yellow River, although he sensed no immediate presence in the temple, but then the Taoists tended to place the principles of living life and harmony with nature above the power of gods, or the lesser powers of spirits, powers, or principalities, which resulted in less concentrated foci of power . . . or should have, since that was not always so.

He could only hope that whoever was behind the tridents had not yet been successful in undermining that dispersion of power among the wider-spread lands of the Taoists and that he would not find a concentration of power growing when he reached Keifeng.

As he left the temple, he sensed a certain presence in the afternoon shadows that spilled onto the stones of the square and paused before linking them to a figure almost invisible in the shade beside one of the granite pillars of the temple's outer walls. Nodding to himself, he deepened the shadows around himself and waited.

A woman with two children walked by the temple and shivered, not knowing why. An older man, preoccupied with either thoughts or communications, strolled by in the other direction, not even looking in the direction of the slightly shadowed woman with the lithe figure, the strawberry-ginger hair, and the close-set reddish-brown eyes that were all too bright.

A broad-shouldered young man walked briskly past the temple, then paused as the woman in the silvery jacket and trousers stepped into the light.

Corvyn smiled and immediately hurried down the steps, calling out, "Dear one, I've been looking all over for you."

The woman turned toward Corvyn, opened her mouth, then shut it as he neared, glancing to one side, as if judging whether she should flee.

"You look like an absolute vixen," he said quietly. Which, in some ways, she was.

The woman froze in place, although her eyes flashed. "I don't know what you mean." She glanced in the direction of the young man, who had already walked past her and continued away from the river, then back to Corvyn.

"Or should I say hulijing?"

"I'm hardly that."

"Just a helpless and powerless vixen, then?" replied Corvyn, not quite sardonically. "Like Su Daji?"

"To one such as you, I am but Hu Mei."

The woman's tone was flirtatious, but Corvyn sensed both concern and fear behind the words. "I doubt that, but I don't intend you harm. I thought we might have an early dinner and a pleasant conversation. Nothing more."

At that moment, Corvyn sensed the arrival of a greater force.

So did the woman, who paled and murmured, "Shui Rong." She looked past Corvyn.

He stepped back and turned, noting the shadows that enclosed and concealed him, the woman, and the new arrival, a massive dark-haired figure with a sweeping black mustache that joined an equally formidable beard. A presence that also wore ancient armor finished in red and black lacquer.

The new arrival turned to the woman. "Hu Mei, indeed. Have I not told you that you are not welcome in the square? Have I not warned you what will become of you?"

Her spine stiffened. "What would you have me do? Return to what I was?"

"That is no concern of mine. One must adapt to nature and what is."

"She has adapted," said Corvyn mildly. "You just don't like how she adapted."

"This is no matter for you, power that you may be. This is not your realm within Heaven."

Corvyn briefly thought about using the shadows and spiriting the woman away, but that would create . . . greater complications. "She has done nothing against your will, except be present in the square. If you had not appeared, we would have left the square, and with that act, she would have complied."

Shui Rong laughed, an encompassing booming sound. "So be it!" He turned to her. "Go with him. Do not return . . . or I will not be so merciful."

The woman shuddered.

Corvyn said gently, "We need to have dinner. Shall we go?" Then he turned to Shui Rong. "As one of the eight and city god of Baiyin, you must have others with whom to concern yourself."

"You amuse me, dark one." Then Shui Rong vanished and the shadows around Corvyn and the woman lightened.

She looked closely at Corvyn and shivered, obviously concerned that she faced even greater dangers with him than with Shui Rong.

"You're thinking I'm worse than he is. Not for you, I'm not. By what name shall I call you?"

"Hu Mei will do." Her voice was firm, but there was even more hidden fear than before.

Corvyn let himself sigh. "Believe it or not, I have no evil designs on you. My only designs are conversational."

"What . . . what can I tell you?"

"More than you think." He gestured toward the side of the square away from the river.

She looked at him warily, then took a step.

He matched her steps and released the shadows gradually so that anyone looking would not notice their sudden appearance—or reappearance. "Suggest a good place to eat, one where the fare is excellent and they won't be too curious."

"I'm not that hungry."

"You don't have to eat, but I'd like to, and you can eat or not, and keep me company while we talk."

"Just talk, is that all you really want?"

"Talk and your feelings and impressions about certain matters. That's all." Corvyn smiled. "I did remove you from the clutches of Shui Rong."

"That's true." She smiled, tentatively. "You can't do any worse to me than he could . . . could you?"

"I'm not interested in doing anything painful or fatal to you, or anyone else, not in the near future, anyway. By the time I am, I'll be gone, and you'll be free to do as you wish."

"That's a rather long answer."

"That's because it's truthful. Now . . . dinner?"

"Is there anything you'd prefer not to eat?"

"I don't care for raw or uncooked meat, fish, or fowl . . . or insects, for that matter. I prefer quality to quantity. Price isn't a consideration."

"The River Pearl, then. They might not let me in."

"They will," replied Corvyn. "Do we need transportation?"

"No. It's only five blocks from here. We'll turn right on the corner."

The buildings immediately north of the square were also stone, in the fashionably commercial style that had bypassed Helios when it had been the latest fad in the more northern reaches of Heaven a century previous, a style that once might have been described as polished stone and angular bronze, and one that did not appeal to Corvyn and never had, possibly because of its ponderous ornateness.

They walked five blocks past largely black stone buildings, in time reaching their destination. The River Pearl's stone façade, unsurprisingly, resembled pearl, and the door was faux pewter with impermite presented as etched glass, a construction designed to resist anything that would not have leveled the building.

Corvyn opened the door for Hu Mei, then followed her inside the foyer, a space of black glass, framed in silvered metal with subdued lighting.

The greeting functionary, clad in a muted green jacket and trousers, looked askance at Corvyn, but only for a moment, most probably because the establishment's systems had detected the information scan block on Corvyn's card, a block that suggested, one way or another, that he should be accommodated. "One moment, sir."

"You've never been here before?" murmured Hu Mei.

"I've never eaten anywhere in Baiyin before. They have ways of telling."

In moments, the functionary returned. "This way, most honored sir."

Corvyn and Hu Mei followed him to a table set in an alcove, as were all the tables. The table linens were a pearled cream that contrasted favorably with the dark green hangings that covered the alcove walls and absorbed most sound. At each place was an ivory-edged bill of fare.

Once they were seated, and he scanned the menu, he asked, "Would you like the duck?"

"If you would."

Corvyn suspected she would be more than pleased with that.

A woman server, also in green, appeared. "Would you like an aperitif, sir?"

"We'll just have a bottle of your best aged Carmenére," Corvyn replied, knowing that choice would be frowned on, but he preferred the character of Carmenére, given that even subtly prepared duck needed a strong red wine to stand up to it. "The mixed appetizers and the duck for two with the pumpkin puree."

"Very good, sir." The server slipped away momentarily, then returned with the wine, opened the bottle, and poured a slight amount into Corvyn's wineglass.

He sniffed and sipped. The Carmenére was good, if not as good as he had hoped, but he was not in a mood to quibble. So he nodded.

The server half filled each glass, then departed.

"It's not as good as you'd hoped," offered Hu Mei.

"No, but it will do." Corvyn took a small swallow of the Carmenére.

"What do you want to know?" she asked.

"How many times did Shui Rong warn you to stay off the square?"

"Just once before."

"But you risked it because that's the one place where men would think a vixen wouldn't be?"

Hu Mei nodded, holding her wineglass, but not drinking.

"And you're afraid of fading?"

"That's not a danger yet."

This time Corvyn was the one to nod. "Is Shui Rong the only immortal who's in Baiyin all the time?"

"He is the city god."

"Have others visited?"

Hu Mei shrugged. "If they have, I've never felt them."

"Then Shui Rong has been gone more often lately?"

She frowned. "How did you know?"

"I just did." *Because you chanced the square.* "You're one of the last vixens, aren't you? In the lands of Tao, that is?"

The hint of brightness in her reddish-brown eyes confirmed that, even before she murmured, "I think so. There are few in Tian, as well."

"How long have you been here?"

"I don't know."

That also did not surprise him. "How have things changed in Baiyin?"

She did not reply.

Corvyn waited.

The server returned with the appetizers and a small plate for each of them.

Hu Mei waited.

Corvyn gestured to her, and she then served herself several of the rabbit bits in the hot bean sauce.

Corvyn added several to his plate, as well as one of the pan-fried dumplings. After several bites, he said, "You were going to tell me how things have changed in Baiyin."

"They feel different. They smell different. There's more of a smell of fear. I don't know how else to say it."

"The young strong men are . . . more desperate, perhaps?"

She tilted her head, as if considering his words, then nodded abruptly.

"Is Shui Rong more restless, wandering the city more?"

"I've felt him in more places."

By the time the server returned, Hu Mei had finished the rabbit bits and shown little interest in the dumplings or the mushrooms. She had drunk a bit more of the wine, and she smiled as the platters with the duck appeared.

Corvyn sampled the duck. It was better than the wine, and he took several bites before speaking again, noting that Hu Mei was definitely enjoying the duck. "Have you run across a singer with a lute-like guitar? Or heard anyone speak of him?"

A look of puzzlement crossed her face, a visage narrower than that of most women.

"Any time in the past several years?" Corvyn added, doubting that she had, but knowing that there was no harm in asking.

"No. I might have heard if one had been here."

"Because you frequent places where there are many young men?"

Her face flushed slightly, but her eyes met his. "It's better if I take only a little from many. Then no one is unhappy or suspects."

"I imagine you've made many young men happy for an evening."

"Until the poetess came."

That surprised Corvyn, although he did not reveal such. "The poetess?"

"She stood by the river and recited poems."

"When?"

"It must have been a year ago."

"What did she look like?"

"She must be old indeed. Her hair had silver in it. I've never seen that. Her skin was almost as dark as mine."

"Do you remember any of what she said?"

"Only a few words. There was one phrase about . . ." Hu Mei frowned and paused, then said, "'Well-worn welcome words twisting souls and minds.' She also said something about men lost in lust call it love because they must." Hu Mei smiled. "I remember that because it's so true."

From those words, especially after what little Corvyn had glimpsed of the poetess, she wouldn't seem linked to the power behind the tridents, except he'd always thought there was some connection because she and the singer had seemingly become more visible at the same time as the tridents had appeared. Her possibly *not* being connected concerned him, because it suggested another power's involvement, and the more powers that were involved, the more the dangers of a loss of control that could lead to another Fall. "Why did that change what you could do?"

Hu Mei shook her head. "She made me think . . . But . . . I still had . . . to do . . . some . . . or . . ."

"You'd fade back into what you had been?"

Hu Mei gave the smallest of nods.

"What else did she make you think about?"

Again, Hu Mei did not answer immediately.

Corvyn took a little more wine and then refilled both wineglasses, not that he had to add much to her glass, then said, quietly, "That you could be so much more . . . if only . . ."

Her face sharpened, and her words were tight, low bites in the quiet. "So many girls . . . they see nothing . . . they want for nothing . . . they only do as little as they can . . ."

"You think that's unfair?"

"Life is unfair. One like me . . . I can't change it . . ."

Corvyn understood what she was not saying, that she struggled on the edge of being, just to hang on to what she had almost become.

"We'll get back to that . . . later. What else do you remember about the poetess?"

"She saw me. Everything was clearer after that."

He nodded. "Do you think any of the others who listened to her felt that way?"

"Some of the women . . . I think. The men . . ." She shook her head.

That clarified some matters for Corvyn . . . and complicated others. "Is there anything else?"

"She looked determined, but there was a sadness there."

"And?"

"That was all."

Corvyn had the feeling that Hu Mei was not hiding anything. "Thank you." He looked at her empty platter and grinned. "For someone who wasn't hungry . . ."

"I lied. Thank you for dinner."

"You're welcome. Would you like dessert?"

"No, thank you. I still don't have a need for sweets. Or a desire." The last three words were added quickly.

"Then we can leave."

"What else . . . do you have in mind?"

"Nothing," he lied. "You told me everything you could about what I wanted to know." Those words were truthful. He gestured to the server, who immediately moved to the table. "That will be all." He lifted his card.

She scanned it, and Corvyn added more than a reasonable amount to the total. Then he rose.

Moments later, the two stood outside the River Pearl.

"Do you need somewhere to stay? Or do you have a place?" *Besides a den?*

"I have a room."

"Then you have credit, and you exist in Heaven?"

She nodded. "Barely."

"Hand me your card."

Her face froze.

Corvyn laughed softly. "You should know by now that I intend you no harm."

She handed him the card, gingerly.

He took it and touched it to his, then used the shadows to make the transfer. He handed the card back. "Go to a town near Keifeng, but not in it." He touched her slightly, with the shadows, in a particular way.

She shivered as the shadows accomplished their task.

"You didn't . . ." Fear again clouded her face.

"No. You'll live as long as you would have, except you're now the lowest of principalities, rather than a barely tolerated half spirit, half woman."

"But . . . why me?"

"Let's say . . . just because." *Because you've existed too long in fear and longing . . . and because you'll make life more interesting wherever you go. Now.* She would also, in time, learn that getting her heart's desire—and more—required much more than she considered. If she didn't, of course, she wouldn't survive. Corvyn hoped she would learn.

He gestured. "Don't stay in Baiyin. Not even for a few days." He knew he was repeating what he said earlier, but it was necessary. "You need to be unknown, completely unknown, while you figure things out."

"How do you . . ."

"Once upon a time . . . I had to learn what you need to learn." He smiled, as he confirmed that she was definitely more than merely human. "Good night."

He watched as she made her way along the street to the northwest. Then he turned to walk back to the Inn of the River's Happiness.

The raven scorns, with other birds,
the wings of white and holy words.

30

Corvyn stood in the west wing of the Musée des Beaux Arts, looking at the three-figure sculpture by Maria diCassatti—Icarus, with a horrified expression on his face as he realizes that the wax in his wings is melting, that the feathers are coming loose, and that he is falling; sun-eyed Apollo in his chariot suspended above, his visage contemptuous, as if suggesting a mortal youth belongs not in the realm of the gods; and the bearded ancient-testament version of Jahweh observing sternly, as if to suggest that the youth deserves what he is getting, if not a great deal more.

"Flight and Faith" was the title of the triptych, which was what Corvyn considered the work, even if it was not technically that, given that the three figures were sculptures and not joined altar boards. He doubted that most of those who came to the museum, the only one of its kind on Ganymede, would appreciate the artistry, from the depiction of the semi-clad Icarus's muscles struggling to keep the wings moving, to the dispassionate arrogance on Apollo's face, and then the unforgiving sternness of Jahweh's countenance.

Only a handful of others stood in the gallery with Corvyn, most of them likely Belters with a few hours to kill, except for the two students who were studying the triptych as if they had some sort of assignment to report on it and the older woman who was trying to sketch the three figures on a lightscreen.

At that moment, shouts and at least one scream shattered the comparative silence of the gallery.

Corvyn turned to see five figures clad entirely in silver—silver singlesuits and hoods, silver-gray gloves, as well as silver face coverings, each a cross between mask and veil that revealed little more than the eyes. The de facto uniforms identified them as Pentecostal Soldiers of the Faith. Four of the five carried stunners, the fifth a heavy sonic disruptor.

"All of you," snapped the first man, "back against the wall."

Even before Corvyn or any of the others could comply, a tall woman in the dark blue of museum staff appeared at the other end of the gallery and strode toward the group.

"What are you doing here?" Her voice was firm and calm.

"Destroying all decadent and blasphemous salaryman pretensions at art," replied the leader.

"This art isn't yours to destroy," the woman replied. "You should leave immediately."

The leader fired his stunner.

The museum staffer didn't even have time to look surprised as she pitched forward, oh so slowly.

Corvyn had the sickening feeling that the stunner's setting was lethal.

"The rest of you! Against the wall."

Corvyn moved toward the wall, if at an angle so that he would be closer to the man who had given the orders. The others joined him, the two students last of all, obviously bewildered by the appearance of the PSF commandos.

The commando with the disruptor set it on the floor, quickly focused it, then touched a stud. The figure of Icarus expanded, cracked, and then collapsed into fragments of rose marble. Next came the figure of Apollo, followed by that of Jahweh. Even the black marble base of the triptych was cracked and ruined.

From elsewhere in the museum, or perhaps from elsewhere in the city, came the sounds of sirens and alarms, loud enough that Corvyn knew all too well that the attack on the museum was but a fraction of what was happening.

In that moment when the leader was partly distracted, Corvyn attacked, moving fast enough to paralyze the leader with his first blow and kill him with the second.

Then there was only blackness.

To see beyond the words and sights
is how the raven guides his flights.

31

Corvyn's sleep was both deep and disturbed, and he woke early, aware of nightmares, the details of which he could not recall, only that they had been disturbing. He took a long hot shower, which helped with the residual soreness, and then dressed quickly, after which he made his way down to the main level of the inn, where he was the first to breakfast in the small dining room. He dragged out eating the breakfast noodles, and slowly sipped his way through several cups of tea before walking, slowly and carefully, to Custom Transport, where he inspected and took a trial drive on his new electrobike before making the final payment. Even the holder for a water bottle and the bottle were as he specified.

In turn, he rode it back to the Inn of the River's Happiness, where he loaded it with his new clothing before departing. Then he disabled three of the four miniature tracking devices, which he located by following minute energy flows.

The sun was higher above the dark green hills to the west of Baiyin than he would have preferred, but there was no help for that. With that white sun shining through the pink sky and at his back, he rode to the river road, joining it on the northwest side of Zhengyi Square. For the next half hour, his progress through the congestion of Baiyin was slow, almost torturous. In the midst of that orderly quagmire, he disabled the fourth tracking device, but it was almost another hour before he reached the far side of the small city, where the volume of bicycles, electrobikes, and small vans dwindled away to a modestly moving line of assorted vehicles heading steadily away from the densely clustered buildings in the middle of Baiyin and toward the small patches of intensely cultivated land on the low rolling hills to the north of the river road.

With each mille that he covered, the traffic thinned, but he knew it would never be less than a steady flow, given the population of the Taoist lands and the necessary decentralization of essential manufactures, even with replicators.

Should he have opted for another form of transport? He shook his head. Electrobikes were ubiquitous in the more northerly reaches of Heaven, and even the most sophisticated sensors in the Pearls of Heaven could not tell one rider in blue or gray from another, not without the aid of the locators he had disabled, whereas any more "secure" transport would be more easily discerned. At this point, Corvyn preferred to keep matters as simple as possible, even though those opposing him clearly had other ideas.

So far it was likely that his new sub-identity remained unknown to any of the hegemons, but there remained the singer and the poetess, whose roles in the subterranean intrigues among and between the hegemons of the Decalivre were anything but clear, as well as what role Ares played.

The air felt fresher well away from the city, and the silence of the electrobike allowed him to hear, if occasionally, the owl-like call of collared doves, similar to and yet unlike Gabriel's doves, for all that they reminded him at times of aerial rats who tended to drive out other avians, even in Heaven.

Four hours passed before Corvyn felt the need for refreshment. From the map he scanned, the next town of modest size was Qikou, a place of which he had no recollection, suggesting that he never lingered there on past journeys. As he neared Qikou, the low hills flanking the north side of the river became more uneven and rockier, with none of the meticulously maintained agricultural terraces he had previously passed, but the river itself was slightly wider, and the current appeared less turbulent.

Before long he saw piers extending into the yellow-green water, several with cargo barges moored there, with a squat tugboat tied up at the adjoining pier. He also saw that Qikou was an ancient town, even by the standards of Heaven, its houses and other structures built largely of sand-colored blocks of stone only roughly smoothed, although the masonry appeared to be precisely laid. The wooden window trim and the doors varied from building to building, but all the colors were bright, unlike what he had seen in Baiyin.

Feeling that any eating establishment near the piers featured fish, he turned onto a road headed toward the hillier west side of Qikou, where he found a jiaozi shop and stopped, carefully securing the electrobike to the old-style bike stock, not only with the standard lock, but also with a hint of shadow, before entering the small eatery. A girl, most likely barely out of school, ushered him to a small wall table, one of the few available seats, despite the lack of bicycles or electrobikes outside, suggesting that people living nearby largely frequented the restaurant.

In the end he decided on pork dumplings with stir-fried bok choy and tea, and the girl server never gave him a curious look. The meal was satisfactory, the tea better than he expected, and a half hour later he was back on the river road to Keifeng.

There is something to be said for less selective restaurants. At least, if he wished not to be noticed.

By late afternoon, it became obvious that he had drastically misjudged the time it would take to reach even the outskirts of Keifeng, a city stretching more than forty milles along the Yellow River, so he reconsidered his options. In the end, he decided to stop for the night in a Gyumgo, a town far smaller than Luoyang.

He turned off the river road onto a street that seemed to lead to a better part of town, where the walls were of a smoother brown stone, only to discover that with every block he rode the walls seemed higher. Then they ended, and he entered what appeared to be a park with very old, well-tended evergreens that reminded him of grown bonsai lining the winding ways. He seemed to be the only one around, and he soon realized that he was on the grounds of an old temple, set on a rise in the middle of the extensive and well-kept gardens.

He left the temple grounds, still heading west, and eventually found what passed as a commercial avenue, and then a very modest hotel—the Pleasant Rest. Corvyn certainly hoped so as he brought the electrobike to a stop under the roof overhanging the entrance. He sensed neither powers nor principalities, and secured the bike before entering the building.

An angular dark-haired man immediately appeared in the spotless but spare foyer. "A room, sir?"

"If you have any."

"We have several comfortable rooms. Our two suites, I regret, are already occupied."

"A comfortable room will suffice." Corvyn tendered his card.

"Are you here to inspect the refractories?" asked the clerk as he scanned the card and returned it.

"No. I'm passing through. I had business in Luoyang and Baiyin, and I'm on my way to Keifeng."

"You'll be comfortable here, sir."

"What about places to eat?"

"Our small restaurant is modestly good, sir. Would you like assistance with anything?"

"I've secured the electrobike in front. Is there a better place?"

"No, sir. It will be quite safe there. Your chamber is that of the two pines on the second level."

Corvyn retrieved the clothing cases from the electrobike and carried them up to his chamber, which he found to be moderately spacious . . . and spare, not that such bothered him. Then he walked down to the restaurant, which had eight booths and three tables.

The single server or attendant simply said, "Any vacant table or booth, sir."

Corvyn immediately noted that all the booths had privacy screens, but that the tables did not. Three of the booths were occupied, one by two women, one appearing younger than the other; a second by a man wearing a gray uniform that Corvyn did not recognize; and the third by two men, the first sharp-featured and more mature than the rounder-faced younger man. The two both wore looser-fitting dark blue jackets and trousers, and something about them worried at Corvyn as he took a booth on the same side as the two men, but with an empty booth between them.

The impermite tabletop displayed the menu. Corvyn studied it and chose the pan-fried noodles with fowl and black tea. While he waited, he considered the pair in the blue jackets, their conversation blocked by the privacy screen, unlike those in the other occupied booths. After a time, Corvyn used the shadows to circumvent the booth's privacy screen, only to find that the older man of the pair had also employed a personal screen.

Two levels of screens in a restaurant? Why in Heaven would he do that?

The only reason that Corvyn could think of was that the man worried far less about powers who could circumvent the screens than residents of Heaven who could not. Still . . . he was more than a little curious, and he used the shadows to overhear the conversation.

". . . what you observed about the man who just entered?"

"He is well-dressed with fashionable and near-new garments. The colors are dark, suggesting a conservative outlook, or that he does not wish to draw attention to himself. His skin is a light tan, and his eyes are gray. That combination likely reflects a Paulist, Skeptic, or Saint background, less possibly a mixed genetic heritage. His carriage is confident, but not boastful. He took a position where he could observe everyone except us. He quickly looked once at each group."

"What does that signify about him? That he's not that interested in any of us?"

"No, honored—"

"Never in public," hissed the older man. "Even with screens, your lips can be read. Go on."

"He is either a man of business or property or an upper-midlevel Taoist inspector, possibly here on a covert investigation of the refractories . . . or for some other purpose."

As Corvyn listened to the younger man try to deduce who and what Corvyn might be, he remembered why the pair seemed somehow familiar. They were very similar to the two men he had observed at the Ridgetop Inn when he'd barely begun his latest travels, and their demeanor also suggested that they were Confucians. He could see why the Confucians might want to conduct observations in Paulist, Saint, or Skeptic lands, but why in Taoist lands, where the customs were similar enough that no one would even likely much notice a single individual from a Confucian background, but where two men studying people and other matters would draw more attention?

Training, perhaps? Or to draw attention away from something else?

Then, again, maybe there was another point to the obvious.

Corvyn turned his full attention back to the conversation.

". . . most likely not an inspector, more likely a commercial spy of some type, on his way to Keifeng . . ."

"Why is he here, then?"

"Because no one would expect him this far from the river."

At that moment, the server reappeared with Corvyn's pan-fried noodles, and he turned some of his attention to the meal, since the pair had turned their attentions to the two women, and seemed to Corvyn not to be as accurate in their assessments of the women as they were of Corvyn, since he was a spy of sorts and he was on his way to Keifeng. It struck him that the younger woman was a junior relation of the older, either being kind or flattering the older woman for some advantage, but then, Corvyn might be just as far off in his judgments as they were in theirs.

The noodles were not outstanding but better than just fair, and that was perfectly fine with Corvyn. He could a use good meal and a solid night's sleep.

Do you not see the raven knows that gold
shines more than lurid truth a god mistold?

32

The room at the Pleasant Rest might have been spare, but the bed was comfortable, and Corvyn slept better than he had in days. He woke moderately early, but refreshed, and immediately used the hotel system to check on news about the *Blue Dolphin*, but there was no additional information. Nor was there any mention of survivors, which puzzled Corvyn, because, surely, someone had discovered that.

Even with a noodle breakfast, where he saw no sign of the puzzling pair of possible Confucians, he was back on the river road in less than an hour. While he could have investigated the two more, he doubted he would have discovered anything significant without possibly making his location known to the power or powers behind the tridents and the destruction of the *Blue Dolphin*.

Four hours later, he neared the outskirts of Keifeng, where the current Laozi ruled in the name of the Jade Emperor. The immaculately sculpted terraces on the hillsides, many of which contained tea plants, slowly gave way to equally well-tended houses, each with a tiled roof, and almost every one seemed to be in harmony with the grounds and gardens surrounding it. But then, socially reinforced harmony with nature had always been an integral aspect of the Tao, and one reason why Corvyn doubted that the power behind the tridents lay in Keifeng. Because it likely did not, he hoped that the Laozi or the Jade Emperor might favor him with what they knew. At the very least, he should be able to find out more about the poetess . . . and possibly even something about the singer, although he had the feeling that the singer might well have left the Houses of the Decalivre for one or more villages of belief.

As he passed through the outskirts of Keifeng, he saw several work gangs in faded blue trousers and shirts toiling on the river wall, cleaning, scraping, and replacing stones. For a moment, he wondered why, then recalled that bankrupt or impoverished gamblers were indentured to public work service until their debts were paid. Upon release, most tended to refrain from excessive gambling, but some spent a life alternating between gambling and toiling, and, in Heaven, that could be a very long time.

Corvyn returned his full attention to the road.

Keifeng was one of the three largest cities in Heaven, the other two being Tian and Varanasi, although Los Santos seemed close to as large with its recent growth. The city proper of Keifeng stretched some forty milles along the north bank of the Yellow River, as it had for more than generations, its growth never rapid and almost imperceptible. It was not for nothing that some referred to Keifeng as "the endless city," as Corvyn recalled when he realized that the center of Keifeng still lay some twenty milles ahead even when he passed the city gates. The city gates were largely symbolic, except to Caishen, the god of wealth, whose powers were curtailed beyond those limits, because otherwise the pursuit of material goods would have dominated all the lands of Tao and the balance between nature, man, and commerce would have been permanently disrupted.

Even with the traffic moving steadily, more than an hour passed before Corvyn neared the center of Keifeng, but despite looking for recent rapid growth, Corvyn did not see any signs of such. Even from the river road he could see the Palace of Harmony, its polished jade walls glowing under the afternoon sun, with the massive malachite staircase rising from the Park of the Way to the yellow gate of the Celestial Emperor that formed the entry to the palace, and which, paradoxically to Corvyn, was the only physical link between the east and west wings of the Palace of Harmony.

In the end, Corvyn chose the Zhongzhou Imperial as his hotel, largely because it had a good reputation and, equally important, he had never stayed there before, although he did find the multicolored dome a bit garish. It was also only a few blocks from the Park of the Way, which was most convenient because he did not intend to remain in Keifeng any longer than necessary . . . unless he discovered something unexpected.

Once in the small suite, he accessed the various news sources through the hotel system, scanning them quickly. There was now a publicly expressed consensus of opinion on the destruction of the *Blue Dolphin*—that it had been a freak accident, terrible as it was. There was also the mention of a possible survivor, based on reports that could not be verified. Corvyn smiled crookedly. That meant that most of the hegemons suspected that it was anything but an accident, but with absolutely no proof, no one wanted to say that. *And whoever was behind it will suspect that you are the survivor.*

It would be interesting to see if the Laozi revealed anything. There had been no more events like the destruction of the *Blue Dolphin*, not that Corvyn expected anything similar immediately. Nor was there any other significantly disturbing news, but there seldom had been in the first stages of any previous attempt to transform the comity of the Decalivre.

Corvyn showered and changed into a dark gray jacket and trousers with a light gray shirt. His second pair of new boots were also dark gray. Then he ate an early dinner at the hotel restaurant, after which he walked out the front door, heading toward the park in the early twilight. He entered the Park of the Way on a gray stone walk that passed through a white stone wall a meter and a half high. The wall surrounded the entire trapezoidal park except on the north and smaller end, which tapered to the width of the malachite staircase, malachite because it was green, and not jade, because it was traveled by common feet.

Once inside the park, Corvyn took one of the smaller stone-paved paths that twisted and turned, sometimes through tree-lined arches and sometimes around ponds, some of which had lilies and other flora, and others of which did not. Even from the south end of the park, Corvyn could definitely sense the emanations of power from the Palace of Harmony, certainly more so than he had felt in any of the Houses he had so far visited, except, of course, Los Santos, although he wouldn't have expected great power in Nauvoo, Marcion, Yerusalem, or Jannah. He expected more power in the northern Houses . . . and in Aethena.

He walked, in circuitous fashion, to the western side of the park and back into the city proper, continuing toward another concentration of power. Two blocks later, he discovered the source of that power—a building lit with cascades of shimmering light. He realized, belatedly, that it was the temple of Caishen, the god of wealth and, not incidentally, also the city god of Keifeng. With a smile, he continued walking, making his way through the brightly lighted entrance and into the casino that was also a temple, or the reverse.

One of the uniformed greeters looked askance at Corvyn, but said nothing, possibly because the temple/casino's detectors registered his shielded card, and such shielding indicated wealth or power, if not both.

Corvyn studied the tables, or small altars, where the faithful made their offerings in various ways, ranging from ancient mahjong to battling quantum random-number generators attempting to build elaborate light structures projected above their particular altar.

Nodding, he turned and walked toward the center of the temple, where a column of light shifted colors. As he neared that column of light, shadows unseen to the various classes of worshippers slowly enfolded Corvyn, cloaking him from all others. The figure who appeared wore a black military uniform with brilliant jade piping. He carried a black whip, one that was not leather, Corvyn knew, but black steel with barbs on the end of the most flexible lash. He also rode a tiger nearly as large as an ancient shire warhorse.

Corvyn waited. He would rather not anger Caishen, especially since the god of wealth appeared in his military attribute, as Marshal Zhao, which was most unusual.

"Why are you here, Raven?"

"Occasionally, I travel to observe what is happening across Heaven."

"In places like Baiyin?"

"I presume that Shui Rong informed you that I might be passing this way."

"You infringed on his perquisites, Raven. You also disrupted the civic harmony of Baiyin."

"I was only passing through," Corvyn pointed out. "I immediately left the area of the temple when he appeared. There are so many temples in the lands of the Jade Emperor that it is difficult to avoid them all."

The marshal ignored the gentle jab and went on, "If you were *just* passing through, why did you disrupt harmony?"

"I had no idea that taking pity on a poor ghost vixen would disrupt Shui Rong's civic harmony."

"You didn't think that elevating a ghost vixen to a minor principality would be without impact?" The marshal frowned. Even his black beard expressed displeasure.

"How could the addition of one very minor female principality even send a shiver of change through the lands of the Jade Emperor? People pray to you for fortune. Sometimes, even Skeptics pray to you. Sometimes, it appears that you answer those prayers. Can you not grant me the same favor? A vixen prayed to become permanently real and fully human. I did my best to grant that wish. If I'd slept with her, that would have happened anyway."

"You did more than that."

"Those things happen, as you well know." Corvyn smiled. "Tell me, did that singer who calls himself Bran Denu ever ask your functionaries here for a job?"

Caishen frowned once more. "You think I concern myself with such details?"

"Not usually, but in his case, you would have noticed a certain aura of power, and that would have piqued your concern." Corvyn did not know that the singer had such an aura, not for certain, but his observations suggested that it was more than possible.

"Oh . . . that one. My people told him that his repertoire was not suited to our clientele. We suggested that he try elsewhere. He sang in a few squares. Despite his . . . abilities, he found the acoustics less than acceptable and departed . . ."

Corvyn repressed a smile at the euphemism for acts by Caishen's functionaries to assure that the singer did not remain in Keifeng.

". . . That was more than a year ago. He should have headed west. The Saints would have appreciated him much more."

Corvyn nodded at Caishen's words, along with the confirmation that the singer had been imbued with some power. "He headed to Tian, then?"

"In that direction. There are rumors that he took over a village of belief in the northeast lands of Tian. I find that hard to believe." Caishen shrugged and continued, "If so, that would suggest that Zijuan's powers are diminishing. I don't see signs of that."

"Have you talked to any of those surrounding Zijuan?"

"Why would I bother? I'm sure that with their great belief in moral improvement they will do as they see fit. They'll just cram another motley power or demigod into their great long march toward moral improvement. Or what they term moral improvement under the revered words of the Twin Masters."

Corvyn merely asked, "The singer had no sense of ziran, then?"

"Like many who fail to understand the essence of what is, he regarded desire and ambition as paramount. Even you understand the flaws in such a belief."

Corvyn did, although his idea of balance was not exactly one with which either Caishen or the Laozi would have fully agreed.

"In your more mortal aspect, shadowed one, will you be worshipping here this evening?" Caishen smiled.

"I have always respected honest wealth honestly obtained, and that is my form of worship," replied Corvyn.

"That is more than sufficient." With that, Caishen and the shadows vanished, and Corvyn stood alone in front of the column of shifting light.

You have one more piece of the puzzle.

As he made his way from Caishen's temple, he wondered how much he would discover on the morrow . . . and whether he should make a detour to the north.

The gods of coins, the gods of wealth,
cannot but fear the raven's stealth.

33

When Corvyn rose after a restful and thankfully dream-free sleep, he did not hurry through his shower and toiletries, nor his breakfast, but composed himself. In time, he walked to the Park of the Way, from the north end of which he climbed the malachite staircase with measured steps until he reached the yellow gate of the Celestial Emperor, also known as the Jade Emperor, the latter term being the one that Corvyn preferred. From there he turned east toward the half of the Palace of Harmony with yellow roof tiles, the half that few entered, and from which few emerged unchanged. He walked through another gate, with a green dragon on the right and a white tiger on the left. While those few who dared enter the East Palace would have taken the left-hand door, Corvyn took the middle door into the Hall of First Enlightenment, a space totally empty of decoration and a reminder that to find the way, one must turn from material distractions. The second hall was smaller, if not by much, and ended with three red doors . . . and three massive guards in black-lacquered armor accented in red.

"Let the shadowed one enter." The disembodied command hung in the air before the red lacquered doors.

Then the center door opened, and the three guards inclined their heads, just slightly, as Corvyn walked through the door, which closed behind him. The small hall was empty, except for a dais holding a simple wooden throne, with cushions of golden yellow. Corvyn's eyes flickered briefly to the black trident burned into the stone wall above the throne. He was less than surprised.

A slender figure in green stood below the dais and turned, watching as Corvyn approached.

Corvyn stopped a yard away and offered a head bow. "Thank you for seeing me, honored one."

"For a raven of power, we could do no less." The Laozi's eyes sparkled in amusement. "Are you the true Raven? Caishen has some doubts."

"Those who count often doubt that which cannot yet be counted, even if by the time it can be counted the cost would be ruinous." Corvyn shrugged. "What is the true raven? The red raven of the Zhou? The raven who survived Archer Yi?"

The Laozi laughed. "You answer my questions with questions."

"Isn't that life? If you say that I am Yangwu, then am I not?"

The Laozi's smile faded. "The raven is known for filial gratitude. What gratitude have you shown?"

"I've always been true to the vision of our distant forebears who founded Heaven after the last Fall. Is there any greater gratitude?"

"One of the few true sayings of the son of the white god," replied the Laozi.

"The one about many mansions?"

"There are many paths to the way and the truth. I am not telling you anything you have not known far longer than I have, ancient one. I am a guide to the way, not the way. If the legends are correct, you also are a guide, of sorts, turning those who think they are gods, the incarnation of god, or merely the voice of their god, from paths better not trod." The Laozi half turned and glanced up to the trident. "Is that why you are here?"

"That is one reason. There may be others that I have yet to find out. There have been tridents burned into sacred structures or books in Marcion, Nauvoo, Yerusalem, Jannah, and Los Santos, and now here. There have also been two Valkyries murdered . . . and a few attempts on me."

"Attacks on ravens are unwise. So are attacks on nature as it is and should be. That has not stopped many from such unwise acts. Or from the price they pay, and the prices others pay for allowing such attacks."

"What are your thoughts on the matter?" asked Corvyn.

"The attacks are meant to force a reaction. They are an attempt to bring change," observed the Laozi. "Who thinks they would benefit from change? Who would be willing to take such a risk? For what purpose?"

"I don't see Lucian seeking change, nor you. I don't see the Prophet of Nauvoo willing to take such a risk. I don't see the Judaics as united enough."

"The Poetics burn for change, but they contend among themselves about which vision related by which relative of the Prophet is the one that should prevail. They also lack the capability to make such a change."

"In the past, they've had enough capability to destroy worlds," Corvyn observed. "They could regain that capability, as they often have."

"That time has passed . . . given certain shadows."

"That still leaves half the hegemons," Corvyn pointed out. "Mostly in the north."

"Then you will be heading to Tian next?"

"It's the closest from here." Corvyn paused, then said, "I asked about a singer who was using song to unite people in belief. Caishen said he found Keifeng and your towns and lands . . . less than welcoming."

"Caishen is not fond of music that has been perverted from harmony with the world and nature."

"Or songs that have not been come by honestly and paid for by the singer?"

"That is also so. Then there are our people. It takes more than musical slogans and simplistic hymns to move the people of Keifeng."

Then they're unlike a great many people throughout the tragedy that's human history. "You're fortunate indeed. Where is he trying to move people now? Do you know?"

"The village is just across the Mekong east of Sunyata and some thirty milles north."

"That's an . . . interesting location, rather far south for a village of belief or rather closer to the center of Heaven than one would suspect. I would have thought that the Disciple of the Twin Masters would have . . . taken notice."

"We have entertained similar thoughts, but if Zijuan has allowed such . . . it must be for some great example of moral improvement." While the Laozi's voice was mild, the ironic tone was there, if just barely.

"Moral improvement is often a matter of perspective," replied Corvyn.

"It could be phrased so."

Corvyn saw no point in pursuing that with the Laozi. The information appeared to be true, and in Laozi's interest for Corvyn to find it so. "What about the poetess? A principality told me that she made little impact in Baiyin."

"She had some effect. That is because she does not argue against nature. Like the winds, she came, and she went. She's likely in Tian. She left here weeks ago."

Corvyn doubted that the poetess was as fleeting as the winds, but he had no facts to back that feeling, and therefore, he only said, "It is hard for one poet or poetess to change a land, especially one so populous as yours."

"The land belongs to the way, not to me," the Laozi replied. "Also, the lands of Tian are now more populous. Perhaps due to efforts at moral improvement . . . or other factors."

"How will the poetess fare there?"

"Less well than here, if I had to judge. In Tian, harmony with nature is only a goal when convenient and otherwise merely afforded lip service."

"Oh?" Corvyn knew that full well, but would like to hear what the current Laozi had to say.

"What we believe is similar in many ways. We do not change what functions well, and we change what does not. That is why we speak the language that proved most useful and not the one of our revered and most distant ancestors." The Laozi paused. "We are more concerned that desire serves nature, and not the other way around, which is what I have seen most recently in Tian." He shrugged, then added, "Most other beliefs subsume too much to desire."

"The Maid does not."

"No. There are other problems there."

Such as the fact that she is a woman. "I would suspect as much."

"Are not all Ravens suspicious?"

"So it's been said by some. Nine sun ravens were not, though," Corvyn pointed out.

"Then you must be the tenth." A pause followed. "What else do you wish from me?"

"Not to change the position of the lands of the Tao, no matter what is threatened or offered."

"Of whom else have you made a similar request?"

"No one else. Until I came to Keifeng, I did not know how serious matters could become."

"You think one of them will risk triggering the Lances of Heaven?"

If limited to the Lances alone, that possibility might be survivable; what the renegade hegemon, or conceivably, even the chief of a town or city of belief, had in mind appeared to be much worse. But Corvyn only said, "I don't think there's any doubt that one of them would trigger the Lances if they could. I just don't know which one. Who do you think might?"

"Those who believe that physical power is the way to understanding, all the while proclaiming the opposite." The Laozi's expression was wry. "Either of the Christos followers. Possibly Shiva. Zijuan is less likely, but lately . . ."

Corvyn smiled. "We have similar concerns."

"Shadowy Skeptics are not that far from the Tao."

Corvyn supposed not, but there was no point in saying so. "I thank you for your time." He offered a considered head bow.

"May your shadow carry you safely." The Laozi bowed in return.

Then Corvyn stepped back before turning and departing.

Once outside the audience hall, he entered the shadows and quickly slipped back to the Zhongzhou Imperial. There was little point in remaining in Keifeng, and he needed to be on his way to Tian.

In Heaven's great and gloried space,
the raven flies to life's embrace.

34

So late in the afternoon that Corvyn could just as easily have called it early evening, he saw a sign at the intersection with a well-traveled road to the south. The sign read WAZHAPING. The name seemed as though it should be familiar, but Corvyn could not remember why. As much because he hated not remembering as needing to find an inn or hotel for the night, he turned toward the large town that seemed to nestle beneath a line of hills running roughly north and south. As he rode past neat, small houses that continued into the town on smaller and smaller plots of land, although each seemed to have a walled garden in the rear, he saw long stone structures rising from the base of the hill beyond the town nearly to the top, and each of those structures was surrounded by solar collectors.

As he saw the solar-electric dragon kilns, he immediately recalled where he had seen the name—the renowned Wazhaping Celadon porcelain. Since he had never been in the town where the ware was fired, he excused his lapse of memory—slightly.

Because he wanted to learn more, he bypassed the larger inn in the center of the town, and chose a smaller one closer to the dragon kilns, appropriately named, he hoped, the Potter's Rest. He secured the electrobike outside the inn and walked inside into a very modest reception area. The clerk could not conceal a frown.

Corvyn smiled, not in amusement, but because there was a restaurant, or public room, with an entrance to the right of the reception area, with quite a few men and women inside, although a quick glance told Corvyn that men tended to be at one table and women at another, suggesting that the public room was a gathering place for kiln workers. He hoped so, but returned his attention to the clerk.

"Honored sir?"

"You do have rooms for the night? Just tonight?"

"Yes, sir."

"Excellent." Corvyn handed over his card.

"Ah . . . we do have a small suite, honored sir."

"That would be even better."

The clerk hid a smile of relief as he handed over an actual metal key with an inscribed "B" upon it. "On the second level at the end away from the public room."

"My electrobike"—Corvyn gestured—"will be all right there?"

"Yes, sir."

"Thank you." Corvyn returned to the bike and extracted his two cases, then secured the bike in more than one fashion before returning and making his way up the wide stairs just beyond the public room. At the top of the stairs, he turned left and made his way to the end. The key did indeed open the door with the stylized greenish-gray porcelain "B" on the door.

Corvyn opened the door, wondering what "a small suite" meant in the Potter's Rest. Once inside, he studied the modest sitting room, then smiled. The "sitting room" was in essence a gaming room, dominated by a four-sided table that could be converted to a hexagonal table, although there was a leather settee against the wall, and a large sideboard. He moved into the bedchamber, which contained an overlarge bed, a small dresser, and two side tables with a padded bench at the foot of the bed . . . and a ceiling mirror.

Corvyn laughed softly and put his cases in the small closet, where he shielded them in shadows, an act that would not be caught by whatever surveillance system was in operation. He washed up quickly, then left the suite and made his way down to the public room, for that was certainly what it was.

No one was directing anyone to tables, so he took a small table against the wall, since all the corner tables were large and already filled.

He had barely seated himself at the dark wooden table with clean polished wood bare of scratches or dents, when a serving woman appeared.

"Drinks . . . or food and drinks?" Her voice was pleasant, her smile professional. Her dark brown hair was pulled back, and she wore a clean brown tunic that might once have shimmered, but was only smooth now.

"Food *and* drinks. What's the best drink?"

"Do you want potency or taste?"

"How about a little potency and an excellent taste?"

"The golden lager."

"What's the best dish to go with it?"

"I'd suggest the pan-fried noodles with crayfish and vegetables. That or the pork dumplings."

"I'll try the lager and the noodles."

"I'll have your lager in a moment." She moved away swiftly, avoiding the roving hand of a younger man at the adjoining table.

At the table behind him, two older men with worn faces and black hair were talking quietly. Corvyn used the shadows to listen.

". . . is a difference between a body and its attributes. Your pots are bodies; their attribute is ugliness."

"And those flat circles you call platters are beautiful? Besides, ugliness or beauty is not an attribute, properly speaking. The celadon green is a characteristic or an attribute. How you see the combination of form and color is a judgment on those attributes. The attributes exist independent of our judgments."

Corvyn managed not to frown. He hadn't expected that kind of conversation in the public room of an inn so close to the kilns of a pottery works.

". . . might be, but the judgment affects the attributes . . . can't make beauty if you're thinking ugly . . ."

Corvyn stopped listening as the server returned with a tall crystal stein filled with a golden liquid. He offered his card.

She scanned it. "The meal's in the scan, sir." Then she was gone, winding through the tables in the direction of the kitchen.

Corvyn decided to listen in on three women, two tables away.

". . . all men know how to do is to make things . . ."

". . . more than things . . ."

". . . the way some of them do it . . . it's things . . ."

". . . They do what they think matters and try to convince us that they know more than we do . . ."

". . . and you try to let them know that you know more . . ."

"Just sometimes."

Corvyn heard a hint of a smile in those words, then shifted his attention back to the two older men.

"Of course the world will end. All worlds end, but the universe beyond Heaven . . . it's a Moebius snake swallowing its tail, and the tail is the end of time."

"Meaning that time never ends?"

"Why should it? Because some teacher or god says so?"

"We have a beginning and an end. Worlds and stars do. How can the universe be different?"

"What we're made of doesn't end. Only the pattern that's us ends."

". . . never convince me of that . . ."

Corvyn didn't quite shake his head, but he was glad when the server brought his steaming platter. He ate slowly, finding the noodles much better than he expected and the crayfish better than tasteless. The lager helped.

He kept eating and listening, catching phrases as the public room began to empty.

". . . time to head home . . ."

". . . nothing much there but an empty room . . ."

". . . better than the full room waiting for me . . ."

". . . too many folks make themselves who they are by what they're opposed to, rather than by what they're for . . ."

". . . all your big statements won't throw a pot or paint a faultless slip . . ."

". . . throw a better pot than the Laozi, or any hegemon . . ."

Corvyn was certain of that, and almost nodded.

The server reappeared. "You need anything else, sir?"

"No, thank you." Corvyn paused just slightly. "Did you ever work in the pottery works?"

"Never did. Pots and vases and even porcelain flowers are all the same. People aren't. That be all for you, sir?"

"That's all, thank you."

As she moved away, Corvyn thought just of the people—and powers—he encountered on his journey. For all the similarities of ceramics, there was also a great variety, from ugly to beautiful and in between. *Are people any different?*

He took a last bite of the noodles, leaving a good half of what he was served, then swallowed the last drops of the golden lager before standing. Only a few scattered tables still held patrons, the others having had their after-work letdown or refreshment before returning to whatever they called home.

As he left the public room, Corvyn smiled to himself. If those he'd overheard were any indication, the people in Wazhaping had ideas, possibly so many that they agreed on little . . . and that might be why the town would remain as it had been and was, a town in a not-quite-obscure corner of Keifeng that produced ceramics both functional and beautiful, with the works of the crafters' hands far more likely to outlast their ideas.

But then, throughout time, for a favored few, the objects they create outlast their names and ideas, and for another small group, their ideas and names outlast them, but most people leave neither beautiful objects nor beautiful and worthwhile ideas.

Corvyn returned to the room, where he not only bolted the door, but added a few precautions of his own, although he doubted their necessity. Whoever might be watching was bound to be bored and disappointed.

All thoughts turned black, feathered and unshod,
the raven flies against the unknown god.

35

A day after leaving Wazhaping, Corvyn woke early and glanced around the bedroom of the small suite in the Hotel Hou Hei in Tian, only several blocks from the Great Square and the Hall of the Analects that dominated the square, and indeed, Tian. Although Tian was a river city, unlike Keifeng, its boundaries proper more resembled a rhombus, so that the city only extended perhaps some twenty-five milles along the Yangtze River.

Days of seemingly unending hard riding over terraced hills that had come to seem unending left him tired even if the electrobike had been doing the work. Still, that had been far less tiring than traveling that far through the shadows would have been, and he preferred to save the shadows for times of greater necessity, because, over time, using them exacted a price, if not so high as others he had paid and would likely pay again.

After showering, dressing, and arranging for two of his outfits to be cleaned, he checked the local news through the hotel system, again. He confirmed that the poetess, whose name appeared to be Erinna, at least that was the name she was using, had been giving readings in the parks at noontime and was scheduled to give another such reading at noon in Beihei Park, close to three milles from the hotel. Corvyn considered the matter, and whether to use the electrobike, walk, or use the shadows to cover the distance.

Should you visit Zijuan in the meantime? He frowned. Reason told him that he should; emotion suggested that it might be better to wait to make an appearance in the Hall of the Analects until after he observed Erinna and discerned who she might be and what power she might represent. That might also give him more information with which to deal with the Disciple of the Twin Masters.

Given that matters usually worked out less disastrously when he followed his feelings, an irony some of the First would not have appreciated, Corvyn decided to walk to Beihei Park. He had the time. He had not been in Tian for many years, and walking would give him a better feel for the city and what had changed and what had not. Also, it would be somewhat less tiring than using the shadows and would not alert any of Zijuan's minion principalities, or others, who monitored the shadows.

Corvyn stepped out of the hotel into bright morning sunlight, filtered by the semitransparent bluish glassy impermite roof over the entry area of the hotel, then turned east, walking for a block before turning south on Qianmen. More had changed than he had anticipated. For one thing, he noticed that, while there was no apparent increase in the presence of police patrollers, the uniforms had changed from pale green shirts and dark green jackets and trousers with red piping to solid black uniforms with a brighter red piping. There was also a sense of what Corvyn could only call "sharpness," possibly because the streets and wide sidewalks were not only clean, but seemed to lack even the smallest of imperfections or dings or dents. The same was true of the array of buildings flanking the street, and although the colors differed, all of them shimmered as if recently built or refurbished, and there seemed to be more shining metallic trim.

Almost militant in appearance. And that bothered Corvyn. *Perhaps you've gotten lazy or too tired when you should have been traveling more.*

The men and women walking swiftly along the ways seemed little changed, but Corvyn noticed that there were no street carts or vendors at all, and that represented a great difference. In the past, such vendors had been limited, but allowed.

While he did see some of those walking who might have been from Keifeng, he did not see anyone attired in the gray of the Skeptics, or the multicolored garments of Varanasi, or the looser tunics and trousers of Sunyata, all of the other nearer lands. He did not expect to see anyone in the greens of the Maid, nor did he. He did see an occasional individual in the whites of Los Santos, and one or two individuals in garment styles he failed to recognize, most likely from towns of belief, or the occasional city of belief without a hegemon, although not from Nauvoo or Ilium.

He kept walking, not quite as swiftly as those hurrying around him, but he had time, even though Qianmen was a long street. Beihei Park was at its southern end, which overlooked the Yangtze River, whose waters were a grayish blue in Tian, but turned brownish blue farther downstream after they mixed with those of the Mekong River.

As he proceeded southward, the shops and the buildings which contained them became somewhat smaller, if no less crisp and clean, and the walks became more crowded and the shoppers less in a hurry. More of those he saw were younger, wearing slightly more relaxed apparel with a greater range of color, but the colors were subdued and certainly not flashy. The obvious outsiders remained few.

In time, Corvyn reached the north entrance to Beihei Park, where he stopped at a kiosk just inside the entry, and asked the blue-uniformed woman there, "Can you tell me where the poetry reading will be?"

"The poetry reading?" She consulted a small screen, then said, "That will be in the Juniper Amphitheatre at noon, sir." She pointed to the map on the counter. "Just take the left-hand walk. It's less than half a mille."

"Thank you." Corvyn studied the map for a moment, then continued into the park, taking the left walk, paved in a light brown stone. He passed several small gardens and a pond with what appeared to be a miniature city on an island in the middle, but he had no idea what past or mythical city the miniature represented. After the pond garden, he came to an open area that might have been a field for some sort of sport, but at the moment, it was vacant except for two women, each with children, walking slowly across the grass.

He slowed his pace as he neared the Juniper Amphitheatre, which could easily have been called a grove theatre, because the five rows of separated wooden benches were each on a different level, surrounded by trees except directly behind the benches. It was still almost a quarter hour before noon, and close to a hundred people, largely younger women and a few older men, already sat waiting.

Corvyn made his way to the end of the last bench on the right side at the highest level, where he stood for several moments, looking over the small crowd and the stage, a stone platform raised about half a meter above the stone pavement between the stage and the first row of benches. He seated himself, not that he wanted to but continuing to stand would have drawn more attention to himself. While neither his garb nor his complexion was outlandish by the standards of Tian, he knew that any who studied him in more than a cursory fashion would find him an outsider.

He waited, conscious that more and more women appeared, and before long, all the seats on the benches were taken, with close to a hundred others standing and waiting.

Just a few moments after noon, at one moment the small raised stage was empty, and the next, a woman seemingly walked from behind a tree just behind the stage and stepped up onto it. She wore bright green trousers and a matching jacket, left open to reveal a cream blouse, suggesting some link or affinity with the Maid. That could have been a deception, since she could have as easily been a sub-identity of Saraswati . . . except Saraswati had never been known for that kind of subterfuge. The poetess also carried an instrument that Corvyn recognized, but had never heard played—a lyre.

Her only prefatory words were, "Welcome to the reading." Then she began, using the lyre.

"I'll sing you songs of men, of women so courageous,
of faith and foibles often most outrageous,
and ask you riddling questions hard to comprehend
in hopes you'll find an overbearing common trend . . ."

Corvyn listened, alert as to whether she enhanced her recitation/song in some manner through the shadows or other power. If she did, it was in some fashion he could not discern, yet he had the feeling that there was something more behind the words and the lyre.

"A woman brave sprang from her father's brow,
with wisdom rare, she cautioned care, and how
the golden fruits for beauty's greatest prize
would shred two empires into death and lies.
No matter that, the feckless hero said,
I'll choose her, claim a queen, and leave well dead
those flowered heroes on a plain stained red . . ."

Corvyn swallowed silently at those words, fearing he knew all too well the identity of the poetess, and wondered why she'd taken the name of the lesser-known poetess from early years. At the same time, the others listening seemed captivated. He waited for the next poem/song.

"We see the iris bloom in spring,
the youngest robins soon take wing,
the sunglow fades to evening light
and stars unchanging shine so bright . . .
relentless through time's cold flight . . ."

Even before she finished that piece, Corvyn wondered just what would come next.

He didn't have to wait that long.

"Men talk of love, of life for two,
but when it's done, and he is through
the sheets so white, the blood so red,
forgotten praises he once said,
rutting men so lost in lust
call it love because they must . . ."

Corvyn had a growing feeling that the reading/recital was not going to conclude well, but he continued to listen and to watch the poetess intently.

"You sing your praises to the skies
to gods, to faiths all made by men,

yet women's truths are held as lies,
debased as straight from evil's den.

We're sisters all in blood and light
and held in Heaven, bound so tight
in faulted faiths from failing flight
and spread across time's endless night . . ."

Corvyn could sense a certain feeling, perhaps a growing anger from the women listening, and at the same time, not too far away, he also sensed a gathering force, but he wanted to hear—and see—how matters played out . . . in both senses of the word.

"*We women sing and speak in rhythms so unheard,*
we've fought and died when we've had little choice
in spoils procured or children's deaths incurred,
but who in Heaven hears a woman's voice?"

At that moment, an announcement thundered from behind Corvyn. "This part of the park is closed. This part of the park is closed."

Corvyn turned his head to see men and women in black uniforms appearing behind him and from each side of the small amphitheatre, moving toward the group seated on benches.

The poetess looked directly at Corvyn with a fiery glint in those gray eyes, then stepped forward to a recently vacated bench and left a single sheet of paper. Then she vanished, so quickly that Corvyn failed to detect the interplay of shadow.

He hurried down to the bench and snatched the paper, calling upon the shadows himself as he saw a uniformed woman turning toward him and lifting a weapon. As he disappeared into the shadows he sensed the stunner bolts filling the area he had just departed.

Using the shadows, he returned to a moderately busy side street near his hotel, appearing close to the wall of a building, since he had no doubt that his rooms were fully monitored, and he preferred not to reveal anything he did not have to, at least for the present in Tian. He slipped the paper into an inside pocket of his jacket and walked swiftly in the direction of the hotel.

Once back in his room, he took out the single sheet, pausing as he recognized it was a poem, but equally important, that the document was actually flexible impermite. The words were a part of the impermite, and not merely placed upon it.

"She definitely made it hard to be destroyed." He also wondered how many impermite copies circulated across the plateau of Heaven, then noticed that the poem/song had no title.

He immediately read it.

The threefold, eternal dream, conscious stream
Winds, falls, through all time, a deceiving seam . . .
Belief in posing honor, lying pride,
And humble faith, deities undeified.

Sequestered sensibilities serve ages
Of strident sycophantic sages,
Ensconced too easily in ivory cages
Their words all penned from puissant plundered pages.
Well-worn welcome words twisting souls and minds
To comfort true believers of all kinds
Weave their webs to warp space-time and define
The Fall as though it were gods' great design.
Do deities die under Heaven's sky,
Or merely deathless do persist and lie?
Their many mansions truthlessly defy
The single truths of those they deify.

O higher ones, tell us now, if you can,
Why of all the Ten, that nine are man?
Or will you declare, as it seems you must.
All stars in Heaven's sky are distant dust?

There was no doubt in Corvyn's mind just who the poetess was, and that she had strong concerns to have done what she had done. There was also no doubt that she had a slightly different agenda than did Corvyn, but her concerns were certainly not antithetical to his, unlike the elusive Bran Denu, whose movements suggested a far different set of motives.

Or is he merely a lure?

That was more than possible, Corvyn knew, but the singer's name was so obviously suggestive that the power behind him might have considered the obvious as concealment and that bespoke a devious approach, not that Corvyn wasn't already aware of that.

Before he set out to meet with Zijuan, there was one more task to deal with—to see if the netsystem had any information on a certain village of belief. First, he called up maps of the area mentioned by the Laozi, and, unsurprisingly, there was a modestly large village located right on the west bank of the Mekong River some thirty-three milles north of the ferry crossing connecting the segments of the main road from Tian to Sunyata. The maps did not provide any name, but Corvyn discerned that one road ran along the west side of the river from the ferry crossing to the town. There were also certain indications that the road was comparatively recent, such as the absence of tall vegetation nearby, and several bridges that appeared newer.

Corvyn nodded. A side trip to the village was definitely in order—with more than a few precautions. But first, he needed to visit Zijuan.

He decided to dispense with an indirect approach and used the shadows to cross the few blocks from the Hotel Hou Hei to the Hall of the Analects and the Great Hall within. Not surprisingly, Zijuan, the Disciple of the Twin Masters of Reason, was not in the Great Hall. Corwin simply followed the flow of power, and appeared in Zijuan's modest private study, a teak-paneled chamber with bookcases on all sides, except for the carved stone frieze two meters wide directly behind the teak table desk and chair. Three books were stacked on one side of the otherwise clear table desk. All the books struck Corvyn more as a nod to tradition or simply an affectation, since none of those who held the position of Zijuan had been known as bibliophiles. Corvyn also sensed that the stone plaque at the top of the frieze with the intertwined symbols of the Twin Masters was new and covered an older plaque, into which a black trident had burned itself.

Behind the desk sat a man attired in a dark olive-green jacket and trousers. His complexion was honey-olive, and his glossy black hair was slicked back. Power radiated from him, so much that he was obviously Zijuan.

Corvyn stepped out of the shadows, but before he could speak, the other did.

"Shadowed one," he said politely, but not subserviently, as if he had sensed Corvyn even before Corvyn emerged from the shadows, which he doubtless had.

"Honored Disciple of the Twin Masters."

"What brings you here, so far from the lands of the Skeptics? Some concern of the Dark One of Helios?"

"You know better than that." Corvyn smiled, even as he sensed and noted the amount of power mustered behind the antique teak bookcases. "He seldom deigns to involve himself in affairs beyond the lands of the Skeptics."

"So it is said. What is said is not always what is, or what is believed. If not for the Dark One, then why are you here?"

"I've been following a certain poetess. I caught up with her, and before I could talk to her, your guards stopped her reading, and she vanished. Then your guards began to stun some of those who had been listening."

"Ah, yes. The poetess. She was becoming disruptive to the social order."

"By reading poetry?" asked Corvyn mildly.

"Words can be disruptive. Literature and art must fit into society and must always unite and educate."

"What about the pursuit of art for its own sake? Doesn't art enrich life?"

"There is no such thing as art for art's sake. Any art that is art has meaning, and those meanings have repercussions . . . as you well know."

"Repercussions?" Corvyn probed. "Such as changing people's beliefs?"

"I noticed that you also vanished immediately after the tool of the Misleading Maid disappeared."

"It seemed advisable, given that your guards were armed."

"Merely stunners. Not something one such as you need worry about. You never did say what your interest in the . . . tool of depravity happens to be."

"She's been reading her works in at least several lands of Heaven. I wanted to see why. From what I heard, she was offering a different viewpoint in her words."

"She was fomenting disruption."

"Questioning beliefs, you mean?"

"Belief is not a poem, nor a dinner party, nor words mouthed out of habit. Belief is a way of life. It is simple. It is only shadowed ones like you that make it complicated. So many forget that he who learns but does not believe is lost."

"What about women? Are they lost, too?"

"You are trying to provoke me, shadowed one. That is not wise."

"I'm actually curious," Corvyn said, his voice pleasant. "I don't see why a woman reading poetry requires suppression by armed guards."

"That is because it is man's and woman's social being that determines their thinking, and the role of the Disciple is to ensure that all social being is in accord with the highest standards."

"The standards written by the Twin Masters and interpreted by the Disciple."

"Precisely. How can there be high standards otherwise? By nature, people are alike. In an ungoverned society they move apart, seeking advantage. Shared beliefs keep people closer together. Totally diverse beliefs have torn worlds apart . . ."

Only because true believers insisted on imposing their beliefs on others. But Corvyn did not voice that thought, as he listened and made ready to depart before it became too painful to remain.

". . . Those who know belief are not equal to those who love it."

And in the original version of that, the word used was "truth." "That's a bit of a perversion of what the more ancient Master said."

"Not in the slightest. A true belief is truth. It cannot be otherwise. How could it possibly be?"

Corvyn managed not to show any reaction. "I think I've heard that before . . . or something like it." *Quite recently, and before that, all too many times, with the same sad results.*

"That should tell you something, shadowed one."

"It does indeed. I also wondered why you're tolerating a village of belief so close to Tian . . . and even closer to Sunyata."

At that moment, Corvyn detected the slightest changes in the power web enclosing the study and dropped into the deep shadows just before the energies converged on the spot where he had been standing.

Through the shadows, he returned to the Hotel Hou Hei, where he immediately noted that his outfits had been returned . . . with certain additions, which additions he removed before he packed them in the cases that fit into the electrobike.

Then he carried the cases down to the main level, arranged for his departure, and reclaimed the electrobike from its storage, also removing more minute devices, and rode it out into the afternoon traffic.

Corvyn concentrated more on the streets and avenues of Tian as he made his way out of the city, heading toward the highway to Sunyata. While he doubted that the followers of Siddhartha involved themselves with the tridents, or in any sort of alliance with either Zijuan or Jaweau, the current Upali might just have some information, and since Sunyata was on the way to Varanasi, where, according to Sunya, something was definitely going on, there was no reason not to make a quick stop there, especially since it would only take a brief detour to visit a certain village of belief that he definitely needed to investigate.

After that, it would be interesting to see if he found Erinna, although that was certainly not the true name of the poetess, in Sunyata.

Corvyn also found it most interesting that Zijuan and Jaweau used the exact same phrase: "A true belief is truth. It cannot be otherwise." If the two weren't communicating, they certainly had some similar thoughts . . . or had read similar old works. Yet by itself, the fact that each had used the same words didn't necessarily mean anything. *Except that both are thinking in a way that has had devastating consequences in the past.*

Zijuan's attempt to annihilate Corvyn was likely as much a way of refusing to talk to him further as an actual attempt to remove Corvyn, although there was no doubt that Zijuan would have been pleased if the attempt had succeeded.

Also, Zijuan had hidden the trident. Then there was the nagging question of who had set Rudianos/Ares after Corvyn . . . and why? All of the hegemons would have known that the Ares avatar was unlikely to have been successful, but that failure most assuredly led to Corvyn's remaining on the *Blue Dolphin.* Also, most gods or demigods of battle tended to overestimate their own capabilities, as well as underestimate the devastation they created, or at least seem unconcerned with the subsequent havoc.

In short, so far most of what he discovered pointed toward devastation, but without much proof of who might have been behind it, and whether it was just one House or village of belief, or even worse and more likely, several.

Music's beauty can so deceive the mind.
The raven's croak, to that, is most unkind.

36

Just past midafternoon two days after departing Tian, Corvyn neared the Mekong River, across which waited Sunyata, but he had another visit to make first. He kept searching for the road that turned off the main way somewhere near the ferry slip ahead. The land was comparatively flat, but that was difficult to see, given the extensive orchards flanking the main road.

Corvyn had just sighted Sunyata across the river, with its largely yellow buildings and the massive stone Buddha, when he spied, perhaps a quarter mille short of the ferry slip, a narrower road that joined the main road from the left. He continued eastward on the main road until he reached the road heading north.

With a wry smile, he turned onto it, studying both the road and the vegetation and terrain on each side. As he rode north, before long, the orchards vanished, replaced by clearly untended trees. The white stone pavement of the road was likely no more than a year old, although there was virtually no way to tell the age of the near-eternal roads of Heaven just by looking. The smooth contours of the land leading down to the shoulders of the road, however, showed little sign of change, suggesting that an older road had been replaced with a wider roadbed, something that happened only occasionally among the lands sharing the great plateau of Heaven. Low bushes and grass grew near the road, but on the west side, beginning some ten meters from the shoulder, were older trees and undergrowth, as Corvyn would have expected at such a distance from

Tian. On the east side of the river, between the road and river, a grassy slope led down to the reeds rising out of the shallow water near shore.

There were no holdings near, unsurprisingly, since the teachings of the Twin Masters focused more on moral and structural improvement than on either rural life or the balance with nature at least rhetorically and theologically emphasized by the Taoists.

Corvyn had only ridden somewhat less than a half hour on the newer north road before he sensed the flow of shadows and power ahead, even though he had not caught sight of the unnamed village of belief, a village that should not have existed so far south in the lands of Tian or so close to the middle of the great plateau, and certainly not so close to Sunyata. Nor should it have displayed anywhere near that many different currents of shadow power. For that reason, he slowed the electrobike, looking for a side lane or path through the wooded lands to his left.

Now that he looked for just such a path or lane, he didn't see one. Because he did not want to ride any closer to the town, he rode a few hundred meters farther and eased the electrobike off the road as soon as he saw a slight gap in the woods. At that slight break in the trees and undergrowth, he dismounted and wheeled the bike farther into the trees, predominantly maples, a species inconsistent with the lands of the Twin Masters. But then, much of what occurred in Heaven, either ecologically or theologically, was anything but consistent, which was in turn, rather consistent with human nature, much as the Laozi and his believers would have liked it to be otherwise.

After concealing the electrobike with the hint of shadows not likely to be perceived by any power or principality except within a few meters, Corvyn donned the semblance of a raven and took to the air, his wings carrying him above the green canopy of the woodlands. The canopy soon gave way to dwellings set along lanes far too regular to have grown in the normal fashion of villages of belief, more like the ordered streets and ways of larger towns, or a town quickly built around a belief backed by a certain organizational ability or structure. Towns that grew rapidly without such structural power were little more than chaotic sprawls of dwellings.

The dwellings themselves were constructed of reddish-tan stone similar in color to sandstone, but likely formulated rather than quarried, seeing as there were no signs of quarries nearby, and sandstone was comparatively rare farther to the north. To quickly construct a town to support a belief, or a singer capable of mobilizing a belief, required resources that a singer alone, no matter how charismatic, did not possess. That meant that Zijuan backed, or did not oppose, Bran Denu and those who supported him for reasons of his own, reasons that Corvyn doubted were necessarily in accord with the motives of the others who had to be involved. Those others were almost certainly from Varanasi, although not necessarily Shiva, along with Jaweau, not that Corvyn had a shred of hard evidence as of yet, particularly since the White One had left few traces, and those only discernible by one such as Corvyn.

As Corvyn flew toward the large building in the center of the town, a building that appeared to be neither temple nor church, but a performance hall, he sensed another presence in the sky over the unnamed town—a massive war eagle that could only be Garuda.

That war eagle was in a stoop toward the raven that was Corvyn. Corvyn banked left, then folded his wings and dropped, before vanishing into the shadows, just for an instant, enough for him to reappear behind the eagle's neck with his claws dug firmly in.

"If you expand to deal with me," Corvyn said, "then you'll have the Lances of Heaven targeting us, and you won't be fast enough to escape. I suggest you just land next to that performance hall that someone built for the singer, and we can resume larger forms."

As Garuda angled toward the ground, Corvyn had no doubts that the fight was not over, wagering that Garuda would either vanish just before reaching the ground or that another presence would be waiting, if not more. So at perhaps three meters above ground, Corvyn again entered the shadows, where he sensed the shades concealed around the wide stone walk leading into the hall.

There were two others besides Garuda, who had acted as Corvyn had predicted. One was so red that he had to be Ares in the form of Rudianos, and the other seemed almost composed of flames.

Before manifesting himself in a form visible to the others, Corvyn twisted the shadows into a portal and thrust the unsuspecting Ares/Rudianos through into the depths below Limbo. Given the Red One's endurance, Corvyn had no doubt he would survive, but it would be some considerable time before he worked his way up to Limbo and around the Torrent to regain Heaven, by which time whatever would transpire would have occurred.

Then Corvyn manifested himself . . . and waited.

After some moments, Garuda appeared as a winged warrior twice the size of Corvyn and asked, "What did you do with Rudianos?"

"I sent him on a journey. He won't be back for a while."

"To Hades, no doubt. He can't hold Rudianos."

"No, but his return won't be that soon."

"You're not a raven," declared Garuda. "You're more like a serpent, half into your shadow hole. You know what I do with snakes."

"Let's put that aside for a moment. Do you have any intention of telling me what you and your demigod henchmen are doing at a false village of belief in Tian?"

"It's as true a village of belief as any other," replied Garuda.

"That's fair." Given what Corvyn thought about most villages of belief, he had to concede that to Garuda. "If that's so, why are three battle gods here? Well . . . two now."

"You might say we're here to protect Bran Denu's freedom of religious expression. Why are you here?"

"If you're going to phrase it that way, I'm here to protect everyone else's religious freedom."

"That's rather amusing, given that your habitat is the shadows."

"Apparently, it's Kovas's habitat as well. At least at the moment. You might tell him to leave the shadows. I could send him to follow Rudianos if he doesn't." Corvyn didn't mention that he could do that no matter where the god of victory and fire might be.

Kovas appeared. "What brings you here, Kutkh?"

"I've been called worse. I'm here to see what idiocy you three were up to. Is Bran in the hall? Practicing? Or is he out somewhere north, using his songs to entice more holy warriors to the banner of faith?" That was the only way Corvyn could phrase it, because he had no idea which banner of faith had co-opted the singer. He only knew why . . . and that it was a very bad idea, as were most based totally on faith.

Kovas turned to Garuda. "Kutkh cannot be trusted, except to further his own ends."

"Tell me something I don't know, small god," said Garuda, almost wearily.

"Are you any different, Kovas?" asked Corvyn. "Isn't your goal always the bright flame of victory, even if the flames are those of an entire world burning?"

"All worlds burn, sooner or later. Triumphing in the struggle is the only victory in life or death."

"Personally," said Corvyn mildly, "I prefer enjoying good wines, good music, spiced with the words of a good poet. All you're left with after your victory fire is ashes."

"We're all still here," Garuda pointed out.

No thanks to all you deities of war. "For now," admitted Corvyn. "But there have been too many plundered and burned worlds, and the universe isn't as young as it once was, and good planets are harder to come by . . . at least given the technology the universe permits. Even gods and this Heaven face quantum limits. Even . . ." Corvyn had been about to say that even the Valkyries didn't want another Ragnarok or Götterdämmerung.

"Given the limits imposed by the Pearls of Heaven, you mean?" snapped Kovas. "Faith has no limits."

"Which ones of you killed the two Valkyries?" demanded Corvyn, his eyes on Kovas.

"The Valkyries?" Kovas tried to look surprised. "What does that have to do with faith?"

"I can see that your mind's made up." Without physically moving, Corvyn wrapped the shadow portals around the ash-loving god of war and victory and transported him a bit lower than he had Rudianos in the nether realms.

"Why do you bother?" asked Garuda. "They'll be back."

"That's true." *But not in time to get in the way.* "I guess it's because I'm kindhearted to tools, even tools who are gods. Now . . . was it you or Kartikeya who killed the Valkyries?"

Garuda did not immediately reply.

"Do you want to follow them?" pressed Corvyn.

"You can't do that to me."

"They didn't even know about the tridents."

"Tridents? You mean trishulas?"

Corvyn sensed Garuda's confusion and knew there was little point in pursuing the deaths of Brynhyld and Kara with the eagle god. He paused, then said, "Shall we go inside and hear the latest battle hymns that Bran has composed?"

"That charade won't change anything."

"You mean in the greater scheme of things? It might. Then it might not. In any case, I'd like to hear what Bran has wrought."

"Why do you bother? It's not as though his songs will change Heaven."

"Then why is history filled with martial music?"

When Garuda did not answer, Corvyn walked past him and into the performing hall, a space that could hold more than a thousand, which was more than suggestive, although it was empty at the moment, except for the singer.

Bran Denu stood upon the stage, fingering the lutelin, almost absently. He looked up as the two figures entered the hall. "Who's your friend, Garuda?"

"You might call him the shadow of the past. For some obscure reason, he wants to hear what you've wrought."

"He should come to a performance then."

"Just one of your latest hymns," suggested Corvyn politely. *Or pseudo-hymns designed to get people to experience religious rapture. The sort of thing that Jaweau wants to draw people in.*

"You can come back later." Denu strummed the lutelin, projecting both voice and a certain power.

"Where have all the powers gone, long time passing?
Gone to graveyards, every one . . ."

Corvyn brushed away the shadow-tinged words as he walked toward the stage. "I'd appreciate hearing one of your real hymns."

Denu stopped singing. "Who are you?"

"You don't want to know. Just sing one of your new hymns."

Denu looked to Garuda, who had followed Corvyn.

Garuda nodded.

Denu frowned, but then cleared his throat and began to sing.

> *"When Heaven's Light shines bright in purpled skies and holy fire,*
> *Amid the shades of greed, and sloth, and sinful base desire,*
> *We know our ancient foe will seek to work us woe;*
> *His shade and skill so great, and, armed with reasoned hate,*
> *He'd praise in song the Liar . . ."*

Corvyn sensed the shadow links to the singer and immediately recognized the pattern, as well as the power behind that pattern.

> *"Should we in our own strength abide, our striving would be losing*
> *Were not the White One on our side, the God of Heaven's choosing . . ."*

Corvyn concentrated, manipulating the shadows to break certain links, and leaving Denu with only the voice and talent he had originally possessed.

The singer stopped, clearly stunned.

"Thank you," Corvyn called out, then looked to Garuda. "I've heard enough." *More than enough.* He eased toward the door, not caring if Garuda followed.

Garuda did.

When the two were standing outside the hall, Garuda looked to Corvyn. "Now that you've ruined Denu and more than inconvenienced Rudianos and Kovas, do you think I'd just let you fly off?"

Corvyn smiled pleasantly. "For your sake, I do hope so." *And for mine, because it will make matters easier.* His eyes fixed on Garuda.

A halberd appeared in Garuda's hands.

"I wouldn't," said Corvyn. "Then, again, maybe it would be better that way. You wouldn't have to explain to Shiva."

"You never carry weapons, Raven."

"That's because I'm much like you."

A puzzled expression appeared on Garuda's face, but only for an instant, before he stepped back, then vanished. Almost instantaneously, a war eagle appeared overhead, winging its way eastward.

Corvyn resumed the form of a raven, and flew back south to reclaim his electrobike, in order to resume his journey . . . and to deal with Kartikeya.

In what distant Heaven's skies
formed Raven's hate of holy lies?

37

From the pale gray sky swooped a deep brown dartship, aimed like an arrow for the angelship whose whiteness radiated from its lifting body and wings, even as the announcement reverberated across the center of Albion, the subsonics beneath the projected voice designed to raise fear in all who listened.

THIS IS THE LAST CHANCE FOR THOSE WHO REJECT THE RULE OF LAW. THROW DOWN YOUR WEAPONS. ALL THOSE WHO SURRENDER WILL BE RELOCATED WITHOUT HARM OR REEDUCATION. THOSE WHO REFUSE WILL BE PURIFIED IN THE HOLY FLAME OF GOD.

Corvyn gathered the shadows about himself, studying the Plaza of the Redeemer, where figures in dark gray had taken cover where they could. His heavy breathing rasped in his own ears as he tried to ignore the smoky oily air that seared his mouth and lungs and glanced toward the middle of the Plaza, where rose the Great Obelisk, a white four-sided shimmering lance that pierced the very sky.

A brilliant blue laser slashed past him, striking the white marble of the Bank of the Redeemer, where white mist boiled off the stone, then congealed into stone droplets that pelted down on the pavement of the Plaza. At the whirr of electrofans, he looked back over his shoulder to see a white-and-gold skimmer of the Seraphim enter the square from the side boulevard, but it barely made it into the Plaza before the men and women in dark gray targeted it, and three violet-white energy bolts converged on the cockpit, shredding it into shards of carbon composite, and disintegrating anything organic within.

Corvyn flattened himself against the smooth white permastone of the Plaza moments before the release of energy from the skimmer flung the remaining nanocarbon shards in all directions, some of which fragments sliced through figures in the dark gray uniforms of the Resistance.

Yet he heard and sensed another skimmer, and one after that, both heading for the Plaza, both crewed by holy jihadists.

The angelship, seemingly secure behind its screens, either did not sense or chose to ignore the dartship until it was too late. Carried by the magwebs of the dartship, angelship and dartship smashed into the Great Obelisk, where their combined energies, mass, and velocity cut through the middle of the obelisk, leaving a truncated stump of a mere hundred meters, still looming over the partly energy-melted and blackened stones wrenched from the edifice instantly and strewn across the Plaza, slamming into buildings and crushing figures in both gray and white.

Two more angelships appeared, and another announcement boomed forth.

THE MERCY OF THE REDEEMER IS NOT ENDLESS FOR THE UNREPENTANT. PREPARE TO MEET IBLIS.

Immediately, lasers began to scour the Plaza and the buildings that surrounded it, vaporizing anything and anyone unprotected.

Once more, if unseen by the angelships, a dartship appeared high overhead and dived toward the Plaza of the Redeemer.

Corvyn understood, almost too late, what that dark dartship carried, and he gathered his shadows around him just before the radiance of a small nova turned the Plaza of the Redeemer—and everything else in a fifty-mille radius—into solar plasma.

When he emerged elsewhere, tears streamed from his eyes, and not from the glare from the now-distant cataclysm that confirmed the first step in the latest Fall.

The latest for now.

The ways that Raven flies are not the roads well-trod
by men whose eyes are chained with lies from God.

38

By the time Corvyn made his way back to the ferry slip on the Mekong River, and waited another half hour for the ferry to arrive, it was definitely late afternoon when he rode the electrobike onto the black ferryboat. He could not help but recall that black was the color signifying evils to be overcome, at least for the Buddhists, which he supposed made black appropriate for crossing the turbulent upper reaches of the Mekong, as well as for what awaited him in the days ahead, one way or another, especially after his encounters at the unnamed village of belief.

On the opposite side of the river lay Sunyata, the yellow city of the Middle Way. Cut into the tall hill farther to the east of the city proper was a massive red stone Buddha, protecting and overlooking the Mayi Devi Temple, an edifice of brilliant white stone, which in turn overlooked Sunyata. The city proper, perhaps half as large as Tian, stretched a mere ten milles from north to south along the Mekong. To the north, Corvyn could just make out the lower peaks of the mountainous hills that eventually gave way to the Celestial Mountains and the howling winds that would make them impassable if the Lances of Heaven did not.

Corvyn's eyes fell upon the handful of travelers scattered across the front lower deck of the ferry, but his thoughts were elsewhere. He doubted that he would discover much from Upali, the keeper of the Vinaya, given that the generations of those who held that name and the powers of a hegemon had been more of the temperament to allow information to come to them, rather than to seek it out, but there was always that possibility. He would visit the Mayi Devi Temple for that reason, among others, including the probability that Mara might be lurking nearby, or perhaps Vajrapani or Mahakala.

As the ferry pulled into the yellow stone slip on the east side of the river, Corvyn debated himself over whether he should cut his journey short—especially since the brief words Sunya had offered him back in the lands of the Saints bothered him even more now than when she had spoken them, and he was afraid he knew why—that some power in Varanasi was part of what the black tridents represented, although he still had doubts that it was Shiva. The trident, more properly the trishula, was Shiva's symbol, and its use was far too obvious, and Shiva was anything but obvious.

Even before the ferry docked on the east side of the river, Corvyn had decided to make his visit in Sunyata as brief as possible so that he could get to Varanasi sooner.

As soon as the ramp extended and was in place, Corvyn eased the electrobike forward and onto the yellow stone lane leading to the upper city. Unlike the buildings in Keifeng and especially Tian, the buildings here were lower, and none seemed taller than four or five stories. While yellow predominated, there were more than a few houses and structures in shades of green and blue.

Before long, he located the Zen Aaraam, a hotel whose walls were a light blue stone and which he had picked because it was not all that far—less than a half mille—from the grounds of the Mayi Devi Temple. He entered the hotel, confirmed the arrangements, and was escorted to the small two-room suite on the side away from the temple. Accommodations in Sunyata were not so sumptuous as those in Tian, Keifeng, Los Santos, or even those he recalled from past visits to Varanasi, but his two rooms looked more than comfortable, despite the largely bare blue stone walls, the simple polished goldenwood blinds that served as curtains, and the plain dark blue quilt that covered the bed for two. In time, he would like a good night's sleep, a sleep where his dreams weren't too vivid, but sleep would have to wait.

After setting his cases down and removing some items, he washed up and left his room, stopping only for a brief bite of noodles and mushrooms at the small café in the Zen Aaraam before taking to the shadows and making his way through them to the grounds of the temple where Upali would be, somewhere, since he was the keeper of the Vinaya, or at least the accepted surviving version of it.

Corvyn had not reached the outer wall of the temple before he encountered within the shadows another presence of power, with a certain residual sensuality. Not far distant was a second power, hard-edged, and most likely endowed with certain powers of possible destruction. He recognized both.

"We should talk, Raven," offered the first.

Corvyn did not ask why Mara hovered around the temple. Mara's mission and function had never changed—to tempt those seeking enlightenment into less aetherial satisfactions. "We? You and who else?"

"Mahakala will join us, whether I like it or not."

"Then lead the way to a suitable place."

"The west garden is empty at present."

"And Upali?"

"You can always seek him out after we talk, even if you choose not to talk. Whether he will choose to listen is another question. I am not the one to guess as to what one such as he will do."

"The west garden, then." Corvyn let Mara lead the way through the shadows remaining between them and their destination.

Mahakala followed.

The three emerged from the shadows nearly at the same time in the west garden, a garden totally shaded in the last moments before complete sunset. A blue stone circle lay in the middle of an oval pool. Framed by the center of that circle and on the far side of the pool was a perfectly shaped and ancient yew tree in the center of a low hill behind which rose a tiered garden.

For several moments, Corvyn studied the stone circle and what it framed, then turned to Mara, who appeared as a well-proportioned man in a bright blue high-collared jacket and trousers. His skin had a slight blue-green tinge, and his eyes seemed to be all colors and none.

Mahakala was black-skinned with flowing yellow hair and beard, bright red lips and eyes, of which there were three, and wore a shifting black cloak that merged with the miasma of black smoke that surrounded him.

"What did you have in mind in talking to me?" Corvyn asked Mara.

"I could say that those who cling to vain perceptions wander Heaven offending people," offered Mara. "Or that all created things perish, even this world that all call Heaven."

"Misquoting Siddhartha again?" said Corvyn, hoping to provoke a response that would prove informative.

"This Heaven is not Heaven, but earth, and that was what Siddhartha meant. But you should know that, Raven."

"I thought you were the tempter."

"You cannot be tempted by the flesh, nor by wealth, nor by eternal life. With what else can I tempt you besides facts and logic?"

"You're more than a crow, raven of the shadows," interjected Mahakala, "but all your hopping about won't bring enlightenment."

Corvyn laughed softly. "Siddhartha said that we become what we think, and Mara has thought long about both temptation and enlightenment."

"You have rejected enlightenment far longer than . . ."

"Than you can believe?" Corvyn smiled. "I haven't rejected enlightenment. Let's just say that I have a different view of enlightenment."

"Your view of enlightenment is based on the idea that the more knowledge about everything that you gather, the closer to enlightenment you will be, but all you gather are the perceptions of reality. The entire universe is nothing but space and energy, and what you gather of it are merely perceptions of perceptions."

"That's a largely accurate description of the universe on a quantum level, if oversimplified," agreed Corvyn. "Accurate, but meaningless. Even Siddhartha, in rejecting the perceptions of his senses, accepted the perceptions of his mind." He turned slightly as flames seemed ready to stream from the Protector. "And you, Mahakala?"

"You cling to those perceptions, Raven, and you only lose what you cling to."

"The root of suffering being attachment?" That was true enough, Corvyn well knew, yet he must persist in his attachment.

But before he could even think of expressing such a thought, most abruptly, both Mara and Mahakala vanished into the shadows.

Interesting, but not exactly productive. Corvyn returned to the shadows, easing his way through the temple until he came to a small room in which were set a table and two chairs. There Upali waited.

Corvyn appeared, noting the teapot and cups set on the table.

Upali was dark-skinned and black-eyed, slight of build, and wore a yellow robe. "I thought you might join me, Raven." He gestured toward the table.

"Thank you." Corvyn seated himself. "Might I ask why you expected me?"

"Why should I not expect you? There is a black trident burned into the main hall of the temple. Whether challenge or declaration, its presence reveals that the hegemons are declining in unity. Those are the first elements of the divination. You are the second. Also, Mahakala knows the ways of ravens, and he said you would be coming. All things often come to those who wait. Not always, but often." Upali filled the two handleless cups with tea and nodded for Corvyn to take one.

Corvyn did so, then waited for Upali to lift his cup. After that, he said, "Thank you. What else can you tell me?"

"You know all that I could say. You've mourned over more corpses created by erroneous perceptions than anyone."

"And you have no advice or information?"

Upali sipped from his cup. "Advice? That suggests you will act, whatever I say. Blameless actions are among the greatest blessings. When dealing with the other hegemons, one cannot be blameless. As for information . . . the trident did not come from here, nor from the lands of the Maid, nor, I can surmise, from the Dark One of the Skeptics."

"Has a poetess of the Maid visited Sunyata?"

"Not that I'm aware of. Why would she? We neither oppose nor support her view of what is. She neither supports nor opposes what we perceive."

That meant that the poetess had not been in Sunyata, for all happenings in the Buddhist lands were known to Upali. And that suggested, even more strongly, that Corvyn needed to set out for Varanasi in the morning. "What can you tell me that's new about Shiva?"

"Nothing. Shiva is Shiva. He does not change, nor does the chaos around him, for it is inherent in all compounded things, not just in his trishula."

Corvyn smiled wryly. "He doesn't accept that existence is impermanence?"

Upali smiled enigmatically and began to fade.

Corvyn stood, waiting until he was alone in the chamber. Then he used the shadows to make his way to the main hall of the temple, where he beheld yet another black trident burned into the stone. He studied it carefully, noting that it was no different from any of the others. Then he dropped into the shadows and returned to the Zen Aaraam.

While Corvyn would have liked to set out for Varanasi immediately, he did need sleep, and, as Upali could have reminded him, he should receive all opinions and evidence equally and wisely, without haste.

But you may not have that luxury much longer.

The raven takes, the raven gives,
and this god dies, and that god lives.

39

After three very, very long days on the electrobike, when Corvyn neared the Ganges River, it was past midafternoon. He rode through gently undulating lands on which a variety of crops were being grown, as well as some rather large orchards, at least one of which, near to the road, held nearly ripe plums. He did not see any apple trees. The houses on the steads were all modest and solar-powered, with occasional outbuildings. The numbers of habitations had not dwindled on his progress toward Varanasi as they had in the lands of Tian.

Less than a mille ahead were low hills that blocked his view to the east, but he knew he was less than fifteen milles from the river. When he reached the point ahead where the gray stone road leveled off before beginning its descent to the river, he should be able to see part of the City of Shiva.

He still wondered whether the poetess who called herself Erinna had come to Varanasi, and exactly what ties she had to the Maid, or if she was a counter to Bran Denu . . . or more. As always, he had more questions than answers.

As far as he was from Sunyata, there was little traffic on the road, although Corvyn was somewhat surprised that there wasn't some coming from Varanasi, but then there had never been much love lost between the two lands, for reasons long lost in history—except to Corvyn and a very few others. The air was slightly drier once he started up the grade toward the low pass in the hills, and with that dryness he became aware of a certain locus of power ahead. Although he could not discern the source, it likely originated in Varanasi . . . but other sources were certainly possible. While that power ahead of him might have been coincidental, Corvyn doubted that, and the fact that its location was in the line of sight from Varanasi was also suggestive, even if the land he now crossed and all that to the west of the river belonged to Sunyata.

Corvyn slowed the electrobike as he reached the flat stretch of road at the top of the hill.

A figure stood in the middle of the road some hundred yards ahead—or rather sat astride an enormous blue peacock. Interestingly, Kartikeya had manifested himself as merely a slightly outsized and absurdly handsome, bare-chested, dark-haired, and dark-eyed human with a single head, rather than the traditional six.

"Greetings, God of Battles," offered Corvyn as he eased the electrobike to a stop some five yards away from the peacock and made certain preparations for what he knew would happen. "To what do I owe your presence?"

"To my sense of propriety, evil raven."

"Even in your faith, I'm only a harbinger. I've never gloried in the slaughter of thousands and millions. I've only warned them of what might come."

"What you think might come, and not what should come."

"As with many events, that is a matter of perspective."

"You are not welcome in Varanasi. I will refrain from destroying you if you return to your eyrie immediately."

"You're threatening me, and doing so on a land that is not even of your faith. That's certainly an example of impropriety, for all your claims to the contrary. It's also against the tenets of Heaven. And killing the Valkyries so far from Sunyata was more than improper." Corvyn managed to reply only in a tone of annoyance, rather than with the anger he felt.

"I say again. You are not welcome in Varanasi." A long and very pointed spear appeared in Kartikeya's hand, infused with lambent blue.

"Ravens go where they must," replied Corvyn. "And not even the god of battles can change that. But before I deal with you, tell me this. Why did you kill the Valkyries?"

"Because once, at least, they were your handmaidens. They refused to return to the beliefs they once held."

"Gods shouldn't lie, Kartikeya, especially the spoiled eldest children of hegemons. You never even asked them."

Kartikeya moved, but long before the spear could reach Corvyn, he drew the shadows around himself and the electrobike, although including the bike took more energy, but he didn't want to go to the trouble of obtaining another or the inconvenience of doing without it—not again.

"I know you abide in the shadows. You cannot remain there forever." The voice of the power was melodic, and yet like thunder, echoing through the shifting quantum forces that comprised the shadows.

"Powerful as you are, Kartikeya, what do you know of the time before time, or the Heaven before Heaven?"

"Would you dare to take on all the Asuras?"

"At present, I have no quarrel with any of the Asuras. Would you create the reason for a quarrel?" Corvyn preferred that Kartikeya see reason, but he had his doubts. It was not for nothing that Kartikeya was called the god of battles, and most likely that would require Corvyn to do what was necessary.

Kartikeya's voice intensified, like massive bells tolling in Corvyn's ears, even through the shadows. "By your presence and your inquiries into matters that should not concern you, you are creating the quarrel. You're a mere annoyance to be removed."

"And what of the Valkyries?"

"They were also an annoyance, by their existence."

Corvyn decided no longer to restrain the white-hot rage he felt, and without speaking further, he gathered certain energies and folded certain quantum shadows around the god of battles, shadows that transported Kartikeya to the depths far, far below Limbo, and below Hades, into the small still molten core of Heaven, where, if Kartikeya could even survive, he would doubtless be engaged for some time in just that, possibly until Heaven itself was either a charred cinder or a frozen airless waste. *And, if not, there's little lost.* For Kartikeya did not deserve the mere inconvenience of escaping from beneath the Great Cataract while avoiding the waters of forgetfulness that roar from Lake Lethe.

When that was done, Corvyn emerged from the shadows, breathing heavily, and soaked in sweat. For several long moments, he stood there before taking a long drink from the water bottle he removed from the electrobike's holder. After a time, he ate the last biscuit and finished the water.

Aren't you getting too old for this? His short burst of laughter was one of wry, self-deprecating humor.

Then he got back on the electrobike and resumed his journey, thinking.

First, Rudianos, except Rudianos hadn't been the first to attack him. Michael had, and Brother Paul hadn't ordered it. *Then* Rudianos had attacked him. The Avenging Angel in Nauvoo didn't count, most likely, because it could have attacked any intruder. *Still* . . .

In Yerusalem, he was attacked by Samael, and in Jannah by both Azrael and Israfyl, and threatened indirectly on the Sands of Time through the death of the nearly but not quite unkillable Valkyries. In Keifeng, though, neither Shui Rong nor Caishen had attacked, but in Tian, Zijuang himself had attempted an attack. And then, at the unnamed village, both Rudianos and Kovas had attacked him, and Garuda had thought about it before withdrawing.

So why hadn't Garuda been with Kartikeya? Because of that fight with Vasuki when Kartikeya saved the serpent?

Corvyn shook his head. Trust gods to carry grudges as close to eternity as possible. He didn't speculate on the difference between duty and grudges. He hadn't for several Falls.

The other question was why war gods from disparate villages of belief had joined with Garuda in support of Bran Denu, particularly Ares in the guise of Rudianos. Had that been Garuda's doing, because he didn't want to deal with Kartikeya? Or because Garuda didn't want to be further eclipsed by Kartikeya? Or because he didn't want Shiva to know? Some form of plausible denial—a term that had almost become a deity in its own right over the eons? Corvyn doubted he would ever know . . . not exactly. Nor did he much care.

Most of those who had attacked could have been termed gods or angels of war, an irony not lost on Corvyn, but in Sunyata, Mahakala had not attacked. *Except he is a defender, not a holy warrior trying to convert through force* . . .

And then there had been the nearly successful attack on the *Blue*

Dolphin, as well as Rudianos's warning, which, coupled with what had *not* happened in Los Santos, suggested that three Houses were involved to some degree, and that the power behind the tridents lay in one of them, which was why Corvyn was on his way to Varanasi. He looked forward to what awaited him there even less than before. He already knew the reason behind the tridents, or one of them, which was to portray doubt, represented by shadows and by an ancient symbol, as evil, as part of an effort to create an artificial distinction between darkness and the brightness of the True Faith, and thus strengthen the attempt to meld all faiths into a shining and united beacon, where no variance from the revealed "truth" was permitted.

As for which hegemon or power was the prime mover behind this effort, the one most interested in the Triumph of His True Faith, Corvyn had a strong feeling about who that was, but he would have to confirm that before he acted, because that was required of him and because acting against the wrong hegemon would be as bad as failing to act. *And that's assuming you're not too late to prevent another Fall.*

He had failed more than once before, and those memories were bitter, and the source of all too many of his nightmares.

He took a deep breath, glad for the air through which he moved and which cooled him and removed the sweat generated by his disposal of Kartikeya, something he would have to explain to Shiva—or avoid explaining, whichever might be the case, depending on what he discovered in Varanasi.

Three milles later, the road flattened into a level grassy plain, stretching toward the River Ganges. For the first time since leaving Sunyata, Corvyn could see no dwellings or structures of any kind, and only loose groupings of cows, not exactly herds, with an occasional herder. For a moment, he frowned, then smiled as he recalled the reason for the grasslands—simply a way for the followers of Siddhartha to keep the Vedic peoples of Varanasi from crossing the river to settle there. While the rationale had never seemed logical to Corvyn, that was because he had never really understood the importance of any sacred animal, including cows, although he certainly understood the behavior of those who believed in such . . . because that behavior so often led to what he was trying to prevent.

When he reached the ferry slip, it was empty.

"How long before the next ferry?" he asked the crewwoman standing by the barrier.

"Half an hour or so, sir."

"Thank you." Corvyn turned to survey the few others waiting—an older couple wearing well-washed khaki shirts and trousers, a bearded man barely more than a youth who moved away from the ramp barrier when he saw Corvyn, and two men in khaki uniforms with visor caps who looked to be military rankers of some sort.

The shorter of the two troopers kept looking at Corvyn.

Corvyn smiled and asked, "Do you have a question?"

"No, sir."

"You were wondering how far I've traveled on the electrobike? I've come from Sunyata."

"That's a long trip on a bike, sir."

"Moderately so. Where are you two posted?"

"Angkor, sir."

"On leave, then?"

"We're due back the day after tomorrow. It's a short van ride from Varanasi."

Corvyn smiled again. "Enjoy your evening."

"You serve, sir?"

"A while back. But not here."

"You put in a full life, then?"

Corvyn nodded. That was an understatement, but one he wasn't about to expand upon.

"Officer, too, right?"

"At the end," admitted Corvyn, which was true in more ways than one.

"Thought so. Thank you, sir."

"Just think it through," Corvyn said, "whatever it is. It's harder in the short run, but worth it."

The taller ranker nodded, and the two eased away.

Corvyn turned his attention to Varanasi, more than a half mille away across the brownish waters of the Ganges. Unlike Tian or Keifeng, Varanasi was a giant semicircle extending some thirty milles along the river and fifteen milles east. The great Lanka Palace dominated the landscape, set as it was on a circular plateau a hundred yards above the city midway between the river and the semicircular wall marking the boundaries of the city proper, seven milles from the Ganges and seven milles from the wall. The plateau was a circle a mille across, all of which comprised the walled and golden Lanka Palace, with its endlessly elaborate sculptures and ornately decorated towers.

Even after his conversation and the survey of his surroundings, Corvyn had to wait almost half an hour for the ferry to return to the western shore of the river. When it finally eased into the slip, only a handful of people walked off, followed by two electrobikes, and one half-filled passenger van.

Then the crewwoman raised the barrier, and Corvyn waited for those on foot to step onto the ferry—except for the ferry at Cammat Landing, the smallest he had utilized on his entire journey—before he rode on and to the far end of the boat, from where he watched and waited.

Another quarter hour passed before the ferry left the slip and crawled across the brownish waters toward the City of Shiva. When it finally reached the eastern shore, it entered a modest slip between two large piers, where cargo ships that dwarfed the ferry moored. Farther north and farther south were other piers, occupied by similar craft, with much activity on the piers.

Corvyn did not recall nearly so much river traffic as the cargo carriers suggested was taking place, and that indicated that even more believers had flocked to the city in recent years. He let the others precede him, then guided the electrobike off the ferry and onto the pier road, and from there onto Saraca Boulevard, one of those radial main streets that converged on the Ring of Shiva, the wide avenue that circled the base of the great and golden Lanka Palace.

Since Kartikeya had known that Corvyn was coming to Varanasi Shiva doubtless knew as well, and, Corvyn saw little point in making great efforts to hide his presence. He ended up selecting the Brijrama Hotel because it was the closest to the Lanka Palace. It was also known to be luxurious, and after staying in places that were anything but over the past days, he was in the mood for a certain amount of luxury.

While the doormen at the hotel were solicitous and one carried his cases, Corvyn sensed a certain disdain over a traveler arriving on an electrobike and not in a chauffeured van or even a palanquin. Likewise, the clerk smiled politely, but his smile widened when he took Corvyn's card and scanned it. "Welcome to the Brijrama Hotel and Marigold Garden, Maitre Corbin. Would you prefer a grand suite?"

"A small suite will suffice, thank you."

"We can do that, honored sir. The Moonflower Suite is on the fourth level."

Corvyn smiled. The assignment of a suite named for a night-blooming flower suggested that the clerk either suspected or knew Corvyn was of a certain power associated with shadows. Whether that knowledge would be passed to the Lanka Palace remained to be seen.

When he and the doorman reached the fourth level, there was no doubt of the clerk's recognition. The suite was far larger than what Corvyn would call small, suggesting that the clerk had decided against creating any possible offense to Corvyn. And that was not entirely surprising, either, given the vagaries of the pantheon gathered around Shiva, as well as the large number of gods, demigods, powers, and their ways of surprising those with only standard human abilities.

Corvyn arranged for all but one of his few outfits to be cleaned and ready in the morning, then washed up, and descended to the hotel restaurant. He was hungry and tired after his efforts in dealing with Kartikeya. No matter where he went, he would likely be watched, and while no one seemed to be watching him, that was an illusion. In Varanasi, as in Los Santos, everyone was watched. Whether they were immediately recognized by more than the systems was another question.

The restaurant was called Pashtarana, and a woman of indeterminate age, wearing a long dark blue tunic with gray trousers, seated him at a corner table that provided a view of the half-filled dining area.

"Would you like something to drink, sir?"

"Just black tea, jasmine, if you have it."

"I'll have that for you immediately, sir."

Corvyn studied the single-sheet menu—on pseudo-parchment, as was common in better establishments in Varanasi, at least from what he recalled—and then decided, setting the menu aside and studying the others in the restaurant. At one table sat three men in jackets of different shades of blue, whose measured and apparently pleasant conversation suggested a certain maturity. Two women in brighter garments talked animatedly. A single man sipped intermittently from a glass, a lime soda, Corvyn guessed, while his eyes continually glanced toward the entrance to the restaurant.

The only aura of power in the restaurant belonged to Corvyn. That should not have been surprising, but it made him wonder.

His tea arrived, and he ordered the butter chicken with saffron rice and garlic naan, then sipped the tea and mulled over the possibilities for what might occur on the morrow. *And after that.*

He ate and enjoyed the dinner, skipped dessert, and finally made his way back to his suite, which, thankfully, faced the river, and not the Lanka Palace. He stood a yard or so back from the window when he sensed an oncoming shadow, out of which stepped a woman in a cream jacket and trousers—the poetess calling herself Erinna, although she was far more than a mere poetess.

"Greetings," he said. "I found the poem you left in Tian most interesting."

She inclined her head. "I thought you might, given that you also write, even if you write only for yourself."

That she knew about the book of verse in his study stopped him for a moment, and before Corvyn could say anything, she went on. "You don't need to visit Aethena, Raven. There's a trident there as well. You've been visiting all the Houses of the Decalivre, and you were on the *Blue Dolphin*, weren't you, when a Lance of Heaven was turned on it?"

"I was on the boat, but how did you know it was a Lance of Heaven?"

"Is there anything else that could destroy a courier boat that thoroughly? And all at once?"

At her words, Corvyn almost stiffened, realizing that the explosion that destroyed the courier boat had not been quite instantaneous, and with that realization he saw that he had almost been led into a trap, unwittingly, by the power before him. He listened as she continued.

"Nothing less could destroy a courier boat. You should also have known that, and so does every hegemon. That means at least one hegemon has access to the Lances. That makes it dangerous to both of us if I'm here with you more than a few moments. I can only block surveillance from the Pearls of Heavens for a short while before the shielded area shows up. You'll have to do what you can with the two of them. I don't have quite the powers you do."

With those words, the poetess vanished into the shadows.

Corvyn had wanted to ask her opinion about Shiva, but her words about "the two of them" essentially answered that question. *Shiva and Jaweau.*

Corvyn just stood there for several moments. First, there was no doubt who the gray-eyed poetess was, especially if she observed him in his study, or even if she only gained the confidence of Ishtaraath, and the fact that she kept moving confirmed that she believed that either Shiva or Jaweau had partial remote access to the Pearls of Heaven, but hadn't been able to get around the fail-safes. From what happened in Tian, Corvyn also was fairly certain that Zijuan was involved in some fashion, although he did not see what the Disciple of the Twin Masters gained from such involvement.

Unless he's convinced that they'll fail and that will strengthen his position. And that was certainly a strong possibility, given the precedents and examples set by the Twin Masters, and from his last meeting with Zijuan alone, Corvyn would be surprised if that had not been Zijuan's objective all along.

There was also the question of whether the Maid was being completely truthful, but if she were behind any of what had happened, then there still would be a trident burned into the temple there as well. Besides, none of the assorted war and battle gods would unite behind her.

And she wouldn't support any of them in anything, which might be why Ares joined the others.

And that left Jaweau and Shiva, and the real question was why either had set up the situation so that Corvyn would believe that one of them had gained remote access to the Lances of Heaven . . . and, as the Maid had said, to the surveillance systems of the Pearls of Heaven. *So you'd lead them there and hopefully disable some of the defenses and fail-safes in the process?*

Corvyn shook his head. The First had been smarter than that.

Corvyn wasn't about to rush into the golden Lanka Palace after the day he'd had, and it was highly unlikely Shiva would leave the protections of the palace to seek him out. Besides, the way matters were unfolding meant that one of the two hegemons, if not both, wanted to force Corvyn into acting, so as to improve their chances of gaining control of the Pearls of Heaven . . . and Heaven itself.

Which means you will have to act, if not exactly as they would wish.

He did not quite sigh.

The black of wings, the eye of night,
no ill escapes the raven's sight.

40

Corvyn woke, neither early nor late, just as the sun cleared the hills to the east. His sleep had been troubled, most likely because of Kartikeya's actions, and because of his own less than temperate reaction.

But how could you have known Kartikeya would have destroyed the Valkyries because they'd once served your predecessor? They would have done nothing. They didn't even know about the tridents.

Trying not to dwell on Kartikeya, Corvyn forced himself to prepare for the day meticulously, beginning by using the hotel system to check the news, noting that there were no further reports on the destruction of the *Blue Dolphin*, nor any reports on anything out of the ordinary. But then, most people wouldn't immediately notice the disappearance of three gods, especially in Varanasi, where there were so many deities. And even of the few remaining ancients descended from Olympus, few cared much about Ares.

Then he showered and dressed, before descending to the restaurant, where he had a modest breakfast of flattened rice with tomato and chilies along with some naan on the side and jasmine tea. After eating most, but not all, of his breakfast, he strolled from the hotel in the general direction of the Lanka Palace.

Corvyn had no way of knowing what, if anything, Garuda had told Shiva, and Kartikeya would definitely be missed, sooner or later, considering that he was Shiva's favorite son, although Kartikeya might not be considered missing just yet, especially if what Sunya told him about

Kartikeya trying to enlist other war deities to his banner happened to be true. For those reasons, among others, Corvyn decided to visit the Lanka Palace sooner rather than later.

He had walked some three blocks and was passing a row of shops when he saw a sign on one: RAJESH GOEL—SECURE TRANSACTIONS/COMMUNICATIONS.

Corvyn couldn't help but be intrigued, given how many ways he knew to unsecure transactions and communications, and a few moments were not likely to change anything. Besides, it might be amusing. As he entered the shop, no more than five meters wide, a young man collapsed an intricate spatial array and stood. Corvyn immediately sensed something about the array, not quite like the quantum shadows he employed, but related, he suspected.

"How might I help you, sir?"

"Tell me how you can guarantee secure transactions and communications. You're Rajesh Goel, I take it?"

"Yes, sir." Goel cleared his throat. "I'd like to say that it's simple, or that it's guaranteed, but neither is precisely true. With time and expertise, any expert can break into any transaction or communication. What our equipment does is to limit the time so that it's close to impossible to pick it out of a message stream. We compress the message or signal into the shortest time signature possible, encrypt it, and surround it with a random quantum flux, call it static with an embedded faux message, and then dispatch it. Upon receipt verification, the message uncompresses. The static conceals the real message in transit, and since the time in transit is almost infinitesimal . . ." The tech/proprietor shrugged.

"That won't stop someone from hacking into the receiving equipment."

"It will if they use our receivers. The best way of describing the system, sir, is that both our transmitters and receivers provide quantum static around the data field. The moment the faux message is touched or disturbed, the entanglement withdraws the data and compares it to the original. At the same time, the system entangles the intruder through the faux message, and uses chaos to scramble his probes or devices."

Corvyn smiled faintly, recalling the systems he would be required to visit if matters did not go well, for they had protocols that were not dissimilar in operation and intent. "Can you demonstrate it?"

Goel frowned. "You won't see anything."

"Humor me, if you will," said Corvyn gently. "You don't have any other customers at the moment, do you?"

Goel offered an almost boyish smile, then gestured to the devices on a side table. "I can send something from one to the other, or I could send a message to our other office."

"Send something to the other office."

"I'll call up a long report. Not that it will matter."

Corvyn watched as Goel transferred the report and then sent it. For all his sensitivities, Corvyn could barely sense the static, and only the hint of the false message, and he might just have been imagining that. Still, it was definitely ingenious.

"You see, sir? There's no sound, nothing."

"I do. Now . . . can you just create the static pattern for maybe ten seconds? No message. Just the static."

Goel frowned again.

"Please."

Goel adjusted the equipment. "Ready. Here goes."

This time Corvyn sensed the pattern. After a moment, he said, "Could you call it a quantum fractal signal?"

Goel looked surprised. "That's essentially what it is. Except it's not a signal."

"You're right, of course. Thank you. What is your time worth?"

"Sir . . . there's no need."

Corvyn extended his card. "Charge me two hours' worth. I'll know if you undercharge. I appreciated the demonstration."

"Sir . . ."

"I insist."

Once Corvyn was certain the funds had been transferred, he inclined his head. "Thank you."

When he left the shop, Corvyn knew that Rajesh Goel would be checking everything to make sure that Corvyn hadn't somehow done something untoward, but, hopefully, the funds would cover that time, since Goel would find nothing.

He continued walking toward the Lanka Palace, thinking and planning.

While he could not personally generate a fractal quantum signal, not without certain technical devices that only existed within the realms of the Pearls of Heaven, he didn't have to. All he had to do was create enough patterns of quantum movement through the shadows around the Lanka Palace that any entry through the shadows would be blurred or lost, inhibiting Shiva's ability to focus or marshal forces at any one point in advance, although he would definitely know that someone was arriving.

Corvyn continued toward the palace, at a pace neither leisurely nor rushed, but he did not approach any of the four gates, since he saw no point in entering in anything close to the normal fashion. In time, he reached the walls girding the artificial circular plateau dominated by the Lanka Palace, walls of golden stone that rose a good hundred meters above Varanasi, one of the reasons why no structures were taller than fifty meters, so that they did not challenge the palace.

Once there, he began to shake the quantum shadows around and infusing the palace, before and while transforming himself into a raven to traverse the shadows and make his way inside. As he traveled, he attempted to see if he could discern a trident burned into stone anywhere. He did in fact find one in the inner chambers of the formal temple, and it was indeed no different from any of the others.

That task completed, he traveled farther, on to Shiva's study, where he appeared as a large raven. He decided against croaking before resuming his usual form, although the thought had occurred to him, as had a single word, given what he would find necessary.

Shiva looked at Corvyn, but did not immediately speak.

Corvyn simply waited.

"You didn't have to rattle the fabric of the universe to announce your entry, Raven."

Shiva's voice was clear, not quite melodic, and even, although his two normal eyes flashed, but not the closed one in the middle of his forehead, which was just as well.

"Not the universe, just a bit of the space-time around your palace. I only shook it gently. I thought it made a better entrance." As he spoke,

Corvyn studied Shiva quickly, taking in his blue throat, his elaborately braided hair, as well as the third eye, and the crescent moon shining just above his head.

"Why did you need to make an entrance at all?"

"I thought it was fitting, especially since this time Parvati didn't give the palace away."

Shiva's face turned cold.

"I also wanted to know why you burned images of your trishula into the places of faith of every hegemon in Heaven." Since Corvyn doubted that Shiva was the one who had done that, for a number of reasons, he waited to see how Shiva replied.

"I burned no trishulas anywhere. Still . . . if I had, I could say that each of the Houses of the Decalivre might be as a single arm of Durga." Shiva's hands made a dismissive gesture.

"But the trishula is your weapon," Corvyn pointed out. "Didn't you give it to Durga, after cutting off the head of Ganesha, not that he turned out any the worse for wear?"

"The trishula is everywhere, part of the fabric of reality. You might as well seek out all who drink water."

"But you know which hegemon planted the trishulas, don't you? And you came up with the idea, knowing that the obviousness would assure that no one would believe it was your thought."

"*You* would question me, Raven?"

"Why not? Isn't it my role to question?"

"The Great Almighty didn't give you that role."

"No. That's true. I assumed it because the various gods in Heaven and before have this propensity not to question themselves, nor to allow their believers any great latitude in that, either. And deities who are unquestioned invariably grow complacent or arrogant, if not both."

"I suppose you're an exception, then?"

"I'm not a deity. You know that," replied Corvyn.

For several moments, Shiva did not speak. Finally, he said, "You dispatched Kartikeya to the depths of Hades. Was that necessary?"

"It was. But I didn't send him to Hades. I sent him to the depths and the core of Heaven."

Shiva's third eye opened, and a wave of chaos and destruction washed over Corvyn, who used the shadows to channel both to the same place that he had sent Kartikeya. That raised the possibility that Shiva's chaotic rage completed what Corvyn had begun. That didn't trouble Corvyn unduly, not given what Shiva and his son had already done and what they'd tried to accomplish.

In time, the third eye closed. A clearly shaken Shiva looked at an untouched Corvyn.

"In addition, as I was about to say, I also sent some other assorted gods of battle and war to Limbo and Hades. Kartikeya seemed to be collecting them. Did he do this and kill the Valkyries on your account . . . or on his own initiative? And, one other thing. He seemed adamant that I not come to Varanasi, almost as if he didn't want me to see you, Auspicious One. Neither did Garuda, apparently. I don't sense him around, either."

"What Garuda and my son did should not concern you, shadowed one."

"In a way, it doesn't. Not anymore. What I'd like to know, if you deign to tell me, is why you let it happen?"

"It amuses me. I also wanted to see what you would do."

Corvyn had suspected that Shiva's answer would be along those lines. "You've seen what I'll do. Why did you do it? To see if One True Faith could arise again?"

"Oh, given men and women, someone is bound to try. The only question is when it will next be successful."

"I can't say I like your definition of success."

"Why not? All you do is stand in the way of the nature of the universe. And destroy my son and your betters."

"They started the destruction business. They've always started it. The only thing I'm standing in the way of is the basic nature of faith. Isn't that more than what you do?"

Corvyn waited for several moments.

Shiva did not respond.

When it was all too clear that Shiva would say no more, Corvyn then entered the deeper shadows.

The raven and his shade
are of the same stuff made,
two linked so by the light
that both or none take flight.

41

Corvyn dropped into the deepest levels of the shadows and struggled across the distances, back to Helios, but not back to his comfortable eyrie, but to a larger and more imposing black villa set at the north end of the Avenue Pierrot, a fitting name for the avenue, given that both his eyrie and the villa were located upon it.

He emerged in the private study, taking on a larger and more imposing form than was his nature or wont, noting in passing, once more, that there was indeed a trident of the same nature as the others upon the black stone wall behind the black and empty table desk. Then he walked over to the desk and stood beside it, before summoning Attar.

In moments, the black-clad seneschal of the villa appeared. "You've returned, sire?"

"Only briefly." Corvyn gestured to the trident. "I'll be dealing with the source of that. Leave it. I'll take care of it when I return."

Attar inclined his head. "Is there anything else you desire?"

"Not at present. You may return to your duties."

Once the seneschal left the study, closing the black door noiselessly, Corvyn glanced around the spare space, shaking his head. There had never been a physical need for a deity of darkness and punishment, not given human nature. But he also knew that without at least a representation of such a deity, people would have invented one even worse, one that would have represented all too accurately the true depths of human depravity, if only to have an entity to blame other than themselves and those around them.

Better an almost empty, seldom-present deity of darkness than an active agent of baseness and self-interest.

With a faint and tired smile, ignoring the sweat and fatigue from the long transit from the north, he dropped back into the shadows.

In instants, he reappeared in his own eyrie, near the southern end of the Avenue Pierrot. He stood in the darkened study, looking at the trident set into the gray stone. He immediately checked a certain signal and nodded.

No disruption yet. And given the time of day, there likely wouldn't be any until tomorrow, if then.

Then he shook his head and lighted the study.

Huginn was the first through the study door, followed by Muninn. Neither spoke. They just waited.

"I'm tired. I'm hot and sweaty, and I'm hungry. I'll also need the flux nerve underwear laid out for when I leave tomorrow," Corvyn said.

Huginn and Muninn exchanged worried glances.

"It hasn't been all that long, sir . . ." offered Huginn, "since you had to travel that far from the north . . . and to go back so soon tomorrow . . ."

"We do what we must. Now . . . I'm going to take a hot shower and get into clean clothes. I'll also like a good meal this evening. Perhaps . . . veal marsala with the Viognier?"

Muninn smiled. "I'll take care of that. It calls up the best memories."

"Who is it . . . this time, sir?" asked Huginn, as Muninn left the study.

"One of the usual suspects. Who else has the arrogance?"

"One could hope for some improvement," offered Huginn.

"I always hope for improvement," replied Corvyn. *Even if that hope is often unjustified.*

"You've been hoping for a long time, sir."

"That comes with the job. Do you regret it?"

"Not in the slightest. The surroundings are far better, and the casualties far fewer."

"That's why we're here." Corvyn's smile was faint, but wry. "I'm going to get that shower. Tomorrow and the next several days are likely to be very long and very exhausting." *And that's the best you can hope for.*

Corvyn didn't even want to think about the worst. He remembered too many times where hopes hadn't worked out. He needed nourishment and sleep, but he also knew he would dream, and the dream would not be pleasant.

That, also, was nothing new.

Black wings bear Raven to his fate,
to stop the hate that lies create.

42

From the unseen shadows that should not have existed on the bridge of the mightiest dreadnought ever constructed, Corvyn watched the array of screens that continually shifted too fast for an uncyborged mind to follow, not that he had any difficulty, although the battle officers before him did not see the screens, for the images fed directly into their thoughts and enhanced information-processing and spatial-manipulation capabilities.

"Energy concentration, sector five, plus three . . ." reported the firm asexual voice, a voice that was unnecessary, given that the battle officers had already received the information and were implementing their countermeasures, measures that would prove too little and too late, Corvyn knew, because of what followed the energy concentration that was the first manifestation of a targeted wormhole, from which would soon emerge a wedge of the shimmering white ships of the Purity Alliance.

As swiftly as Corvyn had predicted the arrival of the attackers, they appeared, almost a blizzard of white stars against the darkness of space, an onslaught met by the gray ships of Home. In the minutes that passed, the gray ships engaged the Purifiers successfully enough that half a gray squadron remained when the white ships were less than traces of ash that would eventually drop onto the surface of the planet named after a god of war. But even as those defenders re-formed and were reinforced, another targeted wormhole spewed forth another wave of attackers bearing the white of the Purity Alliance.

Energy concentration followed concentration, and after each wave of Purifiers there were fewer and fewer gray ships remaining to face the next onslaught. Then, there were none remaining to defend the planet, and the white ships turned upon the planet and boiled away the atmosphere and the shallow oceans.

Frozen in time, the raven that was Corvyn, or Corvyn who was the raven, watched, helpless to forestall what followed.

And follow it did, as before that long, the energy concentrations and the ensuing wormholes surrounded the dreadnought that maintained the defenses for the blue planet farther insystem. The last fleets of gray ships arrived, flat-coated, energy-reflective, each a hammer of defensive destruction thrown in the name of the political entity that was embodied by the dreadnought. Each flashed out and took its toll on the shimmering white attackers, but the attackers were truly endless. Not only that, but each emerging wormhole stressed the very fabric of space-time itself around the defenders, and the rips and rents in time and space swallowed white and gray alike.

Then a concentration of energy greater than all that had preceded flared around the dreadnought, and englobed it with the interlocked waves of gravity, and gravitons like spears of creation flew inward toward the doomed behemoth.

In that moment, Corvyn folded shadows and time around himself and fled, mere nanoseconds before the dreadnought expired, releasing outward the energy of a small sun as it died, shredding the gray and white alike into less than ashes.

Corvyn shuddered away, his skin covered with a thin rime of ice, except for his forehead, which burned so much that the ice instantly melted and flowed down his cheeks like tears of mourning for all the deaths remembered once more.

Yet another variation on the Falls, those before the Fall that was the only one the hegemons of the Decalivre remembered . . . or cared to remember, as if no other Fall had occurred before the forced arrival of the *Rapture*.

Too often, sleep was not the refuge of dark forgetfulness, but the Niflheim of memory.

How long can you keep the past of the pasts from being prologue? How long before the demands of conflicting and absolute purity lead to another Fall?

He no longer knew . . . but he knew, also, that each Fall postponed or averted was one less torment.

Wings black from Heaven's true unholy lies,
Raven lights again the fires of the skies.

43

Corvyn wondered why, when he awoke, he slept better in his own bed because he'd slept in so many beds over the years.

But more in your own dwelling and bed in recent years. And that was some small comfort, although he was unlikely to be sleeping in his bed for the next few days, and that was if matters went well. If they did not . . .

He didn't bother to shake his head at the thought, but concentrated on preparing himself for his departure. That included a long hot shower and dressing, beginning with the necessary nerve-support underwear that ran from ankles and wrists to his neck, designed to block some of the agony to come, and followed by a protective singlesuit. When he reached the breakfast room, Muninn had eggs béarnaise, with ham slices, on the table, along with hot bergamot tea. Corvyn seated himself carefully at the table. He did not rush, but neither did he dawdle, and in less than an hour he stood in the study, nerving himself for what needed to be done. His eyes glanced briefly at the trident, thinking that, even if all went well, he should let it remain.

As yet another reminder? As if you needed more.

"I wish you didn't have to go," offered Muninn. "We'll have everything ready for your return."

One way or another Corvyn would return, but in one way, he would not be aware of it . . . He pushed that thought away.

"Although it's unlikely, Jaweau may already be on his way to the control center. If so, I don't want him snooping around for too long."

"Are you sure he's discovered it?"

"He's known it existed for as long as he's been here. What he hadn't known, until now, or recently, is *exactly* where it is." Corvyn didn't mention the obvious, that the control station for the Pearls of Heaven could not be concealed entirely, given its purpose, only made incredibly difficult to locate and access, effectively limiting its access to those with skills, excessive strength, technical expertise and infrastructure, and particular abilities.

Jaweau had already hinted at finding information in the shadows, but there was one aspect of the station's location that he might not know. If Jaweau did know, however, there would be evidence of that and, if so, that proof would allow Corvyn to act, affording him a slight advantage, one that would allow him to return as he was, at least in good enough condition to be returned to what he was, as he was.

He pressed against his belt, felt the bulk of the special disruptor in its holster. Then he nodded to Muninn and Huginn and dropped into the shadows, heading southeast to Los Santos—to the cavernous spaces beneath the Mount of Faith—where he needed to find proof of what he suspected was certain.

Even before he reached the domain of the White One, he sensed an immense amount of power being collected in the caverns beneath the Cathedral Los Santos—far, far more than had been used when he had visited Jaweau earlier.

Then a particle beam of intense power flared skyward for but a few seconds, leaving a momentary gap in the quantum fields around and beyond the Pearls of Heaven, although that beam had not been aimed directly at the command station that held the intelligences directing the Pearls and their lances, not that the beam would have even strained the station's defenses.

That's one way of doing it, Jaweau. Or at least of reducing the initial agony by disorganizing the shadow defenses surrounding the center.

The White One's momentary weakening of one of the obstacles to gaining the command station might have smoothed his entry to the station, but if Jaweau had worked that out, then he had to have made plans for his return—plans Corvyn needed to thwart immediately. He felt as though he had taken a deep breath, although that was an illusion while he was still within the shadows. He pressed onward.

Moments later, he appeared in the central control room of the quantum intelligences located well beneath the Cathedral Los Santos, but no sooner had he left the shadows than an angel seemingly composed of brilliant violet light appeared.

"You shall not pass, Shadow of Darkness."

"By whose command?" asked Corvyn as he stepped toward the coruscating spatial arrays of colored lights that constituted the manifestation of the masterlinks, from which he could trace what he sought.

"By the Master of the Faith, the White One Omnipotent."

"I'm sorry, but the will of the Master of the Faith will have to defer to the dictates of the First." *As embodied in one Raven.* With that, Corvyn twisted certain shadows and dispatched the violet angel to a position slightly below the surface of Lake Lethe, from where the angel could possibly emerge and recover, without memory, possibly under the care of the Brothers and Sisters of Mercy . . . if the angel was fortunate.

Before there was another interruption—and there certainly would be—Corvyn immediately seized control of the masterlinks, searching for the rejuvenation cradles that doubtless existed within the lands of the White One, since Jaweau had to know the damage his mind and body would suffer from reaching and even staying for a short time aboard the control station.

Corvyn tried not to dwell on the fact that he would face the same problem, that is, if he was successful in what he needed to do. If he was not successful, the pain would be less—for him—but the eventual carnage for Heaven would be far greater. Falls always decimated planets, if not systems, or even entire stellar clusters.

He had discovered the location of the two cradles in the Mount when a second angel appeared, this one of brilliant blue light.

"Depart, Shadow of Darkness!"

Corvyn sensed the disruptor carried by the angel and shunted the energy back onto the aetherial being, then dispatched that angel also to

Lake Lethe, immediately returning his attention to the masterlinks and gathering in two other locations in and around Los Santos.

Sensing the shifting of the shadows, he immediately twisted those same shadows around the third angel, this one of brilliant yellow light, and sent that angel to the selfsame lake as the previous two. By now he was sweating and breathing harder than he would like, but he knew that Jaweau was thorough and patient, and that there had to be other cradles, at least a few, elsewhere within the lands of the White One.

He teased out the last three locations just as the angel in red appeared.

Rather than exert any more energy, he employed the shadows to move to the first rejuvenation cradle in the Mount, appearing in a small chamber deep beneath the interplay of quantum intelligences and energies, and so concealed by them that without the information from the masterlinks, he doubtless would have been unable to find it nearly so quickly, that delay being another form of defense being mustered by Jaweau.

He immediately drew the disruptor and fired, targeting the control system. Then he dropped into the shadows and sought out the second cradle, which met the same fate as the first.

He sensed the red angel following him as he wound his way through the shadows under the city toward the nearest remaining cradle in the city, which he discovered, in a certain irony, rested well beneath Lucifer's Basement. Again, he used the disruptor, but before he could return to the shadows, the red angel manifested itself.

To dispatch the red angel took more time . . . and effort . . . before Corvyn could proceed to the next cradle in the city, located deep beneath the river port coordination center. A quick blast from the disruptor rendered that cradle useless.

Then Corvyn shadow-traveled from Los Santos to the outlying locations that contained cradles.

The first dispersed cradle was located under a white obelisk in a forest to the northwest of the road between Plymouth and Los Santos, followed by another located near nothing that Corvyn could discern, except trees, other vegetation, and a concealed, wide-spread array of solar collectors.

Last was the cradle under the white obelisk in the woods east of the Redstone Inn.

From there, Corvyn returned to the control center under the Mount of Faith, where, before another angel could appear, he twisted certain quantum shadows and immediately withdrew before waves of fire and destruction began to reduce most of the complex to melted materials and ashes. He regretted the handful of deaths, but those deaths were far fewer than those who died aboard the *Blue Dolphin* and far, far fewer than the millions who would die in the years to come if Jaweau had his way and gained control of the Lances of Heaven—and that would be just the beginning.

Corvyn returned to a vacant room in the Domus Aurea, just to spend a few moments recovering. No angel followed him, not this time.

He washed his face and drank some water, then walked to the window and looked toward the Mount of Faith, surrounded by an aura of smoke, and likely the acrid odors of electric and quantum malfunctions. After several long moments of observation, he turned from the window . . . and thought.

Jaweau had definitely believed in redundancy . . . but old as the White One was, Corvyn was far older and had seen and experienced all too many stratagems of would-be purveyors of the One True Faith. He had also survived the agonies of semi-rebirth enough times that he dreaded what he must again do . . . an option that he had foreclosed for Jaweau, and one that Jaweau might foreclose on him, were he not successful in his next actions.

In a way . . .

He shook his head. He was bound by duty . . . and the knowledge of all too many Falls across too much of a galaxy that had far too few worlds suited to the biochemistry and narrow temperature range of human beings.

And if he could have acted sooner . . .

. . . but he had always been bound by proof . . . unlike deities who could act on faith without proof.

So . . . after a few moments, he would have to depart for the control station where Jaweau awaited him.

In a few brief moments.

No single truth convinces Raven's brood,
for solipsistic gods are far too crude.

44

Using the shadows to shift skyward was like climbing a staircase. The first level was uncomfortable, the second irritating. By the third level the pain burned through Corvyn's body, although there were in actuality no levels at all, just an ever-increasing bombardment of radiation, staggered quantum fluctuations, and intermittent and increasing gravitonic pressure. When he reached the command station controlling the Pearls of Heaven, his nerves began to scream from the combined effects that would, within hours if not sooner, limit his ability to function or even to stay alive. Those cellular effects were largely irreversible.

Even before Corvyn reached the shadows surrounding the station, he sensed another organic presence—and that presence had to be Jaweau or, even less likely, Shiva. Rather than emerge from the shadows in the receiving bay, where he had sensed the presence of a hegemon and where he would have received certain treatments to extend his ability to function without pain while he was present in the command center, Corvyn decided to bypass that and go to the control center directly. He located the small chamber off the main control room, the space that had been the admiral's quarters when the Pearls of Heaven were being formulated and strung, wincing as he emerged into the space, noting it remained seemingly the same as it always had been. That, of course, was an illusion, but then reality was also an illusion, if of a different sort.

Every movement hurt. That pain would increase in time, since the station was suspended in what might have been described, nonmathematically and therefore somewhat inaccurately, as a fixed point in a macro-quantum space-time geode, and thus out of phase, slightly, with normal space-time, making it inimical to the long-term survival of carbon-based organic life. It was, however, ideal for the qubit-based AI systems that governed Heaven, operated the Pearls of Heaven, and used the Eyes of Heaven and, when necessary, the Lances of Heaven.

Corvyn gestured, and the door to the control center opened. He took two steps forward into a space filled with intertwined matrices of energies and information flows. For the sake of convenience Corvyn visualized himself on the bridge of a long-annihilated vessel, then connected to the systems . . . and waited.

Although Jaweau likely discerned Corvyn's presence, he would not wait long, patient as he might be, since he was under the same physiological time constraints as Corvyn, as well as the fact that he had no familiarity with the systems, and system access was not possible except through the control center.

In a short while, perhaps only moments or possibly longer, the energy matrix that was Jaweau entered the control center and resolved itself, at least in Corvyn's perceptions, into the ageless blond and blue-eyed figure of the White One and offered words that were not spoken but conveyed, nonetheless. "Raven of shadows, of course. The dark one standing in the way of the triumph of faith."

Corvyn ignored Jaweau's jab. "Why did you plan the explosion of the *Blue Dolphin* to look like a strike from the Lances of Heaven? To see if I'd lead you here? To persuade Shiva that you had partial control of the Pearls of Heaven?"

"Both. Also, to see whether you are as indestructible as you seem."

"I'm scarcely that." The pain coursing through Corvyn reminded him that he was anything but indestructible.

"But you are endlessly replaceable. In theory, anyway."

"With present biotechnology, so is everyone, including you," replied Corvyn, adding, "In theory." *But each individual's unique stream of consciousness is not.* That was why Corvyn needed to resolve the situation between the two quickly if Corvyn wished to continue as the unique stream of consciousness that he had been for longer than he could accurately recall.

"Ingenious, the way the First did it," added Jaweau conversationally. "Using shifting fractal quantum fields to keep any of us from using the shadows to reach this installation. Or rather, to keep us from returning after reaching it. You don't seem surprised, Raven. How many times have you died? You know if you die here, it's the real death for you? The clone of you left behind may have your memories, but *you* will be dead."

"I've always known that. Now . . . why are you here?" Corvyn was well aware of the concealed disruptor that Jaweau carried and what he intended.

"To ensure the triumph of faith and to allow everyone to escape the prison the First created for us. The irony of naming it Heaven . . ." Jaweau shook his head.

"A prison? No more than any other planet. Everyone is free to believe as they wish, to work or not work, to pursue other interests so long as they do not injure others . . ."

"But they can't leave!"

"What would be the purpose of that?" replied Corvyn. "To destroy other worlds, other planetary systems in the endless conflict over which faith, which belief system, should rule the others?"

"The Pearls of Heaven are no more than a collar on aspiration. Men need to be free to pursue their own destiny."

Men? What about everyone else? Women? Those individuals who are either both or neither or some gender in between or even elsewhere? Those who don't share your faith? Corvyn knew there was little point in even bringing up those points, at least not to Jaweau. "And when they had the freedom of the stars . . . what did they do? Squabbled and fought over everything, killing billions of people and destroying planet after planet. You know, really good planets are scarce . . . and they're hard to get to, but that didn't seem to stop them, even with Fall after Fall. All in the name of faith . . . and freedom."

"The Almighty is truth and light. You're the dark side, Raven, representing the lack of faith, and especially the lack of aspiration." Jaweau smiled. "But one way or another, with you here, at last the white will triumph in Heaven below."

"How so?" returned Corvyn, fearing and knowing that the struggle would play out once more to the same conclusion.

"You know. You know all too well. You cannot return. No field or being can transit the screens in both directions, not and long survive. With you here . . ." Following the words was the sense of a triumphant smile.

"And how will you triumph if we both perish here?"

"You'd like to know that, wouldn't you, Raven? There's so much you don't know, and so much you think you know that isn't so."

Corvyn could say the same of Jaweau, but there was little point in saying it. He continued to listen.

"You're not the true Odin, but you're no different. Not you. You're just a construct . . ."

Not just . . . thought Corvyn. *Not for longer than you can imagine.*

". . . You think that in the end, all is nothing. For you, all that matters is the struggle. You and this station, this tin god, have denied the hope of perfection, the glorious whiteness of that perfection, out of life. You've denied the opportunity for any faith to triumph, especially the most worthy."

"Every House of the Decalivre, every village of belief, has a different view of what perfection is," Corvyn pointed out.

"You have never understood. There is only one true perfection, one True Belief, and with you removed from Heaven, there is nothing to stand in the way of that perfection."

Corvyn had heard variations on those words all too many times. He could have sighed. He did not. Instead, he said, "You continue to define me as evil. Tell me. What is good? Besides being opposed to what you declare that you stand for?"

Jaweau frowned. "Faith. Freedom."

"Whose faith? Whose freedom? And, for that matter, freedom to do what?"

"Whatever they want to do."

"Over several tens of thousands of years, first on ancient Earth, and then on every planet or system thereafter, human beings were free to do what they wanted. Tell me what happened."

"This time will be different."

"Every would-be tyrant has said that. The very fact that you tried to destroy me shows that it won't be," Corvyn pointed out.

"There are always casualties in the struggle for freedom."

"Every faith on Heaven has the same rights to try to persuade others to its beliefs. They just can't do it by any form of force. Why is that evil? Or wrong?"

"Because those who believe in false premises and false gods harm themselves and others. If people believe in the wrong tenets, holding to ways and thoughts that will harm themselves and others, how can I not use force to bring them to the light and the truth? Yet you and your tin god prohibit any effective means to bring them to the truth and the way."

"Nothing prohibits you or your believers from trying to convince others of the truth of your beliefs. You just can't use force as a means of obtaining support for your faith and beliefs." Corvyn knew his arguments would be rejected, but even Jaweau should have a choice. He also knew that Jaweau intended to keep talking until Corvyn was too weak and too pain-ridden to act effectively to oppose him.

"And aren't you and the tin god doing exactly the same thing by using force to prohibit us from leaving Heaven?"

Corvyn smiled, painful as it was. "You're absolutely right. The difference is that the way in which the Pearls of Heaven restrain people doesn't destroy planets or kill millions, if not billions of intelligent beings."

"You're no different, and that being the case—"

Corvyn understood exactly what Jaweau was about to do, and, before the other could complete the sentence that he felt he must, Corvyn called on all the powers of the Pearls of Heaven, as he could only do while existing in the control center, cloaking himself in shadow as he did so, knowing that he, too, would burn, even within the shadows, but that pain would end . . . one way or another.

A much smaller version of the Lances of Heaven blazed so brightly within that space that was not just space, within those fields that were both more and less than energy or space-time, that any sun, even that of Heaven, would have been black by comparison.

Jaweau did not even have time to say another word.

And the backlash of the agony of his death—real death—washed over Corvyn, who was paralyzed for a long moment with the experience of that burning pressure.

Even as his body was failing, still within the twisting multiple levels of the shadows, Corvyn concentrated on returning to the only possible place to preserve his unique stream of consciousness and self-awareness, knowing that the moment he left the shadows, death was only instants away. Each mille he crossed, even in relatively empty space, burned more than the previous mille, hollowing out his very being.

When he finally did leave the multiple levels of the shadows, lightnings burned along every nerve in his body, and dull spikes pounded through his skull, but only for the single instant before he collapsed.

Where, now, will the raven go?
Beyond the light, beyond the snow?

45

When Corvyn was next aware, or half aware, his entire body was being jabbed by needles that penetrated through skin, flesh, and bone, and each needle felt as though it was also a set of jaws, except those jaws were ripping pieces out of him even as the needles were sewing him back together. He could not breathe through his nose, and he could not open his mouth to gasp for the slightest bit of air.

Then liquid oxygen flowed over him, and he felt his body turning to stone before the cold darkness settled over him.

When he again sensed himself, he finally could open his eyes, but he was still in the cradle, his naked body surrounded by foam-like nutrients except around his face. Tiny needles still pricked at his skin and into his flesh . . . or that was the way that it felt, but he could breathe. All he could see at first was the transparent shield a few centimeters above his eyes, but as his vision cleared, beyond that he saw Huginn looking down at him.

Corvyn blinked several times, then tried to clear his throat, but those muscles did not seem to be working. As he realized that he had never sensed or felt Huginn and Muninn pick his dying body off the gray slate tiles of the floor and carry him swiftly into the depths of the villa, where the special cradle had waited for him, a warmer darkness settled over him.

For some time—how long it was, he could not tell—Corvyn drifted between painful and sometimes just uncomfortable semi-awareness and total dreamless darkness.

Then, almost abruptly, he was aware and awake, if still in the cradle, but the shield had been removed. Both Huginn and Muninn stood there, looking down at him.

Corvyn swallowed, then managed to ask, "How long has it been?"

"Eight months, sir," replied Huginn with a smile of relief. "We weren't sure . . ."

"There was almost no thread of continuity," added Muninn.

"You'll need a physical conditioning program, although we did what we could through the cradle," said Huginn.

"Can I get out of here now?"

"If you can input the release code, either verbally or through the shadows."

Release code? Corvyn had to think for several moments before recalling the single word. "Nevermore."

Immediately, the restraints relaxed, and the cradle tilted and turned slightly.

Corvyn eased himself out, but his legs were shaky.

Huginn handed him a robe, and Corvyn put it on, all too aware that his skin felt sticky and his stomach empty. He also knew that he would be able to eat very little, but he smiled when he saw the teapot and cup on the table in the recovery room. He was more than glad to sit down and let Muninn pour the tea.

"Is there a new Jaweau?"

"Yes, sir. I believe he was one of the lesser angels of the White Faith. The primary angels did not survive the destruction of the intelligence systems beneath the Mount of Faith. The Brothers and Sisters of Mercy found several men without memories on the Beach of Forgetfulness, and at least one who did not survive." Huginn looked at Corvyn inquisitively.

"I did what I could. Not being able to invade the intelligence systems of a hegemon or to act directly upon any hegemon without proof . . ." He shrugged. "But that's the way the First set it up, and we're bound by it."

Not that Corvyn hadn't found ways, over the centuries . . . and longer, to learn how to accomplish what he must within those parameters.

What had been behind all the Falls was that all too human—and even divine—desire to make something perfect in one single image, and to force it into being with the bright glory of shining arms—except arms were never shining, except in the imagination of unrestrained idealists and fanatics, although in practice the two were the same. That desire always empowered the war gods, the gods of battle, who were more than willing to lead the fight for that single blazing vision of perfection that never was and never could be. And when it was all over, and the Fall had once more destroyed a good, or functioning, society in the name of pure faith and a perfect unattainable ideal . . . the Frost Giants stalked, for a time, before the cycle once more began to repeat itself.

Corvyn took a small sip of the bergamot tea.

EPILOGUE

Corvyn slid out of the shadows near the piers on the River Acheron, piers located almost precisely 231 milles northeast of the gray stone point at Ilium where the Yellow River joined the Acheron. He glanced toward the boat moored to the goldenwood bollard that rose above the smooth golden planks of the pier, the only wooden piers in any city ruled by a hegemon, but that was scarcely surprising, given that as much as possible connected to the Maid was natural, from the wood of the piers to the oak planks of the boat itself to the hemp mooring lines.

For a time, he watched as passengers disembarked from the boat, their garments in all shades, colors, and styles, although a slightly larger proportion seemed to be wearing white.

Corvyn smiled sadly. Many of those in white would be disappointed, because they likely fled from the failure of the former White One to provide a simple shining white truth to follow. Then he turned from the pier toward Aethena proper, where tall dark woods flowed through the city, one of the reasons why it was often called the City of the Forests.

No one even looked at his dark gray jacket as he walked toward the comparatively low white-columned building that appeared to grow out of the only unforested hill in Aethena, one slightly taller than the others, if sprinkled with tall and well-shaped trees rising out of gardens and grass.

In time, after making his way through the winding streets that held a mixture of homes and small shops, with frequent smaller parks, he came to a spreading expanse of gardens and greenery. Before him was a fountain with a circular walk around it. He stopped in front of the fountain and studied it—just a spray of water that looked white against the greenery. Not even a statue, just that spreading fan of water. Around the green-tinged marble of the pool rim grew low flowers, white with diamond-green centers. Just the hint of a fragrance teased him, something between rockroses and lavender, then faded away with a puff of a breeze.

Three paths wound away from the fountain in a general uphill direction. Corvyn squinted, realizing that there was a fourth path, concealed by shadows. With an amused smile, he took it, following the twisting way upward, past gardens filled with flowers of every shade and color. At the top of the hill he stopped just short of the white-columned temple.

One moment he was standing alone in the shadows of the structure, perhaps not a copy of another white-columned building, but certainly a representation meant to evoke similar feelings, when he sensed the shifting of the quantum shadows and she stood beside him.

She wore the same green jacket and trousers with the cream-colored blouse that she had as Erinna, and she smiled but did not speak.

Instead, she gestured to a bench in a shaded glade off the path. The bench was of the same smooth natural oak as all the others he had passed as he followed the shadowed path. Corvyn walked beside her to the bench, where she sat at one end. Corvyn sat at the other, turning slightly to face her. Since she had not spoken, he did.

"I never got here on my last journey. I thought it might be a good idea."

"You didn't need to come. You did what was necessary."

Corvyn didn't want to admit that he was limited by what was necessary. Instead, he asked, "Why did you act as a poetess?"

"Because you're known for your love of poetry."

Corvyn frowned.

"Was I wrong?"

Corvyn laughed softly before saying, "That is one of my weaknesses."

The Maid looked at Corvyn, and for the first time in eons, he felt less than comfortable. He wondered why.

"Because you're not the only one." She smiled enigmatically.

After a moment, Corvyn smiled in return.

ABOUT THE AUTHOR

L. E. Modesitt, Jr., is the bestselling author of the fantasy series the Saga of Recluce and the Imager Portfolio. His science fiction includes *Adiamante*, the Ecolitan novels, the Forever Hero trilogy, and *Archform: Beauty*. Besides a writer, Modesitt has been a U.S. Navy pilot, a legislative assistant and staff director for a U.S. congressman, director of legislation and congressional relations for the U.S. Environmental Protection Agency, and a college lecturer. He lives in Cedar City, Utah.